Kat Richardson is a former magazine editor who escaped Los Angeles in the 90s. She currently lives on a sailboat in Seattle with her husband, and a crotchety old cat and two ferrets. She rides a motorcycle, shoots target pistol and does not own a TV.

Visit her website at www.katrichardson.com.

Also by Kat Richardson:

Poltergeist

GREYWALKER

Kat Richardson

PIATKUS

First published in Great Britain in 2007 by Piatkus Books
First published in the United States in 2006 by ROC,
A division of Penguin Group (USA) Inc., New York, USA

A CIP catalogue record for this book
is available from the British Library

ISBN 978-0-7499-3896-3

Papers used by Piatkus are natural, recyclable products made from
wood grown in sustainable forests and certified in accordance with
the rules of the Forest Stewardship Council

Data manipulation by Phoenix Photosetting, Chatham, Kent
www.phoenixphotosetting.co.uk

Printed and bound by Mackays of Chatham, Chatham, Kent

Piatkus Books
An imprint of
Little, Brown Book Group
100 Victoria Embankment
London EC4Y 0DY

An Hachette Livre UK Company

www.piatkus.co.uk

For Ellen Williams

ACKNOWLEDGMENTS

Writing and publishing a novel is not nearly as solitary as I'd always thought. A lot of people helped make this book more than just an idea and a pile of paper.

First in line for kudos is my husband, who continues to support, encourage, and put up with me in all my moods; make great suggestions; and only laugh at the funny parts. Usually. He also contributed to Quinton's knowledge of arcane electronics and computer tricks.

Many thanks to my dedicated first readers, Nancy Durham and Elisabeth Shipman, who read Harper's adventure when it was still huge and gangling, read it again every time it got pared down, and keep asking for the next one. And thanks to my sister, Beth, and to our friend Joe Ochman, who also read the manuscript and gave me sage advice, encouragement, and help early on.

I owe a lot of thanks to Steve Mancino, who plucked the query from the slush pile, and Joshua Bilmes, "el queso grande" at JABberwocky Literary Agency, who said yes. I've learned my lesson and will never send another manuscript on twenty-four-pound paper. I promise.

I also have a wonderful editor, Anne Sowards, and copy editor, Cherilyn Johnson, who helped me keep my foot out of my mouth and made me look very much more clever than I am. If there's a mistake in here, it's because of me.

Special thanks go to Tanya Huff and Charlaine Harris for their personal charm and gracious words.

I received some last-minute technical assistance from Seattle PD detective Nathan Janes. Even though the specific information didn't make it into this book, it will have its day in the next one.

Beyond all of these, there are a ton of relatives and friends who've seen this through from raw idea to bookstore shelves, offering assistance, persistence, and forbearance in not smacking me with a wet trout on various occasions, while knowing when to go away and leave me alone on others. They are too numerous to list, but I'll single out a few for sticking it out above and beyond all reasonable expectation: Bruce Shipman, Ellen Williams, Bo and Sandy Carpenter, Sharon Langlois, Ken George, Jason Wood, Marci Dehn, Richenda Fairhurst, Joy Huffine,

Bart and Kris Lawrence, Josh Mitchell, Mara Love, Alex Pearson, Jacque Knight, Jay Menzo, Mike and Chris Uyyek, Jessica Branom-Zwick, Mel Shipman, Pamela Hale, Dan Sabath, Glenn Walker, Julie Albright, Becca Hildebrandt, Heather Steward, Melissa Wadsworth, Laura Friend, Rey and Karen Solis, John Barber, Misty Taliaferro, Olwen Palm, Stephanie Lawyer, and Frank White.

I have to mention the virtual communities that have put up with my shenanigans all this time: the rec.arts.mystery newsgroup, the TTLG.com forums, and Seattle Writer Grrls. Special thanks to Jon and Ruth and the rest of the staff of *CrimeSpree Magazine*, and to authors Jane Haddam, Barry Eisler, Robert Sawyer, Louise Marley, John Hemry, Donna Andrews, Brandon Sanderson, Mike Moscoe, Lawrence Watt-Evans, Kurt Busiek, Richard K. Morgan, Keith Snyder, Katy Munger, Lise McClendon, Monette Draper, Karen Irving, Mary Keenan, and Joe Konrath for professional advice and words of wisdom.

And if they were here, a last thank-you for everything would go to Richard Dennis Huffine, Leila Jane Phelps, and Andrew "Fluke" McKenzie, who had to leave too soon.

I am grateful for so much help and friendship from all of these people and from those I may have forgotten who've lent me their support for so long. They've all contributed in some way to this book, but if there are mistakes in it, those are entirely mine.

—KR

GREYWALKER

ONE

I'd been surprised when the guy belted me. Most people don't flip out when they get caught in such a small fraud. I had expected an embarrassed apology and a hasty check to appease my client—his stepdaughter. But instead, the guy leaned over his desk and smacked a sledgehammer fist into the side of my head.

I pitched out of my chair, ears buzzing. I groped for my purse, but he was moving around the desk faster than I could get at my gun. I rolled to my knees and aimed to slug him below the belt.

He dodged and tagged me with another fat fist to the back of my skull. Then a kick in the ribs. I shrieked as my breath rushed out, and prayed for nosy neighbors and paper-thin walls. He raised his foot again.

I rolled, shoved his forward-swinging foot … and both feet slid out from under him. I ape-scrambled for the door. My chest felt as if everything had torn loose from its moorings.

My head yanked back as he jerked a fistful of my long ponytail. I kicked backward. Something meaty met my heel, but not what I'd been hoping for.

"Goddamn it!" He whipped my head sideways against the door-jamb. I thought the side of my skull had caved in.

Everything hurt. I wrenched around, close to his body, using him for support. Hair ripped from my scalp. I batted his head against the wall with one hand and crunched a knee into his crotch. He gasped, letting go of my hair. I jerked loose, spun, shouldering through the doorway, staggering into the hall, scrabbling my gun from my purse as I made for the elevator.

Nothing worked right: my legs felt like rubber bands; every time my hand closed on the pistol's grips, it slithered away; I couldn't get a full breath; my chest blazed agony. All I could hear was buzzing and the swishing of blood through my veins.

I shoved open the folding metal gates of the antique elevator and lurched forward. Another yank on my hair stopped me short. I tried to turn around and shoot the bastard, but my legs collapsed under me. The gun spun onto the elevator floor and slid into a corner.

Clutching my hair, he grabbed hold of the outer gate. I scrambled my old Swiss Army knife out of my jeans pocket. He slapped the gate against my neck. It felt like he was trying to cut my head off. I squirmed and tried to jerk away. The gate smacked into my temple. Blood ran from my ear, hot against the side of my skull. My vision narrowed to a dark, bloody tunnel.

The gate again. Smash! An insistent rattling noise came from the elevator and the inner gate tried to close on me, too. I flipped open the big blade of the pocketknife and jabbed it into the man's hand on my hair. He yelped and let go.

My head thudded a few inches onto the elevator floor and I squirmed the last measure away from the closing gates. I could hear the man rattling the grille and calling me a whole lexicon of dirty names as the elevator started down. Something was still tugging on my hair, but I didn't want to worry about it; I wanted to curl up and pass out. Then the jerking started pulling my head up.

My long hair was stuck in the gates and rising as the elevator sank toward the ground floor. The thought of being hung by my hair upset me enough to move again. My vision had squeezed down to a distant point of dim light, floating on a dark red sea. My grip was weak, but I began sawing at my trapped ponytail. I wished

I had sent the knife out to be sharpened when I'd had the scissors done. I pushed myself to stand against the wall, hacking away, long strands of brown hair falling past my face as the car dropped. I was up on my toes when the last hank split. Heaving, nauseated, and dizzy, I crumpled onto the elevator floor and sprawled through the opening gate.

After that, things got disjointed: people yelling; someone's shoes; aching in my chest and arms; someone flicking something against my eyelids; a man with an accent; a throbbing in my head like a kid kicking a merry-go-round into motion. I think I threw up. Then I slept.

That had been April first...

I'd woken in the hospital a couple of days later feeling so horrible I'd figured I was going to live. If it felt that bad dying, no one would go.

Now weeks had passed, and the aches and pains, the bruises, scrapes, and lacerations were fading, but the bash on the bonce wasn't clearing up so well. The bouts of weirdness after I'd left—some minor problems with my senses still a bit out of whack, some not so minor—had brought me back to the hospital.

Dr. Skelleher was a stranger to me—the only doctor on urgent care duty when I'd come in. He looked barely thirty and in need of coffee. His hair was short and spiky from a lack of style rather than an excess, and the dark bags under his eyes could have passed for fanny packs. His clothes under his white coat were environmentally correct. A narrow leather thong peeked over the back of his collar and disappeared below the placket buttons of his raw-cotton shirt.

The "incidents" ran past my mind's eye like fast-spinning film as I told the doctor about them.

Sometimes things just looked misty and impressionistic—like the reflection in a steamed-up bathroom mirror. At the hospital, I couldn't always tell when people were really in the room. They seemed to float in and out, changing shape and detail. My hearing was just as unpredictable, all buzzings, mutterings, water gurgles, and cotton wool. I'd been told this was normal for concussion patients and would get better. But ... some of it had gotten worse.

And sinking through the hospital bed had been unsettling.

I wasn't supposed to get out of bed without a doctor or nurse around. Call me a bad patient: I didn't like peeing in the cup, so I decided to use the toilet like a human. That part of the job hadn't been so bad, though it was no waltz with Fred Astaire. Getting back to the bed was harder.

Coming out of the bathroom, I'd started feeling sick. The lighting in the room had dimmed a bit and the bed seemed much farther away, deep in the steamed-mirror effect. I struggled toward it, chilled and sweaty, feeling sicker by the minute, picking up a whiff of something like autopsies and crime scenes. I plunged through the cold steam as my vision went gray, then smoky, heading for charcoal. The bed was a vague and shimmery pastel block. I reached it with a shin first, grabbed a steel rail, and dragged myself into it. For a moment, I just lay like a stunned fish on the cold, soggy mattress, panting. Then the bed shifted and I fell through.

The lights had brightened and the room snapped back into focus as I fell. A nurse came in just as I hit the floor. She scolded me, of course. Then she called an orderly and had him scoop me up and dump me into my own bed, which was about four feet away.

I'd thought there were three beds in the room, but the nurse said there hadn't been three beds in that room since the remodel in the 1960s.

Then had come the final-straw incident, just the previous morning.

My face in the bathroom mirror was still scary. My left eye was surrounded by a livid bruise that washed up against the bridge of my nose, seeped over my eyebrow, and sagged across my cheekbone to dribble off over the corner of my jaw into a nightmare dog collar of purple and green. My lower lip and ear were both a bit tattered and swollen still. The general bruising and swelling had pulled my face into a grimace at the hospital that was only then collapsing into tie-dyed puffiness. What I could see of my hair from the front was frayed out at the bottom like the ends of an old straw broom. Most of it was still below my shoulders, though.

But I needed to go back to work—had to pay the hospital bills—and I had an appointment coming up, so I decided to submit myself to a day spa—a combination salon and torture chamber—and hope the staff could make me look more like a human and less like Frankenstein's monster after a night on the town.

With my head in a towel, and padding about in a robe and slippers, I'd been deposited in a tiny steam room to "relax and open the pores" for fifteen minutes. I tried to sit still and relax, but my head felt stuffed with humming insects.

I put my hands up to my temples. I tried squeezing my eyes shut and taking long, slow breaths, but a scent of something like smoke made me open them again. The steam around me writhed and coiled into Chinese-dragon clouds framing a misty doorway.

I stared around. I was alone, no one to tell me it was just a trick of the light. The steam closest to me was thin, tingling warmth on my skin. But the stuff around that doorway was dense as smoke and dark, but chill as fear.

A pale spot of light seemed to twinkle from the middle of the doorway, throbbing a bit, growing into a narrow, pulsing column of watery light. My stomach wrenched and a stab of nausea ripped through my guts. The smoky odor had shifted toward ripe corpses and floodwater.

I put out my hand for balance, then jerked it back. I didn't want to touch whatever that squirming cloud-stuff was. I wriggled back on my bench, thumping my head against the wall as an irrational horror crawled over me.

My chest went tight with sudden anxiety, breath thin and metallic in my throat. I must have yelled, "No!"

Light sliced into the steam, chopping into the misty doorway. I jerked my head toward the light source. One of the perky spa employees looked in from the real doorway.

She asked if I was all right.

I gulped and looked around. Just steam—ordinary steam that smelled of clean water and a hint of pine from the benches. No column of beckoning light. No dragon smoke stinking of death.

I'd told her I was fine, had just fallen asleep. But a frisson had rattled down my spine.

I'd been more than ready to leave the room.

I paused to settle myself a bit before I went on. I frowned at the doctor, who only raised his eyebrows and waited.

I started in on the last tale. "I tried to jog this morning, but I couldn't make it past a trot for more than a few seconds. I feel seasick, smell things, hear things... This cloudy vision ... I keep seeing eyes, shadows, crazy things ... ," I added, petering out. "I'm not sleeping well, either. But I have clients to see tomorrow and I need to get back to work. They told me I should be safe to return to work by now, but maybe I'm not as healed as the hospital doctor thought, or maybe the pills are making me hallucinate."

Skelleher scowled. He'd already poked me with needles and sticks, and made the usual gestures with bright lights and cold instruments. "It's not the pills," he announced, "and your physical signs are fine. There's nothing here that makes me want to challenge your original doctor's recommendations—aside from my personal feeling that the least intervention is best. I'm a strong believer in letting the body and the mind do the work as much as possible." He looked at my chart again and got quiet.

After a moment, he glanced up. "Look, I know this is kind of scary stuff. Head trauma is mysterious and unpredictable. The brain is an amazing thing and we learn more about it every day, but we don't know all there is to know. And what we call the mind—it's still pretty wild country. There are a lot of things that traditional Western medicine is a little uncomfortable with, and the whole issue of life and death, the physical and psychological effects of death on the mind—the metaphysical—is still pretty much in the dark."

I was startled by the turn in his conversation. "Excuse me," I said. "Are you saying that I … died?"

He looked at me with a crooked smile. "Nobody said anything to you?"

"No."

He shook his head. "Jeez … no wonder you're confused. There's supposed to be counseling for this sort of thing. I guess they all just forgot about it, what with the police and all. OK, I guess it's a little late to break this gently, so I'll just give you the condensed version. According to your records, you were dead for a little less than two minutes, about the time the Medic One team arrived. They pulled you back, stabilized you, and got you to the hospital. No other incident occurred. This kind of thing happens with head injuries. Some people have a little trouble … adjusting, sometimes, and some people have some pretty strange experiences, but this is getting into that mysterious and creepy unknown territory medicine isn't very good with. There are psychological counseling services for this, if you're interested…"

I shook my head too fast and felt woozy. I winced.

Skelleher frowned at me. "Would you come into my office for a moment?"

I shrugged and followed him out of the examining room and into an afterthought of an office cramped with a desk and two chairs. He told me to leave the door open if I preferred. I swung it closed and sat down.

He sat back and rubbed a knuckle over his lower lip for a few moments, then raised his eyes back to mine. He took a deep breath and leaned forward again. "I'm going to crawl out on a very narrow professional limb here, because I think there's something more than medical about this situation.

"I have some friends who ... have had experience with similar things to what you're describing. And—I don't like to say this, because it sounds unprofessional—but you might get some benefit out of talking to them. Ben and Mara Danziger. They're friends, not patients. I know him professionally also, and he's a good guy, even if some of his ideas sound like they're straight out of the *Twilight Zone.* If nothing else, they might at least help you determine if what you're experiencing are legitimate phenomena, or something that ought to be addressed by a counselor." He picked a card out of a desk drawer and offered it to me.

Suspicious, I asked, "You're not sending me to a shrink, are you?"

"No," he replied with a laugh. "Nothing like that. I think that you might be experiencing something that most people just can't get in touch with. Not anything bad, just something from that mysterious edge of knowledge. And in keeping with my belief that a lighter touch is better, I'm going to let you make up your own mind. If you talk to Ben and Mara and then decide they're from the land of the loonies and so am I, I'll be glad to recommend a psychologist, a counselor, or even a change in meds, if that's what it takes."

I looked at him sideways.

His smile limped with exhaustion. "I don't think there's anything medically wrong with you or your pills. I think you'd be just fine without them, to be honest. I can't do anything else for you except make some suggestions and tell you to be sure to go to your follow-up exams. Whatever's causing you these problems seems to be outside my purview."

I took the card, skeptical, and dropped it into my bag. He watched me hitch the bag onto my shoulder and stand.

"You probably should switch to a backpack if you always carry that much stuff," he commented. "A load like that can hurt your back if you carry it on one side."

"I don't like backpacks. Too casual, and they're hard to get into in a hurry."

Skelleher shrugged. "You have to make choices. But be good to yourself, you know? Try to sleep. Eat red meat to restore your blood count and proteins. Put wet tea bags on your eyes to reduce the discoloration. Get some regular stretching and exercise. You'll heal faster and feel better. And call me if you have any more trouble."

I said I would and he gave me another crooked, coffee-deprived smile as I left.

Dead. Except for a few family funerals, a required course in forensic science, and a couple of bodies on a case that went nuts, what did I know about death? Bodies are just the leftovers, not the real event of death. I'd never seen anyone die, never been intimate with death—except for that moment in the elevator when it just seemed like a very inviting kind of nap. I wanted to sit and think about that and yet, I really didn't.

I left it to stew in the back of my head, and my brain bumbled around it like a bee in a rhododendron. Dead.

TWO

Roiling gray mist flooded across the floor, pushing against the walls. Lucent wisps spiraled up from the mass, forming a columned portal supporting a hot-white door. My vision clouded, like snow on a television screen. Vertigo gripped me.

The door drifted open on an endless whiteout storm, swarming with almost-seen shapes and moving light. I crashed to my knees in the thick cold, gasping in the sickening death smell of it. Hungry fog boiled out, muttering, whispering, clawing…

I started awake with a racing heart.

Nerves vibrating, I stalked through the entire condo, throwing open cabinets and closets, daring the mist to stream out at me. The ferret watched me from the safety of her cage as I found nothing. My head buzzed from getting up too fast, and black dots fringed my vision. I lay back down, but I could not fall back to sleep.

I gave up and stumbled through my morning routine. The sun struggled up through the early-morning Seattle gloom. I looked out the balcony windows, but I couldn't face the prospect of another fog-haunted run.

I showered and faced off to the bathroom mirror, my pulse ragged as I wiped it clear of steam. In spite of the best efforts of the salon gnomes, I still looked thrashed. Pillow creases and morning puffiness didn't help, either.

Chaos, the ferret, made a pest of herself as I dressed, rumpling up my impress-the-client suit, stealing shoes, stockings, and jewelry, and throwing dancing fits of sound and fury when I took them back. Finally, I tucked her back into her cage. She glared at me as I slipped my pistol into the clip holster in the small of my back and hid it under a suit jacket that almost matched my skirt. I would not be taken by surprise again.

I was in my office before seven, coffee in hand. I started catching up on old business and billing and prepping for my meeting at nine.

My first day out of the hospital, I'd called my answering machine. Most of the messages were old business, crank calls, and hiss, but two had sounded like work.

The first had been a male, accented, bad connection: "Miss Blaine. Grigori Sergeyev. You have come to my attention to recover a family heirloom. I must call again. I have no phone number to give now."

I'd made a note, but still no second call had come in.

The second was a female, controlled, with a mature, Eastside girls-academy voice: "Ms. Blaine, my name is Colleen Shadley. My son is missing. The police have been condescending but no help. They suggested I hire a private investigator, and Nan Grover recommended you. Please call me as soon as possible."

I had called her back and agreed to look into it. I'd have preferred later, but Mrs. Shadley had set the time and place for the meeting. I thanked the gods for coffee. At eight thirty, I shut down my computer and locked up the office.

The morning fog hadn't thinned much, giving Pioneer Square a watercolor look as I headed for the bus stop on First. There was no point in moving my Rover just to pay for parking six blocks away.

As I was crossing Occidental, a man shambled out of the alley toward me. He was draped in layers of dark, shaggy rags that spun vortices off into the mist around us.

He muttered as he approached. "Can you see? Can you see?" He waved his hands, one of them clutching an empty shape, gesturing around like a tour guide.

I could smell him, wafting the odor of dirt and attics. I started around him, peering through the sulfurous mist.

His hand darted out and grabbed my upper arm. He hauled on me and shoved his face near mine. "Dead lady? Are y'dead, lady? Y'see 'em?" He waved his clenched-open hand at me and demanded, "Looka! Can you see this? Huh? Can y'see?"

I twisted, pulling my shoulder down and shoving him with my other hand. The layers of his clothes were warm and furry and gave under my hand, but he stumbled back and I spun away, putting a couple of paces between us.

I shook the smell out of my head, saying, "I think you should back off."

He stumbled another step back, muttering, "No? Can't y'see? No?" He whimpered, confused.

I made an aggressive feint forward, leaning in and glaring at him, my hands coming up, curling.

He darted in, trying to grab for me again, but I roared at him and swung one hand hard over his nearest ear.

He yelped and turned, skittering off into the alley and sliding away in the shredding fog that swirled and sucked behind him.

I let out a breath and hurried for the bus, shaking off a shiver.

I was a fashionable five minutes late. I hate to be fashionable.

Colleen Shadley had picked an espresso bar with pretensions of clubhood, paneled in cherrywood and dark green leather, with clots of business-suited men and women muttering together among the big armchairs and glossy mission tables.

I spotted a lone woman in the rear right corner and headed for her. She was paging through a copy of *Wine Spectator* at a desultory rate and ignoring a cup of coffee.

Her hair was styled in a soft, chin-length bob that curled smoothly forward at the ends, the color a gentle beige. She wore an Audrey

Hepburn sort of black silk dress as if it were armor. A sleek leather attaché case leaned against her chair legs.

I stopped in front of her. "Mrs. Shadley?"

She looked up at me. Her eyes were violet.

"You're Ms. Blaine. Please sit down. And call me Colleen." She waved to the chair at an angle to hers, studying me. I expected to be graded on the grace of my transition from upright to seated. "You're not what I expected, but Nan did recommend you very highly."

Nanette Grover does not give gushing reviews. In two years of running legal backgrounds for her, the best I'd heard was "This is good." I wondered what she had said.

Colleen continued. "Where did you get that blackened eye?"

"Complications of a now-closed case. I can recommend a less scrappy investigator if it makes you uncomfortable." My offer was a little stiff, I admit.

She smiled. "That won't be necessary." Then she beckoned over my head.

I pulled my notebook and pen from my purse. "Let me recap what you told me on the phone. Your son, Cameron, is a student at U-Dub—the University of Washington. He disappeared recently, has not, apparently, been attending classes, and has not been paying his bills, though his ATM card seems to be showing regular use in the Seattle area. You've filed a missing persons report with the Seattle PD, but you don't expect any satisfaction from that quarter."

She nodded. "Very concise. We have a joint account into which I deposit funds to cover his expenses every two weeks. I didn't know anything was wrong until I got a call from his landlord. Cameron has not paid his part of the rent for a month and, since I'm a cosigner on the lease, the landlord contacted me. When I called to speak to Cameron's roommate, the boy told me he hadn't seen Cameron in six weeks or more. He also said Cam had been sick the last time he did see him.

I remember that Cam seemed rather pale and said he'd had the flu the last time I saw him. That would have been just under six weeks ago."

Her recitation was interrupted by the arrival of coffee, preordered.

"According to Richard—his roommate—Cameron left most of his things behind, so it didn't seem that he was going away for any prolonged length of time. I haven't been by to talk to Richard myself, though I suppose I should have done. I just kept thinking Cam had finally caught a wild hare and would turn up again anytime. Then I got the latest bank statement. No checks had been written for any bills, and all the transactions were for cash taken from ATMs in Seattle."

"Is this his normal pattern?" I asked.

"No. He writes checks for almost everything—bills, groceries, clothes, and so on—and only takes out cash for entertainment."

"A joint account is a little unusual for a kid over fourteen or fifteen."

Colleen waved it away. "It was set up a long time ago. When my husband died, we created a very large trust for Cameron until he completed his college degree. I am the executrix of that trust, and it was easier to establish a joint account into which to put his stipend and expense money than to try to set up an individual account. When he got a little older, he chose to keep the account rather than open a new one. I always kept the account records for tax purposes."

She frowned, her mask of expensive makeup creasing like heavy paper. "But now he appears to have left school. As the trust executrix, I must find out if he really means to quit school and give up the money, or if he's just taking a quarter off, which would only put the payments into suspension. Of course, as his mother, I need to find out what's happened to him. This is … unlike him."

I sipped coffee and braced to be rude. "How much money are we talking about in this trust?"

She didn't flinch. "Just under two million dollars."

"That's a nice trust."

She shrugged. "Daniel and I wanted to be sure the children were taken care of if anything happened to either of us."

"What becomes of the trust now?"

"If Cameron goes back and finishes his degree, he'll get a set percentage of the trust to get started on after he graduates, and the rest will be divided among a list of persons and charities. If he doesn't go back to school, he gets nothing and the entire trust is divided."

"Among whom?"

"Well, myself, our daughter Sarah, Daniel's old business partner, Dan's two brothers, and a list of charities." She shifted uncomfortably and bit the inside of her lip.

I just nodded and made a note. "Let's go back to the bank statement," I suggested. "Do you know the times, dates, or locations of any of the transactions, or the amounts?"

She looked startled. "I forgot to bring the statement with me."

She didn't strike me as the scattered and forgetful type. I'd bet she was the president or treasurer of three or four charitable boards around town. A flicker of her mouth and the shadow of sudden small lines gave a hint of unaccustomed anxiety, which she shut down as quickly as I spotted it.

I continued. "What's your son's full name, Colleen?"

"Andrew Cameron Shadley. He prefers to go by his middle name." She reached into her case and brought out a large manila envelope. "I brought some photos and a list of friends and relatives who may be able to help you."

I took the envelope and pulled out two photos and a sheet of typed bond—the thick, cottony stuff that costs forty dollars a box. One of the photos was an eight-by-ten color studio print, the other a standard snapshot.

The portrait showed a beaming Pre-Raphaelite angel in a black crew-necked sweater. His long, pale gold hair would have hung in Shirley Temple ringlets if cut to shoulder length. His eyes, fringed with thick, dark gold lashes, were deep violet like his mother's. Only the vaguest blond down of a mustache kept him from being mistaken for a girl.

Colleen pointed at the portrait. "That picture was taken after his high school graduation. He's lost a little weight since then, and that dreadful mustache finally grew in." She sighed. "He was the most adorable child, but, of course, he hated it." Which I'd figured. "That other picture is from this past Christmas. That's what he looked like when I saw him last."

In the snapshot, Cameron and a girl were standing next to a hearth that was decorated with cedar garland and red-and-green-plaid ribbons. Thinner, his face had lost its cherubic plumpness, and a silky blond mustache draped over his mouth. His long hair was tied back. Now his smile was secretive. The girl looked about the same age, but sullen at having her picture taken. Her hair was asphalt black, but whether it was natural or from a dye bottle was impossible to tell in such a small picture. She had cultivated the trendy, Gothic vampire look. Surrounded by the Christmas theme, she looked like a witch left over from Halloween.

"Is this Cameron's girlfriend?" I asked.

"Oh, no. That's Sarah. My daughter." Her lips tightened a little; then she reached for her coffee and took a sip.

"Would Sarah have any idea where Cameron is?"

"I'm afraid I don't know. We don't talk. Her address is on the sheet. Maybe you'll have better luck with her than I do."

I made a mental note while I sipped coffee and looked at the list. It was short. Each name was annotated "friend" or "relative," followed by contact information—except for Sarah's, which had only an address.

"I wish there was more for you to start from," Colleen said. "Cameron didn't socialize at home much anymore. He was always very independent, but he was never reckless. When I didn't hear from him, I assumed that he was busy with new projects and studies. It wasn't until he missed his birthday that I began to worry. He's the one who always calls. He participates. He's a good son."

Her tone said someone else was not a good daughter. "How old is Cameron?"

"He turned twenty-one on the seventh of March."

"And how long has he been studying at U-Dub?"

"Three years. Though it will take longer than four years to complete his degree."

"Oh? What's he studying?"

"Majoring in human factors engineering and minoring in Japanese."

I made a puzzled face. "Human factors engineering?"

"Ergonomics," she clarified. "He always knew what he wanted. He started college straight out of high school. I thought he would want to go to Europe for a while with some of his friends, but he said he'd rather 'get a jump on them.'" She smiled her pride. "Who could say no to that?"

"When did you see him last?"

"The end of February or the beginning of March . . ." She flipped open a datebook and glanced through it. "The first of March. Yes . . ." Her mouth turned down as she paused, remembering.

"You said he had been ill," I prompted.

"Yes. He looked very pale. Distracted. I remember he told me he was just getting over the flu and he didn't want me to catch it. He kept his distance from me all night and picked at his food. He didn't talk much, either."

"I see. Do you have his class schedule?"

She flushed red. "I seem to have left that with the bank statement."

"I'll get them from you later. Can you think of any places he might hang out?"

"He is fond of Waterfall Garden Park, but it's in such a grubby neighborhood. I can't imagine him 'hanging out' there. Of course, he spent a lot of time around the campus and the U-district. He saw art films at the Grand Illusion once in a while. His roommate will be more help on that."

I knew Waterfall Garden Park. It was only a few blocks from my office. Most of Pioneer Square was grubby, but so were parts of the U-district. The tiny garden was locked at sunset, so I wondered where Cameron was really hanging out when he went slumming in Pioneer—especially since he'd been underage for the primary nightlife down there until March seventh.

"Does Cameron own a car? Do you know where it is?"

"No, I don't. Richard said he hadn't seen it in the parking lot, so he must have it with him."

We could hope that was the case. I kept my mouth shut on the other possibilities.

Colleen continued. "It's some horrendous old sports car, but I can't remember the type." She made a moue of distaste. "He and some friends went to California for a week after their high school graduation, and he drove back in the thing. A money pit."

Colleen interrupted herself with a raised finger. "Wait ... I may have that." She flipped open her attaché case and riffled through some envelopes, then pulled one free and handed it to me. "Cameron's registration" was penciled on the flap in a precise, copperplate handwriting.

I took it, looked it over, nodded. "Dark green, 1967 Camaro, license: CAMSCAM." I didn't roll my eyes.

I shut my notebook. "I think I can get started with this. I'll return the photos to you once I've made some copies. Tomorrow, if that's convenient. And I can pick up the schedules and bank statement from you at the same time," I suggested.

She looked relieved. "Yes, that's fine. I have a lunch at the Bellevue Hilton tomorrow. We can meet at the front desk at one thirty."

"Sure." I pulled out my appointment book. As I flipped it open to write down the note, she was opening her own again. Every date I could see in Colleen's calendar had at least two or three appointments on it. And they didn't look like beauty salons and lunches with the girls.

"May I ask what you do, Colleen?"

She looked me in the eye and gave a practiced smile. "I'm an event coordinator. I work as an independent consultant to arrange weddings, meetings, parties, conferences, conventions, shows, any sort of large function. I met Nan when I was creating an event for her firm."

I nodded. "And your husband? What did he do? When did he die?"

Her motion stuttered, and she went blank. For a moment I was sure I could see the skull beneath her skin before she spoke. "Daniel died five years ago. He ran a small engineering firm in Redmond. His partner, Craig Lee, runs it now, though we still hold some stock. Is it important?"

"Just background."

We wrapped up our business and dealt with my contract. She seemed relieved to be back on a professional footing and disposed of the paperwork and retainer with efficiency.

I didn't expect to make a lot off this case. It sounded too typical: a controlling mother whose kids have finally had enough. The daughter had already cut loose and I'd guess the son was doing the same. It was even money he'd turn up with an "unsuitable" girlfriend, bingeing on something, or chasing psychedelic dreams in the clubs. Or all of the above. The depressing grind.

THREE

I walked back to my office, thinking about Mrs. Shadley's case. I was at the top of the stairs, about twelve feet away from my office door, when a shadow flickered across the frosted glass panel.

I stopped and frowned, watching for the movement again. When it came, I eased over to the wall and along it to the doorframe. I crouched down next to the door and listened. My heart squeezed and fluttered in my chest. There was someone—two someones—in my office, and it sounded like they were searching the place. Without a thought, I reached for my gun.

And stopped.

What was I doing? There were two men searching my office and I was ready to fling open the door and confront them with gun drawn. Had I gone stupid while dead? I'd once cornered a rat by accident and had a neat line of scars on my hands and one leg to remind me. Was I now proposing to stand between these two rats and the only exit? Hell no. Once dead in a month was plenty.

I slid my pistol back into the small of my back and duckwalked across the hall to the offices of Flasch and Ikenabi, accountants. The secretary stared at me as I waddled in—no mean trick in a skirt and heels.

"Can I help you?" she squeaked.

I closed the door, stood up and spoke in a low voice. "Um … yes.

I'm Harper Blaine. I have the office across the hall and there seem to be two men searching it without my permission. I'd like to use your phone to call the police."

Huge-eyed, she pushed a button on her phone and offered me the handset. Gotta love speed dial.

I called it in and warned the operator that my office looked down on the west side of the building, so the patrol should approach with caution. I stayed in the accountants' outer office, waiting.

In minutes, a police car blipped its siren to get through the intersection and pulled up outside—on the west side of the building. Two men exploded out of my office and raced for the stairs. They brushed right past the officers coming up. With a yell that echoed throughout the building, the cops gave chase, but lost them.

The two patrol officers came back up the stairs a while later and met me in front of my office. The door was standing open. The place was a mess. Papers and files were strewn across the desk and floor, and my rolling file cabinet had been pulled out into the center of the room. Its two drawers hung out. My computer was on and the little safe under the desk was open. The burglars had either been here longer than I thought, or they were quick workers.

The cops looked at the mess and looked at the door with its drilled lock. Then they called for a technician to come and collect fingerprints. They didn't lift a single one, though I would have sworn neither man wore gloves.

The two cops questioned me alternately as the tech worked. "Could you identify them?"

"If you'd caught them, maybe. One of them looked like a homeless guy who grabbed me this morning. The usual Pioneer Square alley drunk or druggie—he was babbling—but I'd never seen him before that. The other was pretty generic. Never seen him before at all."

"Great," the shorter of the two muttered.

I shook my head. "I warned the dispatcher that a noisy approach on the west side would spook them. Or didn't he tell you?"

They both looked a little pinker and I restrained an urge to spit.

"Could one of these guys be stalking you?" the taller cop asked.

I snorted. "Stalking me? Oh, yeah ... private investigators are every crackhead's dream girl."

"Maybe someone sent them. Any ideas on that score?"

"Nope."

And that was the truth. My assailant was repentant and hoping to get off lightly. I had no angry clients or frustrated evildoers lurking in my professional closets, that I knew of. Most of my work is boring and mundane stuff people pay to avoid. My nerves itched wondering about it, and my patience for Twenty Questions with the dingbat twins was about to expire.

The cops looked at me as if it were my fault. "No idea? Like nobody you pissed off?"

"No."

The taller one rolled his eyes. "Just get your lock fixed and get yourself an alarm before one of your admirers comes back. That would be your best move."

That was my limit. I snapped at him, "No. The best move would have been for you to think before you came charging in."

He narrowed his eyes at me but didn't respond. They stalked away, muttering.

It was almost one p.m. and I was left with a mess and a broken lock. I strangled the urge to kick a few large, idiot-shaped objects. I slammed into my office and called Mobile Lock Service, then started picking up the mess.

Nothing seemed to be missing, in spite of the thorough tossing. Even the safe had been turned out, but not ripped off. It made no sense, and that bugged me.

I tried to put it out of my mind by calling a contact at the SPD and asking him if Cameron Shadley's car had been impounded recently. It hadn't, but he promised to page me if a call came in on it, if he could.

I returned to the mess.

I was sitting and steaming, after an hour's cleaning and sorting, when the locksmith arrived. I'd worked with Mobile Lock before for my own business as well as clients', so I just pointed at the door. The locksmith nodded and went straight to it.

After a while, he grunted. "Break-in?" he asked, fitting the new lock into the old one's hole.

"Yeah. The cops think I need an alarm… As if I can just pop out to the mini-mart and get one off the rack."

"Huh. Tiny little place like this, you don't need a big alarm system."

"No, but I need something, I need it yesterday, and I need it cheap."

"You get what you pay for."

"And sometimes you just pay," I answered, kicking my trash can in misplaced spite.

He started fiddling with the striker plate. "Huh. Well. Y'know, I might know someone could help you out, cheap."

"Really?"

"Yeah. Kind of a weird guy, but he does good electronics, tinkers around with a bunch of stuff. You should look him up, maybe. Bet he could do you an alarm for cheap and, like I said, he does good work."

"What's his name?"

"Quinton. This time of day, you could probably find him at the library down the street, if you're in a hurry."

"Maybe you could just give me his phone number."

"Nah. You'd have better luck going down to the library. Quinton's the sort of guy you just … find. Y'know? Hey, there, that does it. All done."

He stood up and handed me a pair of shiny new keys. "There y'go. Tougher than the old one, though this crummy door don't do much more than hold it up and look pretty."

I gusted a sigh. "All right. I'll look your guy up. What's his name again?"

"Quinton. Go up to the reference section and ask the librarian for him. She'll know where he is."

Anything was worth a try, and the guy had never steered me wrong before. I thanked him and paid for the new lock, knowing I'd have to fight my landlord for a week to get reimbursed.

FOUR

I trudged up to the main library at Fourth and Madison. The reference librarian knew right where to find Quinton.

I walked down the row she pointed out and saw a man seated at a computer workstation at the end. He was slashing away at the keyboard at a terrifying speed and muttering as he did so. His long brown hair was tied back at the nape of his neck and his pale face was decorated with a close-trimmed dark beard.

He stopped what he was doing, blanking the screen, and cocked his head at me.

"Are you Quinton?" I asked.

"Who's looking for him?" he countered.

"My name's Harper Blaine. The guy from Mobile Lock sent me."

He nodded. "OK. What do you need help with?"

"My office was broken into and I need some kind of alarm system right away and cheap."

"Ah. I see." He grinned. "Yeah, I can get something up for you in about fifteen minutes. It won't be perfect, but it should hold back the Visigoths for a while."

I goggled at him.

He grinned. "It's not that hard. What's your setup?"

"One door, one window, two phone lines," I said. "One of the phone lines is for the modem on my computer."

"That'll be cake. How far away is it?"

"About eight blocks."

"Did you walk or drive?"

"Walked."

"OK. Let's go." He logged out of the computer system and grabbed his coat and backpack off a nearby chair.

I had to hurry after him. I'm tall and leggy, but he didn't waste time and keeping up required a brisk stride. As we headed south to Pioneer Square, mid-April was doing its spring fake-out of good weather. Seattleites seem to forget that it usually starts raining again in May; they were out without jackets, enjoying the beginning of an unexpected clear evening that would probably turn cold by nine and produce more fog by morning. In spite of its capriciousness, this was usually my favorite time of year. But this time, I felt grim.

Turning onto Yesler uphill of Pioneer Square, I found myself blinking against a sudden haze in my vision and rising queasiness. As I was walking across the street to my building, a dusty-looking, bearded man in jeans, boots, flannel shirt, and a broad-brimmed hat glared at me, then walked right into me. He bumped me out of his way. His touch sent a cold shock through me, and his smell was worse.

"Hey!" I yelled after him. He stomped on.

"What's the matter?" Quinton asked.

I blinked my eyes clear and caught my breath. "That guy just walked right into me."

"What guy?"

I pointed. "That one."

We both stood and looked at the empty block where the man had been. A few ordinary pedestrians were about, but my rude man had vanished.

"He must have gone down the alley," I said. But he hadn't. I shook off a qualm, frowning.

Up in my office, Quinton started prowling around the window and the doorway. He took a complicated folding tool out of his pocket, then rummaged through his backpack and laid a pile of wire spools, tape, and small-parts packages on the floor.

"This shouldn't take very long," he said and squatted down beside the open door.

While I watched, he stuck something to the doorframe near the floor. He attached some wire and cut off a long piece of the stuff, leaving it hanging like a tail as he taped it into place and closed the door. He went to the window and began on that.

My phone rang. I turned my back on Quinton and answered it.

"Miss Blaine. Sergeyev. I am calling again. Would you have interest in recovering my heirloom?"

I sat at my desk and grabbed a notepad. "Possibly. It would depend on the circumstances. Perhaps we could meet to discuss it?"

He laughed. "No. I am not in Seattle now. But I would pay very well. Two thousand American dollars up front, as you say. And more to retrieve it to me."

"Then I'm interested. Has the item been stolen?"

"Misplaced, only. So many disruptions here. It has gone astray."

"Where are you?"

"I last saw it in Switzerland. Ingstrom, I think, took the cargo to Seattle, 1970, 1980…"

I was getting confused by his odd speech patterns. I tried to put him back on course. "What is the item?"

"A furniture. A parlor organ. Can you find it? It is not rush."

I jotted down what he'd said so far and looked at it. "Your information is pretty skimpy. Do you have any other leads?"

"I shall consider on it and express you papers with the check. We are agreed?"

"Yes, but it may take some time…"

I thought I heard a chuckle and then, "If you'd like to place a call, please hang up and dial again."

I glared over at Quinton, just rising from kneeling by the phone jack on the wall. "What just happened? I lost a client and I don't have his number!"

"Wasn't me. The line's fine. Maybe he'll call right back."

But he didn't. After a few minutes' waiting, I shook my head. "Damn."

Quinton frowned at the phone. "You think he's not calling back?"

I was miffed. "Not right now."

"I only have to do one more thing. I'll need the phone for a couple of minutes. You have a pager?"

"Yeah."

"What's the number?"

I looked sideways at him and felt a little dizzy, then looked away. "Why do you need it?"

He held up a birthday card in a clear plastic envelope with the words "Record your own greeting!" on it. "I'm going to program the chip to call you with a code if someone breaks in here."

"Oh." I rattled off the number.

He stripped a small, dark object out of the card and placed it next to the phone. Then he placed the handset next to the chip and dialed my pager number and an extension, then hung up. In a moment, my pager went off at my waist, vibrating silently.

"Did you get it?" he asked.

I read the page. "Nine-nine-nine."

"That's the code you'll get whenever the door or window opens. Just ignore it if you do it yourself. I should be able to get a better system up for you in a day or two. Just a couple of quick things and we're done, for now."

He made several strange-looking connections to my phone and electrical system, covering them neatly with white tape so they were invisible to a casual glance.

"That'll do it," he said, putting his tools away and picking up the backpack.

"How much do I owe you, Quinton?"

"How 'bout dinner? I've got a couple of other questions about the permanent system. If you're still interested?"

I thought about it. "I guess I am. Can you make a ballpark estimate?" I asked.

"I don't make estimates as sloppy as that." His eyes were twinkling over a smothered laugh.

I gave him a suffering look.

I got an apologetic grin in return. "Unless the parts have gone up a lot, it'll be under two hundred, including the stuff I used today."

It was only a small gamble. "OK. We can talk over dinner. What do you want to eat?"

"Some kind of dead animal will do me fine," he answered. "I like veggies well enough, but I'm too much the carnivore to give up meat."

I started picking up my things. "Good. I was leaning toward a steak, myself."

"Sounds great."

We walked up First to the Frontier Room. It's divey, kitschy, and the menu runs to barbecue and stiff drinks, but they have a good steak and it's cheap.

"So," Quinton started, separating brisket with his fork, "what situation am I dealing with on this alarm? You don't seem like the type to lock the barn after the horse is gone, to drag out a cliché. Are you expecting more trouble?"

"I'd rather not take the chance."

He glanced at me from the side. "OK. I assume you don't want the cops on your doorstep every time the alarm goes off. Right?"

"Yes. And I don't want this to be out of my control or open to prying by some security company. My clients pay for confidentiality, but I still need records if someone does break in again."

Quinton nodded, a comma of barbecue sauce lending him a quirky smile. "Quiet, reliable notification—no false alarms to the cops—and admissible in court. I think I can do that pretty easily with the setup you've got. I may have to drill a few holes, though. Is that a problem?"

"The manager's a bit of a jerk, but I'll get around him. The owner couldn't care less, as long as he gets his tax credit."

We hammered out a few more details, but by the time we'd finished eating and were chasing the meal down with coffee, the conversation had gotten onto other topics. Maybe it was the glass of wine I'd had, but I felt comfortable. Quinton made easy conversation, and a business dinner turned into just hanging out.

We walked back toward Pioneer Square afterward. Quinton stopped at First and Columbia.

"This is it for me. I'll get in touch as soon as I've got the parts. And ... thanks for dinner. That was good."

"Yeah, it's a pretty good place."

He grinned and started down Columbia toward the waterfront, turning back to wave before disappearing below the freeway ramp on the steep downgrade.

I strolled on, heading for the Rover a few blocks away, feeling warm and full and a little drowsy. It was getting colder, as I'd expected, though. As I passed my office building, a swirl of clammy steam licked up from the street. The cold slither of the mist around my ankle made me shiver and raised the hair on my nape.

I looked around, feeling observed, and started arguing with my paranoia. It was just steam. All the steam covers leaked a little wisp into the cooling air and made tiny ghosts dance a moment on the cobbled street. But this steam slunk up a shape in an alley nearby.

I gave a start. Someone was standing, shadowed, in the alley, watching me. I turned and strode toward the gleam of eyes. The shadow moved, flickering through light from a window above. A female shape and a flash of wine red hair, then she was gone around the next corner without a sound.

I started after her, pursuing the Cabernet gleam of her cropped hair. Alternating heat and cold rushed over me. I darted around the corner into indeterminate light and a deep, low thrumming. Everything was shrouded as if within a dense snow cloud, always moving, almost revealing ... something, then closing up again. The light—hazy gray and impossible to look at as sun-glare in the desert—wiped out detail in a fuzz of visual noise. Shapes seemed to surge and stream just at the knife-edge of perception, flickering with black dots in the corners of my eyes.

I stopped short and whipped around. More of the same. I quailed, gripped by vertigo, and swiped at my eyes as if I could wipe my dimming vision clear and find the way out.

I turned again, but the alley had become an unending plain of cloud-stuff.

I shouted, "Where are you? Where are you!" Panic rushed my breath. I staggered backward in circles, panting and calling.

Something murmured, "Be quiet or it will hear you."

I spun toward the whisper. A face had formed out of the thick atmosphere, glowing with a pale, internal light—a soft-edged human face, but with no defining factors and no real color, just a thicker, more luminous density of the wavering not-mist. My heart stuttered in my chest.

I shook and stammered, "Who are you?"

"I am ... I. I am ... he. I am she..."

I didn't care about philosophy. I waved a shaking hand in front of the face. "Strike that. Just get me out of here."

The face murmured and began to dissolve. "Shhhh ... be patient." The formlessness distorted and writhed as if unseen snakes rolled within it, dragging the face back into its depths. I was alone in my pocket of the haze-world.

A shriek and a moaning howl ripped the thickened light. Shudders racked my spine. Something screamed back. A shape bulged out of the mist, brushing hard against me, spinning me.

A maw of dripping teeth snapped at my head, rushing ahead of a coiling blackness that drove a wave of shock through the mist. It turned, drawing a shape to it, gathering itself—massive, dark, with a snarling, eyeless head. A mane of bone spines whipped the smoky light. It screamed, lunging.

I caught its scream and stumbled backward. Then I felt a touch on my head and another on my chest that resolved into a shove. The unseen force flung me away.

I fell hard onto the cobbled alley. Something roared, and the bright darkness vanished with the sound of a door slamming.

I thrashed around, looking for the black thing or the vile mist. Just an alley, stinking slightly of urine and garbage and spilled beer. Thin wisps of ground fog danced across the surfaces of tiny puddles between the stones, but nothing else.

A door hinge squealed, then trash cans clattered as a busboy heaved bags into a Dumpster next to Merchants Cafe. I swallowed the urge to heave, myself, and slowed my breath. I pulled myself up with one hand pressed on the rough brick wall of the café and brushed at my backside, shaking. Pedestrians went past the ends of the alley. There was no crowd of onlookers. No one had seen or heard what I had.

I wobbled across the alley, found my purse, and faltered away.

I quivered as I drove home across the West Seattle Bridge. Whatever had happened was not a momentary visual aberration from a head injury. What was the thing that had lunged at me? Where had I gone? The only word I had for the creature I'd spoken with was "ghost," and I didn't like that word at all.

At home, I scrabbled up the business card that Skelleher had given me from the bottom of my bag. It was ten o'clock, but I couldn't wait.

A cheery male voice answered. "Danzigers'. This is Ben."

I don't know what I'd expected but it wasn't this.

Shivering, I bumbled into speech. "Uh, my name is Harper Blaine. Dr. Skelleher suggested you or … Mara might be able to help me."

"Skelly! Yeah. What kind of help do you need?"

I hesitated. "I … don't know. He thought … you might have some ideas. Maybe I'm seeing ghosts or something…"

"Oh. I see. Yeah, they're annoying, pesky things when you're not sure they exist in the first place."

"Yes! And there's this living mist..."

"Ah. That's interesting. This—these occurrences are new to you?"

"Yes."

"Hmm." He turned from the phone and I heard a muffled conversation. Then he came back. "Well, I think we can help—at least a bit. Maybe we can help you figure out what's going on, maybe make you a little more comfortable about it. Could you drop by for an hour or two?"

"Now?"

He chuckled. "No, no. Tomorrow. Could you come about ... four? Mara will be home by then."

I leapt. "Four is fine. Where?"

"Upper Queen Anne, above the Center. Let me give you directions..."

FIVE

As I walked toward my office the next morning, I saw the rude man in the hat who had bumped into me the night before. He paid me no attention this time and strode away toward First. Despite the sunlight diluted by a high, thin cloud cover, the day seemed shadowy and dark. I was inclined to write off the vaguely human shapes where no humans stood as an insufficiency of caffeine in my morning-shocked system. I hustled upstairs and wrapped myself in still more paperwork and phone calls, sending Cameron's picture out to be copied.

I detected no watchers in alleys or elsewhere, but couldn't banish the unease itching at the back of my neck. Even in my office, I felt observed.

I was interrupted when an express service messenger knocked and entered my office. She shoved a clipboard at me and I asked what it was for.

"Letter pak from a G. Sergeyev," she answered.

It was a large express envelope. Tearing it open, I found a few sheets of cheap, typed paper, and a cashier's check drawn on a foreign bank. I looked that over carefully, but never having seen a European check before, I couldn't tell if it was legitimate or not. The express routing slip gave a London origin, far from the origin of the check. I figured my bank would know what to do with the check, and I took a break to walk it over.

Coming out of the bank, I pulled my jacket close against a sudden bluster of wind. The air seemed to be getting darker and thicker, misting up despite the thinness of the cloud cover, and my ears were ringing a little. The wind between the buildings whispered, and my hair blew into my face, flickering in the edges of my vision. I hunched a little deeper into my jacket, tucking my chin down into the collar.

As I strode along with my head down, something smacked into my chest. The impact made me catch my breath, stumbling back a step. I stared down, trying to figure out what had hit me. There was nothing lying nearby, but the object, whatever it was, had struck with the force of a thrown ball and left a cold ache in my chest. This was no hallucination; hallucinations don't hurt. I raised my head and felt queasy.

The cold steam-mist was back, rendering the world into pale colors and soft focus. Workers on their lunch hour bustled obliviously through the cloud-stuff, like projections on a deteriorated screen. A shadow with no object moved along the sidewalk away from me. I shook my head, but nothing changed.

A few of the passersby glanced at me, moving out of sync, as if the projectionist had several films going at different speeds. My legs went shaky and I stumbled toward a pink splash in the mist. It was a gigantic metal tulip I knew was painted bright red and green. Public art. I sat down on the granite base and stared.

Stray shapes swarmed among the passing humans. I wanted to jump up and run from the shadow-shapes. The dimmed world of my normal Seattle seemed as oblivious to the shadows as they were to it, plunging through each other without regard. The thin sunlight did not penetrate the mist, but still touched buildings and people, somehow. The other things felt it not at all, moving to a constant thrumming cut with clangings and distant voices.

Even as ice crawled over my skin, I berated myself. I took a deep breath, then another. That seemed to help. What was I afraid of? Nothing was coming for me, this time. The shadows were just going about their business, whatever it was. I shook my head and glanced around. A dark columnar form seemed to be watching me. I stood up and started to walk away. It turned to track me. I ran for my office.

But the historic district enclosing Pioneer Square was thronged with shadow-things. I squeezed back against a building and vertigo shook me as I looked out at the street. Real and past traffic mingled in the misted road. Ghostly horses and motorcars moved heedlessly across the center of the Square about a foot lower than the modern pedestrians strolling there. Spectral shapes rose and sank along the sidewalks, and the shade of a giant tree that hadn't existed in a hundred years whipped its branches a foot from the bust of Chief Sealth.

I felt ill. I needed to negotiate this maze of the solid and the incorporeal and make it to some safety—someplace they couldn't come. Shuffling my feet along the concrete and asphalt of the real world, I crossed the street with a crowd of visitors and their tour guide. I flinched as a horse and rider passed right through the crowd with no discernible effect, then staggered as I refocused on a lamppost menacing my path. Concentrating on objects of the present helped hold the past back for a moment. I thought of lampposts and bus benches and fought my way through the insistent mist-world toward my old Rover. I scrambled into it.

Nothing touched me in the old olive green truck. I sat until I caught my breath; then I started the engine and drove. Once I was up on the freeway, the real present was in complete control.

The Bellevue Hilton was modern and bland. I approached the building with all my concentration on the normal, determined not to be swept up again by anything weird. In the lobby, a signboard directed visitors to the chamber of commerce luncheon, and small clutches of business people drifted toward the lobby doors.

I heard footsteps on the carpet, and someone called my name.

I turned and saw Colleen Shadley walking across the lobby, carrying her attaché case. She moved with a smooth grace, even on her rather tall heels. Without them she would barely break five five. Somehow I had carried away the impression that we were close to the same height. But even wearing flat-soled boots, I overtopped her by more than two inches.

"Harper," she greeted me, extending her hand. "I'm so glad you made it. I have those papers for you." She opened the flap on the case and offered me a plain manila envelope. "Have you been able to get started yet?"

"I've got a little information, but now that I have this, I should be able to get along faster." I offered her an envelope containing the pictures of Cameron that she had lent me. "I'll let you know as soon as something comes up."

She gave me a cool, professional smile and wished me well, then turned away. I got out of there before someone asked her who I was.

I had almost two hours to kill. I craved a cup of coffee or anything mundane and anchoring: comfort food, bad TV, something like that. I decided to try a little shopping. Coffee and lunch and department stores in suburban Bellevue. Not a shadow-thing in sight. I was done and on my way back to Seattle by three fifteen. If I was fast enough, perhaps the strangeness couldn't catch up to me.

I was even feeling a bit smug when I parked near the Danzigers' house. I was ten minutes early. I locked up the Rover and walked toward the pale blue house.

It was one of those square, half-brick, half-clapboard houses from about 1900. It had a deep, railed front porch overhung by the second floor. A favorite-grandma house. A pleasant, if slightly wild, garden overran the yard above a short flight of stone steps and a vine-grown wooden arch.

Closer to, the house glowed, golden and beckoning as a cheery fire. It should have made me feel welcome, but the hair on my neck prickled.

SIX

The door popped open to my knock.

Ben Danziger was over six feet tall, broad-shouldered, bearded, and blue-eyed. His wavy black hair stood from his head in electrified tufts, and he looked like either a mad scientist or a terrified rabbinical student.

"Hi! You must be Harper Blaine," he exclaimed. "Come in, come in. Excuse the way I look. I've been doing the laundry and the static from the dryer always makes me look like a mad poodle."

He held the door open and I stepped inside.

The house did not glow as brightly inside, but it contained a low hum like the contented purring of a cat.

He turned and ducked through another doorway on the left. "Would you like a glass of tea?"

I followed him into the kitchen, dazed by his bouncing energy. "Yeah, sure."

You could have filmed commercials for Grandma's Old-Fashioned Something in there, among the rubbed hardwood floors and polished copper pots on racks.

Danziger excused himself to pop into the back room and toss a pile of clothing into a wicker basket. He paused and called out, "Honey, our guest's here!"

A voice came from a bulge in his chest pocket. "Start without me, darlin'. The baby's being stubborn."

He bounced back in and rattled around, piling objects on a wooden tray. He swept it up, then put it back down on a huge table and looked at me.

"I'm sorry. I didn't ask if you prefer your tea over ice. Do you?"

I was too surprised to say I had assumed that he meant iced tea when he mentioned glasses. "I don't care one way or the other."

"Ah. Good. I like Russian tea. Mara'll join us in the study."

Toting the tray, he led me up the staircase and around the landing to a small door. "Open that for me, will you?"

I opened the door and followed him up a last narrow flight of stairs into what used to be the attic. A large skylight had been installed on the southern slope of the roof, making a bright, comfortable small office—if you didn't mind ducking a lot. Wall sconces bounced more light up against the sloping walls and ceiling. Bookshelves stood wherever the walls rose over four feet. The lower, darker corners were stacked with boxes.

Danziger's desk was built of four wooden file cabinets and a wooden door. An old leather swivel chair stood on one side and an old leather couch on the other. He elbowed a clear space in the books on the desk and set down the tray. The soft, aged leather of the sofa squeaked and settled around me as I sat down.

Danziger began tinkering with teapots and tall, metal-caged glasses. "Water?" he asked.

"Huh?"

"Hot water in the tea? It's really strong, otherwise," he explained.

"Sure. Whatever you suggest."

He frowned in concentration, poured dark tea into one of the glasses, measuring it against some spot on the filigree cage, then added hot water with equal precision.

He handed me the glass, saying, "Skelly sent you to us because you've been seeing strange stuff. So tell me about the strange stuff."

I put up a hand. "Wait a minute. Let's start with some background. I don't know anything about you except that a doctor who seems a bit

... unconventional suggested I talk to you. How can you help me? Just who or what are you?"

"Well, I'm a part-time linguistics professor at the U and I do some other research on the side—which is how I met Skelleher and my wife, Mara. I translate text to and from Russian, Czech, Polish, German, and a few other languages, and do related work in comparative religion and philosophy. I was a philosophy major once, and I got interested in comparative religion and started studying languages, met Mara, and one thing led to another... I used to teach religion and philosophy, too, but budget cuts ... you know." He shrugged.

I looked askance at him. "And what does any of that have to do with my problem?"

Danziger gestured as he explained. "Well, when you really start to tangle with religion and philosophy, you eventually run up against all the mystical stuff about death and souls, the meaning of life, burden, responsibility, unity—all the really big, freaky topics. And then you have two choices: just jump over it and go on to the parts that don't bend your brain, or dive into the bizarre and try to run truth to ground. I guess I just like wrestling with the weird stuff and I ended up writing a book about it. So now I'm 'the ghost guy.' "

I scowled. I had no wish to be an experiment in flaky science. "So you're some kind of parapsychologist."

He shook his head. "I'm just a strange type of philosopher, really. I don't know any ghosts, personally, except for Albert over there," he added, pointing into a corner.

I looked, saw nothing, turned my head and saw a slender, weedy shadow just inside the door. It was not particularly thick, but it had baleful cat eyes that glared at me. I started.

"What is that?" I demanded.

Danziger smiled. "That's Albert. We're pretty sure he was a boarder in this house during Prohibition and died here from drinking doctored gin. Poor old sot." Danziger shook his head and smoothed a hand over his hair, dispelling the last of the static so his dark hair flopped down and made him look like a half-wilted dahlia. "Anyhow, you can see him and that's good. I can't. I only know he's there because I've figured out the cold spot. Fakers always look where I point and swear he's right there."

The door opened beside the ghost. A tall, slender woman with flame red hair stepped into the study. Her eyes were slanted and green as a cat's, and she would have been stunning even if she had not gleamed from within. I doubted she'd been ill a day in her life.

She cocked her head as if to listen to the dark shape, then gave a rueful smile and shook her head. She spoke in a fluting Irish voice. "That's lovely, Albert, but you're blocking the door, aren't ya? Now, shoo." She flipped her hands at the shadowy form and it wafted away.

She turned to look at me and her eyes sparkled. "You must be Harper. I'm Mara. I see you've met Albert, our polygraph." She walked across to the desk and leaned down to kiss Danziger on the cheek. "Hello, love. Sorry I'm late. Brian was being obstinate. Would you pour me some tea?"

She plumped down onto the other end of the sofa with a biscuit and a glass of tea.

Danziger pointed at my own glass. "You should drink your tea while it's still hot, and try the biscuits and jam. The jam goes in the tea, not on the biscuits."

I mucked about with my tea while Danziger picked up a biscuit and studied it, frowning, as he spoke. "I did some reading this morning based on what you told me last night, and Mara and I discussed it. Have you been in some kind of accident recently?"

Startled, I put down my tea, untouched. "Yes. Do I still look that bad?"

He bit the biscuit and chewed, looking at me from under lowered brows.

It was Mara who spoke. "You do look as if someone's smacked you about a bit."

I took a slow breath. "Yes. A man I was investigating."

"Investigating?"

"I'm a private investigator."

"Damn," Danziger muttered.

The Albert shadow slipped behind him, spangling the air around them both with snowy mist. Danziger shivered and asked, "Were you hit on the head?"

"Yes."

"Knocked unconscious or … ?"

Over his shoulder, Albert became more clear. The glowering eyes began to look more like glasses. I watched the ghost evolve and the words tumbled out. "Dead. For two minutes."

I told them about the hospital bed, the mists, the thing in the alley, maybe-ghosts, shadow-things, nausea … everything. By the time I was done, Albert looked almost there. "Your ghost is firming up," I finished.

Mara chuckled. "Ah, no. That's just you seeing him better."

I turned to her. "What?"

She gave a small shrug. "Ghosts exist in a place between *here* and *there*. When you're open to that world, you see them. When you're not, you don't."

Albert faded back a bit as Danziger spoke up. "When you're engaged with that world, your expectation or acceptance affects your perception and access. You've been fighting it, but when you talk about your experience, you accept certain facts—whether you can explain them or not—and Albert there is reinforcing proof that you're not crazy, that what you experienced is real, so you can see him a little better."

I shook my head. "I don't want to see him better. I don't want this stuff."

Mara sighed. "I fear you're stuck with it, since you can't un-die."

She must have seen me recoil. Her expression softened and she put down her glass before continuing. "That was a bit abrupt of me, but it's plain you can see Albert. There's a limited number of satisfactory explanations for that, plus what you've described. Do you think yourself mad?"

"No. I … don't want to think I'm crazy."

Danziger chimed back in. "Unless you think we all share the same delusion—which is statistically unlikely—"

"Then it must be real, or we're all mad as hares."

"All right," I conceded. "Suppose we're not all crazy and that is a ghost." I pointed at the grim column of Albert's ethereal form, wavering between Ben and Mara, as if it was pacing. "Why do we see it? What is happening to me?"

Danziger grinned. "Ah, now that's where things get interesting. You see Albert for a different reason than Mara. Albert, like most ghosts, manifests by bringing an instance of his energy state with him. You're both able to access the energy state at which things like Albert become visible, so you're both able to see him. But you can do more than that; you can move around in that state and directly observe it, operate in it, even though you're not normally at that energy state yourself. It's very rare and really exciting stuff. You don't manipulate the energy state, however—that would be magic. But it's all energy, anyhow. So you experience the energy state of the Grey differently than Mara, but since you both have access to it, you both see Albert." He looked pleased and expectant.

I let him down. "What are you talking about?"

Mara rolled her eyes. "Ah, Ben, jumping right to the conclusion without demonstrating the proof. You must have been the despair of your Maths prof." She turned to me. "He'll be rabbiting on about metaphysics and energy states for hours if we let him."

Danziger looked affronted. "I'm not that bad. But maybe we should start from a different perspective. Has anything like this happened to you before?"

I picked up the glass again and looked into the tea. "No." Weird flights of childhood imagination and bouts of the willies weren't relevant. Danziger nodded, but Mara narrowed her eyes at me and looked thoughtful while he went on.

"OK. So sometimes you seem to just walk in and out of these strange places, these mists, but other times, you just see some weird stuff?"

Mara cocked her head and, before I could answer her husband, added, "Sometimes you seem to hold it off and sometimes you don't?"

I glanced from one to the other. "That's exactly it."

Danziger picked up a book and began flipping the pages with a swift finger.

Mara carried on. "You've talked to a creature in the mist, been pushed on by one, but have you pushed anything around yet? Pushed the mist aside or away from you?"

"No."

"You have no control over the coming and going?"

"Not really."

"And all of this has been growing more frequent and intense since you woke in hospital?"

"That's why I went to Dr. Skelleher. I thought there was something wrong. He says there isn't."

She sat back. "It's not wrong. It's just quite rare and hardly what they're teaching in medical schools these days."

I clenched eyes and fists. "What is it, damn it?"

Danziger had been running his finger down the pages as she questioned me. Now he paused and answered, "It's the Grey."

"What the hell is that?"

He pointed at my hands. "Don't squeeze so hard on the glass. They really hurt when they break."

I put the glass down with exaggerated care and glared at him. I'd have started screaming if someone else hadn't beaten me to it.

"Oh, God. The baby." Danziger pulled a baby monitor from his chest pocket. "We'd better go downstairs and continue where Brian can join in."

Shaking my head, I trailed behind Mara Danziger and the flickering shape of Albert. Ben brought up the rear, peeling away at the landing as Mara and I continued down the stairs.

"Are you confused yet?" she asked.

"Frustrated. Neither of you has answered my question."

"No, we haven't, have we. The *why* is, you're a Greywalker. Which means exactly nothing to you, yet."

"Not a thing."

"Stay for dinner and I'll try to explain while I'm cooking. Ben'll be right down, I'm sure, to help out."

SEVEN

I wasn't so sure this was wise, but I followed as Mara led me into the kitchen and began organizing dinner preparations. Albert shimmered in over her shoulder as she talked. "There's a bit of a place between our world and the next. That's what Ben calls the Grey."

Ben Danziger walked in, carrying a black-haired toddler who was gnawing on the head of a large Russian nesting doll. "Are we ready to talk about Grey stuff now?" he asked.

"We'd started on it," Mara replied.

"Aha! I have visual aids to make this easier. If I can just get them away from Brian." Ben put the baby down and wrestled the doll from him. "OK. First, you have to have an overview. Matter, as we know it, is simply a state of energy. Particle physics and so on. It's all just energetic states and interactions. When you strip out the fancy terms, many philosophical and religious beliefs come down to essentially the same thing: being, existence, and consciousness are basically energy states."

He sat on the floor beside a heavy oak table and pulled the doll apart to show the next doll inside. "Now, if what we perceive is just a state of energy, then it follows that there may be other states we cannot perceive because we exist within a different state. Beside our 'normal' world—our normal energy state—there is a parallel or 'paranormal' world where other energy states dominate, and a transition zone where the world states overlap. Like these matryoshka dolls, nesting one inside the next. This transition zone is the Grey, and it has its own special denizens, all the weird crossover manifestations of the paranormal and the normal together. Things like ghosts, vampires, elemental spirits, stuff like that. They're neither one thing nor the other. They have some kind of physical body too massy for a purely paranormal sphere of existence—or can manifest one—but they also manifest the faster, lighter energy transformations that—"

The baby snatched the dolls back and Ben looked up. "You're frowning. I'm losing you, aren't I?"

"Yes."

Mara sighed and spoke up from her work by the sink. "It's not so arcane as Ben makes it sound. The world is a sea of energy and most people skim along the surface in the normal world. But when you died, you fell into the sea, and when you came back out, you had a bit of it in you, changing your knowledge and sight of the world. You may try to ignore that knowledge, but it persists."

"I 'fell in.' " I gave her a skeptical look.

"As an analogy, dying is definitely the big plunge. When people say you 'pass over,' they don't know half. You drop all the heavy, slow parts of yourself and zip right through the barrier to … something else. That's the paranormal. But you have to pass through the Grey first, and if you aren't quite ready for the next place, the Grey is where you stop a while, because that's where both worlds overlap."

"Purgatory," I supplied.

Mara laughed, tossing her curls aside and glancing over her shoulder. "That's a Catholic idea. This is nondenominational, and it's nothing to do with either suffering or expiation. But it is full of strange things, you've probably noticed, and it's alive with energy. You notice the house glows, I'm sure."

"Umm … yes, I did."

"This house sits on a Grey power nexus—that's why we chose it-which is part of a sort of power grid, though that's a broad analogy. It's the same energy that runs everything psychic or magical. And it may seem chaotic, but it has rules. All you need do is learn the rules."

I sat down at the kitchen table. Mara turned all the way around and leaned on the counter, shaking flour off her hands.

I stared, unnerved a moment, as the flour drifted like a familiar cloud, then settled to the floor. "Why would I want to? I'm fine now. I'm all here, alive, solid. The bruises will fade and then it's over."

They both shook their heads.

"The state change happened," Ben said, "no matter what your state is now. You changed and you can't change back."

The baby flung the Russian dolls across the room, drowning my reply in clatter.

Ben got up and tucked Brian under his arm. "OK, that's enough of that. Your mom'll turn you into a frog if you don't settle down, and then you'll have to live in the yard. Hey … there's an idea!"

Mara twitched a towel at him. "Behave, y'monster, or it's you I'll be turning green and warty. And you can be sure I'll not be kissing you anytime soon for that."

Ben laughed and loped out of the kitchen with the squirming baby.

Mara bent down and picked up the matryoshka dolls, placing them on the table in front of me. "Would you reassemble the universe, please?"

She went to the counter and began rolling out pastry dough. She spoke over her shoulder. "I imagine you find this upsetting."

"Yes. Look, I don't understand this. Even if I accept that I can see a ghost, what about the rest?"

"It's all bundled up together. You see ghosts because you can see and walk into the Grey where they live. That's very rare. Most of us who can see it at all can only stand on the edge of it and cast lines, or draw up water in buckets, or shout across the water and hope someone answers. We're very limited, weak and in danger of attracting the wrong sort of attention, if you know what I mean. If we want to go in, we're leaving our bodies behind and traveling only with our minds. It's exhausting and dangerous, and few people can do it for more than minutes."

"Psychics and mediums, you mean?"

She laughed, dumping fruit into the piecrust. "Among others. But you, you see, you have the strength and safety of your body when you go there. You don't leave it behind now. You could, if you knew how, walk right through until you found what you were looking for. You wouldn't be asking for intermediaries or hoping the right thing heard you calling. You do have other problems, but the strength you have in the Grey, as a physical person among things that are mostly energy, is very powerful. There are some creatures of the Grey who do have bodies—and they can be strong—but they'll have other weaknesses in exchange."

She carried the finished pie to the oven and waved her hand over the top crust, muttering to it. Her words fell on the pie in a drift of blue.

I noticed. "What are you doing?"

She looked surprised. "Oh! Just sang it a little crusty charm against burning. I hate burned crust."

"A charm?"

She blushed. "Well, you see, I'm a witch."

I blinked at her. "Of course, an expert on the paranormal would be married to a witch."

She grinned and blushed darker. "It's not quite as easy as that. Ben and I don't always see eye to eye on theory versus practice. Fascinates him, of course, but he doesn't take in the real shape of witchcraft so well. He's more interested in ghosts and things like that. And we've had a few goes over it, I'm afraid."

She turned away and bustled for a few minutes, then went back to the stove, putting something into a pot. "Well, that's better. You see, this Grey thing isn't so awful. If you can see that little charm, and Albert, you should come along a treat in no time."

"I can see you cast a spell—a charm—because of … this?"

"Yes, of course. If you have the right skills and you can touch the grid, then you can use that energy for work. Magic is just a way of drawing up some of that energy and directing it. But it requires quite a lot of mediation, and how you have to mediate it determines the sort of magic you can do."

My skepticism deepened. "I can?"

"Oh, no! Not you, actually. As I said, you're a Greywalker. You don't manipulate the material of the Grey. You're in it. And that's a thing we should be discussing. You'll need to learn what you can do and what you can't. And how to protect yourself from the things which will be attracted to you. And there already are a few, I'm sure. Because, like this house, you glow a bit."

I was still skeptical, or perhaps I was tired of wrestling the idea, but it crept into my voice. "I glow? How do you know? Can you see that?"

"Just as you can see me work magic, yes, but as to the rest, that's a bit of guessing. I'm one of those who just stand by the edge of the water and cast lines or haul buckets. And Ben is purely a theoretician. We aren't you. We can't know what you know or experience. We know a lot, and can make best guesses, but it's not quite the same."

"If you don't know, how can you help me? I don't want to be a witch or a psychic or a medium or … whatever."

"You shan't be, for you aren't any of those. But you still need to be learning the principles. Ben and I can teach you what we know about the Grey and how it works, what lives in it, how to fend them off. You'll have to improvise here and there, but you'll have a good foundation. But you'll have to accept that this is real, that it is not going away, and that you must learn to live in it, not just with it."

"No." I stood up from the table. "My brain won't stretch to this right now. It doesn't fit!"

Mara's shoulders slumped a bit. "It does fit. No luck getting out of it. But I will help you, if you let me."

I shook my head hard enough to hurt. "Not today. I need to think. I won't make a leap of faith when I don't have any. And this is still—this is too strange for me to swallow."

I picked up my bag and walked out of the kitchen and met Ben coming in.

"You're not staying for dinner? Mara makes great food."

"I don't think I could digest it. I need to digest something else first."

"Oh. Well. We'll be here if you need us. I know this is a lot of crazy stuff to try and chew up all in one shot."

I looked him hard in the eye. "What if I don't?"

"Then you'll laugh me off as a kook. You won't be the first. I don't think I'm nuts, though, and I don't think you do, either, but you have to make up your own mind. Nothing works if you don't start there. I hope I'll hear from you, though. You seem … nice."

I snorted. "Haven't heard that in a while. Thanks."

Albert trailed after me to the gate and hung in the arch, fading and flickering, until I drove away.

EIGHT

Friday morning I put the strange conversations of the night before out of my head, choosing to concentrate, instead, on my work. I had no doubt about how to do my job, and if I did it with all my concentration, I would not be spontaneously transported to uncanny realms … I hoped. The lurking shadows didn't disappear, but they stayed on the edges and were easier to ignore.

Colleen's list was mostly a bust. When I could reach anyone, the response to my questions about Cameron's whereabouts met with universal ignorance. Most of his friends and relatives had not seen him in an even longer time than his mother. Whatever events had caused him to vanish must have started a lot earlier than the first of March.

I did have one stroke of luck: Cameron's roommate agreed to meet me for lunch between classes.

Richard "RC" Calvin waited for me in front of a Greek café on University Way. He was short and muscular and unremarkable otherwise. We ordered at a counter and sat down nearby.

I put my notebook next to my coffee cup. "I know you think you don't know anything, but you might be able to give me a start. When did you last see Cam?"

He rolled his eyes as he thought. "Uh … sometime around the end of February, I think. It must have been a Thursday night, 'cause that's when we were usually both home at the same time. See, Cam didn't have any Friday lectures, like I do, so he'd usually stay up late on Thursdays and be hanging around when I got home from my late class."

"Didn't he go out?"

"Oh, yeah, he'd blow out of there after we talked about the rent and bills and stuff. You know, it's funny, I really didn't remember till just this second, but he said he'd be gone for a while, so not to worry. I guess I really took him serious, huh? 'Cause I didn't think anything of it till his mom called looking for him. Huh! That's kind of weird, isn't it?"

"Not really. Did you ever think that he'd returned to the apartment?"

"Uh, yeah. About a week ago or so some of his stuff disappeared. I was going to borrow a book from him, so I, like, went into his room, and most of his stuff was gone. Little stuff, like clothes and paperbacks, a couple of big things, like his laptop, but a lot of his stuff was still there, so I didn't think he'd, like, skipped or anything. His duffel bags were missing and his backpack, so I figured he'd gone on a trip, y'know?"

"He never called you after that?"

"Well, no. We're just roommates. We're not buddies or anything. We're kind of from different worlds, y'know?"

I nodded. "Was he distracted, seem to have something going on? Did his behavior change suddenly, or his schedule, anything like that?"

"Um … well, I thought he might have got a girlfriend or something for a while, 'cause he got a lot of calls from a chick and he was going out a lot at night, but he told me it was just his sister, so I didn't think any more about it. Then some guy called for him a couple of times, usually late, like when I was about to go to bed. Cam was home both times, so he took the phone to his bedroom, like he didn't want me to listen in. I don't know, maybe he's gay or something. Anyhow, the guy never called again."

"Could the man on the phone have any connection to Cameron's disappearance?"

RC shrugged his beefy shoulders and dug into his souvlaki. He hunched over the food, eating as if the plate was going to be jerked away any second. He talked with his cheek stuffed with food. "I don't know. Wouldn't think so. Cam had the flu about then, so he was sleeping all the time. Could have been someone from the U, I guess. The guy sounded older—forty or fifty, maybe. Hard to tell, y'know, and it wasn't any of my business anyway."

"Do you remember the man's name? Did he give it?"

He took a swig of his soda before answering. "I can't remember. I think he told me, once… Everett. Something like that. Something snooty. Just can't remember."

"If it comes back to you, let me know. You said Cameron had the flu. How could you tell?"

"It's pretty easy when the guy's been puking his guts up for a week. He was really white when I did see him—pasty, y'know—and kind of thin and wasted-looking. If he hadn't been worshipping the porcelain god, I'd have thought he was on drugs or something. He looked like, y'know, in those old movies when someone's got a terminal disease—all white with big eyes. Couldn't keep anything down. Actually, I don't think he was eating at all for a while, just drinking water and some kind of nasty-smelling soup." He looked up at me and noticed I wasn't eating much myself.

"Did I gross you out? Sorry. Nothing makes me queasy anymore. I'm premed. He was starting to look a little better about the time he took off, but he was still pretty pale, y'know?"

"You're pretty sure it was the flu, then, not some other disease or drugs?" I asked, sipping my coffee.

He shrugged again. "Could have been something else, I guess—I mean, I'm not a doctor yet, so what do I really know?—but flu can be pretty nasty. People think it's, like, just a little thing, but it can kill you, y'know. And there really isn't such a thing as a twenty-four-hour flu. That's usually mild food poisoning. Real all-out, balls-to-the-walls flu is a killer. The Spanish Flu epidemic of 1918 killed millions, and it's just a different strain of the same old bug that makes the rest of us answer the call of the great white telephone. Pretty disgusting, huh?"

I agreed, nodding. "Disgusting. Did anyone come to see Cameron while he was sick? Girlfriend drop by, classmates, anything like that?"

"Nope. Didn't have a girlfriend that I ever heard of—except for the sister thing, like I said. Nobody came around except a couple of my buds and the landlord. Nobody's been around since, either." RC shoveled a last bite of rice pilaf into his mouth and chased it down with a swallow of soda. "You just gonna leave that spanakopita?"

I looked down at my untouched plate. "Uh, I'm not that hungry. Why don't you have it?" I offered, pushing the plate toward him.

He nodded his thanks and forked up a large bite. I watched him, bemused, as I sipped my coffee. I'd read a newspaper article once that claimed interns often suffered from malnutrition and sleep deprivation. Obviously, Richard Calvin was determined to get ahead before the medical profession had a chance to break him down. I wondered if he spent his days off sleeping.

"So you've never heard from Cameron again?" I asked.

"Nuh-uh. Not a word."

"What did you do with the rest of his stuff, and what about the rent?"

"Well, his mom paid the back rent and bills, and she asked me to pack up his stuff and store it till he came back. In the meantime, I'm going to see if I can get another roommate, 'cause I can't meet the rent by myself. Cam's mom said that was OK with her."

"You talked to her on the phone recently?"

"Yeah, I called her and I told her I was going to be talking to you, 'cause, y'know, I didn't know if you were really legit or not. But she told me I should tell you everything I knew, so, like, I guess I have. I mean, I don't know very much about Cam, really. Is there anything else you want to ask me?"

"Not much. Was there anyplace he hung out, where he might have headed, or anyplace where he might talk to people about where he was going?"

RC grunted. I couldn't tell if it was a thinking noise or appreciation of the food. "I don't know exactly, but I do know he was kind of into music, and I think he said he was going to meet his sister downtown once, but other than that, I don't know."

"OK," I said. "Let me give you my business card, and if you think of anything—like that guy's name—or if something comes up, give me a call, OK?"

"OK," he said, swallowing the last of the spanakopita. He ran his tongue over his teeth, eliminating any wayward bits of spinach, and guzzled down the last of his soda as I fished a business card out of my bag.

I handed him the card. "You've been a lot of help, RC."

"I have? Cool." He tucked it into the pocket of his shirt, grabbed his bag and headed for the door. "Hey, thanks for the food."

I watched him go; then I headed down to the administration buildings. I rounded up a list of offices for Cameron's instructors, then walked to the engineering building.

Only one of Cameron's instructors was available. In answer to my question, he blinked and snapped at me, "No. I haven't seen him in class or elsewhere. Haven't heard from him, either. He's failing, at this point. Hasn't shown up in ..." He flipped through a notebook. "At least a month. If he doesn't make some kind of arrangement with me, he will not pass. I don't give NCs. What he will get is an F. And you can tell him that."

"When I see him, I'll be sure to let him know. Thank you."

I left his office grateful I was no longer in college.

I was walking across one of the many quads when my pager went off. I couldn't see any phone booths around, so I entered the nearest building and found a pay phone near the math department office. Someday, I swear, I am going to get a cell phone. I called my pager number and listened to the voice message.

"Hi, Harper, this is Quinton. I've got the stuff to set up your alarm system, though I've still got a couple of questions before I install some of it. I'd like to get onto it today, if that's convenient for you. Give me a call," he added, rattling off a phone number, "but do it before two, if you can, because I'll be leaving this location then, and may not get near a phone for a couple of hours after that. Thanks."

I checked my watch. "Ah, hell ..." It was 1:55. I punched the number and waited through the rings.

Through the noise in the background, I just made out a male voice saying, "... garage."

"Is Quinton there?" I asked, raising my voice.

"Hang on."

In a second, a slightly quieter environment reigned as Quinton answered the phone. "This is Quinton. How can I help you?"

"This is Harper Blaine. I'm returning your call."

"Thanks for getting back to me so quickly, Harper. I can go ahead with your project whenever you can get me access. When would be convenient?"

Was I talking to the right guy? I could almost hear the necktie strangling him. "Are you at work?" I asked.

"Not precisely, but that's a good suggestion. Three o'clock would be fine."

"Actually, I was going to head downtown to do some research, so I might be a little late back to my office. Could you wait a few minutes if I'm not there?"

"Certainly. I'll be seeing you then. Thanks for calling." The connection cut off with a click.

I went back and climbed into the Rover, trying to concentrate on what I planned to do next, rather than obsessing about Quinton's odd behavior and odder job. He was just not in the same game as the rest of us.

I turned onto the freeway and headed back downtown. I thought about the job, the job ... but phantom images seemed to press in harder than before, trailing their cold mist and rushing around the truck. When I got off the freeway downtown, I was firmly back in Ghostville. I parked the car and shouldered my way, shivering and queasy, through a thin fog of shadow-things, toward the main records repository in the county building.

A cold gust blew through me. I shuddered and leaned against the Metro tunnel facade to catch my breath. Several scruffy panhandlers cast suspicious glances at me. I figured I'd better move on before they took exception to my sullying the tone of the neighborhood.

Once in the records room, where even ghosts fear terminal boredom, I started searching for any sign of a furniture company, importer, or freight handler doing business under the name Ingstrom in the last twenty-five years. The list was short, but discouraging: a shipwright, a real estate office, and a bakery. The residential listings were more daunting. There were a lot more private citizens named Ingstrom, since one-fifth of what is now the city of Seattle had been settled by Norwegians and Swedes. I paid for photocopies of the listings.

By the time I'd finished, it was nearly three fifteen. I trudged back toward my office. I'd taken Sergeyev's money but done almost nothing so far, and that rankled. I hadn't done more than glance at the papers he'd sent. The hour-plus I'd just spent could be a washout. Maybe the Ingstrom he wanted wasn't even in King County. Seattle may have been just an unloading point for a pickup. The guy could have driven from Pullman, for all I knew, and then taken the parlor organ away again. I didn't even know for certain what a parlor organ was.

Quinton was sitting on the floor just down from my door, leaning against the wall, reading a paperback copy of de Tocqueville. He was wearing a button-down shirt and trousers under his jacket. No sign of a tie. Without even glancing up, he got to his feet and fell in beside me. Finishing his paragraph, he marked his place with a ticket agency stub for the Paramount Theater and stuffed the book into his backpack.

"Hi," he said. "I was starting to get worried. There were a couple of two-legged rats scratching around your door when I came up, about half an hour ago. When they figured out I wasn't going to leave, they slunk off, but I thought they might have been waiting for you downstairs. Did you see them?"

"No," I answered. "What did they look like?"

"One nondescript in a very concentrated sort of way. Very beige, very bland. Very spooky. The other was scruffier, but nothing unusual for this neighborhood," he added as I unlocked my door.

I nodded. "Probably the same guys who tossed my office. Either that or tax collectors."

He nodded. "Yeah, I thought they were thugs."

I raised an eyebrow at him. He grinned back.

"I've got everything I should need to get this job done in a couple of hours at the most," he said, putting his pack down carefully by the file cabinet.

"I've still got some work to do," I warned. "You're not going to need me to leave or anything, are you?"

"I don't think so. I need to drill a couple of holes and I'll need to work on your phone line at some point, but I should be able to do the installation without much noise or mess. Oh, I'll need to load some software onto your computer, too, but that'll only take a minute, right at the end."

"Let me know when you need the phone line. I need to make calls."

"No problem," he agreed and began to scramble around in his pack.

I settled myself behind the desk and called the Shadleys' bank. It took a few minutes after I introduced myself and explained my business to get me connected to the person with the lowdown on ATMs.

The ATM expert asked me for the numbers. I read them to her and she clacked away on her computer.

"Hmm ... some of these are other companies' machines, so I can't give you any more information than I have right here. They all appear to be in Seattle, looks like downtown. Of the ones that belong to us—let me see—there's the First and Cherry location, Main, Pine and Seventh, and the South Industrial."

"Where are the Main and South Industrial ATMs, exactly?" I asked.

"Main is around the corner from the Pioneer Square branch at 300 Occidental, and the other is First Avenue South at South Forest, just down from the baseball stadium."

I thanked her and wrote the information down. Then I pulled out my laminated map of Seattle and dotted all the known locations on it in whiteboard marker.

I got out of Quinton's way for a moment while he did something to my desk; then I called a few more major banks and got the same information from them, adding more dots to my map. Most of the dots were in downtown, clustering around Pioneer Square. If I could figure out what Cameron was up to, or get a line on his car, I'd stand a chance of finding him soon.

"I'm going to be working on the phone line now for a minute or so," Quinton said from somewhere near the floor in front of the desk. "If your computer hiccups, let me know." His head popped up for a moment, adorned with a pair of headphones and some dust kitties. "OK?"

I pulled out the papers Sergeyev had sent. "OK. I'll be reading. Let me know when the lines are back up."

He nodded and disappeared again.

I read. The parlor organ was about six feet tall and three wide, made from carved European walnut, according to the description. Built by the Tracher Company of Bavaria in 1905, it had a lot of bits and stops and railings with ivory and gilt decoration, a built-in cabinet for storage behind the music desk with a plate glass mirror, and red and blue tapestry covers over the pipes, which matched the mats on the pedals. Sounded pretty garish.

An incomplete shipping bill was included with the description. The date had been torn off and some lines of information were too blotched and stained to read. It looked as if the organ had been shipped to Seattle by boat from Oslo, along with other household and office furniture. How it had gotten to Oslo wasn't documented. There was a partial ship's registry number, a bit of letterhead that read "-gst-" and the signature, "Ingstrom." There was a little squiggle in front of the last name, but it could have been an *e* as easily as an *n*, a *u*, or a *w*, maybe even an *i*.

As information, it gave only hints. The shipping bill seemed to originate with the shipper in Oslo. If Sergeyev was wrong, Ingstrom could be the sender, not the recipient. I didn't relish trying to find a shipping company in Oslo that had employed someone named Ingstrom over thirty years ago.

I picked up the phone, absently thinking I should call the port authority or the coast guard about ship registries, but it was dead. Then it hiccuped as if on call-waiting and I jiggled the cradle switch.

"Hello?"

"Miss Blaine?"

"Yes." Quinton must have finished with the line.

"Grigori Sergeyev. I am calling as I said."

"Yeah, I was just looking over the information you sent. It's still a bit thin."

"I have forgotten some small information. Also, I have a phone number that you may leave me messages."

"All right. What's the number?"

It sounded like a Tacoma prefix.

"You have questions?"

"Yes. This information you sent includes the name Ingstrom, but it doesn't indicate if he was the shipper or the recipient of the shipment. He could have been an agent in Oslo. There's not enough information here to be sure."

"Ah. The ship was damaged. The paper is listing cargo for salvage to pay the repairs. This Ingstrom, he takes the cargo, for the ship repairs," Sergeyev explained.

"I see. Well, there was or is an Ingstrom Shipwrights in Seattle."

"Excellent to start. I must go. Leave me message of your progress."

And I was holding a dead line.

"Quinton!" I barked. "What are you doing to my phones?"

Quinton's head emerged above the desktop with the headphones half off. "I just spliced in the components. Your lines should be just fine now."

"Now, yes. What about thirty seconds ago?"

"Out of commission."

"Well, the phone line worked just fine."

He shrugged. "Huh ... should have been dead. Doesn't matter, though. The automatic sender is on the modem line, anyhow."

"Can I use the phone now without getting cut off?" I asked.

"Sure. I'm going to run a quick electrical test, but it shouldn't affect your call." He vanished back to his station on the floor in front of the desk and I picked up the phone.

I called Ingstrom Shipwrights of Seattle.

A very young male voice answered. "Hello? Can I help you?"

"I'm trying to reach Ingstrom Shipwrights. This used to be their number," I said.

"Oh, yeah, of course. The company's out of business. I'm helping out with the auctions. I think all the business records are with the family and the lawyers."

"Actually, I'm trying to track a piece of furniture. What's this about auctions?"

"Business and the estate, both. McCain Antiques and Auctions."

"Estate auctions? Someone died?"

"Yeah. The owner and his son died in a boat accident. Kind of creepy, huh? They fix boats and their boat sinks. Gives you the chills."

"That's pretty ironic. Umm ... hey, I don't want to be crass, but I need to talk to someone about the furniture."

He hesitated. "We're pretty hectic right now... If you come down for the preview, you could ask Will or Brandon in person. That would probably work. Preview started at three and closes at seven."

I got the address and said I'd be there. I glanced at my watch. It was a quarter to six.

"Quinton. I have to get going. Are you almost done?"

He hummed as he stood up and came around to my side of the desk.

"Yep. Almost done." He poked a floppy into the computer's disk drive. "Let me just load this software."

The machine hummed and grunted a bit, then blinked up a message. Quinton typed in a string of commands and watched it respond.

"OK. Looks good. Should run just fine. Now, to arm the door and window circuits, you just go to your menu bar and pull down this new menu here..." He ran me through the arming and disarming routine and explained the function and parameters of the new system.

He pointed at the underside of my desktop. "See this red LED I installed under the lip? It will flash slowly at you if something disturbs the motion detectors, like someone trying to sneak up on you. You'll get the nine-nine-nine code on your pager if any of the sensors are set off when the active system is armed. There's also a passive component to the system and a panic button. When you enter the remote panic code, or hit the button, here"—he pointed at another thing under the desk—"all hell will break loose. You can also call your computer and look at the office via that remote fiber-optic camera I installed over the door. And there's a reed switch on your safe door that will let you know if anyone has opened it. You like?"

"Oh, yes. I like very much. What do I owe you?"

He waved that off. "I don't have my bill printed up yet. I'll drop it off another time, OK?"

"All right. Now I've got to run. Can I drop you off anywhere?"

"No, thanks. I thought I'd catch a movie or something. Would you ... ?" He raised his eyebrows.

I was already gathering my stuff and heading for the door. "Can't tonight, thanks. I'll see you when you drop off the bill, though."

He hesitated, then grabbed his pack and came through the door in a rush. "No problem. You can always try the library if you need me." He shouldered his backpack and sauntered off.

I stopped and watched him go. I just didn't get him. Sometimes he seemed like a friend I'd known for years; then he flipped right back into being a stranger. It bugged me, but not enough to keep worrying at. I had to get moving; I was going to find out what had happened to Ingstrom Shipwrights and Sergeyev's heirloom. I hoped.

NINE

I drove up around Lake Union and found the Ingstrom Shipwrights warehouse on the north end of the lake, east of Gasworks Park. I had to cruise for a parking space. The small, graveled parking lot was full, and a misty rain was starting to patter harder as I circled. A generic sedan was also hunting for a parking space. I pulled into a tight spot and ran for the warehouse doors, huddling my leather jacket closer around me. I wished I'd had the foresight to wear my raincoat instead.

I skittered into the warehouse and shook myself off like a dog. A teenage boy stared at me from his post behind a laptop computer on top of a long, collapsible table.

"Hi," I said. "I'd like to talk to Will or Brandon."

He perked up. "You're the lady who called, aren't you? Brandon took off. But Will's in the office with the family. He'll be out soon. You want to walk around and see if you spot the furniture?"

"Sure, though I'd think it would be pretty obvious…" I looked out at the packed stacks of goods and crates under cones of dusty light. The masts of a wooden sailboat reached for the ceiling near the back. "Or maybe not. That's a lot of stuff. You don't know if there's a parlor organ in this mess, do you?"

He shook his head. "You'd have to talk to Will. There's a lot of cool stuff, though—there's even a whole boat! Want to register to bid?"

He must have seen the auction-junkie gleam in my eye. I like getting neat old stuff cheap, like my Rover. My reaction against my mother's insistence on all-new everything, maybe. I prefer good, solid, old things, even if I have to fix them up myself. That kid knew he was looking at a sucker the moment I came in.

"Sure," I said.

He entered my name and office phone number into the database and gave me a printed catalog and a cardboard paddle with a number on it.

"Don't lose your paddle or I'll have to register you again," he warned.

I tucked it into my bag. "I won't. Now, how can I catch up to Will?"

"Oh, just wait and watch for him. He'll be out in a minute and he usually does a walk-through before we close up in a place like this. You can't miss him. He's tall and he has white hair. I'll point him in your direction."

"I'll keep an eye out for him."

The kid nodded and went back to something on his computer. I strolled off into the aisles of stuff.

I did not spot anything that looked like it could be a parlor organ. Among the piles of rope and wood, crates of boat parts, woodworking and machine tools, there were a lot of desks and drawing tables, filing cabinets, chairs, objects of use, and even a few objects of beauty. And a boat, as promised: a complicated little thing with two short masts and a lot of carved woodwork. There was also a great collection of model ships—some of which appeared to be Ingstrom design models—and a lot of yacht furniture from the 1920s. There was also some antique furniture that must have come from the executive offices, including a table you could land a Boeing on.

Deep in the piles, I spotted a small cabinet jostled in between two much larger pieces. It wasn't a parlor organ, but it pulled at my attention. So I pushed my way to it, chiding myself against buying another piece of needy furniture when I was a bit needy myself.

The cabinet was old, short, narrow, painted a ghastly red, and in terrible condition. It didn't need a home as much as it needed a trip to the dump, but I marked the lot number in my catalog anyway. It might turn out to be wonderful under the grunge. I've always had good luck with oddball items.

The rattle of the warehouse door coming down made me turn. It was five to seven, according to a big clock on the wall.

High over the stacks of stuff and ranks of file cabinets, passing quickly under the dim cones of light that sliced the aisles, flashes of silver and black caught my eye. Someone quite tall and slim moved toward me with a long stride that painted white arcs in the air where the light reflected off silvery hair. This had to be Will. From a distance, I guessed he was fifty.

He corrected his course and strolled up the aisle I was standing in. Then he stopped in front of me and I stood there, poleaxed. Not fifty. Two-hundred-watt smile. "Hi. Michael said you were looking for me."

My heart did a little changeup and my stomach turned a sympathetic flip. I just wanted to stand and stare at him. Angular face and hazel eyes behind rimless spectacles, shades of freakishly premature silver, white, and gray in his glimmering hair. The black turtleneck and jeans he wore didn't obscure the flow of muscle and limb beneath them. Worth watching in action. A crooked grin full of slightly crooked, very white teeth. I got ahold of myself just in time to correct an imminent stammer.

I put out my hand, dazed. "I'm Harper Blaine. I'm a private investigator."

He wrapped my hand in one of his. "William Novak. Pleased to meet you. What can I do for you?" His hand was so big it could have gone around my own good-sized paw twice. I'm five ten in my socks; not many men tower over me. Even fewer make me like it.

I wet my throat and coughed. "I'm trying to locate a parlor organ that may have come into the possession of Ingstrom in the late seventies or early eighties. Is there a parlor organ in this sale?"

"Early-twentieth-century grot? Curlicues and bad reeds? Normally, I'd be thrilled to say 'No such item here,' but you make me wish there was one."

I felt the prickling heat of a blush. "It belonged to my client's family. Do you think anyone else might know anything about it? Is there someplace else it might be stored?"

"Possibly at the house, or it might have been sold already, privately. Have you met Mrs. Ingstrom and asked her? The senior Mrs. Ingstrom, that is."

I had to shake my head. "Neither Mrs. Ingstrom," I replied.

"Hmmm ... well, I could introduce you at the auction. I assume you will be coming back for the auction," he added, eyeing the paddle peeking out of my bag.

"I was planning on it. I thought I might bid on a few things for myself."

"Like what?"

I pointed over my shoulder. "That silly cabinet over there, lot 893."

He crinkled his brow and strode over to it. "This one? Kind of an ugly little thing, isn't it? Surgeon's cabinet. Doctors and dentists used to keep their instruments in them, in the good old days before scrubbing and autoclaves. Nasty concept, isn't it? Still, you could find a treasure in there, if you can break it free of all that paint. A ten-dollar gold piece or one of Doc Holliday's own teeth," he added with a wink.

"With my luck it'll turn out to be just the right size to fit between the toilet and the sink. It's ugly, but it sort of ... talks to me."

"Didn't your mother tell you not to talk to strangers? And I doubt they come much stranger than this bit."

"Talking to strangers is what I do, and the stranger the better."

He laughed, and the round, brandy-rich tones rolled over me like velvet blankets, sending an electric jolt of lust down my spine. His eyes sparkled as he laughed, deepening the sketch of wrinkles at their corners. I revised my mental estimate of his age to between thirty-five and forty. I also added, sexy. And I was in trouble.

"Well, you're certainly standing in the right place for strange." He chuckled. "I'll talk to Mrs. Ingstrom and look for you tomorrow. All right?"

"That would be great. I appreciate it."

He gazed down at me with a half smile, then shook himself. "Mind's wandering, I guess. I'd better finish locking up. Would you like a guide to the door or can you blaze your own trail through the maritime wilderness?"

I blushed again, for some reason. "I can manage."

He grinned. "I'll see you tomorrow, then."

I started walking backward, smiling like an idiot, before common sense reminded me that eyes should be pointed in the direction of travel. I shrugged the jacket up around my neck and turned, hurrying toward the front.

I heard Novak call out behind me. "Hey, Mikey! Unlock for this lady, will ya?"

An answering shout: "Michael! Not Mikey, you attenuated stick insect! No waffles for you!"

As I got to the desk, I saw that Michael was grinning the same grin as William Novak. He unlocked the walk-door in the larger rollaway door for me. "See you tomorrow, right?"

"You bet," I answered as I stepped through.

He waved to me as I started across the gravel.

The rain was taking a breather, as it often does, now coming down as just a fine drizzle, wetter and fresher than the dry, uncanny mist with its accompanying vertigo and unpleasant reek of dead things. The moist, uneven ground slithered under my feet as I made my way across the now mostly empty lot. All the cars were gone except my Rover, a bland sedan, and a recent-model pickup. The car was just starting to pull out of the lot as I got near my truck. Headlights swept over me and I put my head down to avoid the glare.

The gravel crushed and clattered under the sedan's tires with a screech from the clutch and a roar of the engine. It was loud. And getting louder. I glanced toward it, blinded by the headlights, but neither deaf nor stupid. The car hurtled toward me.

TEN

Screwed, big-time. The car was a blur of headlights in motion toward me, safety just too far away. My fingers, under my jacket, hooked round the pistol grips. I pushed myself sideways, through thickened air … through fear, with a runaway-elevator sensation as I dropped …

dropped …

and fell …

through coiling fog stinking of rot …

and landed rolling. A hot gust, like the breath of a monster, blasted into my face and body, shoving against me as the car churned past. Wet gravel slashed my leather jacket, stung my cheek.

I dug my toes in and crouched, leveling the pistol.

No safe, clear shot. The car fishtailed out of the lot and turned onto the access road. I spun, lunging to my feet, slamming the gun back into the holster, snatching truck keys from my pocket. I dashed to the Rover, fumbled the lock. By the time I was in the driver's seat, the sedan was out of sight … last seen joining the stream of headlights on Aurora Avenue North.

I yelled and pounded the steering wheel. "Damn it! Damn it!"

I slumped back into the seat, shoved my hand through my hair, and vibrated for a minute or so as the adrenaline dispersed. Then I got back out of the Rover and went to retrieve my bag. I felt like I'd had too much to drink or not enough, shaking a little and shuddery in the knees. I stuffed spilled items into the bag and trudged back to the Rover.

At 7:34, William Novak came out of the warehouse. I was still trying to reengage my brain. He started toward the lonely pickup truck, then changed direction, coming toward me through the drizzle. He tapped on my window.

I rolled the window down and he asked, "Problem?"

"Not now."

"Sure? You've got blood on your cheek."

"Yeah, well. Somebody tried to run me down."

"And that's not a problem?"

"Not at the moment. I'm still alive and he's long gone. But I didn't get the license number. And I really want a drink."

"There's a decent Italian place nearby that's open until ten. They serve drinks, but their bar's the size of a French provincial commode. I was going to get a little supper myself. I'd be glad to take you."

I hesitated. My innards were still jumping in syncopation with my nerves. "What about your youthful assistant?"

"Mikey? He's got some work to do and he knows how to forage. See, there he goes." He pointed toward the warehouse.

A small motorcycle grumbled out from the building's shadow. The slender, helmeted figure on the back waved to us and went slowly out the gate. The machine whining and coughing, the unsteady firefly of the taillight jounced away. We watched it until it vanished into a curve.

"So, you coming with me or you prefer to follow?" Novak asked.

I sighed. "I'll follow."

He grinned. "You shouldn't have any trouble—I give great signal."

I had to roll my eyes. "You'd better."

I followed him around the perimeter of the lake to a scruffy-looking little building just off the lakefront industrial area. The rents are affordable and so was the food. If we leaned our heads a bit, we could still see the lake in all its famous nighttime beauty. The water looked like polished obsidian, reflecting the lights of the city and the boats. I could just glimpse the Space Needle pointing its green-glowing crown at the clouds.

The scent of food reminded me that I hadn't eaten since lunch with RC, and that was mostly coffee.

As soon as we were seated, Novak ordered antipasto and then looked at me for my drink order. "Can I guess?" he asked.

"What I drink? Sure, give it a shot," I allowed, leaning back on the padded bench.

"I'll bet you used to drink white wine, but switched to something more interesting… Scotch?"

I made a face. "Irish. I don't like peat smoke."

He looked at the waitress who had one eyebrow raised and a cynical crook to her mouth. "Bushmills?"

"Double?" she shot back.

I just nodded. Novak ordered a local beer and the waitress stalked off.

He glanced at me and gave an embarrassed smile. "The service here stinks. Luckily you only pay for the food."

"So long as she doesn't put ice in my drink, I don't care."

"She won't—that would be extra effort. Can I ask what happened?"

"Back at the warehouse?" I clarified, and he nodded. "Not much, really. Some jerk tried to run me down. I jumped. He missed. He fled. Pretty much the whole tale."

"Not the first time, I suspect."

"You think weirdos in light-colored sedans chase me down every day of the week?"

"No," he said. "But I also don't think most women wear makeup that looks like bruises, so I'd assume that the marks on your neck and cheek are the real thing. Since you're not wearing a wedding ring, I assume they aren't there because your husband beats you."

"No husband. I can't believe you can still see the bruises."

"Faintly. I thought it was the lighting in the warehouse. Same guy?"

"No." I didn't volunteer any more and turned my eyes to the menu instead. Novak did the same.

The waitress returned and put down our drinks. She nearly spilled Novak's into his lap and gave him a curt little "Sorry" and an insincere hitch of the mouth before she handed me my drink. No ice. We ordered food and I asked where the restroom was.

"I'll show you," she offered.

We were crossing the tiny foyer when she said, "If some guy smacked me around I'd serve him one to the crotch and scram. You don't have to put up with that, you know."

"'Scuse me?" I asked, catching her arm. "You think that guy back there hit me?"

She faced me square-on and crossed her arms over her chest. "Well, look at ya. Face all scraped up, bruises, he bullies you ... Think I'm blind? You don't deserve it, you know. Don't have to take it just 'cause he's got the dangly bits and you don't."

"Hold on," I said, digging around in my pockets. I found a business card and handed it to her. "I'm a private investigator. I got these bruises at work. That man had nothing to do with it and if he did, he would be suffering a lot worse than a beer in his lap."

She stared at my card, then peered at my face. "Really? You're not just trying to cover up?"

I nodded. "Really."

Our gazes locked and her mouth formed a little O, but no sound came out. Memories leave a light in the eyes, just as plain as scars.

I shifted expression and smiled. "Now, where's the restroom? I really need to pee." She pointed and I headed for the door.

I looked at my face in the restroom mirror. The bruising wasn't that bad, but I'd acquired a new graze on my left cheek. My jacket was roughed up and stained with mud. My hair stuck out in tufts. I looked like Ophelia three days after the river. No wonder the waitress thought someone had hit me. I'd have been indignant, too, if it happened to be true. I straightened myself up before I headed back to the table, much cleaner and looking a little less like a tragic heroine.

I slipped back into my seat and reached for the plate of appetizers. I snarfed down three in short order and caught Novak grinning at me.

"What?" I demanded.

"I never expect skinny things like you to eat like that."

"It's not every day you cross the line between life and death, you know," I said. "You should dive in. You ordered this stuff and you're not exactly hefty yourself."

"You have a point, Ms. Blaine," he conceded, digging in.

But I had stopped talking or listening. The angle of the car, the speed … it could not have missed me. At the very least it should have clipped my hip, my leg, my foot… I shivered and felt gravity drop out from under me. It had been drizzling thin, wet drops with the brackish smell of the lake. But I had stepped sideways through stinking fog and back into rain. Somehow. Through the Grey to avoid the car.

"You OK?" Novak asked. "You seem to be drifting off."

I shook myself. "I'm fine. Just getting ideas about … various things."

"Work related?"

"Yes."

"Were those bruises work related, too?"

"Yes, but that's not a normal occupational hazard. Most of what I do is pretty low-key paperwork chasing."

"Mind if I ask, anyway?"

I was rattled. With the whiskey and the warm room and a man not hard to look at giving me puppy eyes, the urge to talk was overwhelming. I told him how I got the bruises. He looked horrified.

"And you say that's not an occupational hazard?" he asked.

"I said not a normal one. People go off the deep end sometimes.

You just push the right button and that's all you get. You must know people like that."

He nodded. "My boss is like that, lately. Irrational about the oddest things."

"Like what?"

"Oh, business things. Doesn't like me to touch things one day, demands that I do all the cataloging, tagging, and hauling the next, while he schmoozes up the clients. Shows up late, then chews me out for taking an extra break. Other days, he just sends me home with no explanation. I've been putting money into the company for a couple of years, but stupid things like this make me wonder if I'm doing the right thing. Are you going to eat that, Ms. Blaine?" he added, pointing his fork at a lonely hors d'oeuvre.

I sat back to allow the waitress to put my dinner in front of me. "Are we still on a formal basis here, Mr. Novak?" Novak stabbed the last antipasto. "Don't we get to graduate to first names once we've shared a drink, salami, and garlic breath?"

He laughed. "On the first date?"

"If you're not prepared for any eventuality, don't take a date to an Italian restaurant. Something about all that marinara sauce and finger food just leads to trouble."

"All right, then—my friends call me Will." He extended his hand to me as if we were meeting for the first time.

I took it. "I'm Harper."

"Funny name."

"My mother has funny ideas. She wanted me to be a dancer or an actress—pushed me into it straight from the cradle. She thought that if I had a movie-star name, I'd have a movie-star life. The road to obscurity is paved with classy names."

"And she named you Harper? Not Marlene or Jean or Rita?"

"Do I look like Rita Moreno?"

"I was thinking of Rita Hayworth."

"I don't look like her, either, but they were both dancers."

"So was Gene Kelly, but you don't look like him, either."

"Thank the gods. He had a cute butt, though." The booze was talking … I hoped.

"Never before have I been envious of Gene Kelly's butt."

I sprayed whiskey, fluffing a laugh, and started to choke. Will reached over and pounded on my back—the advantage to long arms. I managed to swallow and catch my breath. He stayed leaning forward, peering at me with anxiety.

"You OK?"

"Fine. I'm fine. You shouldn't say things like that to a woman with a mouthful of whiskey."

"Yeah, with these rotten candles and the way you spit, we might have set the place on fire."

I broke down, giggling. Shadows and shapes flickered in the corners of the room, but I was laughing too hard to do anything about it, or care.

Will looked mock grave. "I can see that my flirting technique is rusty. I've reduced you to painful laughter and choking. Can you breathe? Are you going to expire? Should I call a doctor?"

"No, no. I'm fine," I gasped. "I'm not even wearing my dinner yet. Everything's fine."

"Good," he said, sitting back. "I'd be embarrassed if you choked to death."

"Imagine how I'd feel."

He looked at me and a wicked grin spread across his face; then he slowly turned red and looked away. "Umm … maybe I'd better not." He got very busy with his dinner and didn't look up to see me gaping.

No one had flirted with me—real, serious flirting—in a very long time. Maybe both of us were rusty, but I had to admit, I liked it.

"Another stupid question," he said, watching his knife diligently as he cut through a chicken breast which would have surrendered whorishly to a spoon. "Why private investigator?"

"I'm a mystery freak. And it was as different from my mother's ideas as I could get, which pisses her off to this day. I danced all the way through college to keep her off my back, but I ditched my jazz shoes the minute I had my diploma in my hand."

He looked up. "You entered a potentially dangerous profession to spite your mother?"

"No. But it does have that satisfying side effect," I explained. "I suppose, if I was less of a loner, I might have been a cop. But I'm the solitary puzzle-solver. I don't really care about street patrols and drug busts and gang shootings and traffic duty—all that necessary and cooperative community stuff that cops do. I like figuring out the puzzle. If it's interesting enough, I'll work a problem twenty-four hours a day. I get to exercise my obsessive-compulsive streak that way. Want to guess what my favorite movie is?"

"The Maltese Falcon."

"To Have and Have Not."

"That's not a mystery."

"I know, but I still like it better. I adore Lauren Bacall. *Falcon* comes in second, though, closely trailed by *The Big Sleep.*"

"Bogart fan, eh?"

"Big-time. Bogey got all the great tough guys," I said. "Who did it better?"

"Jimmy Cagney, Alan Ladd?"

"Both very good, but not Bogart. Did you know Cagney started out as a dancer?"

"Yes. So did George Raft."

I stared at him.

He shrugged. "I like old movies, old things. That's how I got into the antique business. Sometimes I think I can hear them talking to me." He blushed. "Too much imagination, I'm sure."

"Better than not enough, in my book."

He shrugged, changed the subject, and we finished dinner talking about old furniture and old movies. I didn't want to leave, but I could barely keep my eyes open. He smiled and walked me to the Rover and watched me go. I was glad I would see him the next day. But the warmth of his company didn't stop me from driving home paranoid.

Nothing happened. The drive was ordinary, and the condo and Chaos were waiting in good order. I flopped down on the couch and called the Danzigers.

Ben answered.

"I know I'm calling pretty late, but I have a question."

"It's not too late yet. What do you need to know?" His voice moved away from the phone. "Hang on." I heard him call for Mara. I heard another phone click and clatter.

"Well … tonight a car tried to run me down. I jumped out of the way and fell pretty hard. I was OK, but there is no way the car could have missed me. The space was too narrow and the car was moving too fast for me to clear the area. It was drizzling. But when I was trying to get out of the car's way, I was in mist. That Grey mist. And then I was in the rain again. And the car hadn't clipped me. So, what the hell happened?"

Ben's voice sounded excited. "Wow … for a second, you must have seemed to flicker or even disappear, I think. Oh, that must have scared the driver!"

The ferret scrambled into my lap and tried to steal the phone. I put her on the floor. "I can only hope. You're saying I disappeared?"

"Not completely. You're a physical being and the Grey is an overlap zone, remember? For a moment, you were basically in both places, switching energy states."

I barked over his enthusiasm. "But how? I don't understand how I can be in two places at once or how I get there. I didn't do anything but try to run away!"

Ben fell silent. Mara slipped into the hole in the conversation. "It's the nature of Greywalkers to move through the Grey, which, as I said, is a bit *here* and a bit *there*. But as to how you did it without meaning to, I'm thinking that your mind whizzed through the possibilities and latched on to this one."

"You opened a door and went through it. You've done it before, but you never did it voluntarily until now. Now that you know you can do it, you did," Ben added.

Mara resumed. "True. But it worries me that it wasn't conscious. This time it was a good choice, but it might not be so safe next time. You're not hurt, are you?"

"Only where I hit the gravel. And why didn't I get hurt worse?"

"I'm not quite certain. You got off lightly, though. You'll need to be controlling it. You can't go blindly popping in and out of the Grey, or being dragged in and out higgledy-piggledy. Something worse than a car might be on the other side."

I didn't respond. I picked up Chaos and teased her with my fingers.

Ben broke first. "Harper, even if you can't quite buy it, at least try to play along, just in case."

Chaos scampered away to wreak havoc elsewhere. My fingers weren't interesting when they stopped fluttering. "What if you're wrong?"

"If we're wrong, you're no worse off. If we're right, then things get better. It's not surgery. And if you didn't think we might be right, why did you call?"

I loosened my shoulders. "What do you suggest that I do?"

"Let Mara help you. I'll get off the phone so you two can work it out."

I could hear Mara hesitating. "It isn't all that hard, really…"

"Yeah. Well. Let's try it."

"All right. You'll need to recognize the barriers of the Grey first. We can try a concentration exercise to narrow your focus. Ever done any yoga?"

I felt a little silly admitting to it. "A little meditation breathing."

"Then you'll be having no problem. It's a bit like mindful breathing. So sit and breathe like that, then remember the sensations you had just before you crossed to the Grey. They're the clues. When you can recognize the barrier and re-create the sensations at will, you should be able to open a doorway and just step across. Or not. As you wish. Shall we give it a whirl?"

"Hang on." I got comfortable, taking off my shoes and sitting on the couch with a pillow in the small of my back. "OK. Now what?"

"Just breathe and feel. When you have the balance of it, then try re-creating the sensations of the Grey. Then open your eyes and try to spot it. Then close them and push the barrier away again. I'll be right here, on the phone, until you've done."

It had been a while. I put the phone on the couch beside me. I closed my eyes and tried to narrow my concentration to one small part of my body, until I was no longer aware of any other part. That went all right. I started clearing my thoughts, putting away every thought and feeling I didn't need this moment, breathing, reaching for poise.

When I felt empty and balanced on that point, I turned my concentration to the feeling of falling through the thick, stinking air, the Seattle mist dissolving from my face, giving way to the Grey. I opened my eyes and looked straight ahead, searching for the overlap of worlds.

It looked like a curtain of clouds and mist—literally gray, the intersection of the ordinary with the extraordinary rippled with an energy glitter that sparkled like fat raindrops falling in fog.

I closed my eyes again and pushed the sensation away. It resisted at first and I started to pant; then I calmed down and tried again. The vertigo, the smell and the chill receded. I opened my eyes to my plain old living room.

I picked up the phone. "It worked."

"Wonderful! Now again. But this time, go in."

"No!"

"It won't harm you. It's you who must be controlling it, not the other way about. Just open the door, step in, then turn round and step out. Then push it away and we're done. You'll be feeling much better for it. I'm sure of it."

I wasn't. But I tried. I sat up, relaxed, mindful, feeling for the barrier. I floated and felt warm. I opened my eyes and it was there again. I rose and walked toward it, stroking my right hand over the small warmth in my left. The interface got thinner as I moved forward, becoming insubstantial as smoke. I stepped through into the living fog of the Grey.

It surged and pressed on me. My stomach pitched and twisted like spaghetti around a twirling fork. I breathed deep and held on tight. Chaos gave an angry chuckle.

I looked at my hands and the Grey writhed around me. I was holding on to the ferret. She must have crawled into my lap again. I cursed. The ground? the floor? bucked, and I looked around, on the edge of panic. No sign of the big ugly this time, nor of the strange human/not human creature that had spoken to me before. This time, I was alone in the restless mirror-steam mist.

"Slow and easy," I muttered and took a couple of steadying breaths, which did little to steady me. I was queasy with trepidation as well as from the whiff of rot. "OK. OK, little fuzzy, let's get out of here."

I turned around, looking for the edge of the curtain, but couldn't detect it. I couldn't see my living room from here at all, yet I knew *here* was *there,* too. I was tired, frightened, and I just wanted out. I was losing concentration, panting. Unthinking, I squeezed the ferret and she screeched, chittering and wriggling.

I felt a breeze, a rippling of the Grey around me. I thought I could see the Grey edge. Close, and very thin. I started for it, then felt a dread cold sweep me, like a wind coming up on the Sound with a noise of storms: cold with an old chill that cuts like glass. I twisted around trying to escape the wind. The edge of the Grey fluttered an arm's length away. Chaos chittered again and dove into my shirt. The weight of something dark and furious was massing behind me.

I lunged forward, thrashing for the edge. The roiling black beast roared, struck me in the back and shook me. Chaos screamed. I yelled and leapt as hard as I could. Something rigid and cold scraped across my flesh as I dove away …

and then I was tumbling onto the living room rug. Exhausted tears streamed down my face as I reached for the ferret, rolling onto my back. Chaos struggled out of my shirt and bolted for her cage. I looked back, ready to grab on to whatever might pursue me. There was nothing to see, nothing to smell. Just the living room like it always was and me lying on the floor, panting.

I rolled slowly to my knees and knelt. My chest ached.

Mara was shouting my name on the phone, a tiny tinny voice of terror. I snatched the phone and yelled into it, "Goddamn it! Something tried to eat me in there! I couldn't get out! It was going to eat me!"

"Harper! Harper. Harper. It's all right, you're out. You're out and you're alive. It's all right." She babbled at me until I stopped freaking. Then she asked me what happened and I told her.

"Oh, my. It wasn't going to eat you. It just wanted to push you out of its territory. Look, you'd better stop by tomorrow and we can discuss this. We'll need to be working out a way for you to protect yourself."

"What is that thing?"

"A guardian beast. But never mind it now. It's gone. You're OK. You got distracted and things went to Halifax, but you did well. Really. You did marvelous. Are you hurt any? Is your pet all right?"

I looked down at myself, feeling weak and stupid. My torso was covered in slime. I crawled to the cage and checked on the ferret. She gave me a dirty look and then snuggled down deeper in her nest of old T-shirts, not deigning to spare me another glance. Fine. I closed the cage door and crawled back to the phone.

"Some kind of slime all over me …"

"Heavens! That's unusual."

"I didn't want to hear that."

"Come for breakfast tomorrow. We'll have to talk. Now you need to rest. Sleep is the best cure."

"All right. All right." I hung up. Shaking, I crept to the bathroom. I loathed the feel of my skin where the slime touched me. Even exhausted, I couldn't face sleeping in that feeling. I peeled off my gooey shirt.

As I turned my back to the mirror, I noticed the redness: a large semicircle of small punctures, starting into shallow scrapes across my right side. It looked like an unsuccessful bite by a very large animal with needle teeth. I shuddered at the thought of legions of hungry Grey things, waiting to rend me. Tears of frustration and fear scalded under my eyelids. I wanted to give up and hide.

"Stop that," I gulped. I glared at myself in the mirror. "You can't quit," I hissed. "You can't quit." A lot of ugly memories crashed past my mental eye. I had no choices and no place to retreat to. There was no place to hide from a creature who stalked the edges of death itself. I would have to learn my way around it, and I would have to watch my back.

ELEVEN

I slept in fits and woke to a Saturday morning clear and blue and mild. I argued with myself all the way up to Queen Anne. What was I doing? Did I really believe in ghosts now? Monsters, witches? It was nuts. But the bite on my side itched and even the hottest shower had not washed the eerie marks off my skin.

I parked in the same place and stared at the Danzigers' house. Ben came out onto the porch with the baby in a backpack and trotted down the steps. The baby squealed in ear-piercing delight.

Ben spotted me and waved, shouting, "Brian and I are going to the park for a while."

I gave a token wave back. Couldn't get out of this now. I forced myself out and up the steps to the door. Mara let me in.

We went into the living room, a bright, warm space lit by a bank of windows, and sat on matching sofas facing each other across a low table. A tang of lemon oil and recent baking floated on the pale green light filtering through the spring leaves outside.

Mara tucked her feet up under her skirts and looked at me, biting her lower lip a bit. "Last night wasn't such a grand success, was it?"

"No."

"Still. Not a complete disaster."

"I don't see it that way. I got attacked by some … thing and chewed on like a rawhide bone. I don't even know what happened. Or how."

"You got stuck because you lost your concentration. You were fine up till then. You found the Grey on your own, instead of slipping, and you pushed it back, as well. It was the second time things went badly."

I snorted. "Tell me something new."

Mara narrowed her eyes at me. The air felt a touch chillier. "That is part of the problem."

I looked askance. "What is?"

Mara shook her head and made a motion with her hand. Albert filtered into view. He almost looked like a whole person this time, wrapped in a buffer of swirling mist, like a cloud of impending snow. "You're looking at a ghost. And you know it's as real as … as that sofa. But you've closed your mind to it, telling yourself you'll not believe it. When you dig in your mental heels, that's when things go bad. Ceasing to believe and panicking when you're in the thick of it, that's dire. You lose control, for how can you control something you'll not believe in? And so long as you're fighting it, you'll not be able to protect yourself or control your slipping."

"Slipping?"

She nodded. "Moving in and out of a magical field, rather sideways, without meaning to. I used to know a young fella at home who did it all the time he was thirteen. Disconcerting, seeing him popping about. People made up all sorts of explanations for themselves, claiming he was just so quiet you'd not hear him sneak up on you, or he was so quick, you'd not see him go. But they didn't like it."

"He was a Greywalker?"

She laughed, an unexpected whoop of laughter. "My, no! He was just a witch like me."

I leaned forward, bemused. "But he stopped slipping eventually, didn't he?"

Her face blanked and she looked down. "Yeah. He slipped in front of a lorry on the N59." She squeezed her eyes shut, swallowed. "So. You see why I'd not like you to keep on slipping."

Slipping away from a car, slipping into the path of a truck— all the same thing as far as the Grey was concerned.

I nodded. "Yes, I do."

"All right then. Shall we try that exercise again? Albert and I will be here to help you."

I bridled. "Albert?"

She grinned. "Of course. You see him and he can go into the Grey, just like you. He'll be your spotter, so to speak."

I started to object. "But—"

"You'll see. We'll not let anything harm you." She tilted her head, raising her brows. "Give it a go?"

Self-conscious, I sat back into the couch and closed my eyes, breathing carefully until I relaxed and felt quiet.

"Open your eyes," Mara murmured.

I lifted my eyelids. A man in a plain, dark suit stood in the table. His hair was parted in the center, slicked back on each side around his long, angular face, and a pair of small wire-rimmed spectacles teetered on his nose. I could almost see through him. A snowfall of Grey hung around him and spread as I stared.

"Close your eyes. Push it back, and come back here."

And that's what I did.

Mara was grinning at me when I opened my eyes again. "That was grand!"

Albert was still standing in the table. I shuddered. "That's disturbing."

"Is it?"

"Albert looks like he's been cut off at the knee and is standing on the table on stumps. You can't see that?"

"No. He's quite a bit less corporeal to me. I imagine you see him better than almost anyone. When you're in better touch with the Grey, ghosts and some of the other things may look quite normal and solid to you. You'll be seeing them both here and there at the same time. Two partial images superimposed. The farther you are from the Grey, the thinner they'll look. Try it again, but keep your eyes open as you get near this time."

I felt a little dizzy and tired, but I tried.

As I slid closer to the familiar cold queasiness of the Grey, Albert looked more and more present. The details of his face and clothing grew surreally clear as the hungry pall of cloud-stuff around him expanded. I cringed from it. The Danzigers' living room shifted and faded to pale smears of gold and sage in the thick, desert-cold haze. A sharp whiff of alcohol and organic rot bloomed in the air.

Distantly, I heard Mara. "You've slipped. You'd better come back now."

Albert moved and I jerked to watch him. My head spun from the motion in the directionless roil of the Grey. I flailed out a hand to catch my balance. I didn't recall standing up. My fingers dug through Albert, a shock bolting up my arm to ring my skull with a stench of raw chemicals. I pulled my arm back against my chest, appalled.

Albert blinked at his arm, then knitted puzzled brows at me. He mouthed a word and patted the mist between us. I could no longer hear Mara. I stared at Albert, my eyes wide and too afraid to blink.

The word was "sit." He made it again and again, until my ears caught the faint sound in the roar of my fear. I sat. He motioned me to be quiet and close my eyes. Cold electricity tapped my shoulder. My stomach lurched.

But I could hear Mara now, far away. "Just breathe and balance. Then push it away. Just breathe..."

Her voice got stronger and I felt the queasy chill and smell slide away. Then a little push ...

I felt as if I had plunged from the ceiling into the couch and I lurched back, panting, opening my eyes.

Mara looked flustered, her hair a bit disheveled and her face white. "That was a mite rough. Do you feel all right?"

I swallowed bile and croaked, "I'm OK." I swallowed again. "I think."

"You look flah'ed out."

I shook it off. "I'm fine." I got to my feet and looked at my watch. "But I have to go."

Mara gave me a shrewd look. "Don't push yourself. And please be careful. You know how to come and go now, but you're not strong or steady at it yet. You need practice."

I nodded and started for the door. "I know. Trust me. I won't be bungee jumping off any Grey cliffs, if I can help it." A flurry of shivers scurried over my skin and I kept my eyes turned away from Albert.

Mara followed me and caught me at the door. She gave me a hard, sober look. "Be sure you don't. Lorry grilles are unforgiving."

I returned a wan smile and said I'd be careful, then hurried away, cursing myself.

Immersion in the Grey induced a panic in me I hadn't experienced since grade school. I just had to get far away from it, into the comfort of the familiar, for a while. The longer the better, though I doubted it would be long.

I got to the Ingstrom warehouse after the auction had started. Michael grinned at me and waved as he registered new bidders. I headed for the sound of Will's amplified voice, breathing normal dust and dirt and feeling relieved.

Bidders' paddles flapped in the air as Will spieled on. He knew how to gauge a crowd. In minutes, he'd closed a set of wooden file cabinets at seven hundred dollars. It was still early in the day and already the crowd was catching bidding fever.

The buyers were the usual assortment of shop owners and auction addicts. But there was a knot of blank-faced men and women huddled in depressed passivity near the back wall. I guessed they were former Ingstrom employees gathered to watch the carrion birds fight for the bones of their livelihood. The buyers pressed forward, ignoring them, impatient for the choice lots.

A box full of glass gewgaws came up and an intense bidding war developed between a thin, blond woman and a pudgy man with bad hair transplants. I couldn't recall names, but they were familiar to me from other auctions. Rival antiques dealers. She, I remembered, was unpopular with some of the other dealers for her sharp ways. I wondered if the man bidding against her merely wanted to drive the price up—he didn't look like the glass curio type.

The price had risen to ridiculous when I saw her hesitate. Will called for another ten dollars. Both bidders looked around. The man grimaced.

Will leaned into the microphone slightly and scanned the crowd. "Antique deck prisms in perfect condition. Highly collectible in today's market," he stated, letting his eye rest on her. "Last chance. Do I hear any more?"

Biting her lip, the woman flicked her paddle up. Will's gavel came down so fast you'd have thought the building was collapsing, though there was no chance of anyone taking pity on her and making a last-minute bid. A sigh and a ripple moved over the crowd as the lot closed. Will moved on to the next one. I could see a scowl spread across the woman's face as she began to suspect she'd been cooked. Then she turned and pushed through the crowd to the door.

About a dozen lots later, Will declared a forty-five-minute break for lunch. I followed him to the back of the warehouse and caught up to him at the registration table in a clutch of the grim men and women.

He looked down at me and beamed. "Hi! Nice to see you again." He slipped his arm around a deflated-looking woman of sixty-and-some and drew her forward. "This is Ann Ingstrom—the senior Mrs. Ingstrom. Mrs. Ingstrom, this is Ms. Blaine, the investigator I mentioned this morning."

She was wearing a well-made navy wool suit that hung on her as if she had lost twenty pounds overnight. Mrs. Ingstrom looked at me with watery eyes, but said nothing. I offered her my hand and she folded her own around it with a stiff, jerking motion. Her touch felt like fine sandpaper.

"I'm pleased to meet you, Mrs. Ingstrom. I want to ask a few questions. Maybe we could get some lunch and chat?" I suggested.

She answered very softly. "Oh. Yes. That would be pleasant. All right. There's a ... a sandwich shop just down the road..."

I glanced at Will. He shook his head. "They're going to be very crowded. People from the auction, you know. Why don't you two go up to Speedy's? It's only a couple of blocks away and you can have a table, if you hurry."

She looked blank, but nodded. I got directions from Will and drove the two of us in my Rover.

Speedy's was the sort of workingman's café that could easily have been called a diner or a dive. We did manage a table near the back and got some coffee while we waited for our food. Ann Ingstrom looked a bit better after a few sips of very sweet, white coffee.

"That William is a very nice man, isn't he?" she offered in her thin voice.

"Yes. He's very nice. I hope I'm not disturbing your day by taking you away like this."

"Oh, no. I ... it's good to get away. I've been practically living at the warehouse since all this happened." Her voice wavered, but held up. "Since ... since Chet and Tommy were drowned. There. I've said it, haven't I?"

"Yes, ma'am. I'm so sorry," I murmured. No matter how much of it I've seen, other people's grief leaves me feeling embarrassed, as if I've peeked through their bedroom windows.

"Well," she said, sitting back to let the waitress slide plates onto the table, "fishermen and sailors. The sea takes them away. They don't come back. You just ... you know, you don't expect it to happen to you."

"It's terribly sad," I offered.

She nodded. "It stinks. But you wanted some help. What was it you wanted to ask?"

"I'm trying to find a parlor organ the company might have salvaged from a damaged ship in the late seventies or early eighties. Do you remember anything like that?"

She chewed slowly and swallowed, chasing the mouthful down with a gulp of coffee. "A parlor organ. I think—well, I'm not sure how we got it, but we had one in the house for a while. I hated it. We finally got rid of the nasty thing when we redecorated. In 1986, I think. I'm not sure of the date, exactly. But it's long gone now."

"What did you do with it?" I asked.

"Oh, I'm not really sure. Chet took care of it. I was just glad to see it go. It always made me feel … unsettled. Isn't that funny?" she asked. "It worked all right. Chet played it a couple of times." She shuddered. "But it always sounded to me like the old thing was screaming and crying." Then she coughed out a laugh. "Silly of me, wasn't it? To be afraid of a piece of furniture? So I never asked him what he did with it."

"Could you find out?"

"Well … there must be some papers, so I suppose so. It will give me something to do. Shall I call you when I find out?"

"I'd appreciate that." I found one of my business cards and scribbled my home number on it as well before handing it to her. "You can call me anytime."

She tucked it into her jacket pocket. "Thank you, dear. I'll let you know what I find."

We finished our lunch and drove back to the warehouse.

I offered her my hand before leaving her in the care of Michael and the mourners. "Thank you again for your help, Mrs. Ingstrom."

This time, she squeezed my hand as if we were conspiring together. She smiled a bit, her face pleating suddenly into once-familiar lines. "I'll do my best," she whispered.

I returned to the auction floor. A different man was at the podium. He was older than Will, sleek as a salmon-gorged sea lion, but not much fun. He took himself too seriously to get the crowd whipped up and his performance was distracted and sloppy, closing a beautiful mahogany console far too fast. He shrugged the grumbles off, then turned the microphone and gavel back over to Will. The paddles began to fly again.

Will took another short break just before the surgeon's cabinet came up and resumed the podium a couple of lots afterward. No one was interested in the crusty thing but me, and I got it for twenty dollars.

About six thirty, the final gavel rang down on a massive bronze propeller and the auction was over. I'd acquired a client's chair with rotted upholstery as well as the surgeon's cabinet. I wandered over to the table at the back to pay for my lots and wait for a word with Will. A man in a raincoat got into line behind me.

Will had just stopped by the table when the lady who'd bought the deck prisms stormed up and shoved her way to him.

Her voice was carbide-tipped. "I'd like a word with you, Mr. Novak!"

Michael took my check and looked up at her. "Which word would you like?"

She shot him a withering look. "Not you! That one!" she spat, jabbing a red-tipped finger at Will.

Will stepped forward but kept the table between them. "Is there a problem, Mrs. Fell?"

"You know there is, William Novak! You know I was tricked into overbidding on that glass," she shouted. "And you did it! You—you massaged me into going that last bid!"

The raincoated man tried to butt in. "Excuse me, I think I'm next…"

Will shot him a pleading look but stayed with the woman. "Mrs. Fell, no one forced you to bid. You know it's part of my job as the auctioneer to get the best price I can for the client, and encouraging faltering bidders is part of that job. If you felt the bid was too high, you could have dropped out whenever you wanted. Now, we have other customers to—"

"I was going to drop out! You tricked me! You—you tantalized me, like a fish on a hook!"

Will started to answer, but the man in the raincoat leaned forward. "I believe I am next!"

"Sir, I know you are, but—"

The second auctioneer stepped up behind Will. Up close, he had broad shoulders and an incipient paunch. He was approaching sixty, not entirely without grace, but his dark gray eyes were chips of flint over his Irish nose and tight mouth.

His voice was much less bland now. "What's going on over here, Novak?"

Will spread his hands. "A small misunderstanding, Brandon. Mrs. Fell is unhappy about her bid—"

"I can see that." He looked at the man in the raincoat, who pouted and began his lament again.

"I am next!"

"Of course, sir. Mr. Novak will assist you."

Brandon shot a black glare at Will, then turned to face Mrs. Fell. As he turned, his face flicked into a soft smile and his voice dropped half an octave and several decibels. Downright Svengali of him.

He slipped his hand under her elbow, easing her close to him and away from the table. "Hello, Jean. Always a pleasure to see you. What's the trouble?" He bent his head down over hers, looking straight into her eyes with warm sincerity.

She whimpered like a puppy. "Well, I—I think Mr. Novak finessed me into overbidding. I'm very upset. It just isn't fair." She didn't seem to notice that Brandon was moving her to the end of the table, out of traffic flow.

I looked at Will and Michael with an incredulous expression. They made identical shrugs and Will turned to the man in the raincoat.

Two more customers had come and gone before Brandon returned. Mrs. Fell was nowhere to be seen. Brandon hooked Will's arm with a much rougher grip than he'd used on Jean Fell.

A few feet from my end of the table, the men stopped. Being a professional eavesdropper, I listened. Brandon's profile had no trace of warmth or charm now.

He growled at Will. "Do not—ever—argue with a customer like that, Novak. What do I pay you for? And when I tell you to take over a customer, you do so! You are not a customer here. You are not a partner here. You are an employee, and when I say 'Do this,' you do it! Do you understand me?"

Will remained cool. "We have an agreement, Brandon—"

"That agreement doesn't mean squat if I say it doesn't! Get it?" He glowered at Will.

Will said nothing. I could see his jaw tighten as Brandon continued to bore his furious gaze through him.

"Yes."

"Good." Brandon turned and stalked back to a glossy blond woman someone had told me was the younger Mrs. Ingstrom. The smile was back by the time he reached her, and he strolled off with her arm through his, his head bent to her every word and a fond laugh trailing behind them.

I leaned over and whispered to Will, "What a piece of work."

He gave an embarrassed shrug. "I'd better get back to work. Then we can talk after."

He moved behind the table. He had a genuine smile for every bidder, and I could see that people liked William Novak. They stopped to chat for a moment as they paid; they smiled back when he smiled at them. He even looked good as he got increasingly dust-covered and dirty, with his hair falling down over his glasses as he carried out boxes and furniture.

He worked well with Michael, too. They joked around and laughed and took turns with the computer and carrying out the stuff. They acted more like buddies than father and son.

Finally, the last of the customers was taken care of. Mikey returned from carting out some boxes and offered to help me with my chair and cabinet.

Will forestalled him. "Why don't you finish up your paperwork, Michael? I'll help Harper and then I'll come back and help you and Brandon close up. OK?"

Michael gave a knowing grin and turned back to his laptop computer. Will picked up the chair and I grabbed the cabinet. He followed me out to my truck. We shoved the two pieces into the back.

He looked around the almost empty lot. "Well, looks like there's no one waiting in ambush for you today."

"It makes a pleasant change. Oh, and thanks for introducing me to Ann Ingstrom. She remembers the parlor organ and is going to look for some papers that may give the name of the current owner. I could be only one step away from finding the benighted thing."

"That would be great." He looked around and his face turned pink. "I was wondering..."

I raised an eyebrow. "Yes?"

"I was wondering if I could ... if you would like to have dinner with me."

"Tonight?" I asked.

"Yes, tonight. After I finish up here. It shouldn't take long."

I sagged with disappointment. "I'd love to, but I can't tonight. I've got some momentum on a missing person and I need to take advantage of it while I can. Could I take a rain check?"

"Does that mean I'm on for dinner the next time it rains?"

"Even sooner, if I can manage it. Can I have your phone number?" I felt like a teenager asking such a question.

He fished a card out of his pants pocket and wrote something on the back, then handed it to me. "My home phone's on the other side. Call me when you can."

"I will."

"No. I, Will—you, Harper," he said and winked at me before jogging back into the warehouse.

Well, that was interesting. Maybe Mr. Novak found me as sexy as I found him. I'd just have to wait and see, wouldn't I? Damn, but he looked good in jeans and a sweater. I wondered what he looked like first thing in the morning…

I drove back home and hauled the chair—it seemed to weigh a short ton—and the cabinet up to my living room. I debated letting Chaos out to run around, but decided that the chair was far too attractive a hazard. Unsupervised romps would have to be put on hold until I could fix it. I took a shower and put on fresh clothes more appropriate to my evening's plan.

First I drove around a bit while it was still light and located the ATMs Cameron had been using. They were all within a dozen blocks of the historic district. Then I drove to my office to pick up copies of Cameron's photograph. My pager started jiggling at my waist as I unlocked the door. Quinton's alarm system was working, though it took me a little while to remember how to disarm it. Nothing more drastic than pager palsy occurred.

I walked down to the Dome Burger for a bite of dinner. While I munched through a burger big enough to choke a Doberman, I asked the young Asian woman behind the counter if she'd seen Cameron.

She looked at the picture but shook her head. "I don't think so." She sang out in Vietnamese to her husband behind the grill.

He came out and looked at the picture while she ran off my story to him. He also shook his head.

That's the way this sort of operation goes: six hours on your feet for a return rate of one yes for every seventy-five to one hundred nos. Still, one positive can be all it takes.

I thanked the couple, finished as much of the burger as I could manage, and started onto the slow work of the evening.

Saturday night in the Square was hopping, but as I worked, I had that observed feeling again, though I couldn't spot a watcher in the crowd. But so what? It's not like this job was going to be exciting. I figured they could watch me work all they liked, so long as they stayed out of my way.

I canvassed the bouncers and bartenders at every club in Pioneer Square and every night clerk in every late-closing restaurant and shop I could find. Most gave me a no. From a few I got a maybe. Several took my card and agreed to contact me if they saw Cameron. Then a bouncer at one of the clubs said, "Yes."

TWELVE

His name was Steve, and he was sitting on a stool just inside the door to Dominic's. He looked at the photo, then raised his eyes to scan for obnoxious drunks and underage partyers. "Yeah. I think I've seen this kid. Not in a while, though. Came in a couple-few times."

"When was this?"

Steve shrugged. "January, February, like."

"You card him?"

"Musta done. He don't look legal."

"He wasn't. Birthday was March seventh."

"Damn it, don't tell me that. My boss'll kill me. Card said he was good. He was good. OK?"

My turn to shrug. "Why do you remember him if it was so long ago?" I asked.

"Patterns. That's what you look for. You know—certain panhandlers always hang on the same corners, certain guys always get real quiet just before they try to bust somebody in the chops. Can't watch everybody in a crowd like this, so you get to know the signs, look for the disruption in the patterns. This kid, he was a pattern breaker. Didn't fit. Slow time of year—shoulda known he was a freakin' minor. Showed up, like, two or three nights a week. Come in right after dark, stay a while waiting for some people, then leave, usually alone. Then he stopped coming around. Haven't seen him in a while."

"Who were the people he waited for?"

"Harder to say. They were more like a type. Not so much regulars as clubbers—you know, the ones who hit the circuit every night or every Friday and make the rounds. Not really anybody's regulars and not really anybody's friends, but they're there all the time and you sort of know who they are."

"Be more specific—what type?"

"Uh-huh—hey, you! ID, please." He broke off to block a young guy and his twitchy date at the door. He stuck out his hand, snapping his fingers and giving the "come on" wave.

Nervous, the guy handed the bouncer his driver's license.

Steve glared at it. "According to this, you won't be legal until after midnight."

The kid shifted and whined. "Aw, come on, man. It's my birthday! Show some class."

"Hey, you're still underage until twelve-oh-one a.m., man. So why don't *you* show a little class and take this pretty lady out to a nice dinner and come back after midnight?"

The birthday boy slumped and led his date away.

The bouncer turned back to me. "What type, huh? Gothies. The black hair and white makeup crowd. But there's a couple of 'em always scare the crap out of me—though, you say so and I'll deny it. You know, kind of guys look at you like they're looking through you, but not like they're ignoring you. Like you're nothing but meat to them. Be just as glad to hack you up." He gave a hard nod. "That kind."

A shiver rushed over me. "Any names you could give me?"

He shrugged. "Don't know any of 'em personally. Don't want to, either, you know? But I'll keep my eyes peeled and my ears open. Give you a call if I find out anything, OK?"

I handed him my card. "Good enough."

I hit several more places before calling it a night. My feet were complaining, and I wanted a drink myself, but I headed back toward my office instead, too tired to worry about anyone who might be trailing me. But I stuck to well-lit streets, rather than crossing through the alleys.

The ghosts were thick around the Square, and being tired and distracted, I had a hard time remembering to dodge only the normal traffic. Pushing the Grey edge away constantly was exhausting, and I wasn't very good at, anyway. I almost got hit by a car while trying to avoid a sudden ghostly gap in the sidewalk. I paused under the pergola on the Square to read my watch. It was 11:22. I knew I'd missed some places, but at that point, I didn't care.

"Hi, Harper. You out partying, or working?"

I glanced up and around. Quinton was standing beneath the next iron arch, grinning at me from under a much-battered drover's hat.

"I was working, but I'm quitting for the night. What about you?"

"Just goofing off. Can I buy you a drink?"

"If you know someplace quiet where no one will complain if I take my shoes off," I replied.

"You bet I do. Come with me, fair maiden," he added, motioning me along.

Quinton struck off east, then turned and led me into a saloon along the angled block of rather disreputable buildings on Second Avenue Extension. The name of the place seemed to be some kind of double entendre that I was too tired to puzzle out.

From the outside, I expected low, dim, and smoky, but it wasn't. Broad, deep, and high-ceilinged, the original carved turn-of-the-century backbar and brass-railed front bar still dominated the room. The place was pretty empty. Of the three men at the bar, one was the bartender. A couple sat at a front table and conversed with the guys at the bar. Across the room, another couple shot pool, observed by two single men seated on high stools, bantering and kibitzing. The place hadn't changed since it was built.

Quinton noticed my assessment. "It's a dive, all right, but it's quiet, decent and the owner"—he pointed to the bartender—"doesn't care if you take your shoes off, so long as you keep your socks on. What would you like to drink?"

"Whatever you're having. Oh, and ask the owner if he's ever seen this guy," I added, shoving a copy of Cameron's picture into his hands.

Quinton returned with two large glasses of beer. He handed me the photo. "He said he doesn't recognize him."

"Thanks. Hey, you never left me your bill," I reminded him.

"Haven't gotten around to writing it up yet. I'll drop it off Monday. In the meantime, I got my own pager, so if you need me, you can page me." He handed me a card with his first name and number printed on it. "Do you shoot pool?"

I blinked at the non sequitur and shook my head. "Never learned how."

"Come on, I'll show you."

He wasn't a great teacher, but I wasn't a great student, so we had fun making mistakes and sending pool balls everywhere but where intended. I was a little tired and a little lit. I giggled a lot and forgot to worry about ghoulies and ghosties, and they seemed to forget about me.

I lined up a doomed shot. "What do you do, Quinton? I mean besides rescuing damsels in distress?"

He watched me miss completely. "I pretty much do whatever comes up. Jack of all trades and master of none, and all that crud. Got an electronics degree once, hung around college, did some programming, worked on cars, did a little wiring and construction, whatever was available."

"So, no steady job?"

"Nah. Steady jobs are for slaves. You just trade hours for dollars. I don't like that. So I don't do it." He bent over the table and muffed a long shot. "There's always someone around who just needs something quick and dirty and I'm the quick-and-dirty expert."

I sank the wrong ball. "Sounds criminal."

"Heck, no. All aboveboard and honest, I swear. Sometimes I get a bit of contract work, sometimes things come up that are a little longer term, but I never let myself become a cog, you know?"

I sat down and drank beer and watched him make a run of three balls.

"Freelance troubleshooter?"

He tipped his head and smiled thoughtfully. "Pretty much. Got a lot of esoteric information stuffed in my head, so I'm often a better guy for a small but complex problem than a guy with a specialized degree and a ton of specialized experience. Flexible. That's the best thing to be."

"Yeah," I agreed. "Flexible is good."

"Yep. Rigidity is death. Hey, you doing OK? You look about to fall over."

"I'm getting drunk, I think. And I'm tired. I'd better quit and head for home."

"All right." He took the cues and put them away in the wall rack. "Want an escort back to your car?"

"Sure."

I was grateful for the company. I was so wiped out I could hardly tell normal from paranormal, but walking with Quinton to blaze the trail, I just let it wash over me.

We stopped at the Rover. "Are you sure you're OK to drive home?"

"Yeah. I'm just tired, so I'd better get going before I get worse. This was nice. Thanks. Do you need a lift?"

"No, I just live a few blocks away." For a second he seemed poised for something, then settled back. "I'll see you Monday, all right?"

"OK," I agreed, wondering what he'd almost said or done.

He watched me drive out of the parking lot, waving before he turned and walked off.

It seemed like a very long drive home.

I woke up in a mean mood. The bells of the Catholic church next door were bonging away like Quasimodo was having a heart attack.

Down the road, the Baptist and Lutheran electronic pseudo-carillons were giving forth with Protestant zeal. Most Sundays I find the sounds pleasant. This morning I was ready to hunt down the men in charge and tie them beneath their own thunderous devices.

I did the morning thing with bad grace and grumbling and let the ferret out to play while my hair dried. There was only one name left on Colleen Shadley's list, and it had no phone number. I'd be making another drive to the Eastside.

I felt a little guilty for having left Chaos in the cage all day, so I packed up the ferret's traveling kit and took her along for the ride to Bellevue.

There was a mild, intermittent drizzle as we crossed the lake, but traffic was light, so we made good time to the 405. I had to consult a map to locate the address Colleen had provided for her daughter. It was not far from the mall, located in an unexpected fold of land that cut the area off from the business and light-industrial development nearby. The houses were mostly from the early 1950s: small bricks, wide cedar-stained clapboards, and crank-out windows. Sarah's had a small, weedy yard in front. I transferred the sleeping ferret into my purse and started to pick my way up the driveway, around scattered parts of a dismembered motorcycle, to the front door. I heard distant music. I knocked.

Steps sounded inside and the peephole darkened. The door opened to the depth of the safety chain.

"What do you want?" Her voice was bland, wafting to me on the supporting strains of classical music. She didn't show her face in the gap.

"I'm looking for Cameron Shadley."

She scoffed. "He doesn't live here. Who sent you?"

"I know he doesn't live here. I want to talk to his sister. Are you Sarah Shadley?" I asked.

The door closed and the chain rattled against it. Then the door opened again. A thin slice of a thin face peered around the edge. "Why do you want to talk to me? Is Cam in trouble?"

"Cam is missing. Are you Sarah?" I repeated.

She opened the door all the way and stared at me. She could have been a Charles Addams sketch. A little shorter than me, she was skeleton thin. Her dyed-black hair was lank and faded below two inches of blond roots. Even without makeup, her face was glow-in-the-dark white with lavender circles of sleeplessness deepening her eye sockets into pits. But her eyes, unlike her brother's and mother's, were hazel green. She wore a black-and-white-striped tunic over black leggings and bare feet.

She mulled her answer. "I'm Sarah. Who are you?"

"My name is Harper Blaine. I'm a private investigator, and your mother hired me to find your brother. He's been missing for about six weeks. I thought you might be able to help me. May I come inside?"

She stood aside and I walked in. She closed and locked the door behind me and led the way into the kitchen, then pointed to the tiny drop-down table mounted to the wall opposite the fridge. The dried-blood red varnish on her short nails was chipped and bitten. I headed for one of the two chairs by the table and settled myself with my bag in my lap.

She looked at me a moment, gnawing her lower lip, then said, "I was making coffee. You want some?" She went to the sink, pulled the plug and water gurgled away down the drain. The garbage disposal growled, cutting off my reply. She glanced over her shoulder at me, drying her hands on a cotton dish towel.

"Sure. Thanks," I replied.

She reached across the sink and pushed a button on the small stereo on the counter; Vivaldi's *Gloria* swelled. In a minute, she came back with a small, painted tin tray and dipped like a cocktail waitress to unload it. A garish picture of the Space Needle from 1962 was painted on the inside. Sarah returned the tray to the counter before she sat down across from me. She wouldn't meet my eyes. She took a book off her half of the table and placed it on the floor; then she pushed a mug of coffee in front of me and arranged a neat little barrier of milk jug and sugar bowl between us. She dawdled over mixing her coffee, keeping her head down.

I sipped my coffee black. It tasted like brackish water run through oil-soaked sawdust.

Sarah swished her spoon around in her cup. "So, you wanted to talk to me … ?"

"Your mother hired me to find Cameron. I've got some ideas about where he might be, but not why. I was hoping you could help me out with that."

She raised her head and glared at me. "Oh, so 'Mummy' thinks that if something bad has happened it must be Sarah's fault, huh?"

I stared back in silence until she blushed and lowered her eyes. "No. Cam's roommate mentioned that you called a few times and that you two seemed to be close." I let that hang.

She poked at her mug.

"When was the last time you talked to him?"

She heaved her skinny shoulders, defensive and sullen. "I don't know. Sometime in March, I guess. Haven't seen him or talked to him since, so I don't know where he is."

"In March, did you see him in person, or talk on the phone?"

"In person."

"Where did you see him?"

"In a bar."

"Where?"

"Pioneer."

"Pioneer Square?" I clarified.

"Yeah."

"Which bar?"

"Don't remember."

I sighed and sat back in my chair. I drank my bad coffee, then put it down on the table. "This would be a lot easier if I didn't have to play Twenty Questions with you."

Again the glare.

My purse shuddered and Chaos exploded from it, scratching and scrambling to look over the table edge. Sarah started and stared at the furry apparition hoisting itself onto the table.

The ferret poked her nose into my coffee mug and I scooped her up. "Chaos! No."

She sneezed and shook her head in annoyance just as Sarah lit up and reached for her, too.

"Sweet!" Sarah cried. She offered a finger for sniffing. Chaos licked the fingertip after a careful snuffle. "Does it bite?"

"No."

Sarah stroked the ferret's head as I put her down again. Then Chaos skipped off to investigate Sarah's coffee mug.

"Don't let her into the sugar," I warned.

"Can it—she—have some milk? Is that OK?"

"Only a little," I allowed.

Sarah dipped her pinky into the milk jug and offered it to Chaos, who licked up the milk with a rapid tongue.

The girl beamed at me. "May I pick her up?"

"Uh, sure."

Sarah lifted the ferret with care and brought her up to her shoulder, cuddling the animal against her neck. "What a sweetie!" Chaos nuzzled her jaw.

Sarah exclaimed over the wonderfulness of my pet for five minutes while Chaos endeared herself, trotting along Sarah's shoulders and offering whiskery, tickling kisses—the attention hound.

Brimming over with the joy of mustelid nuzzling, Sarah began pouring out a story. "I don't know if this is related to Cam going missing, but I suppose it could be. He helped me out of a bad situation back … in February, I guess it was. I was really stupid to get into it in the first place, but I was mad, you know?"

I prompted her. "What happened?"

"Well, first you gotta know the family thing. Cam's not the oldest. I am. But because he's a boy—a male—everything is for him." Bitterness crept into her tone. "The car, the trust fund, the education ... everything. I only get an allowance out of it until I get married. If I never get married and never have any kids, I'll get an allowance for the rest of my life. It's like being on some kind of parental welfare! When I asked my mother why I didn't get a trust fund for college, you know what she said?"

"Tell me."

Her voice swooped and rattled in fury. "She said that she and Daddy didn't want some man to marry me for my money! How antediluvian! Mom is always on about all that upper-middle-class-masquerade crap! It is so Mrs. Robinson. And you know, I tried it. I really did. But it's not what I want. So I decided that if I couldn't do what I wanted, I wasn't going to take her money."

She sneered. "You can probably imagine how well Mummy liked that! And she had a lot of ways of letting me know just how much she disapproved. So I got mad. I started doing things I knew would piss her off, just to irritate the hell out of her. Cam tried to give me money so I wouldn't have to work, but there was no way I was going to take it."

She waved her hands to indicate her hair and body. "So I did all of this. The whole Gothic-dead thing. I pierced my nose, my eyebrow ... and a lot of other parts, too. I talked about getting a tattoo, but really, the idea kind of squicked me—and branding is right out! I even had a pair of red contact lenses I used to wear." She cackled. "They really weirded Mom out. I started hanging out with some rough guys, playing the slut, taking drugs—all that teenage rebellion crap. Except I didn't get around to doing it until I was twenty-one, so it's not like drinking was going to be a big deal. I had to be totally vile. And manage to keep just inside Mom's tolerance level, because, if she threw me out, how could I keep on making her life as miserable as mine was?"

Her voice began to slow and she caught the ferret, petting her with repetitive strokes. "But right after Christmas I finally broke the camel and Mom threw me out. I bummed around and slept on friends' couches and all that. And then I met this guy..."

THIRTEEN

Sarah lowered her head and stared at the memory. Her words wafted out like a cloud of drug smoke.

"I used to see him in some of the clubs and I was just kind of drawn to him. He was beautifully scary, like a perfect knife. He used to say things that frightened me, but I was … fascinated. I guess I was just so low, I had made myself into this despicable thing so well, that it seemed like the right thing for me, like I deserved to be hurt." She was holding on to the ferret with both hands and tears began to roll down her face. Her voice slowed until it barely trickled.

"And one night I saw Cam in one of the clubs with some musicians we used to know and I just wanted to be with him. I wanted to get away from the man I was with and get back to what I really was. I thought, 'What the hell am I doing here?' I tried to catch Cam's eye, but he didn't see me. So the next day, I called him and we met and I cried all over him and told him all about it and he said he'd help me get away." She stopped talking and stared at the table.

Silent, melancholy thoughts weighted the air between us.

I barely breathed. "And Cameron did help you get away?"

She shivered back into speech. "Yes. He did. I'm not sure how. I don't know what he did, but one night, the guy just said he didn't want me anymore, that I could go." Chaos turned in Sarah's grip and began to lick her face. The young woman sniffed and snuggled the ferret closer to her face, shaking out quiet sobs. Chaos kissed away the tears until they stopped.

"He said that you could go? Were you living with him? It almost sounds like he was keeping you prisoner."

Sarah let Chaos onto the tabletop and picked up her now-cold coffee, keeping her eyes turned from me. Chaos scampered for the milk jug. I grabbed her. Sarah picked up the milk and sugar and carried them to the counter without meeting my gaze.

"Kind of. I guess. I didn't start out living with him—not the first night or two—but then things started to get kind of strange and kinky. You know, it's hard to remember details now." She came back to the table with a saucer of water and a plateful of cookies. She handed the cookies to me and put the saucer on the table for Chaos. Sarah sipped her tepid, sweet coffee, ate a cookie, and offered the crumbs to the ferret.

"Did you ever read *The Story of O*?" she asked.

"No," I admitted, "but I know about it."

Chaos decided it was nap time and jumped down into Sarah's lap. Sarah stroked her warm, furry body while we talked. Bit by bit, stroking the trusting little creature in her lap, Sarah calmed.

"Sometimes I felt like I was O, but it wasn't quite the same. It's so hard to remember... He used to tie me up and leave me that way all day, he made me sleep in a box ... things like that. He had the role of Master, but I wasn't really Slave. I was more like ... Plaything, or Toy. It was like living in a Fellini film. I was so relieved to get out, but sometimes, I—I almost miss it. God, am I some kind of sick puppy or what?"

She raised her head and gave me a wavering smile. Any smile was more than I had expected.

I had my notebook out. "What was the man's name?"

"Name? I can't remember his last name. Maybe I never knew it. His first name was Edward. That's all I can remember."

"Did he give you drugs?"

"No. That's one of the funny things about it. He absolutely would not let me take any drugs—not even pot or aspirin—only a little wine or tea once in a while. Maybe he was doctoring the tea? I don't know why the details are so fuzzy. Maybe I just want to forget it, so I do."

"Can you remember any details about Edward himself? Where he lived, what he did for a living? Physical description?"

"I never knew where he worked. He was gone all day and came home at night—if he came home—and that was when things would happen. I slept during the day a lot, too. I stayed in a condo downtown. One of those fancy buildings with a doorman near the Paramount Theater."

"You remember the address?"

She rattled it off. "But I think it's leased by a corporation. I can't remember why I think that… Maybe Edward told me." She shook her head. "It's hard to remember stuff about that time."

"It's all right. I can find out. What does Edward look like?"

"He looks like James Bond."

"Excuse me? He looks like Sean Connery?"

"Not Connery. The new one. Sort of, but not quite. I think his hair is thicker and his face is thinner and he's a lot scarier. But, you know, that dark-haired, movie-star look, only cruel."

I made a note. I couldn't believe I might be looking for a Pierce Brosnan look-alike. Crazy. "You don't know what he does for a living, but what was his lifestyle like? Did he seem to have money? Did he ever say anything about family or where he was from? Did he have an accent? Anything like that?"

"No. He just sounded rich and American. You know that super-clean, no-accent voice? He had that. Always sounded so cold and remote …" Sarah shuddered, then shook herself and resettled.

Her voice was clear and calm when she continued. "I don't think he had a family, though he had a lot of friends who were all as creepy as him. He did seem to have a lot of money and a lot of people who hung around him—I think they were kind of scared of him, or, like, his employees or something. Really subservient. Total pack behavior. Edward is definitely the top dog. I think he's from Seattle, though, because sometimes his friends would talk about stuff that happened around here when I was a little kid or before I was born, like they saw it. Like the World's Fair and stuff like that."

"Well, if he's a local boy and he has connections to a local corporation that leases that condo, I'll find him. What do you think Cameron did to get you away from Edward?"

"I'm not sure. I think it took a while. I think they met a bunch of times before he let me go."

"Edward, you mean?"

She nodded. "Uh-huh. I think, at first, Cameron tried to frighten him, or pressure him somehow, blackmail, sort of. You know, 'Leave my sister alone or I'll sic the cops on you.' Or maybe he said he'd have someone break Edward's legs—that's one of Cam's favorite mock threats, because he's so skinny and wimpy-looking. But I think they must have made some kind of deal. Maybe Cam paid him off. Cam lives pretty tight for a rich kid, so he has plenty of spare change, if you know what I mean."

"Why would a rich man take money from your brother?"

Sarah shrugged. "I don't know. It's just a guess. Some people are greedy, no matter how much they've got. Or Cam could have offered him something else. He's a smart guy. He'd have found out what Edward wanted."

"Do you think Edward could have anything to do with Cameron's disappearance?"

Her face became bleak. "He could." She leaned toward me. "Do you think my brother's dead?"

"No, I don't. I think he's alive, but in hiding or unable to let anyone know where he is. Could Edward arrange something like that for Cameron?"

She frowned. "I think he could kill someone. And I know I wasn't the first plaything he had, so he could do that, too, but I can't imagine it happening to Cam. He's very strong-willed. And he's smart, like I said. Not very many people ever put one over on Cam. If he's not sick or locked up in some fashion, he'll find some way to save himself. But it's good someone's looking for him. You'll find a way to help him, won't you? You'll find him?"

"I'll do my best. I think I will find him. Soon."

Now she was fierce. "Good. You know what I said before, about how Cam gets everything? Well, it's not because I hate Cam. I don't think he even wants it. It's what Dad wanted and what Mom wants. That makes me a little pissed, still, and sometimes I really could hate Mom and Dad—if it was worth the energy—but I don't. None of that is worth my time. But Cam … Cam is worth my time because I was worth his. You find my brother. And when you do, let me know. I owe him a lot. And I love him a lot, too. If I can help, you just say so."

"I will." I handed her one of my cards. "If you think of anything, call me."

She looked at my card as if memorizing it before reaching down and placing it between the pages of her book: *Divina Commedia* by Dante. She reached into her lap and picked up Chaos, raising her to her face for one more nuzzle. Chaos yawned, nipped lightly at Sarah's nose and licked her. Sarah kissed her and offered her to me. I took the ferret and put her into my bag, where she stuck her head out of the top for a good view.

Sarah walked me toward the door. I stopped in the doorway, unable to resist.

"Can I ask you a personal question?"

"Sure," she answered, shrugging and reaching to stroke Chaos's head with a finger.

"What are you doing here? What is this place?"

"This?" she asked, looking around. "This is my place. It was my grandparents' house. I inherited it a couple of years ago when the trust matured. My family's really into trusts. Right now I guess it's some kind of therapy. I'm trying to fix it up a bit. It's a lot better than it was when I came here in March."

"What about the motorcycle parts?"

"Those belong to my sort-of boyfriend. He's in Italy right now, visiting his family, and I kind of like to have the mess around to remind me of him."

"Oh. So that's why Dante in Italian."

She blushed and looked away. "No. That's why the Italian boyfriend. Can I ask you a question?"

"Sure."

She surprised me. "Do you think I would be good with ferrets?"

I smiled at her. "I do." I gave her the name of the shelter where I'd found Chaos and told her to call them. She smiled, looking twelve years old.

As I drove away, I waved. Sarah waved back. I found I kind of liked the girl, but I felt more drained than by any other interview I'd ever been in. Despite my tendency to feel instantly chummy with any other ferret person, leaving was a relief.

By the time I reached my office, it was raining in earnest: big drops that hit with a splat like a thrown water balloon. I bundled Chaos into the bag and tried to run between raindrops. We both got wet.

The answering machine was blinking. I pushed the button as I set down my bag. Chaos jumped out, tumbled onto the floor, and began exploring.

The voice on the single message was familiar. "Hi, Harper. This is Will Novak. I was thinking … well, it's started raining, so I was wondering if I could cash in my rain check for dinner. If you're interested, please call me." He rattled off a phone number.

An impatient suitor. Let's face it, I had a bad case of lust for him, but dating someone connected, even tangentially, to a case can be complicated. I thought about my options as I set down some food and water for the ferret. Chaos fell on the bowls as if starving.

"What do you think, fuzzy? Should I have dinner with Will, or play it safe?"

Chaos crunched down on a mouthful of ferret kibble while I stroked her shoulders.

"You're right. Food is always important. I'll call Will."

He couldn't come to the phone. Michael took a message and my home phone number and assured me he'd tell Will to call me. He chuckled a bit as he did so, which made me smile, for some reason.

I sat at my desk, satisfied, and checked my watch. I could finish up my typing and get home in time for a decent shower. I plunged into my notes. Chaos crawled into my lap while I typed and was dopey-faced and limp when I packed her up to leave.

At home, Chaos was content to settle in for a good sleep, exhausted by five hours of exploring and working her wiles on Sarah.

The ringing phone dragged me out of the shower about an hour later. Dripping and towel-wrapped, I sprinted to catch it. My answering machine started reciting into my ear at head-splitting volume as I picked up the receiver.

"I'm here, I'm here!" I yelled into the phone, slapping the OFF button. "Hi."

"Hi. Um … this is Will."

"Hi, Will."

"Hi. So, you're available for dinner this evening?"

"Yup. Are you?"

"Of course I am. We're just closing up here. Should I pick you up or would you rather meet somewhere?"

"It would be easier to meet. I'm not presentable at the moment. Where and when?"

We agreed on Dan's Beach House at seven. I'd never been there before. The original house on the bluffs had been a notorious rendezvous for bootleggers in the 1920s. The shale heights afforded a view of the whole Sound—including the coast guard station at Elliot Bay—

while the mudflats below created a difficult approach, which still sank or stranded a few careless boats every season.

I grinned at the phone and slithered to my bedroom to dry off and dress. It took me a while to decide what to wear. At the last minute, I decided that I didn't want the evening to get too serious, so I threw on a good jacket over a cotton sweater and fresh jeans with loafers instead of my usual boots or sneakers. I looked good. Even the bruises weren't too bad. But, still paranoid, I put my pistol in my purse before I left. It didn't feel right to wear it on a date, but I didn't want to go without it.

I had no trouble following Will's directions and arrived ten minutes early. I spotted his pickup truck in the parking lot. Will was just getting out. He stood beside his truck and waited for me to catch up to him, the misty remains of the rain clinging to his hair and clothes in a jeweled nimbus. I parked a couple of cars away and walked over to him. He caught my hand and we jogged for the doors.

Once inside, he said, "I hope you like fish."

I didn't get to answer before a hyperefficient host bustled us to a booth away from the windows. It was a little more intimate than I had expected and a bit darker. My defenses started to rise. I slid around so I was facing into the room while Will was forced to turn his back to the other diners.

I murmured, looking at my menu, "So, what do you recommend?"

"Everything. The cook does a spectacular salmon with ginger and lime, and all the shrimp dishes are wonderful. Did you know that people who eat a lot of shrimp have a higher baseline radioactivity level than people who don't eat shrimp?" Will added.

Shrimp? What did I care about radioactive shrimp? Then I realized that Will was babbling about crustaceans because he was nervous. That was kind of sweet. Most people who get nervous around me have something more to hide than first-date anxiety.

I grinned at him. "Maybe I'll go for the salmon, then. I wouldn't want to glow in the dark."

He laughed and ordered drinks and food, then started in on the serious chatting and flirting. We were interrupted by a musical beeping from Will's waistband. He snatched a pager out of a fold of his clothing and looked at it.

I watched him study the number, then put the pager away. "Is it something important? I can wait if you need to make a call."

"Nothing like that. It's just Mikey's code."

"Your son pages you?"

"Son?" Will began to laugh and I quivered. The sound of his laughter was like a warm touch on my spine. "Michael is my little brother. He pages me with this code when he goes out. Lets me know he arrived safely."

"Oh," I muttered.

He shook his head in amusement. "It's OK. Lots of people make that mistake. I am old enough to be his father, technically. The relationship is kind of somewhere in between, though. He was a late baby and I was already out of the house—in Europe, in fact—by the time he was a real human being, so I missed a lot. When our folks died, I got the responsibility for raising him. So now I'm Father Goose. I keep tabs on him all the time, which is a little paranoid, but I guess I'm afraid I'll misplace him or something. We both carry pagers so we're never out of touch. Overprotective, right?"

I shrugged to cover both my surprise and my chagrin. "Can't ask me—I'm an investigator, not a family counselor. So you always know where he is? Or at least where he should be?"

"Pretty much. He always knows where I am, too. We're like two weights on a rubber band—we always bounce back toward each other."

"I wish more people were like you and Michael. It would be a lot easier to find some of them."

"You mean your clients?"

"No. Their kids and spouses. Most missing persons are routine," I explained. "There's often a strong clue in their past behavior or habits that will lead me right to them, once I've figured out the habits in the first place. Most people don't have any idea how to disappear. Most don't even mean to. They leave tracks like elephants in mud. But I have one of the other kind right now. Kid just broke his routine and habits completely and disappeared."

Will blanched. "Oh, God, I'd go crazy if anything happened to Michael, if he just disappeared someday… If somebody took him, I'd—I'd lose it. Do you think someone took this kid?"

I reached over and touched his arm. "No. I think he went for a reason and I'm getting an idea of where he might be. But I've got to admit, I'd really like to know why. That's what's bothering me. When I know why someone's vanished, I can make a good guess of where, but the why often turns out to be the most important question. I wouldn't want to have to approach someone in, say, a crack house, without knowing what I was getting into first."

He nodded. "I can understand that." He played with his glass. "You've got a dangerous job," he added, trying to steer the conversation back to my lane. I accepted the transfer, for the time being.

"It's not so bad. A lot of what I do is hunting down paperwork, filing forms, and waiting around. But it beats milking cows."

He grinned and raised his eyebrows. "Cows?"

I nodded. "Yeah. When I was little, I went to visit my Mom's family in Montana. They lived on a cattle ranch, but they kept a few milk cows for themselves. One morning—about four thirty—my cousin got me up to help him milk the cows. I think it was supposed to be fun. But I am not a cow person—my favorite cow comes on a bun. I was sleepy and the cows were large, smelly, and scary. And milking is nasty—which is the real reason they invented automatic milking machines."

Will chuckled. We chatted on about inconsequential things. Around the time our dinners were served, I was starting to have a strange, queasy feeling in the pit of my stomach. The feeling was familiar. I looked around out of the corner of my eye as I bent over my fish.

I saw a face flicker in the edge of my vision like one of those persistence-of-vision tricks you can only see when you look away. I pretended to remove a fine bone from my boneless fish, lowering my head and breathing slowly until I could settle the Grey and look without falling in.

A ghost, staring at me with a long and dour face, stood against the wall beside the prosaic RESTROOMS sign. He was thin and weedy, dressed in a suit long out of fashion.

I stared and whispered, "Albert?"

He beckoned to me with an impatient gesture.

I looked up at Will, who was frowning down at me. "Excuse me. I've just remembered a client I needed to call. I'll only be a minute."

Curiosity quirked the corner of his mouth, but he didn't ask. "OK. I'll wait right here."

I smiled and slid out of the booth, grabbing my purse, and headed for the restrooms.

As I walked down the hallway across the back of the building, I looked for Albert.

FOURTEEN

What was the Danzigers' ghostly housemate doing here? My stomach was flipping and roiling as if the fish I'd eaten had come back to life, but I forced my concentration toward looking for Albert without being sucked into the Grey completely.

I spotted him stopped ahead in a doorway of dragon smoke. I didn't want to go in there, but he motioned me forward. I gritted my teeth and caught myself hyperventilating. Then I stepped across into the cold and the smell of the Grey.

I staggered and Albert flickered solid, then rain-thin, beckoning impatiently. I felt the fluttering edge of the Grey nearby. The world seemed darker and overlaid with a wavering silver projection on fog. I groped after Albert, pushing through smoke doors and down staircases built of dry-cold mist, holding myself as close to the normal world as I could. Albert was a flickering match light in the down-drawing darkness ahead.

I must have left the restaurant, because the space sounded like a tunnel now—wet and dank and lit only by ghost lights that came and went. There was noise ahead of me, a distant, raucous clamor and a roar of music.

Reality wavered and pitched. I hesitated and my concentration stumbled. Couldn't panic now. I had to keep going, had to keep chasing Albert, concentrating only on Albert, because it was the only thing

I could think of to do. I didn't know what would happen if I jolted out of the Grey into some unknown place: the middle of a wall or three inches from a speeding truck. And I hoped that the presence of a ghost—a creature who belonged here—would keep that dark beast away. I held on to the idea of Albert and kept going, quivering inside and wet with ice-water sweat.

I followed a flight of twisted steps down a dim shaft to a heavy door and along a short, narrow tunnel. I trudged on, tight with fear.

The dim flicker ahead winked out. The sounds died.

"Albert? Where are you?" My ears throbbed in the silence.

"Albert!" I howled, whipping around. I lost my balance in the shifting world and yelled, falling . . .

And crashed into a solid wall. I tumbled and sat down hard. I huddled on the cold ground and panted and held back tears of relief and exhaustion, and a desire to throw up.

Finally I looked up and around. I was in a basement storage area. There was a sound now, one I had been ignoring for a while: a burglar alarm going off.

I swore and promised under my breath, "Albert, I'm going to get you for this."

I crashed around in the dark for a minute or two before someone opened the exterior door to the basement. I breathed a thankful sigh and moved toward the shaft of streetlight illumination striping the floor. A body cut off most of the light and I slowed my steps.

"Police. Stop where you are and leave your hands in plain sight."

My relief soured to resignation and I raised my hands to shoulder level, open and empty.

The arresting officers were quite polite until they found my gun. Then the chill came on. They drove me to the downtown police station for processing, without a word beyond Miranda. The booking officers weren't happy, either, but they did concede that I had all the proper paperwork. They still put the gun in an evidence bag before they would let me use the phone, though.

It took only moments for the restaurant to find Will, who was still sitting at the table.

"Hi, Will, it's Harper. Look, I'm sorry. Something work related came up and I had to go. I didn't mean to leave you in the lurch like that."

"Something work related," he repeated.

"Yes. What? Do you think I just ran out on you? It was something I couldn't control."

"All right," he said, but it didn't sound all right.

"Will. Don't be angry. My job is like this. Weird stuff comes out of nowhere and I have to chase it down when the opportunity arises. If I hadn't wanted to have dinner with you, I wouldn't have called you back." There was a lot of silence at the other end of the line. "Will, I'm at the police station, so I can't stay on the phone. I don't know how much longer this is going to take. I'll have to call you later. OK?"

"All right," he said again. "If you call me later, we can talk about it." Then he hung up.

Great. Well, there went that romance. This was not turning into the sort of evening I'd had in mind.

I'd been booked and fingerprinted and had gone through a carefully edited version of my story once. The owners of the property weren't home when the alarm went off, and when they arrived to press charges, they wanted to hear what they'd missed.

I lied. I told them, as I had the cops, that I had been tailing an insurance fraud suspect from the restaurant and had stumbled through the remains of an old bootlegger's run into their basement. The owners of the house—now a bed-and-breakfast—were kind of charmed by the idea that their house might have a secret past as a speakeasy. The cops, on the other hand, were not charmed by the discovery of a rotting tunnel behind a bit of broken plaster, but that thin evidence was a lot more comfortable than explaining that I'd somehow managed to get into a basement which was still locked from the outside.

It was after eleven p.m. when they decided they couldn't hold me.

The cops returned my stuff, including the pistol, and I went downstairs to call a cab and get my car back.

When I paid off the cab, I was relieved to see that Will's truck was gone from Dan's parking lot, and then I got angry with myself for feeling relieved. I damned Albert with catholic breadth as I slammed the truck door behind myself. I sat still for a good two minutes, calming down before starting the drive home.

I pounded up the back stairs to burn off my lingering fury. I slammed out of the stairwell onto my floor to see my front door standing open. I stopped and gaped, then bent down and snatched up the ferret as she tried to scamper past me.

I stared into my living room. Chaos dove out of my arms and raced across the floor in wild, ferret delight. She danced across the face of disaster. The burglar alarm was off and the living room was a wreck. The ferret's cage was tilted on its side, the door hanging open. The surgeon's cabinet had been knocked over and the chair was dribbling stuffing from the underside of the cushion. Books and paperwork drifted around like autumn leaves.

I caught the ferret one more time and stuffed her into my jacket before going to knock on my neighbor's door. I left the place just as it was. It couldn't get much worse, after all.

"May I use your phone?"

He let me in and I called the police, asking for a detective I knew, but was told he was off duty. I'd have to take potluck.

I slammed the phone down and waited for the cops while watching my neighbor's half-breed pit bull sniff and whine in the direction of the lump of ferret moving around under my jacket. Once they showed up, my neighbor Rick let me wait in his living room eating cold pizza while the evidence crew found nothing. Once they were gone, I thanked Rick and his dog and went straight back to my place. I slammed the door, locked up, and headed to bed. And threw my damned, silly loafers against the bedroom door hard enough to dent it.

In the morning, I called Mara, my mood very little improved.

She answered the phone herself.

I started straight in. "Mara, I don't know what's going on, but Albert popped in to see me last night and I got arrested following him. What the hell was he doing?"

"You were following Albert … through the Grey?"

"Yes! And I ended up in someone's basement with their alarm going off like a teenage girl at a Hanson concert."

I heard her smother a giggle. "As bad as that?"

"Not funny. I got arrested, got dumped by my date, and had an interesting time fending off the blandishments of a beer-and-pizza-addled neighbor."

"I shouldn't laugh, it's just the image… But there is a problem and I'm afraid Albert has made a bags of the situation."

"What situation? A 'bags'?"

"A mess. I'd rather discuss it in person. Can you drop by? I've a geology lecture to give at one, so if you can come before eleven …"

"Geology?"

Mara sounded harried. "Yes. I also teach at the U. Can you come up?"

I growled. "All right."

I rushed my routine and drove up to Queen Anne. I was barely through the Danzigers' front door when Albert showed his shadowy face in a swirl of snow-threat Grey.

I jabbed a finger at him, too furious to consider how utterly stupid it was. "You! You are so lucky you're dead."

Mara blinked surprise at me as Albert blinked out. "It does no good to be threatening a ghost."

"It's not a threat. It's a fact. If I hadn't been following his incorporeal ass, I wouldn't have gotten arrested. Normally I'd take that sort of thing out of his hide. If he had one."

"Then it's me you should be angry with. Not Albert. It's my fault he showed up and acted badly."

"Is it? Why? What did you do?"

"I sent him looking for the source of the problem, but he came up with you!"

I threw my hands into the air in frustration. "What problem?"

"There's something wrong with magic."

FIFTEEN

Something wrong with magic?" I echoed. "There's a lot wrong with it from my point of view. But I assume that's not what you mean."

Mara made a sour face. "Not hardly. I know you've still some trouble with all this, but it is a serious problem. The house has its own nexus, but outside, things are running a bit slow, as if the power is dammed up. So I sent Albert out to find the source of the blockage, but he somehow followed it to you—he says you're a knot in the thread."

"What does that mean?"

"That you're connected to the problem, though you aren't the problem yourself. And that's a relief. When Albert found you, he got confused and tried to bring you straight to me. Unfortunately, Albert's idea of straight seems to mean straight through the Grey. Can't say I'm pleased with him for that. Whatever this is, I do need your help to find it and fix it. Can you see that you're the only person who can help me?"

I sighed and shook my head. "I'm not sure about that, but I can try."

"You'll find this much easier if you can accept what you are."

My annoyance had dropped, but it was starting to notch back up. "What I am able to accept is that most people in my situation wake up every morning in a padded room."

It was Mara's turn to sigh now. She took a few steps away from the door and sat on a wooden bench in the hall, tired and frustrated with me. "It's fighting it that will drive you mad. That's why you slip and stumble and why Albert couldn't stay with you. You burn up energy needlessly fighting to do something you'd find so much easier if you accept and relax into the Grey."

I crossed my arms over my chest and leaned against the doorframe. "A couple of days ago you were trying to show me how to push it back, now you want me to let it in. Which is it?"

"That's access-control, not denial. The normal and the Grey are different states, and you can't go on struggling against that fact once you're in the Grey. You'll exhaust yourself, and you'll not be able to protect yourself or concentrate or do any work. You must connect to it to control it."

"And how do you suggest I do that without ending up like your friend?"

Mara gave me a look which must have quelled rooms full of rowdy undergraduates without raising her voice. "Sit down, Harper."

I considered it. What did I lose by giving in?

I sat down on the bench.

"Are you going to help me?"

"Yes."

"Then you shall have to learn to relax into the Grey. It's not so bad as you think. It's not hard. But it's only in the Grey that you'll be able to understand the problem and track it down—as you would a missing person or a stolen object, here."

I turned and peered at her. "You want me to try this, right now?"

"Yes. It's simple. Do what you did before, but once you're in the Grey, just relax. Don't fight."

I had strong reservations, but I tried it.

It wasn't too bad, at first. I'd had enough practice last night to have a feel for the edge of the Grey pretty well, though it rippled and moved like a flag snapping in a stiff breeze. Each time I approached it, a wash of nausea flooded over me and my heart raced.

Albert crept in and I yelled at him, "Don't help me!" The break dumped me back into the hall with my head ringing. A combination of fear and fury left me shaking.

I settled myself back down and tried again. The writhing curtain wall of the Grey flooded up very fast and I pushed across the edge before I could change my mind. The snowstorm light twisted and heaved around me with a blizzard howl. I clapped my hands over my ears and staggered as the steamed-mirror world budded with the suggestion of monsters and armies of formless dead. The cold pushed through my skin, trying to touch me someplace deeper, frosting my flesh with ice.

"No!" I yelled and yanked myself backward, away from the rain-mist wall, crashing back to the floor of the Danzigers' front hall on my knees.

Horrified, Mara was on her feet, reaching down to me. "Harper!"

I pushed her hands aside. "No. Don't touch me." I smacked my hands onto the plain, solid wood of the bench and shoved myself up to my feet. "There's something in there. I cannot go in there and let it at me."

"That's your fear. You're fighting so hard, you only see what you expect to see. You have to let go."

"I can't."

She glared at me. "You mean you won't."

I snapped back. "All right. I won't."

"You must. You're just afraid and it won't—"

"Damned straight! Damned. Straight." I shoved a hand through my recently chopped hair and almost cried when the hair ended too soon. I swallowed a vile lump in my throat.

I bit my lip and grabbed my bag. "I can't do this. I can't. I won't. Whatever word you want to use. I—"

I wrenched around and reached for the door. Albert, looking solid as a plank, intruded.

Behind me, Mara was saying, "Harper, don't bolt. You have to try or your fear will eat you!"

I shot her a look over my shoulder which sent her a step back with wide eyes. "I. Can't. Do. What you want me to do! I can't!"

I felt hot with terror-fed fury. I whipped back to Albert and hissed through clenched teeth, "Get out of my way or I swear I will find a way to hurt you."

He slipped away. I slammed out the door and ran.

I drove and I didn't know where or why I wasn't arrested. I couldn't see anything but flooding, pressing Grey around the windows for minute-eternities. Shock-cold chilled my nerves. I pulled to the curb until I stopped shaking.

I couldn't remember ever saying that before: "I can't." Even as a kid being pushed to perform, the phrase never came from my lips. "I don't know how," "I'm afraid," "I'm not good enough," all kinds of propitiations and excuses, but not that one. Not "I can't." I felt sick.

I closed my eyes and took slow breaths until my chest and throat stopped aching. I was tired, but I pulled the Rover away from the curb and headed to the office, where I left it in the parking lot.

I didn't want to sit in the middle of the routine haunting, so I started walking.

I walked up Third for a while, paying very little attention to where I was going, trying to ignore the flitter of Grey in the corners of my eyes. I looked up when I reached the Bon Marché and realized I was only a few blocks from the address Sarah had given me for Edward's condo. I'd nearly forgotten. Good, old-fashioned work.

I used the ladies' lounge at the department store to clean up, then started toward the Paramount Theater.

The condo was in a swanky building. It had started out as a hotel in the thirties and been converted into expensive condominiums in the late eighties. The lobby had an electronic security lock and call system at the door and a husky majordomo at the desk inside. I pushed the call button.

"May I help you?" came out of the speaker. I could see the man behind the desk talking into a white telephone handset. His mouth moved just ahead of the voice from the speaker. The effect was a bit like a poorly dubbed film.

"Yes," I replied. "I was wondering who the leasing agent for this building is."

"There aren't any vacancies in the building at the present time."

"I'm not interested in leasing. I just want to talk to the agent about something related to the building."

There was a pause. "Stanford-Davis Properties."

I'd never heard of them. "Would you mind giving me the phone number?"

The man hung up. I was just thinking up nasty words to call him when he marched over to the door and opened it. He was huge. He was not any taller than me, but he filled the doorway. On purpose. He held out a business card that looked like a chewing gum wrapper in his massive paw. I took it.

I looked at it. Stanford-Davis Properties information card. "Thanks."

"It's nothing," the man replied. Then he stepped back and closed the door between us. He stood there to watch me go. His steady, remote gaze set off a feeling like ants crawling up and down my spine. I backed from the door, then turned to go down the steps.

I tucked the card in my jeans pocket and walked back to my office. I wanted a cup of coffee, but what I got was a message from Mrs. Ingstrom.

"Miss Blaine, I found a bill of sale for that organ. If you'll call me back, I'll give you all the information I have."

I wrote down the number and listened through the rest of my messages, including my landlord complaining about the charge to change the locks. The bliss of the painfully mundane. I made a note to call him back, then dialed the number for Stanford-Davis.

A perky receptionist answered. "Stanford-Davis Properties. How can I help you?"

"I'd like to talk to the agent who manages the Para-Wood condominiums, please."

"That's Mr. Foster, but he's not in today. However, I do know that the building is fully leased and no new leases are expected to come available before 2010."

"I'm not interested in leasing myself, but I am trying to discover who is leasing a specific unit in the building. This may pertain to a future criminal investigation." I let it be ugly.

She squeaked. "I ... I just don't know. I'll have to have Mr. Foster call you back tomorrow."

"I need the information as soon as possible. Is there someone who can look up the file for Mr. Foster? His secretary? I could come to the office for the information."

"Oh no. That won't be necessary. Give me your name, phone number, and the unit number, and I'll have Mr. Foster's secretary call you."

"All right." I gave her the information and she assured me she would have the secretary return my call before close of business. The surfeit of butt kissing was discomfiting.

Secretaries know everything and run everything, but they are often clueless about the import of what they do. They are also great sources of information, if you can get one to talk. I hoped Mr. Foster's secretary would be a talker, but I wasn't expecting it. I stood and stretched and left my office to get a large cup of coffee.

When I returned, I set down my coffee and called my landlord. He wanted to argue about the cost of the new locks. I told him he was being a skinflint. He'd never heard the term before. We were in mutual midharangue when the call-waiting beep interrupted. I switched calls.

"Harper Blaine."

"Hey, it's Steve. From Dominic's. Remember me? Couple of nights ago you were looking for a blond kid? Well, I think I saw him last night."

"Hang on a second, Steve, I've got a call on the other line. Be right back." I popped over to my landlord. "Look, the lock was broken and I couldn't go off and leave my office unlocked, so bill me. OK?"

He muttered, but I ignored him. I was afraid Steve would have hung up, but he was still on the line when I toggled back to him.

"Thanks for waiting, Steve."

"No problem. So, that kid you were looking for? I think—no, I'm sure—I saw him last night."

"Where?"

"Outside the club."

"Why were you at the club on a Sunday?"

"Moving stuff around, just helping out. It was just getting dark when we knocked off. So I went out into the alley to throw some garbage in the Dumpster. And I see somebody out there. So I look around and then I see him kind of way in the back, in the dark."

"How did you recognize him? Did you get a good look?"

"Pretty good, yeah. You know that feeling you get when somebody's staring at you? Well, I got it, and I turned and there he was. So I stared back at him."

"Why?"

"Usually works. Sometimes we get junkies hanging around the alley and if you just stare hard, right at 'em, they go away. Or they jump you. But either way, it's something. So I stared at him and he took a step toward me. Then he just kind of faded back into the alley and ran away."

"You're sure it was him?"

"Or some other cupid-faced kid with yard-long blond hair, yeah."

"About what time?"

"About … seven thirty, eight o'clock."

"Why didn't you call me right away?"

"Didn't have your card with me."

It was more than I'd known an hour earlier. "Thanks. By the way,

I was told he might have gotten tangled up with a guy called Edward who hangs around the clubs. Sounds like an aging Goth, from the description. Ring any bells?"

"Uh … no. Can't come up with any matches from that description. Sorry I can't give you any more."

"What you've given me is great. Oh, hey, how'd he look?"

"Look? The kid? Not good. Kinda gave me the willies, you want the truth."

That raised my eyebrows. "I do. Thanks again, Steve. There's ever anything I can do … that's legal …"

"Round about midnight on a Tuesday I could really use a triple skinny."

I laughed. "I'll remember that."

I hung up the phone and sat for a minute. My guesses had been good: Cameron Shadley was in the Pioneer Square district and something was wrong. Now I just had to bring us together. That might be hard.

Someone had told me once that the Pioneer Square historic district completely covered the original downtown of the early 1880s—small by modern standards, but still a city within the modern city, stretching from the new baseball stadium to the Cherry Street bend and from the waterfront to the train stations flanking Seventh Avenue. About fifty square blocks, and every inch of it crammed full of nooks and niches, basements and alleys. You'd need two hundred cops sweeping through with elbows linked to stand a decent chance of flushing one individual. Luck and shoe leather wouldn't be enough; I needed something specific to catch Cameron. But my brain resisted working. I sighed and put the problem on my mental back burner, trusting my subconscious to boil up an idea.

While that cooked, I'd concentrate on Sergeyev's missing parlor organ. I returned Ann Ingstrom's call.

Mrs. Ingstrom sounded stronger and more confident than she had on Saturday. "You know, it seems we got rid of the wretched thing more recently than I thought. It was 1990."

"Who bought it?"

"A man named Philip Stakis. It's not someone I know, so there's not much else I can tell you. Let me give you his phone number."

She rattled off the number and I wrote it down. "Thanks, Mrs. Ingstrom. Could I get a copy of the receipt from you, just to be thorough?"

"Oh, certainly. Should I mail it to you?"

"I'd rather come pick it up, if that's OK."

"Oh, fine! Today? When would you like to come?" She sounded as if she were inviting me for tea.

I glanced at my watch. It was just about one o'clock. I doubted I'd hear from Stanford-Davis before four. "I could be there by two, if that's all right."

"That will be just fine." She gave me her address and directions. I had just enough time to grab a bite to eat. I snatched up my stuff and locked up, then went out for food and lots more coffee.

The amount of coffee may have been a mistake because, while it helped perk me up, I was nearly cross-eyed with the need to find a restroom by the time I got to the Ingstrom house in north Ballard.

It was a pleasant Victorian, the kind in which families raised generations. Mrs. Ingstrom answered the door herself at my knock. She asked me in and I requested the use of her bathroom.

"Oh, the one down here is a mess. Go to the top of the stairs and turn right. It's at the end of the hall. Watch out for all the boxes and don't mind the cat, he likes to sleep on the heat register there," she explained.

I shot up the stairs past a row of packing boxes and into the large bathroom, where I was greeted by the beady glare of a single yellow eye.

"'Scuse me," I said to the three-foot mound of white fur. It huffed and tucked away its eye for a few more winks of catnap.

The bathroom was clean and depersonalized. Only a small bottle of aspirin and a cardboard box of adhesive bandages still sat in the open medicine cabinet. Rust marks on the metal shelves showed where other things had been not long ago. The room was silent on the matter of the lives which had passed through it.

I was leaving when the cat rose like a thunderhead and stretched with a head-splitting pink yawn. I looked back toward it as, with no apparent acceleration, the cat sailed out of the room past me, waving its plume of a tail. A cat-shaped shadow, fluttering Grey, remained lurking on the heat register. I shook myself and went back downstairs.

Mrs. Ingstrom was in the kitchen at the rear, making coffee in an old drip Melitta. She glanced at me as she picked up the pot and a couple of thick-sided white mugs and started out of the kitchen. "We'll have our coffee in the front room. I've got all the other things out there. Everything else is packed or tagged for the auction this weekend."

I regretted the lunchtime coffee more than ever. I'd be vibrating by the time I got back to the office, at this rate of consumption.

I followed her out to the living room—"the parlor" when the house was new, I supposed. She waved me to a seat in front of the unlit fireplace. All the knickknacks and personal bits were either gone or sported prominent lot tags. Most of the furniture had been shoved to one side.

She started pouring coffee. "Help yourself to the shortbread."

I picked up a small piece and I could smell the butter at arm's length. I could gain weight just breathing near it. I nibbled.

Mrs. Ingstrom put a mug of coffee down in front of me and pushed forward a sugar bowl and matching creamer. She gave me a small, strained smile. "It's a good thing I hadn't packed up the sugar, yet."

Sneaking up on the scalding coffee, I asked her about the organ.

"I was surprised at how easy it was to find," she said. "Chet had quite a few papers on his desk and I had to sort through them first. I thank God he was such an organized record keeper. But I just ... If I had to go through every piece of paper, I'd never make it. It's been awful, just ... awful," she quavered, and then began to cry. "Oh, why? Why, why?" She buried her face in her hands and sobbed.

I froze and sat there a moment. Self-conscious, I scootched along the sofa next to her and put my arm around her shoulders.

I patted her arm and murmured automatically, "Please don't cry. It's all right."

She sniffled and wiped her eyes with the hem of her skirt and hiccuped, "No, it's not."

I handed her a napkin from among the coffee things. She blew her nose and dabbed at her eyes again, talking while she covered her discomfort with pats of the napkin.

"It's just terrible, is what it is. The company always seemed to be doing so well, and we're not extravagant people. We never lived above our income. Chet was always frugal. It ran in the family, I suppose. And then so many things went wrong all at once and, somehow, the company just couldn't stay afloat. All the bills and the creditors and the contractors with their lawyers and lawsuits, and then the tax men. It was a nightmare. It's still a nightmare—it's worse! If Chet had just died, then the company would have been sold all as a piece, but instead, this horrible bankruptcy was already tearing the company into shreds. And then this! Well, all I can say is thank God Chet had a will or we'd be in a dreadful mess..." She sniffled again and shook her head.

She mumbled past the napkin, "I'm afraid I'm making a spectacle of myself. I'm just overwhelmed... At suppertime I keep expecting to hear them coming up the back stairs and into the kitchen, stealing a taste out of the pots, their clothes smelling like bilgewater and diesel oil, laughing and teasing me for complaining about them. And do you know what's worst?" she asked, turning toward me.

Her eyes seemed to look into someplace I'd been too recently. I was startled and stammered, "No, what?"

"I'm afraid they will! It's not that I don't believe they're gone—I can never, for a moment, forget—it's that the house can't seem to forget them … like the shape of them is worn into it, the same way walking up and down wears away the front step."

She leaned forward, glancing about as if she thought someone watched us, and whispered, "I'm almost glad I'll be selling the house. What would I need it for, except to plague me with these awful ideas?"

She sat back. "There. Now you think I'm a crazy old woman."

I remembered the shape of the cat upstairs, and shook my head. "No, I don't. Is it safe to guess that Tommy and your husband were both born in this house?"

She nodded and sniffed.

"I'd probably leave, too, if I were you. It's hard to live with ghosts."

She sighed. Her shoulders loosened. "Thank you. I'm glad someone understands. I'm afraid to tell my friends and family. I'm afraid they'll think I'm trying to make Chet and Tommy disappear. They all think it's the bills that are making me sell, or the sheer size of the place."

"Let them believe what they want. It doesn't hurt you," I suggested.

Mrs. Ingstrom nodded, then straightened her skirt and sniffed one last time, seeming to shift a weight off her shoulders. "Well, now you've put up with me acting like a watering pot, let's see what I can do for you."

She picked up a manila file folder that had been lying on the table and handed it to me. "The bill of sale is in here and a copy of the original bill of lading for the lien that was attached to it. I thought you might want that, too. I don't need it, since it's so old and long gone that not even the tax men are interested in it."

I flipped open the folder and scanned the papers within, then smiled at her. "Thank you for all your help, Mrs. Ingstrom. I'm sorry about what you're going through and I appreciate your digging into your husband's records for me at a time like this."

"It was pleasant to be doing something that wasn't for an estate lawyer or a bankruptcy lawyer or a tax accountant, for a change. I hope it helps you."

"I'm sure it will," I said, rising. "Thanks again and thanks for the coffee, also."

She rose to escort me to the door. "It's the least I could do. And it was so nice to see you again." She saw me out, acting the part of hostess on autopilot.

Once back in the Rover, I sat in the driver's seat and fiddled with the seat belt, tired. From the corner of my eye, the Grey flickered, giving the house a writhing patchiness—its own personal fogbank. The cat, who now sat on the porch, was solid as a stone and staring at me with malevolent yellow eyes. Mrs. Ingstrom waved to me. I waved back and drove away.

I just drove for a few blocks and let everything in my mind drift. I felt a bit out of sync with something I couldn't place and still under the weather. Maybe I had the famous flu RC had gone on about. Frowning, I headed back to the office. It wasn't a solution to the problem of Cameron Shadley, but all I could think of was to call this Philip Stakis and try to make some ground on that case while I could.

No further depredations had been attempted on my office and no shady characters lurked in the alley or my hallway. I flopped into my desk chair and tried the phone number I'd got from Mrs. Ingstrom. No answer, no voice mail. I would try again after six. I typed up my notes, poked around my computer a bit, then checked my messages.

"Hi, Harper, it's Mara." She sounded more Irish than usual and rather hesitant. "I'm after wanting to mend our row this morning. I've been more the head teacher than the friend, I'm afraid. Anyhow, the little one's at Granna's and Ben and I were hoping you'd come for dinner this evening. A nice, grown-ups' evening with no dirty nappies. I do hope you can come."

Interesting. I couldn't say I was angry at Mara. It wasn't her fault I'd freaked. OK, yes, she pushed, but . . . what could I expect?

I looked at the phone and thought a while. Stanford-Davis hadn't called and none of my other messages included dinner invites. I wanted to talk to the Danzigers, anyway. I picked up the phone and dialed.

"Hello?"

"Mara?" I checked.

"Harper! I'm so glad you called. Did you get my message?"

"Umm ... yeah, I did. Look. This morning ... sucked, but it's not your fault. And dinner would be nice."

She let out her breath. "Good. Food will be ready about six or six thirty. Ben's on for lecture until five and I thought—that is, I was hoping you might come just a touch early so you and I could get in a chat before Ben's oratorical powers are fully recharged. Sound all right?"

"Fine," I answered. "Should I bring a bottle of wine or something?"

"Ooo, that would be lovely!"

"Red, white ... green?"

She whooped her wild laugh. "Green sounds brilliant! But I'd settle for white or a nice light red. OK?"

"OK. I'll probably get there between four and five."

"Grand! We'll see you then. Bye."

And so I found myself on the hook for a bottle of green wine. I was trying to imagine where I could find some when the phone rang.

"Harper Blaine."

A deliberate, East Coast voice replied. "This is Ella with Stanford-Davis. You wanted to know about one of our lessees?"

"Yes. Are you Mr. Foster's secretary?"

She sniffed. "I'm his assistant." My back went up. "I want you to know that while commercial leases aren't confidential, I'm not required to give you this information. I called Mr. Foster about this and he told me to go ahead."

I disciplined my bristle. "Thank you, Ella. I appreciate it. Could you tell me who the lessee is?"

"Mr. Foster doesn't like this sort of thing, you know. This is not part of our usual policy."

"I understand," I said and then clammed up.

The silence dragged a moment or five.

"It's TPM," Ella admitted.

"Is there a specific name on the lease?"

"No. It's a corporate lease, signed by their legal representative."

TPM is a private corporation with fingers in a lot of local pies. They also have political connections that go back a long time. I got no other details from her, so I thanked Ella and hung up. Then I sat and thought dark thoughts about famous wrestling matches with TPM from which their opponents had staggered counting their remaining limbs and thankful for retaining their lives.

Time dwindled as I banged on the implications of TPM.

I jumped in surprise when someone knocked and entered my office. My pager wiggled and the light under my desk flickered. I jerked my head up and looked at the doorway. Quinton was standing there, grinning at me.

"Hi."

"Hi yourself. The alarm works—you just set it off."

"Good thing, too. I just came to drop off my bill, like you suggested," he said, brandishing a torn piece of computer fanfold. He thrust it toward me and I leaned forward to take it. "If it didn't work, you wouldn't be so interested in paying me."

"Thanks," I said, glancing at the page. "Quinton, this doesn't look right."

"What, billed too high for parts?"

"No. This seems sort of low, considering all the work you did."

"You're complaining? The parts were cheap."

"You only billed fifty bucks for labor. I think you spent a little more than the two hours you've got here."

"I spent about an hour here and some time on the program at home."

"It only took you an hour to write the program?"

He shrugged. "It's not as elegant as you think. Mostly I just cut and pasted from programs I'd already developed. Besides, now I've got another routine I can plug into someone else's program down the line. It's paid development time."

I pulled out my calculator. "Let's see here ... parts plus actual time on-site, plus development time, plus consultation ..."

"What consultation? Will work for food, you know. You bought dinner."

"OK, but you still shorted yourself by sixty bucks."

"Call it an introductory offer."

I shook my head. "I don't like to end up behind favors."

"Investment in the Bank of Karma?"

"Quinton ..."

He flipped his hands up. "Hey, look, I like you. I don't mind doing a little work for friends, cheap. I wouldn't feel right about charging you more." He hesitated. "Unless you want me to charge you a business rate."

I felt like a fool. "Umm ... is this the 'just friends' rate, then?"

He smiled and nodded. "Yeah."

"Will you take a check?"

He looked a little uncomfortable. "I prefer cash."

I looked at him sideways a moment and he stared right back.

I shrugged. "OK, but we'll have to go down to my bank."

He grinned and shrugged.

We went. The manager looked a bit askance at Quinton, but didn't say anything. Flush with cash, Quinton headed off for the main library while I went back to the Rover and headed for home for a quick wash and brushup.

I put on a skirt, blouse, and heels, for a change. I felt much better than I had in the morning, if a bit tired. I played with Chaos for a while and gave her a chance to shed on my clothes until I had to leave. I put her back into her cage with her food dish under her nose, and she hardly noticed.

I stopped at an upscale grocery in Queen Anne. The clerk restocking the wine department actually knew something about the subject and managed to find a wine that was, he assured me, pale green and not bad. I broke down and bought a backup bottle of Chardonnay as well.

Mara opened to my ring of the doorbell. Once again, her hands were floured and she still looked stunning.

SIXTEEN

"Oh, you're as good as your word, aren't you?" she exclaimed, seeing the wine bag in my hand. "I hope you don't mind the kitchen for a bit, I'm still rolling out crust and I hate to yell at my guests just to have a conversation. I felt I should be making a pie, since you missed the last one."

We adjourned to the kitchen, Mara in the lead. "Have a seat, open the wine and we can have a sip while I finish up the crust. Corkscrew's in the drawer of the table, glasses right there on top."

I hung my purse and jacket over the back of a chair and tackled the first wine bottle. With the wine poured and distributed, I leaned against the counter and watched her drape pastry dough into a deep pie plate and cut off the edge.

She started to sip her wine, then held it away, staring at it. "Oh, my! This is green wine. Wherever did you find green wine?"

"Larry's. It doesn't seem too bad."

She sipped, then glanced at me out of the corners of her slanted eyes. "It's wicked green, though, isn't it?" Then she let out that wild whoop of laughter, her eyes squeezing to merry slits.

I couldn't help laughing with her. She was more relaxed and outrageous now that we were on a social footing, rather than a … what? Magical one? Student/teacher?

I noticed she was paying a great deal of attention to the pie preparation and biting her lower lip.

I was about to speak when she beat me to it. "Harper, this morning I was rather too pushy. You're right to be wary and I didn't think of it. You see, I'm used to this sort of thing and I forgot that I'm not like you."

I shrugged and drank wine before answering. "No one's like me, I guess."

"Indeed. And there's quite a lot of guesswork to being what you are. Theory and philosophy are all well and good, but reality can rather rear up and bite you on the bum. It's not a field chock-full of scientific validation, you know—not astrophysics or chemistry, after all—and it attracts sharpers and loonies, if you know what I mean."

"Spoon benders and people who write paperback science about ancient astronauts building the lost city of Atlantis," I suggested.

"Exactly the sort of thing. And that brings me to a point I should make before Ben gets home. You see, he's rather enamored of some theories authored by people who can't be proved wrong any more than they can be proved right. It's impossible to resolve any clash between the theories or practices, or even to sort out the possible from the ridiculous when the scientific world as a whole is skeptical. And Ben, ironically, is just as doubting-Thomas as the rest, at heart. Only someone like you can know for certain—not that science would listen to a word you said—but you'll not know until after one of Ben's pet theories has left you with the baby. Do you see my concern?"

I nodded. "So why don't you just tell Ben that you know some of the theory and philosophy is bunk? You can prove it yourself, can't you? As a witch, I mean. Hell, I would."

She leaned back and narrowed her eyes at me over the rim of her glass. "Never been married, I see."

"No. I'm not even very good at dating," I admitted.

"Many of us aren't. We see too much, and it's difficult to dissemble all the time."

For a moment, I could imagine the look that must have been on Will's face when I called him from the police station. "Yeah," I replied.

We both sipped wine and I decided to wade in with both feet. "Why do you glow?" I asked.

"Do I? It's a glamour, I suppose. A habit. I was a spotty, gawky child, and though Ben is always at telling me I'm lovely, it's hard to get over the idea that I'm not just as awful now as I was then. You know how that is, I'm sure."

I nodded. "Oh, yes. I was fat."

She gave me a sober look, then grinned. "Childhood's a bugger, isn't it?"

Mara and I were sitting at the kitchen table, giggling like longtime girlfriends at a sleepover by the time Ben got home. He stuck his head through the kitchen doorway and smiled at us.

"Hi! I see you two are getting on like the famous house on fire."

"Oh, passing fair," said Mara, rising to kiss him. "How were all the budding little linguists?"

"Lugubrious, possibly even mummified."

She tousled his already unruly hair. "Well, go scrub the tomb dust from your hair and dinner will be ready in about fifty minutes, all right?"

"*Sehr gut,*" he said and smooched her before ducking out. We could hear him ascending the stairs.

Mara and I drank more wine and chattered while she finished up the dinner preparations. As her husband descended toward the main floor, she turned to me with a look of concern.

"You'll not say anything to Ben, will you? About my doubts."

I frowned at her. "Of course not. Who am I to break up a marriage over a theory?"

She was still laughing when Ben entered the kitchen.

"What's funny?" he asked, patting himself down. "Did I forget something? Hair sticking up, soap in my ears?"

"No, darlin'. Harper's just very funny, you know. Go pour yourself a glass of this green wine our guest's brought us and have a chat, while I set the table."

Mara whisked out of the kitchen, leaving me alone with her husband. He settled himself at the table and poured wine into a glass. "You two seem to be getting along."

"Mara's lovely."

"That she is. First-class researcher, too. We met over research." He made a goofy grin.

"What sort of research?"

"Mara was doing some geologic studies in a dig out in Ireland that I was also on, doing some ancient religions research. She had some religion questions and I had some questions about ley lines, and we ended up sitting in the pub all night, talking about everything under the sun."

He chuckled. "Sometimes, I'm too much the scientist for Mara's taste." He made a rueful shrug. "I get enthusiastic and bury myself in all the squirrelly little details. Probably can't see the forest for the trees half the time, but she keeps me looking up often enough that I don't go completely into the woods. And speaking of being lost in the woods, how are you doing? Getting any more comfortable with the Grey?"

"Yes and no ... there is something I need to ask you—"

Mara came back to the kitchen and we moved the conversation to the dining room.

Once we had food in front of us, Ben prompted me.

"What were you going to ask me?"

"Oh. Why does this seem to be getting worse? More frequent?"

"Well, I think it's kind of like gum on your shoe. Every time you go into the Grey, a bit sort of sticks to you and it keeps on building up."

"But if I'm building up this Grey ... covering, why would the guardian beast-thing attack me sometimes and not others?"

He thought about it, and Mara frowned.

"I'm not certain," Ben replied at last. "Maybe you don't appear to be a threat sometimes."

"I don't see how I could have changed."

"I'm afraid I don't know what triggers acceptance or rejection, but there must be something. There isn't much known about this creature—or creatures. We don't know if it's one thing or a bunch of them. But everyone agrees that it's stupid as a rock. It does its job by a set of rules. So ... " He leaned his head back and stared at the ceiling.

Mara glanced at me.

"So maybe," Ben continued, "it has a hierarchy to follow. Bigger apparent threats get its attention and it lets small things go, if it has to. So if something is more foreign or threatening than you, it would chase that instead."

"But if I'm a Greywalker, why would I be foreign at all? What kind of threat do I represent?"

Mara looked at Ben, who was stroking his beard in thought. "I'm wondering ... ," he started. Then he looked at Mara. "Maybe you're bright, for some reason. If you're still not very comfortable in the Grey, maybe that makes you look more foreign and bright to it. What do you think, Mara? Does Harper glow?"

Mara glanced at me. "I suspect she does."

I gave her a sideways look, but she went on. "So long as you're uneasy in the Grey you'll be creating some disturbance. The beast is like a spider and the Grey is like a web, so if you're thrashing about, you probably attract its attention."

I frowned at her and she made a "sorry" face. My pager went off, jittering against my hip. I glared at it and excused myself to use the phone in the kitchen.

My friend at the SPD had left a message: Cameron's car was about to be impounded from a garage near Pioneer Square. He couldn't hold the call. I had thirty minutes to get there ahead of the tow truck.

Yet another great dinner down the tubes. I went back out to the dining room to excuse myself to the Danzigers.

"Something's come up that can't wait. I seem doomed to miss that pie."

Mara smiled at me. "We'll put some aside for you. If you've finished by ten, come back and join us again. We'll still be up."

I exceeded the speed limit, but the old Rover took the twists and turns of Queen Anne Hill nimbly and roared down the Viaduct to Pioneer Square in ten minutes.

There was no sign of the tow truck when I pulled into the garage. I circled down to the lower level, searching for the dark green Camaro, and spotted it in an isolated, dark corner. There were more cars than I'd expected and I had to go around the ramp looking for a place to park. I ended up farther away than I would have liked and had to walk back up.

As I approached, I noticed two young men moving around near the car. I stopped and looked them over from the shadow of a pillar. Neither of them was Cameron. One was black, the other white. Both looked unkempt and dangerous. The black guy, the slimmer and shorter of the two, was hanging back, crouched, acting as the lookout as the taller, white guy tried jimmying the trunk open with a crowbar. I didn't like the look of it, so I hung back, slipping my hand toward my pistol.

The trunk lid flew up with a sudden jolt and a pallid blur exploded out of the dark hole beneath. With a scream of rage, a pale whirlwind descended on the man with the crowbar. I darted forward, hand closing around the grips of my gun, not quite sure who was in more trouble: the two car breakers, or the willowy apparition that had erupted from the trunk.

The taller thief dropped his crowbar with a howl of pain as he was grabbed and flung backward. His smaller companion, darting panicked glances between the sudden assailant and me rushing toward him, snatched up the crowbar and tried to smash it into the skull of his attacker. He connected with a forearm instead.

I heard the bone shatter. The chalky one let out a shriek and doubled over, vanishing under the open trunk lid. I had my gun out and started to bring it up.

The dark-skinned man whirled toward me with the crowbar raised. I put the sights on him and held. His eyes met mine for a nanosecond.

He panted a moment, then flung the crowbar at me and spun away, running like a scalded dog. I ducked and the crowbar hit the cement with a clang that echoed long after the thief had vanished up the ramp. I could have chased after him, but I wanted to get a look at the guy with the broken arm a lot more.

I edged toward the Camaro. "Hey. You OK?" I called out.

He moaned.

"Cameron? Cameron Shadley?" I led with my left hand out and the gun pointing straight up. I didn't want to take any more damage, but I was prepared to dish a little out, if I had to.

The pale violence leapt at me with a yowl of pain. Hands like a raptor's talons flashed at my face. I backpedaled as fast as I could, turning, my right arm swinging down, left reaching to lock my grip.

"Hal—" I didn't get to finish the warning.

A clawed brick struck my shoulder and scraped up under my hair, yanking out a few strands. Losing my balance, I squeezed on the gun and felt it buck in my hand.

The fury shrieked and flopped onto the ground. He sat there, a haystack of fair hair, cradling his limp right arm in his left hand. Even through the ringing in my ears, I heard him. "You shot me?" he wondered. "Ow! Oh, fuck, that hurts! It's not supposed to hurt!" He lifted his face and glared at me between matted strands of hair. "Why did you shoot me?"

I stayed my distance, the gun firmly gripped, muzzle pointing at the oil-stained cement between us. "You attacked me. I fight back." Everything sounded a little distant to me, still.

"With a gun?"

"It's a much better tool than a stick. Are you Cameron Shadley?"

"Yes," he moaned. "Who the hell are you?"

"Your mother suggested you were a gentlemanly, soft-spoken boy. Now I discover that you swear and hit women," I mused aloud.

"You'll have to excuse me. I'm not at my best when I'm sick and scared out of my socks," he growled. "So, who the heck are you?"

Sarcasm usually indicates a drop in threat level. I put my gun away. "My name is Harper Blaine. I'm a private investigator. Your mother hired me to find you. Are you bleeding badly?"

"It's not too bad now." He winced. "It's closing up already. The bullet must have gone all the way through."

"Let me take you to a hospital."

"Oh, yeah." He started laughing. It didn't sound too rational. "A hospital's going to love me. 'Excuse me, Mr. Shadley, are you aware you haven't got a pulse?' "

I stepped closer. "Are you all right?"

"No!" he spat, throwing back his tangled hair. His bloodred glower sent a bolt of sickening ice straight through my chest. "I'm not all right! I'm a goddamned vampire with a goddamned hole in his already broken arm. I am not fucking all right, all right!"

Wary, I knelt beside him and looked at the arm he cradled. As I stared, the torn flesh of the bullet wound eased closer together, knitting up like a sweater sleeve. Only a couple of millimeters, but enough to convince me that Cameron Shadley was not operating within original design specifications. I looked at him and he glared back. I had to swallow hard a couple of times to work up enough spit to speak and keep my dinner down at the same time.

"I have to get you and your car out of here right away."

"I'll be fine."

"Not once the tow truck gets here."

"Tow truck?"

"Yes." I stood back. "I heard about your car because it's on the impound list. It'll be towed in the next couple of minutes if we don't move it."

He groaned like a soap-opera diva and hung his head back. "Great! Just great! How'm I supposed to drive with one hand? It's a manual."

"I'll drive."

"What about your car? You've got a car, right?"

"My car isn't going to be towed yet. Come on. Let's go. Give me the keys."

Grunting, Cameron reached into the left front pocket of his jeans and flipped me the keys. Miserable, he oozed into the passenger seat as I tied the Camaro's trunk shut around the broken lock, then got into the driver's seat. In five minutes, we were at the payment kiosk.

"Ticket?"

I looked at Cam. He looked back and shrugged.

"Lost it."

"Lost ticket pays the maximum—twenty dollars."

I handed over a twenty and asked for a receipt. We passed the tow truck a block away. I parked the car under the Viaduct and turned to Cameron.

"You stay put here while I go back for my truck. I don't want to have to hunt you down again."

"I'll stay right here," he sighed. "Promise."

I got out, taking the keys, and walked back to the garage. The man in the payment kiosk gave me an odd look when I pulled up again.

"Weren't you just here?"

"Yeah. Had to drive my kid brother's car out. He's so smashed he can barely walk."

He grunted and jerked his head, taking my money. "You want a receipt this time, too?"

"Yes. I'm going to make him pay me every cent."

He chuckled and handed me the receipt. I drove away and parked next to Cameron's Camaro. It was right where I'd left it. Cameron didn't seem to be in the front seat, though.

"Cameron?" I yelled, looking around. I didn't see him anywhere around the car. I stared at the passenger seat, furious and grinding my teeth. Something flickered. I breathed deeply and looked harder along the wavering edge of the Grey. I reached out and jerked the door open.

Cameron rolled onto the ground.

"Hey!" he yelled, jumping up. "You're not supposed to be able to see me. That's my best trick!"

"I didn't have to see you, just your Grey shadow."

"I don't cast a shadow anymore."

"You do if you know where to look."

"Huh?"

"Never mind. I can see you. What I want to know is why can I see you in the paranormal?"

"I told you—I'm a vampire," he snapped. There was that glare again. This time I was better prepared, but it still felt like an arctic wind had blown through my rib cage.

I studied him a little harder this time. His skin had a pallor that went beyond merely ill, all the way to waxy, and his eyes seemed to have an opaque glaze over the irises, deadening the vibrant violet I had expected to a pastel lilac. His grin was a dead giveaway: his canine teeth were prominent points and the gums had drawn back. I caught a whiff of something and gagged.

"Jeez, Cam, don't you brush?" I asked.

"Kinda hard to see myself in the mirror, you know."

"Not your hair, your teeth."

Embarrassed, he rolled his lips over his teeth and looked abashed.

"OK, now tell me if I'm wrong. You've been sleeping in your car and cruising the Square at night for over a month now."

"Mostly. I had another place for a while, at the beginning, but I got thrown out."

"The beginning of what, Cameron?"

"Are you thick? Since the beginning of this vampire thing. I wasn't born this way, you know."

"Yeah, I figured. Your mother and sister seem pretty normal. So what happened?"

"I got into some trouble with a guy down here."

"Getting turned into one of the living dead is the current rage in payback?"

"No," he drawled at me as if I were not too bright. He stood there looking grim, then glanced around. "Could we get out of here? I feel kind of conspicuous."

As he mentioned it, I remembered how often I'd felt observed lately myself. "We can go over to my office. It's not far and we can park your car nearby."

He gave a reluctant nod and we both got back into the Camaro. I drove to my building, concentrating very hard on looking calm and thinking fast. We parked and I led him up to my office, ignoring the alarm.

"Listen," I started, sitting behind my desk. "I'm going to deal with your most immediate problems first and get the long story afterward, but you are going to tell me the story, one way or another."

Cameron threw himself into the client chair. "Fine."

"I take it you don't feel safe, or you'd have gone back to your apartment, right?"

"Right. I was afraid I'd hurt RC, if I did. I get really hungry and kind of irrational right after I get up."

I narrowed my eyes. "Hungry. How are you doing right now?" In the back of my head I was gibbering, but had no time to listen to that voice now.

"Not so good. Those two guys woke me up."

"Tough. I'm not opening a vein for you. What else can we do? What do you normally do?"

"Well," he mumbled, looking around the floor, "I catch rats, sometimes."

"What?"

"Rats," he repeated, looking anywhere but at me. "I eat rats a lot."

"That's kind of disgusting."

"Yeah, it's pretty gross, but I figure it's better than attacking someone on a street corner. When the bar crowd gets pretty well lubed, I start cruising the drunks. Usually I can find someone who'll help me out."

I started to ask, then decided I didn't want to know right now. He saw me shake my head and looked relieved.

"It's a long, nasty story," he said.

"I can imagine. In the meantime, it looks like your trunk is broken. That a problem?"

"Yeah. See, I sleep in there."

"You sleep in the trunk?"

"It's good and dark and I don't get rousted by cops. Besides, my dirt is in there."

"Dirt?"

"Haven't you ever heard about the native earth?"

"No. What about it?"

"A vampire must sleep in his native earth every day. Well, or at least close to it."

"Why?"

"I don't know. That's just what I was told."

"You ever tried to sleep without it?"

"No. I'm afraid to try. What if I shrivel up or something? It's not a great life—or unlife if you like—but it's mine and I'd like to keep unliving it a little longer, if you don't mind."

"Sounds like you need a more secure place to stay."

"What do you suggest? The county morgue?"

"No. Give me your car keys."

"Why?" he asked, reaching for them again.

"Because I'm going to take care of it while you go out for something to eat. Also, this way I know you'll come back."

"You're not very trusting," he said, handing me the keys as he stood up.

"I'm a professional not-truster," I answered. "Now go out and do what you need to do, but don't break any laws I'm going to hear about."

"Yes, ma'am," he replied with a sarcastic salute as he marched out.

I paged Quinton. In less than a minute, he called me back.

"Hi, Harper." I could hear him smiling. "What can I do for you?"

"I've got a weird situation and I need some kind of security system rigged in a car ASAP."

"Can't wait, huh?"

"No. Not really."

"What sort of thing are you looking for?"

"Ignition cutout, lots of noise, armed and disarmed from the trunk, and extra security for the trunk itself."

"The trunk?"

"Don't ask. Oh, we probably need to add some kind of handle inside the trunk lid and fix the lock."

"What kind of car is this?"

"'Sixty-seven Chevy Camaro."

"It'll take me a couple of minutes to collect my stuff and get over there. OK?"

"Great. Thanks."

"For you, no problem."

Quinton showed up before Cameron did. I took him down to the parking lot.

"Very nice car. Who's Cam?"

"The owner. He's in some trouble and he's worried about the car. I think he's been living out of it. He hides in the trunk to dodge the police—that's why we need a handle and an arm/disarm switch in there."

"He wants to get in the trunk and stay there for a while with the alarm on?"

"I think so."

Quinton rolled his eyes and blew a strand of hair off his face. "That's going to be a bit more complicated. This could take a little longer than I thought."

"Like how long?" asked Cam, looming up behind me. I spun and glared at him. Quinton just blinked.

The silence began to stretch. The males stared at each other.

"Hey, that's enough," I said. "Cameron owns the car. Cam, this is Quinton. He's going to build an alarm for the car so it's safer for you to use. Any problems?"

I glanced between them. They each shrugged. "Good. I have to go move my truck. Cameron, you come with me. Then we'll have a chat in my office. Quinton, if you need anything, come up and knock." I pivoted and stalked away.

So long as I was boiling, the discomfort of Cameron's Grey presence was easier to ignore. It only took a few minutes to move the Rover and get Cameron back up to my office. I kept my temper on simmer.

"OK," I started, sitting again, "the car is taken care of. Now let's deal with the rest of this mess."

Cameron stared down at his hands clasped in his lap. He sighed in disgust. "It really is a mess, isn't it?"

"It could be worse, but it's not good. Why didn't you get in touch with anyone?"

"At first, I thought I was just … sick. I didn't believe all that vampire junk. I thought I might have something really nasty, but I figured I'd either get better soon, or I'd have to go to a doctor. When I found out what was happening to me—I mean when I believed it—I panicked."

"You seem to have adapted. If you'd called your mother, you could have avoided panicking her, too." I wanted to kick myself for sounding like a stereotype.

"What was I supposed to say? 'Hi, Mom. Sorry I can't make the birthday party, I'm a vampire and I wouldn't want to upset you by biting the guests'?"

"How about 'I'm sick, but I'm going to be fine and I'll see you soon'?"

He sighed again and lowered his head even farther. "I guess I didn't think, but I don't know what I'm doing. I'm not very good at this vampire stuff."

"You mean you don't just wake up one night and know how to be a vampire?"

"No. Usually you have somebody around to take care of you, teach you, until you can take care of yourself."

"So, what happened to your … tutor?"

Cameron shrank. "He threw me out," he whispered.

In a cartoon, the wooden desktop would have slammed into my lower jaw as my mouth popped open. Cameron squirmed and snuck a peek at me out of the corner of his eye. I clenched my eyes shut and smoothed out my face.

"Threw you out?" I repeated, choking on a dry throat. I swallowed and restarted. "Why?"

"He said— He didn't— I didn't want— I—" Frustrated, he plunged his face into his hands. "I can't do this!" he howled. "I suck at this!"

I didn't laugh. I stood up and walked over to put a reassuring hand on his shoulder … and fell straight through to the Grey.

I couldn't breathe. I was cold, frozen, falling, sliding through something writhing, oozing, squeezing into me. Black cold. Cameron raised his head and looked through me with a gaze like a razor. I yanked my hand away from that burning cold/hot, live/dead flesh…

and stumbled backward, falling against the desk and sitting down hard on its top, gasping.

"What's wrong?" he asked, jumping up to offer assistance.

I pushed at the air between us. "Don't touch me!"

He recoiled as from a blow, drawing his hands back against his chest.

I gnawed air and fought back to some kind of equilibrium.

"I—I really wasn't expecting that." I straightened myself up and tried to smile.

"What happened? Are you OK? You … flickered." He peered at me, ducking his head to squint at my face. "What are you?" he asked, backing away a step.

I laughed. "Are you afraid of me?" I waved a hand over my body. "Look at me—an ex-dancer with a run in her stocking and rips in her blouse. Why should you be scared of me? You're the vampire, the transcender of death. Who the hell am I?"

"You … you're something—I don't know. You're—you're more here than most people."

"I'm more somewhere. Look, Cameron, I'll tell you my nasty secret, then you can tell me yours. OK?"

SEVENTEEN

Cameron gave a slow nod.

"I seem to be able to see things most people can't," I started. "I met a couple recently who said there's a … another sphere of existence sort of parallel to, or on top of, the normal one. The paranormal. In between here and there, there's a place where things like ghosts and vampires exist, the same way ordinary people do in the ordinary world. Making sense?"

"I get it."

I nodded and made my best stab at the story, dawdling over my words. "I got into an accident a while ago, and afterward I started seeing, moving, into this … place. It's called the Grey. Sometimes I just see things like film projected on fog. Sometimes I can go all the way in—but I try not to. I don't know if I leave the ordinary altogether or not. But I'm getting pretty good at catching sight of things that sort of waver in the Grey, even when I'm here."

"You mean like ghosts?"

"Yeah. I see a lot of ghosts. And a lot of other stuff. I can't say I like it. And I can see you. You seem to exist in both places at the same time. I think that you see me with both sets of eyes, so I seem more solid or more real to you than a lot of other people do."

"You do seem more real than most people have in a while. So what happened just now?"

"When I touched you, I … fell in."

"Whoa. That's pretty weird."

"It's not a lot weirder than being a vampire."

His head bobbed as he thought about it.

"So what's your story?" I asked.

"Um, well … can I skip over some of the details?"

"Sure. For now." I leaned back against the desk and crossed my arms. I could feel the molded edge digging into my butt, but I wasn't about to move.

"Yeah, OK. See, I was down here in the Square a lot a while back, trying to help out a friend."

"Your sister, Sarah?"

He hesitated to confirm or deny.

"She told me about it. She said she'd been some kind of possession for a while. A guy named Edward kept her as a toy."

He closed his eyes and looked tired. "Yeah." His lids rose, but he didn't refocus on me. "I finally got ahold of Edward, and I tried a lot of things to get him to give Sarah up, but he wouldn't." His voice was starting to growl and resonate. "He was so damned amused about it. I was ready to smash his face in. I couldn't have done it, but I wanted to. I got pissed off and asked him what would induce him to let Sarah go. And the son of a bitch said me!"

My stomach did a flip. I put my palm out toward him. "Calm down a little, Cam. You don't need to boil the atmosphere."

He glared at me, then slumped a bit and took a couple of deep breaths. "I didn't mean to get so wound up, but it really wound me up at the time. Anyhow, I was kind of creeped out about it. But I had to help Sarah. It was like she was fading a bit more every time we met.

"Anyhow, I—I said he could have me." Cameron looked down at his hands. "I didn't know he was a vampire. I thought he just wanted to have sex with me. I didn't know he wanted to … make me."

Now he looked up. His eyes glimmered. "I thought he was just some kind of kink and I figured I stood a better chance of holding him off than Sarah did. I'm not hung up about sex, so I didn't think it would be a big deal. I figured he'd find me boring after a while and let me go. But that's not how it went.

"At first it was just sort of weird... I don't really want to discuss that part." He tucked his head sideways and looked at me with a grimace.

"OK. Go on with the part you do want to tell," I encouraged.

"Anyhow, so ... Edward's a vampire and now I'm a vampire."

"Why isn't Sarah a vampire, too?"

"I don't know. I think he was having a lot more fun just sort of playing with her. Or maybe he doesn't like girls. I don't know."

"And then what happened? Why did Edward dump you?"

He tilted his head back and stared at the ceiling. "Oh, I pissed him off. I had a meltdown, got nasty, lost my temper, and he tossed me out and told me to fend for myself. I've tried to get some help, but I don't know who to turn to besides Edward, and he won't even look at me. I mean he literally doesn't see me. I'm really in a mess. There are other vampires around town, but I think Edward is a big man in the local community and he's got them all scared or something. I've been cut out, I guess. It's kind of scary. I could get killed just because of the things I don't know, but I don't know how to learn them. There is no *Vampirism for Dummies* handbook. I tried reading the folklore sections in the library but most of that tells you how to destroy a vampire, not how to be one."

He lay back in the chair for a few more seconds, still. Then he jerked upright and stared at me. "You could help me!"

"Me? I don't know even half as much about vampires as you do."

"You could be my ... my intermediary. You're a neutral party. Maybe some of the others will talk to you. You could talk to Edward."

"I don't think th—," I started.

Cameron jumped up. "Yes! You could do it. You don't need to be a vampire expert. I could point out some of the people and you could ask them. They'll talk to you, I know they will!" He was almost capering with excitement.

"Why—why," I repeated, raising my voice with each rep, "why would they talk to me?"

He stopped and stared at me. "Well, because … because you've got great legs. Who could resist a smart PI with good legs who can spot a vampire without a mirror? Please try. Please? I can pay you. I've got lots of money. I'll pay you double your normal rates. Come on. Is it a deal?"

I had a strange feeling about this. "Let me think about it."

"OK. How 'bout twenty-four hours?"

"Make it twenty-eight hours. I've got a life, you know."

"Yeah, rub it in."

"Cameron …"

"OK, OK. Twenty-eight hours. What do I care? I'll still be up."

My riposte was interrupted by a knock on the door.

"Come in!"

Quinton opened the door and stuck his head into the room. "I'm having a little problem."

"Come all the way in and tell us about it," I suggested.

Quinton closed the door behind himself and perched on the edge of the shabby chair next to Cameron's.

"I can't get this system functional tonight. I've got most of the work done—the lock's fixed and all that—but one of the alarm modules I brought with me is toast and I can't get another one until morning."

"Can you rig something temporary?" I asked.

"Not for this. There has to be a brain of some kind for a multi-input, multistage system like this," he explained. "The fried module is the brain, but it's the one thing I don't have a spare for. I can fake it, but no guarantees, or I can get the correct part in the morning." He glanced at me, then looked over at Cameron. He twitched a stiff shrug. "Sorry."

Cam's face wrinkled up and he pursed his lips. I could almost read the swear words forming around his head. But all he said was, "No problem." Then he looked at me. "You got any suggestions?"

I shook my head and looked at Quinton. "You?"

"Well, if you guys both trust me with her, you could leave the car with me and I can take it down to a friend's garage first thing in the morning. I'll get the module from him, finish up the work, and bring the car back. Be done by nine."

"A.M.?" Cameron asked.

Quinton nodded. One corner of his mouth rippled.

Cameron looked at me with rising panic. "I'm not much of a morning person."

I waved him down. "I'll take care of that. I can pick up the car and pay for it. You'll have to pay me back. Assuming that I can find you a safe place to sleep, that schedule sounds OK to me." I looked at Quinton.

"All right," said Quinton as he pushed to his feet. "Any problems, I'll page you. Car's all locked up. Should be safe where it is till morning." He looked at Cameron. "You need anything out of it before I take off with the keys?"

"Uh, no. I can make do. Thanks."

"No problem," Quinton replied, slipping out the door.

When he was gone, Cameron shot me an expectant stare. "What am I going to do? Where am I going to sleep?"

"Hang on. I have to make a phone call."

I dialed and waited.

"Hello?"

"Mara, it's Harper. How do you two feel about vampires?"

"Never met any. Why?"

"I have a young man in my office who doesn't have a pulse, sleeps during the day, and needs a place to hide out while the sun is up. He seems all right, but he's got some problems we're dealing with. I only need a place for one night. Would it put you out if I dropped him off with Ben?"

"Oh, no. I'm sure we can work something out. There's a little finished room in the cellar that's quite cozy and the light doesn't come in during the day. That might do."

"All right. Now let me talk to Ben."

"You do catch on quick to this wife/husband business," she said, before turning away from the phone to call for Ben.

"Hi, Harper. Are you coming back for pie?"

"Let me tell you what's come up before I answer that. I need to find a place to hide a vampire for one day, and I'm in a bit of a bind about it."

"I don't understand."

"He's a nice kid, but he's new to this vampire business and his normal sleeping place won't be available until tomorrow. Mara thinks you might have a place he could hang out until sunset tomorrow, but I wanted to OK it with you first. Is this safe?"

"Safe? Sure. You're not worried about all that 'has to be invited' junk, are you? Folklore. That's all. But are you sure this kid's a"—he lowered his voice—"vampire? Really?"

"You could almost pass him off as normal except for the teeth and the eyes and the fact that he doesn't have a heartbeat."

"Wow. This is kind of exciting. We can manage. Yes, sure. Brian's at my mother's until tomorrow, so that's no worry."

"Thanks, Ben. I couldn't think of anyplace else. And he really needs more help than just a place to crash for a day. I thought you might want to talk to him."

"Oh, God, yes! When are you coming?"

"I'll be there in about twenty minutes."

"Great! We'll fix some things up and see you then."

I hung up and looked at Cameron. "What do you think?"

"I'm not sure. Who are these guys? They didn't seem too freaked out by the idea."

"I'll tell you on the way."

Cameron followed me to the office door. "Are you sure this is a good idea?"

"It's the safest option I can come up with on such short notice. They won't be any threat to you, except that Ben might keep you up till dawn asking questions. Do you eat pie?"

"No. Solid food makes me spew. I drink a little alcohol or coffee every once in a while."

"Coffee?"

"Yeah. It has just the opposite effect it used to have. Now it smooths me out."

On the drive back up to Queen Anne, I explained Ben and Mara Danziger, to the best of my ability.

"A real witch? Sweet," said Cam, leaning back in the passenger seat. "This could turn out all right."

"I hope so. The only thing I'm worried about is Albert getting agitated. I don't know if he could cause you any kind of trouble."

"I'll do my best to snake-charm him," Cam said with a smile that was both winsome and horrifying. It had to be the teeth. "Who's Albert?"

"He's a ghost. He … lives there."

Cam was still puzzling on that one when I pulled up in front of the house and parked.

"Come on," I urged, grabbing my bag as I stepped out.

We started across the sidewalk together. Albert materialized in the arch at the foot of the steps and glowered at us.

I sighed. Folklore. Right. "May we come in?"

He didn't move, and I was loath to walk through him. He stopped looking at me and directed his baleful gaze onto Cameron.

Cam stepped forward and held up his empty hands. "I promise I won't do them any harm," he said. "I … I give you my word. I just need some help and I hope your friends can give it to me. OK?"

Albert looked at him a moment longer, then nodded and whispered away.

Cam glanced at me. "Tough customer. Must have been a bouncer."

I grinned and we went up the walk.

Ben Danziger opened to my knock. He looked Cameron over as hard as Albert had before stepping back. "Come on in."

Mara stuck her head out the kitchen door. "Would either of you like some coffee with your pie?"

"I would love some coffee, thank you, Mara," I said.

"Coffee would be very nice, thank you, ma'am," said Cameron.

"Oh, heavens, call me Mara. Even my students don't call me ma'am." She smiled and vanished back into the kitchen, calling out, "Go ahead. Ben will catch me up on anything I miss."

Cameron and I exchanged a look as Ben led us into the living room and waved us into seats. He sank himself into a big wingback chair by the fireplace. Cameron took a corner of the couch and I sat next to him, in spite of the vertigo his proximity caused me.

"OK," Ben started. "You think this young man's a vampire?"

Before I could reply, Cam let out a barking laugh and grinned to bare his teeth. "Harper can think what she likes, but I know. Three months ago I had perfectly ordinary teeth. Now I've got these. I used to get up in the morning with a pulse. Now I don't roll out of bed until sunset and you couldn't time the motion of a glacier against my heart rate."

Ben looked at him with a combination of skepticism and excitement fighting on his face. "Are you sure it isn't just a mental aberration?"

"I'm pretty sure."

"Come over here."

Cam ambled over to Ben, who reached out for his wrist.

"Damn, you're cold!"

"Yep. It takes about two hours for my skin to rise to room temperature if it's cold outside."

"Hmmm … I wonder why."

"Thermal inertia, I think. If it gets too warm, I start to smell a bit unpleasant up close. Summer's going to be a real treat."

"Well, you've got no discernible pulse in your wrist." He raised his hand up toward Cam's neck. "Do you mind?"

Cam bent forward. Ben placed his fingers against the side of his neck. "No pulse at the carotid."

"That's the jugular side. Trust me—I've learned my veins and arteries." Ben wrinkled up his nose. "Oops. Harper says I have bad breath. I don't know if that's part of the condition, or if I've just forgotten to brush in a while. I've sorta lost track of time. This thing kind of bums me out."

"I can imagine." Ben leaned back in his chair and Cam came back to the couch. "Well, you certainly seem to be … undead. Do you know what your body temperature is?"

"Not sure. Most regular thermometers won't register at all. I think it hovers around sixty, but that's just a guess."

"I think that alone would qualify you for dead. It's the undead part I'm wondering about. Maybe you're a zombie."

"Don't think so," said Cam, sitting back. "I do seem to have a will of my own and I don't have any interest in human flesh, just blood—though I don't really need much more than a cup or so most of the time. I don't like the sun. I don't cast much of a shadow, or a reflection—at least not that I can see. Sometimes I can make people think I'm invisible. Except Harper."

"What happened to your arm?" Ben asked. "You keep cradling it."

"Some jerk broke it earlier tonight with a crowbar, then Harper shot me."

Ben glared at me. "Shot you?"

I glared back. "He started to attack me."

"Hey, it's all right," Cam cut in. "I deserved it. Besides, it'll be OK soon. I heal fast."

Ben started toward Cameron. "Let me take a look at that."

He was staring at the closed bullet hole when Mara came in. He jumped when she spoke.

"What are you up to, Ben?" she asked.

"Looking at this wound. It's amazing."

"Ben. He's not a specimen. He's a guest. Don't be rude."

Ben looked sheepish and retreated to his chair as Mara set a tray of pie and coffee on the table. She handed out mugs and plates as she spoke.

"Harper says you're in need of a place to stay. How did that come about?"

"I … was sleeping in my car and a couple of featherless bipeds broke in," Cameron explained.

"Featherless … oh," she added and began laughing. "That won't do."

"He seems trustworthy enough," Ben suggested. "If it's all right with you, I'd be glad to have Cameron stay."

"You shan't stay up and examine him all night, now will you?"

"Mara …"

"Oh, all right. I don't mind. Albert says he's promised to be good and you can't make promises lightly to ghosts."

Cameron looked startled. Mara gave him a stern look, then broke up. "It's all right. Albert won't task you, though he'll probably follow you about. He's very protective. Do you need anything special?"

"Um, no," Cam stammered. "I don't think so. I'm kind of nervous without my dirt, but I think I'll be OK. This is still Seattle, after all. Especially in the basement, I think I'll be close enough to the dirt to be OK."

"What's this about dirt?" Ben asked.

Cameron was about to launch into an explanation about native earth when Mara passed him a slice of pie. Cameron gazed at it with nostalgic longing and refused.

"No?" said Mara.

"Oh, no. It looks delicious—it's just that … uh, I can't … ," he stumbled.

"Allergy?" she asked.

"No, I puke."

Ben and I cringed, but Mara laughed.

"You're not very good at lying, are you?"

"Terrible."

"You'll have to learn. All right?"

Cameron nodded.

"Ah, well. I'm certain Ben will find a spot for this slice, too."

Ben looked up from his already half-eaten slice. "Hmm … well, OK."

"What do you do, Cameron?" Mara asked. "Aside from the obvious."

He sipped his coffee and answered slowly, "Um, I was a student at the U."

"Are you graduating, then?"

Ben fidgeted. "Mara …"

"Oh, Ben. I shan't embarrass the lad by asking him awful questions like your sister did me. Don't be so silly. So," she continued, turning her bright green stare back to Cam.

"I … I'm on a leave of absence from school for a little while. For medical reasons."

"That's better."

"Thank you."

"What are you studying?"

"Well, I'm not sure if I'm going to go back."

"Whyever not? Learning's a marvelous thing, if you can manage to avoid an education."

"What?"

"The indoctrination. The interchangeable parts result. You know what I mean, I'm sure."

"Oh, yes," he replied. He played with his cup and sipped his coffee again. "That's one of the things that's been bothering me. I don't know what to do with myself—if I survive this. What do I do with my … life?"

"You've a few things to work out first, I imagine. Still, knowledge for its own sake is worthwhile, if you can afford the tuition. There's a gentleman in one of my lectures—he's fifty-nine, I think—who's working on his fourth degree. He's got loads of credits, so he just keeps taking classes, and occasionally he completes a curriculum quite by accident and they give him another piece of paper. He's having a grand time."

Cameron looked thoughtful. "I hadn't really looked at it that way. I … have time."

"What are you going to do first?"

"I need to solve some problems. Harper is going to help me."

"Hey," I objected. "I haven't said yes yet."

Cameron grinned at me and the pie tap-danced in my belly. "You're not going to say no."

I found myself pressing back into the couch and starting to nod.

Mara cleared her throat as Ben leaned forward. Albert formed in heavy mist by Cameron's elbow, flickering like a wet flame.

Cam jumped. "What?" I relaxed.

Mara had narrowed her eyes. Albert drifted toward her.

"Um … Cameron," Ben started. "Whatever you just did, I don't think you should do that."

"What? What did I do?"

"That was a geas," Mara said. "Persuasion by psychic force. Bad form to try it on your friends."

"I can do that? I thought that was a myth."

"Apparently not. You have power—or you will have. You mustn't abuse it."

Cameron's eyes grew round. "I didn't mean to. I really didn't."

I stood up and grabbed my cup and plate. "It's all right," I lied. "No big deal. I'm just going to take these to the kitchen."

Mara got up, too. "You lads chat. I'll help Harper with the dishes."

Mara closed the kitchen door behind us.

"Are you all right?"

"I'm fine," I assured. "He didn't mean to do whatever he did. I just needed to get away from it. Have I done the wrong thing, bringing him here?"

"Not at all. That lad needs help. Between us, I'm sure we'll get it all settled just fine. Ben and I were busy before you arrived. There'll be nothing to worry about. So long as we make it through the night safely."

I slept poorly with Mara's comment in my head and, having agreed to meet Quinton at nine a.m., I had to rise at seven, but I did not shine.

Quinton was waiting with the Camaro outside my office building.

"Morning!" he greeted as I walked up. "Figured you'd be punctual. She's all ready to go."

"What did you do, get up at five?" I asked.

"Nope. Didn't go to bed."

"You stayed up all night to work on Cameron's car?"

"No. I was going to be up all night anyway, so I just tacked on a couple of hours at the end. It was pretty easy once I had the part. We tested the system out about an hour ago and it works just fine. Your guy should be happy with it."

"Why don't you like him?"

He glowered at me. "I've never been very fond of his kind. They put my hackles up. I didn't mean to be a jerk, it just came out."

"That's OK, but try to be a little smoother about it next time."

"You think there's going to be a next time?"

"Well," I said, "I'm beginning to think there could be."

"Oh? Are your clients getting shady?"

"More than you can know."

"Judging from this one, I can guess. Well, I'm always available. There are some things I won't do, but I can't imagine you asking me to do them."

"Don't be too sure, Quinton. You don't know me and my business as well as you think you do."

He gave me a Cheshire-cat smile. "Don't hesitate to call."

I bought him a cup of coffee—more because I needed one than because he wanted one—and he gave me his bill and explained the system to me. We disarmed and armed it twice, just to make sure.

"Thanks, Quinton. Could you drive the car up to Queen Anne with me?"

"Sure, if you'll answer a question for me. What's with the dirt?"

"Dirt?"

"Yeah. The trunk has an inch-thick layer of dirt in it under a blanket. I had to move it to run some of the wires. So I ask you—who keeps dirt in their trunk?"

"Someone who's very eccentric."

He quirked an eyebrow at me, but didn't argue.

We drove up to the Danzigers' house and I asked Quinton to wait in the Rover. Ben answered my knock.

"I brought Cam's car," I explained, pointing it out and offering him the keys. "How's he doing?"

"Uh, fine, I guess. No problems last night and he seems to be … asleep. You just missed Mara. She had a faculty meeting this morning."

"That's all right. Did you stay up all night? I don't see those jackass ears you swore Mara would curse on you if you did."

"No, no, she was fine with it, but … Look, Harper, there are some things I'd like to discuss with you."

"Anything drastic?"

"No, but there's something really weird going on. Mara said something about ripples. She's afraid things worse than the guardian may be attracted to you."

"Make my morning, Ben. Am I in danger this second?"

"She didn't think so."

"Then it'll have to wait."

"It can wait a little," Ben conceded.

I handed him Cameron's keys. "OK. The little doodad on the key ring will disarm the alarm. Make sure you tell Cameron about it when you give him the keys or he'll set off the alarm and your neighbors will be all over you. I'll call you when I'm free," I added.

Ben looked bemused, but I couldn't take time to chat with him while Quinton was giving me the hairy eyeball from my own front seat.

On the way back, Quinton frowned at me for the first five blocks.

"What is it?" I demanded.

"I'm just worried, that's all."

"About what?"

"Just got a bad feeling about this situation."

"Oh, yeah?"

"Yeah. Call it a prejudice of mine. I just don't like your boy, I guess. Bugs me a bit to see someone as nice as you get involved in things that are ... creepy."

"I can manage creepy just fine, Quinton. I work in Pioneer Square. I've seen plenty of creepy."

He shrugged and went silent, but kept glowering all the way back.

I was glad when I was in my own office and Quinton had wandered off. Skulking about on business for the undead made me feel like a character in film noir, and Quinton's comments about the creepiness of it all hadn't made me feel any better. I was also wondering how I was going to write this up in my case notes.

Though I had found Cameron, I still had questions itching at my brain and an irresistible desire to scratch them, especially if I was going to take on Cameron's proposal. I called the TPM corporate office and started digging to discover who had been using the condo during the dates Sarah stayed there. I finally found a real estate lawyer named Sweto with a chip on her shoulder that could have supported a couple of single-family residences with room for large backyards. We talked misconduct, lawsuits, and criminal charges, and it was no fault of mine if she got the impression we shared a profession.

"TPM has interests in many real estate ventures in the Seattle area," she informed me. "In point of fact, we own the building and lease several suites in it back from the management firm for tax reasons. We also have investments in nonresidential commercial property and many other business ventures not related to real estate."

"And who was using this particular suite at the time in question?"

As fast as she'd opened up, she clammed shut. "That information is privileged."

"Oh, come on, Sweto. It's not like I can't find out."

"I'm sorry. You won't find out from me. Not unless you have a subpoena."

"A what?"

"What sort of case was this again?"

"Misconduct."

"Sorry. I can't talk any further. You'll need a subpoena for me to release that information. Have a nice day." And she hung up on me.

My native curiosity was now leavened with irritation. I went up to the records office and killed several hours looking for deeds and business licenses. They wouldn't give me the names, but they'd give me a start on cracking TPM's shell.

The corporation was privately held, so deep information on TPM was difficult to find, but I made phone calls and one of my contacts offered to fax me everything he had. Another came up with a list of newspaper articles that mentioned TPM. By the end of the day, I expected to be adrift in TPM-related paper.

While those bits of information dribbled in, I tried Philip Stakis's number again.

A woman answered. "Hello?"

"Hello, I'm trying to reach Philip Stakis. Do I have the correct phone number?" I asked.

The woman gasped. "Oh, my God," she shouted. "Can't you just leave us alone?"

"Please don't hang up!" I begged. "I'm not a solicitor or a lawyer or anything like that. I'm a private investigator and I'm just trying to find a piece of furniture." What the hell ... ?

"Furniture? Oh, yeah, right," she snapped.

"No, really. My client is looking for an old parlor organ that Mr. Stakis bought from Chet Ingstrom of Seattle back in 1990."

She was silent a moment, then said, "Really?"

"Yes."

"Oh. Well, we don't have it anymore," she stated in a Long Island drawl.

I restrained my urge to swear. "What happened to it? Do you know, or should I ask Mr. Stakis?"

She laughed harshly. "You'll have a hard time. Phil's dead."

EIGHTEEN

"Dead?" I echoed. Another dead guy? "I don't mean to pry, but could you tell me what happened?"

"To Phil?"

"Yes."

"Lung cancer." I sat back, relieved that it wasn't something mysterious and sudden. Then she added, "Or pneumonia, really, but that's what happens when you're too sick to move after being a two-pack-a-day smoker. Died in the prison hospital a little over a month ago, sudden-like. And he'd been doing so good. Hadn't been in trouble since the navy, hadn't smoked in over a year. But he couldn't care anymore."

"What was Phil sent up for?" I asked.

She laughed her raw, barking laugh again. "Being a jackass. Grand theft—he stole a truck full of furniture, only he thought it was a truck full of TVs. Him and a couple of his jackass buddies from back in the day. So you can understand why I was kind of flipped when you said furniture."

"How long had Phil been in prison?" I asked.

"This time? About six months. It was just before the holidays he got convicted. Then he got sick just after New Year's. Missed the Super Bowl and everything."

"That's terrible, Mrs. Stakis," I said.

"Oh, I'm not Mrs. Stakis. My name's Lenore Fabrette. I'm—was—

Phil's sister. My son and I moved out here to live with Phil when I got divorced. Phil was retired from the navy and he was all the family I had left except Josh, and now it's just me and my boy."

"Do you mind if I ask you just a couple more questions?"

"No. You seem OK, like you actually care, not like some of the creeps who've been calling."

"Creeps?"

"Local jerks. Some reporter's been trying to make a big deal out of the story, like it's gonna win him a Pulitzer or something. Just a bunch of middle-aged farts being stupid. Phil's criminal past is big news in Anacortes, though. He joined the navy back when we were kids so the court would seal his juvie record, but he got in more trouble in the navy and barely stayed in to retirement. I don't know how they found out, but it was all over the local papers, and me and Josh have been hounded like we had something to do with it."

"That's rough. Umm ... what happened to the organ?"

"Oh. Phil gave it away. He said it wasn't worth much, but because it was an antique, taxes on it would be through the roof after he died, so he donated it to some historical society or museum or something like that. I don't know which one, though."

There was hope. "Do you have the tax records for the write-off?"

"No. All that stuff's with his tax guy."

"Could you find out for me? My client really wants that organ. He might be willing to pay you a fee for the information."

"Oh? I don't like to sound greedy, but I could sure use the money. Tell you what. I've gotta go down to Bremerton Thursday. I'll call the guy and see what he says. If he's got the stuff, I'll swing across and drop it on you then. OK?"

I agreed, gave her my numbers and address and hoped she'd come up with something. I left a message for Sergeyev asking if he'd pay for information from Fabrette.

I blew the rest of the day in mundane tasks, like billing, meeting with a lawyer who needed to find a witness, and making more phone calls and trips to the county records office—professional meat and potatoes that were strictly hamburger and home fries.

I finally stopped for some dinner and returned to my office. Cameron drifted in just a step or two behind me. I sat behind my desk and waved him to a seat, straightening up a few things as he sat down.

"All right," I started. "You want me to act as your agent in attempting some kind of reconciliation between you and this other vampire, Edward. Is that right?"

"Um … yeah. I mean, I don't care how Edward feels about me-that's not the issue. I just want the information and help that he should have given me, and I don't want to be a pariah with every other vampire in Seattle. I don't care if Edward helps me, or if he passes the job to someone else," Cam explained, "so long as I get some kind of help."

"What makes you think I can do this job?"

"Who else is going to believe me and not be on Edward's side? You're neutral. And I don't know who else to ask. And even if I had other options, I'd rather work with you. You're … you're tough."

I laughed at that. I felt as tough as wet Kleenex. "I'm new to this world myself, Cameron. You've already exhausted all my contacts among the undead." And if I took this case, I would have no choice about associating with the Grey and its residents.

"I'll give you some names. I think they'll talk to you, just because they're bored. I know I can't expect you to work a miracle, but, hey, it's worth a shot. I'm not doing so great at it."

"Why would Edward even be willing to negotiate with me? What can I offer him?"

"Well, that's what I'm hoping you can figure out by talking to the others. Y'know, maybe once you have a better idea of what the others think, then you'll know what Edward's buttons are and we can push them."

"You've got a lot of confidence in me," I observed.

"Why not? You tracked me down."

"That wasn't as hard as you seem to think. This idea of yours is a different situation. I'm also not quite finished with your mother's case, either. There's still the matter of informing her of your situation," I reminded him.

Cameron squirmed in his chair. "Can't that wait a little longer? Until after we fix this?"

"Have you ever heard the word 'unethical,' Cameron? We have no idea how long it will take to solve your problems with Edward and the rest of the local bloodsucking brotherhood."

"Hey, they're vampires, not lawyers," he joked.

I gave him a thin smile. "I'm willing to try this, but you have to help me with your mother first."

"That kind of sounds like blackmail to me. Isn't that unethical?" he demanded.

"No. It's a contractual obligation. You're the subject of an investigation right now. Until that status changes, I'm not inclined to do anything for you. You want to change that, you need to call your mother and tell her you're all right."

"But that's not true!" he protested.

"Didn't Mara tell you to learn to lie? Start now. It's true enough. But whatever you choose to do, I am going to call Colleen first thing in the morning and tell her I've found you and you're OK. Technically, as your trust's executrix, she's not entitled to more than that. As your mother … that's another matter. You're over twenty-one and not of diminished capacity, but morally … What you choose to tell her is up to you, but you'd better come up with something satisfying, or she'll be on you worse than me."

"Thanks a lot, Harper! What am I supposed to say? 'Hi, Mom, I'm a vampire'?" he shouted at me.

I shook my head and pushed myself deep into my chair. "Cameron, sometimes you are a whiny little brat, you know that? You're spoiled. Oh, and there's something else you should deal with," I added, stabbing a finger at him. "Sarah. You did all this for her, remember?

Leaving her thinking you might be hurt or in trouble is cruel and selfish. And don't start in on another pity-wallow with me. Of all people, Sarah is the most likely to believe your story. She could have ended up the same way. Or worse. If you go and tell her the truth, not only will you be helping yourself, you'll be helping her. She doesn't understand what Edward did, and she's beaten herself up about it. You got into this by playing hero, so play on or take a hike."

He started to say something, then shut his mouth with a click and looked at the floor. "All right. You're right. Do you know where she is? I haven't seen Sarah since this started. I assume she's not staying with Mom."

"She's living in Bellevue, over by the mall."

"At Grandma's house?"

"That's the place. No phone, so you'll have to go there in person."

"I'll go. Right after we're done, I swear."

"Good. She might have some suggestions about talking to your mom, too."

He burst into a megawatt grin. "Yeah, she might!"

"And when you call your mother, ask her to call me," I said.

"You don't trust me?"

"Not one hundred percent. Not yet. Trust isn't a gift, Cameron. You earn it, and it's not cheap."

He shook his head and looked at me sideways. "You are tough."

"So I hear," I said. "Now, give me your list of names and how to get in contact with your vampires. I'll start working on it as soon as I hear from your mom."

He gave me a short list of names and places and we worked out a contract for the job. I shoved my copy in a file and returned my attention to Cameron.

"All right. Now tell me what put the wedge between you and Edward." He looked anywhere but at my eyes and began to fidget. "If you think I'm a bigot who's going to be offended that you went to bed with a man, you can forget it. Half this town's gayer than Paris in the spring."

"I'm not gay," he protested.

"I don't care," I pointed out. "Do you want me to repeat that?"

"No, I get it." He took a deep breath he didn't need and launched in. "He's an arrogant ass."

"How very diplomatic of you to tell him so."

"I did, too."

"Was that all?"

"No. I didn't say that much more, but it was all pretty much on the same theme. I mean, I had figured out that he was weird, kinky, sadistic, and a major control freak before I even got close to him, from what Sarah told me. It took me a while to get how psychotic he is. He just doesn't believe that the consequences of any of his actions are ever going to boomerang on him. He's beyond arrogant. He's a sociopath. Nobody's rules apply to him."

I gave a slow nod. Maybe sociopathy was in the eye of the beholder, in this case. If you're not a mortal, why care what they think? I started mulling the implications, then stopped. Cameron was staring at me, as if he could see the processes revving up in my head. He made a bitter little stretching of his mouth and went on.

"He didn't give a damn about what he'd done to Sarah. It was five minutes' diversion for him, and then he forgot it. He didn't give a damn what he did to me or what he's done to me. He never asked for anyone's consent."

"You said you went along with him willingly in exchange for Sarah," I reminded him.

"I did, but I didn't understand the whole thing. How could I? But he knew I didn't know what I was getting into. I was stupid for jumping into a situation I didn't have a real handle on. But what happened was not what I agreed to. Somewhere along the line, he changed his mind. I didn't know he was going to—to turn me into a vampire! I don't think he meant to, at first. But he just went ahead with what he wanted and he didn't care about what I thought.

"I wasn't mad at first. I was too scared and confused. I didn't know what was happening to me. I still wasn't sure that he was a vampire. I mean, how do you wrap your mind around that concept for the first time? For real?"

I shook my head and shrugged. I hadn't wrapped my mind around it yet, either. Broken contracts I understood. The rest would have to wait.

"When I told him what was happening, he laughed at me," Cameron continued. "He thought it was funny that I was sick and puking because I was trying to eat regular food. Then he explained it to me and he laughed even harder. I was humiliated and upset, but I was so sick I begged him to help me. He agreed because I was 'amusing.'

"I was like a trained monkey that he liked to show off to his friends. I listened to them, though, and I figured out that they knew things weren't going too smooth for me because of Edward. Except for the humiliation, I didn't even care. I was getting through it and that was what mattered to me. But Edward ... likes messing with people. Does it like a sport. I mean ordinary humans who have no idea. He can be cold or nasty to other vampires, too, but it isn't the same. He's got a whole collection of butt kissers and flunkies. He treats anyone he thinks is inferior like an animal or a toy. And he seems to think all ordinary humans are just dirt to walk on.

"When I started to feel OK, I told him I didn't like it. I told him, y'know, what comes around goes around. But he was still laughing at me. He said I didn't have any idea what I was talking about, that I was a 'foolish little boy' who was still more animal than vampire, that I should shut up, mind my betters, and do as I was told. He also told me that I should stop thinking that the rules and morals of 'stupid animals' had any hold on a higher species. 'Higher species,'" Cameron snorted.

"I flipped a bit. I told him he was scum. That he wasn't any more evolved than a protozoa whipping its tail through the mud of the primordial ooze. That he wasn't any better than an oversize tsetse fly, sucking the blood of creatures better than him and infecting them with his own brand of sleeping sickness. I said that every society had rules of some kind and that it was only bullies who preyed on those weaker or less fortunate than they and that any reasonable society would pitch someone like him straight into the nearest volcano for recycling."

Cameron slumped back in his chair, the agitation of his recitation seeming to drain him of energy. "He beat the crap out of me. Then he dumped me on a street corner in Tacoma and told me the next time I spoke to him, he'd stake me out on the top of the Washington Mutual Tower for the morning sun. And that's the last word I ever had out of him."

I had to take a couple of breaths and slow my brain back down before I could say anything. "That was quite a speech."

"Yeah. The one time in my life I was eloquent," he admitted.

"And after that, no one else was willing to talk to you, either?"

"That's right. Alice warned me off once, but even she won't look at me anymore."

"Alice?"

"Alice Liddell. Another vampire." Cameron waved away the details for now. "Doesn't like Edward, but even she said I might have gone a bit too far."

"You regret what you said?" I asked.

"Yeah, I do. Not the sentiment, but … losing it like that. He could have killed me. It was just stupid. I should have found some other way to get out of the situation." He was fidgeting again.

"So what you're so embarrassed about is that you lost your temper?"

"Well, yeah … it's a pretty ugly temper."

I leaned forward and gazed at him until he looked back at me. I managed to hold his stare even while the sensation of cold knives shredded me. "You're an idiot," I said.

"Hey. That's a little harsh, isn't it?"

"No," I replied. "You dove into a situation you hadn't fully evaluated and didn't understand. Under the circumstances, that makes sense. But after that, you only made your own situation worse. You should be embarrassed. Your temper got you into deep kimchi with Edward and it'll get you in just as deep with me, if you don't keep a lid on it. You ought to be scared out of your damned mind. I am."

I sat back, tired out by my own annoyance and underlying fear.

"I am scared," he muttered. "I'm scared of everything. Daylight. People. Myself. I'm afraid that I'll hurt someone. What if I attack my sister or my mother? What if I flip out and kill someone? I don't need to kill for food, but what if I do it by accident? All my friends come down to the Square, you know. What if someone figures me out and … and … I don't want to be like this. I don't want to be a monster!"

Who does? I sighed. "Oh, for the gods' sweet sakes. You're not a monster. You didn't harm the Danzigers, did you?"

"No, but they knew and they were prepared. They had … magic and stuff."

"So do you, if what the Danzigers said is true. You are a creature of magic, a denizen of the Grey. This is going to be hard," I added, shaking my head.

"Why?"

"Because I'm not good with this ghosts-and-magic stuff, so I can only do things in the way I already know, and that's the ordinary human way. Investigation and legwork and shuffling papers. If that doesn't work, I don't know what we'll have to do, but I hope it won't get us killed."

"It has to work … I know you can make it work. You just have to."

"Thanks for the vote of confidence. Luckily, it seems that Edward used a condo that belongs to TPM to house Sarah. I'm already trying to track down his connection to TPM. You wouldn't happen to know his last name?"

"Edward's? I don't know if I ever heard it. But TPM … Wow. They're pretty heavy."

"Yes, they are. And here's a funny coincidence for you. In addition to the condo building, they also own several clubs in Seattle, including two in Pioneer Square."

"They do?" Cameron leaned forward. "Which ones?"

"The After Dark, which I've never heard of, and Dominic's, which happens to employ the bouncer who confirmed that you were in Pioneer Square just last night."

"Jesus H—I thought Edward owned Dominic's. But if he's connected to TPM . . ."

"Edward can't be the principal of Dominic's. Steve the bouncer told me he'd never heard of Edward."

"He's lying. Maybe he never heard his first name—that's a possibility—but he sure knows him on sight. TPM. That might explain why so many people kowtow to Edward, though. And he seems to be a very important guy among the vampires. Lots of bootlicking there, too. He said I was out and by the next night I might as well have been the invisible man."

"So you don't know what his connection is to TPM? Or exactly what his position is relative to the vampire community?" I clarified.

"No, I don't, but I'd guess if he's not the top dog, he's very close to him."

"Oh, terrific. I've just agreed to take on Seattle's top bloodsucker. Thanks, Cameron. I always did like to live dangerously."

"Well, I didn't say it was going to be a normal job."

NINETEEN

At seven a.m. Wednesday morning, I rolled out of bed to stagger around the water tower. It was the worst I'd felt in a week, but I was doing much better at keeping the Grey at bay—at least when there were no ghosts or witches or vampires around. It was an ever-present thin mist dodging around the edges of my vision now, throwing occasional ghost-shapes over the landscape ahead. The constant flickering at the corners of my eyes left me a little dizzy.

When I stumbled home, I called Colleen Shadley to say I'd found Cameron.

Silence sat on the line a while before she asked, "Under what circumstances?"

"Living in his car down in Pioneer Square."

"Why? That's not like him."

"He had a personal problem and he panicked."

"Ridiculous. Why didn't he call me? I certainly could have taken care of it."

"He was scared but wanted to take care of the problem himself. He got in a little over his head. I've agreed to help him deal with it," I explained. "He should be calling you soon. If you don't hear from him, please let me know."

"It must be drugs," she stated. "It's the only way I can account for this behavior."

That sounded familiar. "This has nothing to do with drugs. He's just young and his situation was more complicated than he realized."

"What is this situation you keep talking about?" she demanded.

"Cameron wanted to discuss it with you himself." I was biting my tongue pretty hard as my temper rose. Sarah's view of her mother snapped into focus.

"I paid for this investigation. You have a contractual obligation to tell me."

The temperature of my voice hovered near freezing. "No, Colleen. The contract gives me discretion on matters not directly bearing on the job, and I'm exercising that clause. You paid for me to find your son, not to spy on him. If he doesn't call you within twenty-four hours, then I'll be glad to discuss whatever you want. But your son asked for some time to straighten out a few things and I'm giving him that courtesy."

"Will I be billed for this 'courtesy'?"

"No."

"I'll call you as soon as I hear from Cameron. Or not." She cracked the phone into the cradle as she hung up.

I slithered out of my sweats and running shoes and flopped back into bed. I felt like a Chihuahua in a wind tunnel. Flat on my back, eyes closed ... I was more tired than I should have been, but the constant wearing nausea was gone. I couldn't see the Grey. I was aware of it, but it wasn't immediate. Without the flickering, the treacherous false ground, the heaving, unstill world on top of the world, only fatigue remained. It was the Grey that left me queasy and worn, the uneven, sporadic view, the constant expenditure of energy to figure out what was real and hold back the rest.

Groaning, I got up and called Mara. Inside an hour, I was back in the Danzigers' kitchen.

I held on to a cup of coffee, but I wasn't drinking it. "I have to get a handle on this. I know I'm a lousy student, but bear with me. I agreed to help Cameron with his problem, but I'll have to get closer to the Grey to do it."

Mara started to say something and I waved her down. "And much as I don't like it, you were right. This isn't going away. I don't want to be a witch or a psychic or a Greywalker or anything else. I just want to do my job, but I can't seem to without help. Cameron is … well, he's not quite like the rest of us, and I'm going to have to deal with more like him. And this other investigation keeps turning up dead men. I've never dealt with this many recently deceased in my life. I'm at three now and the coincidence is bugging me. What's with the dead guys?"

Mara swallowed a bite of muffin. "I've been considering that. You're like a pebble in a pond, putting out Grey ripples, and all the fishes in that pond come swimming to see. That's part of the difficulties you've been having. They swarm around and frighten you. And perhaps a few of them are pushing you in some way you can't yet discern."

"You mean like that geas thing?"

"No. What I'm wondering, now that it's come up, is this. If a vampire, like Cameron, can have problems which need help solving, why not other creatures of the Grey? Some of them can't communicate well, and others may need help which cannot be easily found. And here you are. Perhaps the number of dead you are turning up is no coincidence at all, but a sign that you're dealing with something out of the ordinary. And as they're attracted to you, so are a lot of other Grey things."

I forced a laugh. "I hope not. The last thing I want is a client list from a horror novel."

"If they choose to come to you, how will you turn them away? And is it even fair to do so?"

I put the coffee cup down. "Don't start on the ethics. I'm already tied up about this as it is."

She shrugged, but she'd made her point.

I picked apart a muffin, scattering the bits around my plate.

Mara pushed hers aside. "I looked up a couple of simple tricks and I'm thinking they might help you out."

"Not more trips to the Grey today, please, Mara."

"No, no. These are truly simple. In a way, you already know one and the other's not any harder."

I sighed. "What've you got?"

She grinned, her eyes sparkling with excitement. "You've learned to push the Grey back so it's just a bit of a flicker on the edges, right?"

I nodded.

"So, if you look sideways and concentrate on that Grey flicker you should be just seeing into the Grey. Sort of a filter."

"Hey … I think I did that, in a way, when I was looking for Cameron in his car."

"Then all you need do now is refine the technique. Don't look straight on, just peek out of the corner of your eye."

The first few times I tried it, the Grey just slipped around and disappeared, but I got the hang of it pretty quickly.

As I peered from the corner of my eye while the sensation of the Grey barrier raised the hair on my arms, a tiny slice of the world went cold silver. I could see white shapes squirreling along the floor and up the walls like vines, weaving glowing lattices through the house.

I gasped. "That's why nothing gets in here! That's why you weren't worried about Cameron. The house has a … a …"

Mara whooped. "Tender's Lace. It's a protective charm, just very large. Let's try the other. This time, you'll need to sort of grab the edge of the Grey and bend it round you."

"What? I thought you said I didn't need to go in there."

"You don't. You can do it from either side if you can catch the thing. That'll be the tricky part."

I narrowed my eyes. "Why would I want to?"

"Because, while the edge of the Grey is no barrier to you, it is to some of them. If you can bend a bit of the edge around you, it'll act like a shield. Not for very long, I suspect, but it should at least bounce things back from you, if they aren't too solid. Wouldn't have much of an effect on Cameron, but should keep a ghost back. You could try it with Albert."

"I'd rather take your word for it than invite Albert to cuddle up, if you don't mind."

"Why? Do you think he's angry at you?"

"I'd rather not find out today."

"Try the trick anyway. I can test it, if you prefer."

"I'm still not so sure…"

I felt around for the edge of the Grey, but since I was trying to grab it, naturally I couldn't. I could only find it as a rippling wall of here/there. Every time I tried to catch it, it bulged away.

"It's not physical," Mara reminded me. "It's a mental trick. Just push it around."

I pushed. The cloud-mist in front of me curved, leaving a clear bubble between me and it. I moved my hands to grab it, not thinking. The Grey gleamed like glass in front of my hands and slid a bit, keeping the same distance as before. I stared at it and moved my hands apart.

The gleaming bit of Grey grew. It felt heavy, as if the Grey not-mist had developed weight and was pushing back on my hands. My fingertips went white from the intense cold. I jerked my hands back and the Grey slumped back into its usual roiling storm-light.

I moved around and pushed on it again, feeling the deformation stiffen and grow heavy with cold. I pushed harder and popped through it, tumbling into the chill, instantly swamped in the cold, writhing haze. For an instant I was disoriented and afraid, but I caught my breath and a whiff of weird chemicals and pushed my way back out. Mara put out a hand, as if that would help.

She looked me over. "That almost worked. Try it again."

I shook her off. "No way. Not right now. It's wearing me out. I don't feel so good around this stuff, anyway. It smells bad, it's cold, and it gives me vertigo. There's no up and down in there."

"Is it really that appalling? I had no idea."

"The difference between theory and practice, I guess."

She laughed. "Ha! Hoist on me own petard! Still, you should try—"

"I'll practice, but not right now. Thanks for the tips, though."

"Glad to. Should help you keep the beasties at bay. And there will be more. You're making waves, remember."

"I do, but I have one question. Why do they seem to go away when I'm in my truck?"

"Do they? They never really go away, so if you're not seeing the Grey, it's because the truck's material acts as a filter. It's got no connection to the Grey. It keeps them out, but it also keeps you in."

"That's fine. I can't start thinking about monsters from the Grey descending on me, or I'll start screaming. Even if I can make myself believe in them."

"But Harper ..."

I waved through her words. "I know, I know, but it's one thing to say you do and see one or two bits of proof and another to get your head around the whole, enormous thing. I'm trying to keep my balance. I'm not used to this brand of open-mindedness. I'm a cynic by nature and training and likely to stay that way."

Mara heaved a sigh. "I know. But so long as you're fighting it, the Grey will be a minefield for you. Be careful. Learn to accept it."

"I'm working on it, Mara. I am."

I wished I didn't have to.

I was just ahead of rush hour all the way to Bellevue.

Nothing seemed to have changed at Sarah's house. The motorcycle parts still reposed outside, the lawn still played dead. Sarah answered my knock before I finished. I almost rapped on her forehead. She didn't seem to notice. She was grinning.

"Hi, Harper! Cam said you might drop by. Come on in. I've got some coffee on, if you want some," she added, holding the door wide.

"So Cam got in touch with you?" I asked as I settled myself at the tiny table.

"Yeah," she called over her shoulder as she gathered up the coffee things. "He came by kind of late last night. Like, about two a.m."

She brought the tray and sat down with me. "I was kinda surprised to see him. I mean, you said you thought you'd find him pretty quick, but I didn't expect it to be that quick. And then he starts telling me this crazy story, and I thought he was jerking my chain, at first. I mean, that is one weird tale. A vampire? Like I think that's likely..."

"What do you think now?" I asked.

"It sounds crazy, but I believe him. It ... it kind of fits. Mom is not going to be cool with this, though. I'm still a little out of it on some of the details myself. Cam couldn't stay a real long time, y'know. He said you're making him call Mom tonight. Is that right?"

"I'm not holding a gun to his head. I told him it was the reasonable, responsible thing to do. If he had called her a month ago, I never would have gotten the case. Even if he'd made up some kind of lie to tell her, your mother would have at least known he was around."

"I know," she said, rocking her shoulders in a queer, rolling shrug. "It's just going to be hard to tell her the truth and get her to believe it. Mom's imagination is limited to interior design and party planning."

"We'll have to wait and see."

"Yeah, I guess. I got the feeling there's still some kind of problem, but like I said, we didn't have a lot of time. Is he going to be all right?"

"I think so," I replied. "Something needs to be resolved, yet, but once that's taken care of, things should be OK. But this is pretty strange stuff to be going through on your own."

"You got that right." She shuddered. "It makes me pretty creeped out to think about it. Edward could have gotten me, too, y'know."

I shook my head. "I haven't gotten a handle on this guy yet, but I don't think he would have done the same thing to you. You're not the same sort of person as your brother, and I think the personality clash made all the difference. At least, that's what I think right now. I could change my mind by this time next week." I didn't add that I suspected the natural path of Edward's games with Sarah would have led to the county morgue.

"In the meantime," I continued, "I'm going to try to help Cameron resolve his problem. Can I call on you if I need your help?"

"Sure," she said. "Anything you need." She got a notebook out of her purse and scribbled on a page, ripped it out, and handed it to me. "That's my boyfriend's cell phone number. He left it with me while he's in Italy."

I cocked a quizzical look at her. "You've had a phone all this time?"

"Yeah, but I wasn't going to let my mom know that." She grinned and became a very pretty girl with very ugly hair.

"I won't tell her," I promised.

"Thanks."

Back across the water, I stopped at the office to check my messages.

"Ms. Blaine, of course paying for information is no problem. Up to … five hundred dollars? This will be acceptable. Please keep me informed." Sergeyev really wanted this thing.

I wrote myself a note, then headed home.

I checked Chaos when I got home and found her sleeping, ignoring me with a will. I looked toward the chair and the narrow, awful-red cabinet and let them wait. I flopped onto the couch with a beer and indulged in total, potato-headed TV-watching.

I was fascinated by some kind of nature show about Australia when the phone rang. I answered and was ambushed.

"I just talked to my son, thank you," Colleen Shadley started, "and he told me some … cockamamie story about vampires and nightclubs and I don't know what. Now, you—you tell me what is really going on!"

"I'm not certain myself yet," I answered. "It's complicated."

"That's hogwash! Why is he doing this to me? Why is Cameron lying to me? I hired you to find my son and you seem to have found some kind of nut!"

"Are you saying that the man you just spoke to was not your son?" I asked.

"No, I am not!"

"So it was Cameron who called?"

"Well, it sounded like him. Except for this wild tale-telling. Now, you tell me the truth, damn it!"

"Well," I drawled, "I am pretty well convinced your son is a vampire."

"What!" she shrieked. "Have you gone completely insane!"

"No." My speech was like molasses. "I don't want to upset you, Colleen, but, as the Bard said, 'There are more things in heaven and earth ...' I wasn't inclined to believe it myself, at first, but Cam has said and demonstrated some things that convince me that he's ... not factory spec anymore. And he still has some problems to resolve."

She barked. Well, it sounded like a cross between a growl and a bark, and it wasn't the sound I was expecting. "I want you over here—now!" She spat out the address and slammed down the phone. I pushed the disconnect button. The phone rang again before I could even put it down.

Cam sounded about eight years old. "Harper? Did my mom call you?"

"Yes. She just hung up."

"Is she still upset?"

"Upset would be a very mild description. I have been ordered into the presence at once. How 'bout you?"

"Me, too. Umm ... do you want to go together? I could pick you up."

"I think separate cars would be better. There's no guarantee we'd be leaving at the same time."

"All right. I'll see you over there."

I hung up and went looking for my shoes. I tickled my computer and got it to spit out a copy of my bill, just in case.

On the way to Bellevue, I considered what I was heading into. I hadn't really expected Cameron to try the truth on her quite so soon, and I hadn't any idea how Colleen Shadley would react once I arrived. I supposed that she wanted me out there so she could fire me or demand answers she liked better than her son's. I didn't think she'd like mine any better, but since I'd already completed the task, she couldn't fire me.

She could refuse the bill, though, and that would be unpleasant. I hadn't had to remind a client of nonpayment in a long time and I didn't look forward to it. Colleen was the lawyers-and-litigation type, without a doubt, and Nan Grover wouldn't like having to choose between a friend and me. No matter what happened, it wasn't going to be fun.

The Shadley house sprawled in one of the horse-trail suburbs where the yards run to an acre or two around houses of equal size. I had to wander a bit to get into the nest of twisted streets and up the curving, grumpy rises to the rambling stone house that hung back from the street like a shy child behind a screen of cypress trees. Cameron's green Camaro stood in the driveway.

The air near the house flickered a bit to my gaze and familiar, cold nausea slid a bodkin along my ribs. I looked sideways at the curtain between *here* and *there,* probing the dark spots until I thought I had looked into them all. I caught the shape...

"Hi," he said, and I twitched, not quite prepared. Cam was waiting in the shadows of the trellised entry. "I didn't want to go in without you."

"Afraid your mother will eat you?" I asked.

"Sort of. I've never heard her this mad. I mean, she yells at Sarah once in a while, but not like this. She's hot."

"I noticed." I took a few deep, slow breaths before continuing. "All right. Let's beard the lioness." I rang the bell. The porch light came on and the door wrenched open.

Colleen glared at both of us and directed us in. Cam, the coward, let me go first. She led us into a stiff, formal room. I shot a glance at

Cameron and he made a grimace. This must have been the child-free zone of his youth, approached only on formal occasions or under parental indictment. We were being called onto the antique Chinese carpet.

Cameron's mother sat down on the pale cream sofa and pointed us at narrow-backed chairs without armrests. I sat on the love seat across from her instead. After a second's pause, Cameron sat next to me.

Colleen reined in a scowl, but didn't comment. "I would like an explanation out of both of you. Now."

Cameron started to answer, "Mo—"

I cut him off with a hand gesture, presenting his mother a bland face. "Of what, Colleen?"

"Of this phone call I had from Cameron this evening. Of what is really going on. Now, please."

"I think we need some clarification first," I suggested, sitting back and stretching out my legs to their full, space-hogging length. I crossed my booted feet at the ankle, heels pointing at her in insouciant despite. "You hired me to find your son and I have, unless you claim that this young man is not your son. Is he?"

"Yes, of course he is," she replied. "But—"

"Then you agree that I've supplied the service you contracted for."

She hedged. "Up to a point."

"There was no other point agreed on in the contract or our discussion, Colleen. As his mother, you were concerned for your son. As the executrix of his trust fund, you were concerned for your trustee. Here he is—son and trustee, whole and sound. I'm willing to discuss the case with you insofar as it doesn't intrude on Cameron's privacy—even further with his permission. But, professionally and ethically, that's all I will do."

She glowered, but she also knew I had her, as far as contracts were concerned. "Very well, then. You can send me your bill and go now."

Cameron was vibrating with tension, his flickering making me dizzy. "I want her to stay. Mom, I'm sorry I tried to run away from my problem and that I didn't get in touch with you a lot earlier, but I knew you would have a hard time with this. I had a hard time with it, and I'm still having a hard time. I wish you'd cut me some slack."

"Slack? You sound just like your sister. You think you'll be handled with kid gloves if you just whine enough."

"I'm not whining. I'm trying to explain," he said, shooting his arms out to the side and nearly smacking me. I refused to flinch.

She snapped back at him. "Evading and lying is more to the point. You can't imagine how disappointed I am in you."

"Actually, Mom, I've got a pretty good idea. I got in over my head. I did some stupid things. I'm disappointed in me, too. But that doesn't change the situation. I'm still . . . what I am," he finished, dropping his hands between his knees.

"A vampire? Cameron, really!"

"Smile, Cameron," I suggested.

He rolled his eyes at me and made an ugly grimace. His lips peeled back from his teeth and his too-sharp canines glinted in the light. Colleen recoiled and stared.

"Andrew Cameron! Stop that. Who did you persuade to mutilate your teeth like that?"

"They're not fake, Mom," he said. "They came with the outfit, so to speak. So did this." He shimmered a little and became Grey. I spotted him right off this time, and grinned.

Ignoring me, Colleen jerked forward. "Cameron! Cameron! Stop that! Stop it!" she yelled. She turned her glare on me again.

I shook my head, stone-faced again. "No smoke and mirrors here."

She reached out and flailed at what seemed to her thin air. She slapped her son on the shoulder.

"Ow!" he yelped and shimmered back into the normal.

She grabbed on to him with both hands, which pulled her off the sofa. She crouched on the floor in front of him and held on tight to his upper arms.

"What did you do? Where did you go?" she demanded.

"I was right here, Mom. You just couldn't see me. I don't know how it works. I just concentrate on being gone and I disappear." He tried to shrug, but she held him too hard. "It just comes with the job, I guess."

"Can you do it while she's touching you?" I asked, half curious, half hoping to prove something to Cameron's mother.

"I can try." He shimmered away again as Colleen held on for dearest life.

She let out a wail and plopped onto her backside. "Cameron!"

He came back. "I'm still here, Mom."

"Oh, my God," she gasped and put her hands up to her face. Oblivious of her makeup, she rubbed her cheeks and temples and smeared her hands up into her hair. "My God, my God." She crumpled into a ball and began sobbing.

"Mom! Mom, it's OK. It's all right. I'm not going to hurt you or anything." He crouched down on the rug beside his mother and put his arms around her. "Mom? Are you OK?"

She wailed and pressed the top of her head against her son's chest. He rocked her and babbled soothing words. I stood up and looked around.

"Kitchen?" I asked.

"Out the other door and through the dining room," Cameron whispered, jerking his head toward a door we had not used before.

I nodded and went out.

Somehow, Colleen Shadley didn't strike me as the sort to resort to hard liquor for shock. I made tea. While it was brewing, though, I hunted up a bottle of cognac and put a good dose of the stuff into one of the cups. I juggled three full cups back out to the sitting room.

Cameron had gotten his mother back on the sofa, though she was still clinging to him a bit and sniffling.

I handed her the cup with the potent brew. "This'll help. Better drink it."

Cameron found her a box of tissues as she snuck up on her first sip. She shuddered and made a face, but took a scalding gulp and then another. Then she took a tissue and dabbed at her smeared eyes and blew her nose in a delicate, ladylike fashion.

"I—I—that wasn't good of me," she said.

Cameron patted her arm. "Mom. It's OK. You were … shocked. It's OK."

She nodded her head and drank some more tea. She set the cup down on the glass-covered table beside the sofa. "I'm sorry," she said. "I can't take any more of that muck. I need a drink."

So much for my assessment of character.

Cameron got up and went looking for liquor. Colleen, face streaked with mascara and lipstick, looked at me and raised her eyebrows.

"What am I going to do?" she asked.

TWENTY

"Improvise."

Her eyes were chasms of confusion. She started shaking her head. "No, no. I don't 'improvise.' I plan things, I prepare for contingencies. This is—this is not something I have any plan for."

I started thinking out loud. "I suppose you could think of it as if Cameron had an exotic medical condition that requires a change of lifestyle. He's still your son. He's still a decent, intelligent young man. He's just … different."

Her mouth turned down in distaste. "You sound like a counselor."

Cameron came back with the cognac bottle and some glasses. He poured generous measures for all of us. I gave him a sharp look.

He returned a "what?" look and a shrug. "It's alcohol. I can practically absorb it through my skin. It's not going to hurt me." He sat down next to his mother.

We sipped. Colleen Shadley gulped. She shuddered and finished off her drink.

"All right, Cam," she gasped, setting the glass down, "tell me how this happened. Help me understand it."

He refilled her glass, avoiding meeting her eyes. "Well, Mom, the details are kind of unpleasant. I did something I felt was necessary, but I did it badly. Can't we just say that it happened because I thought I knew more than I did?"

"All right. Someday I expect to get the whole story out of you, but I can let that go for now. Go on with the rest."

"I met someone who wasn't very pleasant and he took advantage of me, because I wasn't as clever as I thought."

Colleen stiffened and began to cough on alcohol fumes. She waved Cameron away as he tried to help and caught her breath on her own. "Go on," she repeated. Her eyes watered. She dabbed at them as her son talked.

"I got sick."

"I remember you were ill for a while after Christmas."

"More like February, Mom, but it doesn't matter. Anyhow, I was megasick and I didn't know why. And when I found out, I didn't know what to do. So I tried to get some help, but things haven't worked out so well. I've got a few problems to settle before everything will be … acceptable. But the plain fact is I'm a vampire, and that's not going to change. It can't be undone. I just have to live with it—or unlive with it," he added and laughed.

His mother made a face.

"Oh, come on, Mom. It's a joke."

She mumbled her discomfort.

"Mom, can you live with it?"

This time, Colleen played with her glass. "I suppose I don't have a choice. You're my son. I can't just pretend you've ceased to exist. I can't—I couldn't bring myself to … do anything to you. Are—are you really all right?"

"As all right as this gets. Better, now that you know. Harper and I are working on the rest. See, I have a plan now, like you always tell me to. So it's going to be OK. But I could use some of your help, too, Mom."

"My help? What can I do?" She sounded younger than her son.

"We'll have to work out some new arrangements with the trust—I can't go to classes in the daytime. And I need to make some new living arrangements, too. My car's nice, but the trunk is kind of cramped."

Her smile wobbled. "I'm sure we can think of something. Oh, Cameron, why couldn't you have gotten into some normal kind of trouble?"

"Just precocious, I guess."

We sat around the white room for another hour, working out details—including my billing. By the time I left I was envying Cam his cozy bed in the trunk of the Camaro. I dragged myself home to my own, head bobbing like a somnolent drinky-bird's all the way.

When I got out of bed, noon was cracking overhead with the *bing-bang-bong* of the Catholic clock. I rushed for my office.

My first job was contacting Lenore Fabrette to say I could pay for the information. She replied that she'd gotten it and would bring it on Thursday, as planned.

I tried to make a little more sense out of the TPM papers I already had and the new ones that came in over the fax, but most of it was too dense with corporate legalese to plow through with speed. I set the pile aside and made more phone calls, phone calls, phone calls. I had a date for dinner with a friend and I didn't want to miss a moment of normalcy before diving into an evening of interviewing vampires.

Even at a quarter to eleven, it seemed that the vampire community was still just waking up. It was nearly midnight before I found Alice in the top-floor lounge of a downtown hotel.

The host at the door pointed her out to me: a petite woman with deep red hair and the same shadowy, filmy-gleaming eyes that Cameron exhibited. She lurked at a corner table, watching. I skirted around the dance floor and approached.

"Hi," I started. "Are you Alice Liddell?"

She looked up from under arched brows. "At the moment." She stretched one corner of her broad mouth into a smile and floated a hand at my side of the table. Alternating waves of heat and cold flushed over me. "Why don't you sit down?" she offered. My knees resisted a bit as I sat across from her, frowning as I wrestled with my sense of familiarity.

Her amused, silent evaluation hammered my spine with spikes of frozen fire. I didn't have to look sideways to see that all light around her seemed to have been sucked away, leaving a pulsing corona of dark red around her pale face. I checked my shudder and stared back at her. My stomach did a slow roll. Apparently, vampires brought their Grey effects with them, whether I liked it or not.

Her voice was chill velvet, stroking over my skin. "How do you happen to come looking for me?"

I had to swallow before I could talk. "Cameron Shadley sent me. My name is Harper Blaine—"

She seemed to be on the verge of laughing—a sound I did not want to hear. "Yes, I know. Do you smoke?" she purred, picking up an old-fashioned cigarette case from the table. "Oh, no. Of course you don't. You're one of those delicious, healthy people." She extracted a pale cigarette from the case with the tips of her long, manicured nails and placed it between her lips with all the slow tease of a golden-age movie siren. She could have ignited it with her own heat. Instead, she used a slim gold lighter and let her first drag ooze out of her mouth. It made a rising blue veil between us. "What does Cameron think I can do for you?"

"You know about his problems with Edward?"

"Of course."

"I think he was hoping you could offer some kind of entrée."

She chuckled and I felt a pain in my stomach. "How delicious," she said, twisting my meaning. Her teeth showed a little. They seemed very wet and very sharp. "Just how well do you know Cameron?"

"Why? Are you not in the habit of dining on the friends of friends?" I shot back. "Cameron is my client and I know a vampire when I see one." I glared at her and refused to drop my eyes, even though her gaze razored my spine. I wanted to throw up, or scream, or anything that would make her stop looking at me, but I clenched my teeth and sat still.

She played with her cigarette. "What an interesting proposition you are, Ms. Blaine. I wonder if you appreciate it."

"Probably, considering I believe you could snap my spine before I could see you move," I replied. "But Cameron knows where I am and how to find me just as well as you do. So, do you want to break my neck or do you want to help us?"

She hummed a cloud of smoke at me and propped her pointed chin in her hand. "Oh, I want to help, believe me. Cameron's a … sweet boy." She smirked and sat back in her chair, sipping at her glass of … something. "What does he think I can do for you?"

"Cameron has been having problems … adjusting. He's hired me to help make some kind of reconciliation with Edward and work out a way to receive the mentoring he didn't get. He suggested that you might be sympathetic to his position."

"Sympathy is expensive. What are you offering in exchange for my help?"

"That depends on what you bring to the table. If you can give information or make a suggestion that helps me out, I may be able to help you. So … ?"

"Kill him."

"Edward?"

"Of course."

"Is that your suggestion or just what you want?"

"Both." She leaned forward, trying to snare me with her stare. "Edward's been in charge long enough, and he's getting long in the tooth, making mistakes. Just look at Cameron. And he doesn't even know about you. And what kind of leader is that, who can't even protect us from one little boy and his"—she looked me over again, licking smoke from her lips—"very interesting friend."

I felt like something nasty was sliding over me as I looked back into her eyes.

She continued, grinning very slightly. "I think it's time we had someone a little younger in charge. Someone more capable of sympathizing with a young man in a hard spot. Someone with sharper teeth." Her lips closed slowly over the knife-edge gleam of her canines.

I felt myself leaning forward, breathing shallow, numb breaths. "You hate him."

She raised her eyebrows. "Hate? Oh, yes." She hissed voluptuous delight. "With every drop of borrowed blood. It would be so easy for you to attack in daylight when he's weakest. You don't even have to kill him, just show his weakness."

"I'm not getting it."

"Let me tell you the way it is with us. We're like wolves, and the toughest wolf gets to lead the pack. But if he shows weakness, instability, insanity, the pack will shred him. He must be strong and his actions must be in our best interest. Attack him, show his weakness, and they will kill him for you."

"I see."

"Yes," she hissed. "You do. Once Edward is truly dead and I am in charge, I will, of course, be very, very grateful."

Something crawled over my skin. Twitching my gaze aside, I caught a red thread of movement in the Grey and pulled back from it, taking a deep breath and shaking my head. The red thing slid away, dissolving onto the air. I blinked rapidly, shedding a sudden sleepiness, but unable to get the ringing of Alice's voice entirely out of my head.

"What's to stop him from killing me first?"

She laughed, and I tried not to cringe. "You don't look like a threat. Who regards the twitching of insects? Once the mud is stirred up, it'll be too late and killing you off won't clear his waters. Quite the opposite. He'll be far too busy to squash you. When the pack turns on him, they will rend him limb from limb." She paused and licked her lips before taking another sip of her drink. She shivered and smiled horrors at me. I swallowed bile.

"I don't see how Cameron benefits from Edward's demise."

"By my gratitude," she growled.

I shook my head. "No. I don't think so. Not inclined to rely on the generosity of vampires, considering Edward's example. Who protects me from you?"

She ground her teeth. "I assure you you'll come to no harm if you do what I say."

I managed to shake my head. "I won't kill anyone. I'm not a hired gun and I'm not interested in playing in your political pool."

Alice leaned forward and her eyes blazed. "Then what good are you to me?"

"I'm not here to help you. I'm here to help my client. I'll find Edward's weaknesses, his mistakes, rake up the muck, but the rest is up to you. And you'll owe me."

She laughed and stabbed out her cigarette with a hard jab in the ashtray. She sipped her drink and watched me over the rim, smiling razor slashes. "All right, we'll do it your way, for now. But I will still be watching you." Then she sat forward and put out her hand, palm up. "Let me see your list."

"What list?"

"The list of names. Cameron must have given you one, else how would you have found me? Hand it over," she demanded, beckoning her crimson-clawed fingers at me.

I dragged out the list. Alice snatched it and read it. A new gleam entered her eyes. "Oh, very interesting ..." She pulled a fountain pen from her tiny purse and wrote a new name at the bottom: Wygan.

"There," she said, flinging the page back to me as dismissal. "Start with Carlos. That should loosen up the dirt under Edward's feet. And don't worry—I'll keep Edward's attention off of you. I did promise. By the time you've finished with that lot, his problems will have just started."

I got up from the table and walked out. I could feel her gaze on me all the way to the elevator, like freezing water rolling down my back.

I did not want to follow Alice's orders, though I felt a mental nudging to do so. I stared at the list as the elevator descended. Unfortunately, the closest vampire was Carlos. If I was going to talk to anyone else tonight, it would have to be him.

I was crossing the lobby when my pager went off. I used a desk phone to call the number. Cameron answered at the other end.

"Where are you?" I asked. My head throbbed and a matching ache had grown in my innards.

"I'm at Sarah's place. Uh, she says to say hi and she got two ferrets instead of one."

"I'm happy for her. I just finished talking to Alice and things are … well, they're trickier than I thought. Could you meet me tonight?"

"Not tonight. Tomorrow. Call it an hour after sundown, which is … eight twenty-seven, so, nine thirty?"

"All right. I'll see you then. For now, I'm going to see Carlos."

"Oh, man … be careful, Harper. If I don't see you tomorrow, I'll know who to ask, at least."

"Thanks for the vote of confidence, Cameron."

I checked my watch as I left the lobby; it was twelve thirty-nine and dread was twisting in my stomach. I did not want to precipitate a palace coup, but Alice's point about the protective behavior of vampires was giving me an idea. I didn't know if I could manage it, but my other options seemed feeble. I had to trust Alice to cover my tracks as she'd said. If she hated Edward enough, she would. I was banking on hate.

The list said I could find Carlos at Adult Fantasies, a sex shop just behind a strip of businessmen's motels from which they probably culled most of their clientele.

Less than ten minutes' walk from the swanky shops and condos of downtown, the tangled area of odd-shaped blocks housed a strip joint, two all-night bar-and-grills, and Adult Fantasies in their own little commerce park of public embarrassment and private greed. Efforts to move them off or shut them down were never completely successful. Even a plan to make the area into a park had come to naught; eighty years of industrial dumping had made the ground too toxic. So the nighthawks' wasteland remained and Seattle's history of making money off sin continued in all its tawdry glory.

The Adult Fantasies building was a sharply pointed triangle. Full-height windows at the point opened up a view right through the fetish wear and lingerie. I pulled open the plate glass door, went past the stairs that led to the video parlor and "home of live girls," and into the store proper. To my left was the clothing: on my right, the stuff even a sex shop doesn't put in the window. Ahead was a glass counter of X-rated impulse items, guarded by a cash register and a Goth girl.

Her hair was deep, oily purple, her face rice-powder white around black lips and battered-raccoon eyes. Two small, black niobium rings pierced her right eyebrow and a fine silver chain connected the ring in her left nostril to one in her left ear. For balance, the earring on the right was a heavy black spiderweb with its ruby resident dangling within. A studded leather collar with swags of chain imprisoned her neck. She glanced at me over a notebook she had spread on the countertop. Realizing I was coming straight to her, she closed the book and put her pen down on top of it.

She looked midtwenties, though she sounded like a teenager. "Hi, did you have a question?"

"Is Carlos in?"

"Oh, he's around. Probably upstairs. Just a second." She looked around the store and spotted a young man over in the only dark corner the store had, crowded between vibrating plastic penises and the green-painted dressing-room doors.

She called to him. "Jason, is Carlos upstairs?"

Jason raised his head out of a cardboard shipping container filled with videotapes and looked in our direction. "I ... um, yeah, I guess I saw him go up there about half an hour ago. One of the girls came downstairs to get him."

"Would you go up there and tell him someone down here wants to talk to him?" she asked, displaying the kind of patience mothers have for backward children.

"What about my box?"

"I'll keep an eye on it," she assured him. "OK?"

"Sure. OK. I'll go get him." Jason slumped off toward the door.

We stood there in the vague thump of music from the rooms upstairs. Her gaze kept flickering down to her notebook. "You can look around, if you want. Sometimes it takes a while for the guys to get back downstairs. I don't know why. I mean, they've seen tits before."

I nodded. "What are you studying?"

"I'm writing an article for *The Stranger,* about safe sex."

"That should be a winner." I wondered what qualified as safe from the point of view of someone who felt the need to chain her nose on. Not wanting to cramp her writing style, I wandered around.

I was examining a black and purple leather bustier with marabou feathers around the top when I felt my stomach fall toward the floor. I turned my head. A slab-bodied, bearded man strode toward me. He wore a clot of darkness like a cape, riding on the broad shoulders of his black leather jacket. His eyes were a couple of pits under lowering, clifflike brows. He stopped a scant two feet from me and looked me over. The desire to run far and fast, shrieking, electrified my legs and caught at my throat. I quashed the urge and pivoted to face him.

He clasped his hands in front of himself. "You wanted to see me?" he rumbled.

The breath. I tried not to flinch. "Alice sent me," I stated.

"Alice." Glaciers react more.

"Liddell." I stared right back at him, even though it racked me. A tremor of fright moved under my skin.

He grunted. "Let's go to the office." He turned, assuming I would follow him. As we passed the counter, he glanced at the Goth girl. "Keep Jason out."

"OK," she agreed, barely raising her head from her page.

A door next to the dressing rooms led to a small storage room with a desk and a couple of chairs shoved in among the boxes and files. Carlos went behind the desk and pointed at the chair on my side.

"Sit down."

I did.

He folded his arms on the desktop, cupping his left elbow with his right hand. His fist was as big as a billboard against the black leather sleeve. "Now. What do want with me, ghost girl?"

I bridled. "Excuse me?"

"You got 'em hangin' all over you," he growled, reaching toward me. I shied, but he hooked something out of my hair and pulled it back to the desktop. A wisp of Grey, like a steam-spun cobweb, wafted from his fingertips. He wadded it up and shoved it into his inside breast pocket. "Now, what do you want?"

"I—I'm a private investigator and I'm working for Cameron Shadley."

"Edward's little blond toy? That Cameron?"

"Yes, that Cameron." I gave a sharp, annoyed nod. "But he's not Edward's 'toy,' as you put it, anymore."

He sketched a shrug.

"I need to know more about Edward before I attempt to meet with him about Cameron," I continued. "Alice suggested you might have something to say that I could use."

Carlos raised an eyebrow and started laughing, bellowing shocks like a gale against a plate glass window.

"You have an ax to grind?" I prompted. I was quaking inside.

He lowered his laughter to a seismic chuckle. "You bet I've got an ax to grind, and when it's good and sharp, I'd like to bury it in that bastard's skull."

"Why?" My voice did not shake, though by rights it should have.

"You wouldn't like the story very much. Or understand it. And if I take you into my confidence, daylighter, I cross a line most of my kind would find unforgivable."

"I can't ask you to jeopardize yourself for my client's sake." I started to get up, relieved to have an excuse to leave.

"What do you plan to do with this information you're seeking?"

"Raise trouble."

Carlos frowned in thought. I shuddered at the rolling weight of his mental processes grinding over me. The Grey had been an encroaching sea near Alice. It was an inescapable drowning pool in his presence.

"You will tell no one what you learn from me."

I fought the compulsion to agree. "I will tell my client, if he needs to know, and I will use whatever I have to to get to Edward."

His stare ripped into me. "The details shall not go farther than this room until you face Edward."

I swallowed dust and shuddered. "Yes. All right." I sat back down, my knees shaking and my heart thumping weird syncopations.

TWENTY-ONE

Carlos leaned across the desk and pinned me to the chair with his gaze. He spoke in a low, intense voice that enthralled and smothered me.

"It's not mere blood that sustains a vampire, but the life force that flows with the blood. Our own is weak. We must take this life force from others or we fade to crippled shadows, fall into madness, and drown by slow agony to the true death.

"The most vital and powerful of creatures offers the greatest quality of life. That is why we prey on daylighters, like you. You offer us so much that we need not hunt too frequently and death is not always necessary to acquire what we need. A vampire uses this energy to replace what he cannot produce himself. All creatures need it. Some rare few can give up this energy by will and use it for other purposes.

"When it is given up, it eats your own life as well. If the power required is great enough, it may devour every shred of life and death within you. You must have other lives—other blood—to draw upon. If the undertaking requires great power, it may require many lives. Or the blood of a vampire, which commingles life and death. Neither blood nor this power are to be coerced or commanded. The price for them is too high. But Edward demanded them—ripped them—from me.

"We met in Lisbon. Edward was still young, but his ambition burned like an equatorial sun. He schemed and clawed to raise himself, but only antagonized the rest of our kind. He had few friends but I—fool—was among them."

His voice fell into older rhythms as he spoke, and I felt the past rise around us in a Grey curtain I could not turn back.

"He had a plan to destroy his enemies at a single blow, but it required that power which he, himself, did not command."

His words began to press on me.

"He brought his plan to me. I told him it was too risky. The blood required, the deaths, would be noticed, and the spells were dangerous. We argued over it. I would not give up blood for him—nor would any other—but he agreed to a smaller conflagration bought with mere human lives.

"I went a safe distance, to Seville, and began gathering the men and women we would need, the materials, the place… I kept our prisoners and began to craft the great spell into the very walls. Edward arrived and I helped him to build the machine until I was near exhausted. He sent me away to rest until we were ready."

Something half memory and half vision coiled around me. I shied from it, but it clutched me. I could see shadowy faces of the men and women in eighteenth-century rags and feel his labor burn in my own muscles.

"On All Hallows Eve, he came for me. We walked to the cathedral and descended into our cellar near La Giralda. New symbols lined the walls and floor in chalk and charcoal, gold and blood. I did not study them, for I was distracted by the sight of what we had built."

Excitement. A hundred arcane words and shapes hemmed me in, glimmering on dark stone.

"Deeper in the cellar, the two dozen men and women—all children of the streets, the unnoticeables, the lost—knelt on a platform, bound within the machine which poised silver blades to their necks, holding them in the spell, directed toward a single instant and purpose." Cold, the edges kissed the back of my neck and the hair rose. "They would know no pain nor the horror of watching their fellows die. I did not require torment, only death. Some had whimpered and moaned in distress as we entered, but they fell into enthralled silence when Edward passed them. Such has always been his power. We walked into the center of the room, to a place in the floor which was the focus of the machine and of the spell's power. All the symbols in the room led to it and from it and already it throbbed with the potential of magic."

I felt the humming of it in my bones, the sudden calm of the men and women smothering Carlos's anticipation and creeping unease.

"He stopped beside a rope which hung from the ceiling, well away from the machine, leaving me to stand at the focus.

"A few of the glyphs disturbed me—black things, like mourners at a wedding feast—but I had no time to protest.

" 'Begin!' he commanded.

"I spoke and the threads of the spell wove together, ghostly, in need of power. I opened my arms to the machine and Edward pulled the rope."

Power thrummed and shook, then roared, and I felt the quick shock of the blades.

"Their heads tumbled and the hot, liquid force of their lives gouted forth, drenching me. My skin drank them, my body and mind absorbing them in life and death conjoined in that shocked instant. Their unvoiced gasp pushed into me and out my own mouth, staggering me, shivering through my flesh. The power of them flooded me and I reached into the spell, giving it their life through me."

I trembled with his memory, quivered with the orgasmic flow of life and death through a body that was and wasn't mine—then shocked into pain and despair.

"The ecstasy of their swift, clean deaths shattered as Edward drove a blade into my back. He spoke a word and flung the black blood which welled from my wound into the focus. The final, dark symbols flared and I fell to my knees.

"Edward stood above me and plunged his knife into my chest.

"I cried out and the newly murdered cried within me. He twisted the knife, ripping into my heart which beat with them."

Agony. No way to scream. He continued.

"I screamed and died for them. Died each death at once, more horrible than they had died, each screaming, all screaming. Their blood, now my own, poured out again. And the power of their souls flashed like white fire, flooded into the cellar, blazed into the symbols, and the cellar erupted in the phosphor white burn of the spell, blinding me as it spent."

Silence.

"I felt something break within my chest. Darkness shrouded me, but I heard him, moving, laughing. He knelt beside me and touched my head.

"'You have done very well,' he said. Even blinded, I could see the fleeting nimbus of his stolen power pulsing around him.

"I reached for him, and agony tore through my chest. I fell to the floor like an injured babe, unable to move or speak.

"'I shall always be in your heart.' He laughed again and left me."

The touch of his telling began receding, draining me as he finished.

"I was awakened by the earthquake and the pealing of La Giralda's bells as the tower shook. The sun had risen, shining through rents in the walls and ceiling. I crawled to a niche in the basement to hide from the overwhelming fury our spell, powered by their deaths and my blood, had poured into the earth. It was far more, far worse, than I had meant. It was a grandiose and pointless rage of destruction fit to Edward's own spite.

"Lisbon collapsed beneath the earthquakes, flood, and fire that swept it. Sixty thousand of your kind and mine ceased.

"And all for naught. Those of our kind who remained in Lisbon left the city and Edward was king of nothing.

"He ripped the sweetness of their souls from me and used it for himself, bled me, then left me bound to die. The tip of his knife is still lodged in my heart. When I find a way to remove it, he will die those two dozen deaths for me. One by one."

He stopped speaking and I lurched up. I stumbled forward. He didn't touch me, but walked me to the shop door and to the edge of the street. He rolled his shoulders and settled back into his modern guise as he stood beside me.

"Feelin' OK?" he inquired.

I choked on an answer, gulping in normality and trying not to throw up.

"You're resting your hand on your belly and I can tell you're not pregnant. Weak stomach?"

I stammered against the bile in my throat. "I'm not a horror-movie fan and I've got too good an imagination."

"You asked. You'll be all right?"

"Just peachy," I gritted.

"Good. You need anything, call me. I want to watch him writhing in agony, the same way he left me."

I stepped away and walked to the corner, crossing the street against the light. I wanted to rush, to run, but didn't dare until I could no longer see Carlos.

I hurried to the Rover and crawled in, locking the door behind me. My belly clenched with cramps and nausea, my limbs shook and my headache shrieked.

Halfway across the bridge to home, the cramps began to ease, but the rest stayed with me.

Once in bed, I slept hard, but not restfully: first too deeply, then tumbled by nightmares. I got up once to vomit, then collapsed into bed again until eleven.

I felt only a little better when I finally got up. I showered for a long time under near-scalding water. Chaos looked into the tub, but chose not to join me. When I got out of the shower, she licked my feet and ankles dry while dancing around me. The water is always sweeter off of someone else's feet, and I laughed at her antics, even though it made my abs and head hurt.

I finished dressing, feeling bruised, putting on a skirt when the restrictive touch of jeans reminded me of ropes and sweat-tight sheets. Chaos and I contested for my breakfast until I declared victory by putting her back into her cage before I left for my office.

Lenore Fabrette called at 3:12. She was waiting to drive onto a ferry in Bremerton and needed directions. I gave them and said I'd look forward to seeing her soon. She tapped on my door a few minutes before five.

She was a too-thin woman with straw hair, her shoulders hunched against routine cruelty.

I stood up and extended my hand. "Ms. Fabrette? I'm Harper Blaine. Please sit down."

She sagged into the client chair. "Can we just get this over with? I've been arguing with the navy all day and I just want to get home."

"Sure. Can I ask you a question?"

"Oh, sure. I guess."

"Do you remember anything unusual about the organ?"

She pinched her lower lip with nicotine-stained fingers. "Aside from how ugly it was? Not much but that it was god-awful and it used to give my boy nightmares."

"Nightmares? How old is your son?"

"He's twelve now. He was six when we moved in. And I just hope that museum isn't having any trouble with it. 'Cause I don't want it back." Fabrette picked at her lip. "So, do you want to see these papers or what?" she asked, laying her hand on her purse in her lap.

"Sure."

She pulled out an envelope and slapped it onto the desk.

"There. Take a look, then tell me what you think."

I pulled two sheets of photocopy from the envelope. One was an insurance appraisal, which put a value of twenty-five hundred dollars on the organ. The other sheet was the receipt for the donation of an organ with a description that seemed to match the one I had from Sergeyev.

"Damn," I snickered, staring at the letterhead on the donation receipt.

"What's the matter?" Fabrette demanded, reaching for the sheets.

"The organ was donated to the Madison Forrest Historical House Museum, here in Seattle," I said.

She cringed back a little. "So what's wrong with that?"

"Nothing. It's just ... The organ was in Seattle for twenty years, moved to Anacortes for ten, and then came right back to within three miles of where we're sitting."

"Does that mean you don't want those papers?"

"Oh, no. I want them and my client wants them and you've been very helpful to bring them to me." I shoved the papers into a drawer and pulled out a check I'd already prepared. I held it out to her. "That's the payment my client authorized. I just need you to sign this receipt for me," I added, pushing over the form and a pen.

She looked at the check, then stared at me. "That's five hundred dollars," she whispered. "Are you sure that's right?"

"Yes, that's right. Just sign the receipt, please."

Mute, she clutched the pen and scrawled quickly on the form.

She raised her eyebrows as she handed the paper back to me. "Are you sure?"

I took it and put it in the drawer with the donation receipt. I smiled at her. "Yes, I am. Thank you for coming down here, Lenore. You've been a lot of help."

She nodded, mute, and got to her feet, edging out the door as if I might turn on her and snatch the check away.

As the door clicked closed, I shook my head, swallowing pity she wouldn't have appreciated.

An hour later, I'd put Fabrette out of my mind as I plowed through routine chores. I was down in the lower drawers looking for more fanfold paper for my printer when I heard the door. "Just a second," I called, grabbing the paper and pulling it up with me. I knocked my skull on the bottom of the desk. I raised my head, shaking back momentary giddiness, and found a man standing just behind the client chair. I blinked at him.

He was still and cold as wax, wearing a very plain dark suit and a white shirt with a strange collar that was buttoned all the way to his throat, but no tie. He was skinny, but had a round face with broad, flat cheekbones and slightly tilted eyes in translucent skin. His hair was dark brown. He blinked back at me. His left hand fluttered up over his coat buttons and rested on his chest.

"I have startled you," he said. His odd accent gave him away.

"Mr. Sergeyev. I didn't know you were in town."

"For little time, only. You make progress? Of my request?"

I sat down and waved him to the other chair. "Well, yes, I have," I started. Some partially formed thought flashed into my brain and vanished before I could apprehend it. "I just spoke to the woman who had the information I asked you to authorize payment for," I said, trying to shake my brains back into their normal function.

"Ah. Good." Sergeyev sat very upright on the chair, not quite leaning forward, but stiff nonetheless. I wondered if the airline seats had hurt his back.

"I ... " I trailed off, thoughts slipping sideways. The day and the night before were catching up to me; my stomach was clenching and my head throbbing again. Something flickered in the corner of my vision. I turned my head a little to find it, and Sergeyev vanished. "Huh?" I grunted and turned my head back toward him.

He was frowning at me. "Something is wrong? You do not feel well."

"It's nothing." I turned to my computer and tapped at the keyboard a moment, buying time, feeling unsteady.

The thin world of the Grey flooded up in cold steam as I peered sideways at my client. He was there, layered on himself like a multiple exposure, the mist-world rippling around him. I yanked myself away from the flood, and it reduced to a trickle and a transient flicker. After last night, the figurative gum of the Grey must have been pretty thick on me, and I didn't want any more building up. And I wanted my unsettling client out of my office as soon as possible. "I have a further lead, which may be the last link in the chain of ownership."

"Then you know where is my furniture?" he asked. His voice rose with excitement.

"I might."

"Tell me." His voiced pushed on me, resonating in my chest and head. I pushed back against it. I'd been pushed on a lot lately, and I wasn't in the mood for it. I dug in my mental heels and resisted his demand for all I was worth.

"I want to be certain. It could turn out to be just another link and I don't want to get your hopes up for nothing."

He scowled and I shivered. "When will you know?"

I poked my computer, which showed me a picture of rolling static.

"I'll be blunt, Mr. Sergeyev. I can't do anything about your case until Tuesday. The party involved won't be available any earlier. Then I still have to confirm that it is the organ you want and see if the owner is even willing to negotiate on it. They might not be."

He seemed surprised. "They would not?"

"I don't know yet. Let me find out a little more, then we can discuss it. I'll do what I can. Trust me—I'll call you when I have something more to tell you."

"Ah, well. So be it." There was that push again, but I could taste anger and annoyance in it this time. "I expect hearing from you Tuesday evening." He rose to his feet like a piece of spring steel unbending.

I got up, beat him to the door, and opened it for him. He went out with a cold little nod to me. In the dim light of the hallway, he seemed bigger. The darkness swallowed him up as he descended the stairs. The bang on the back of my skull seemed to have rattled something loose in my head and I felt a little stupid. I went back to my chair behind the desk and stared at the computer screen.

The screen prompt asked if I wanted to view recorded video. I clicked on YES. I saw the room on the screen, the desk, myself at the desk, the empty chair on the other side. Maybe the last fifteen minutes had not been saved? I didn't like it. I'd have to call Quinton, but I had a feeling he wouldn't make me feel any better.

My head hurt, but the butterflies in my insides calmed. I wondered if I was just hungry. I trotted out for a bite. It was a little chilly and the evening breeze was kicking up, but I decided to sit outside for a few minutes while I ate, hoping to clear my head a bit. But I just got cold and wolfed my food, which made my stomach ache, and I wished I'd worn the jeans after all, instead of the skirt.

Cameron drifted into my office a few minutes before nine thirty. I noticed he didn't exude the halo and draining Grey effects of Carlos and Alice. Odd.

"How's it going?" I asked as he sat down.

"It's OK. Sarah and I worked out a sleeping arrangement at her house, but it's only temporary. I'm going to have to find something of my own before her boyfriend gets back."

"Any idea when that will be?"

He shrugged. "Not sure. Could be as early as June."

I gave him a faint, false smile. "We'll just have to work fast then. I told you I talked to Alice last night, right?"

"Yeah. How'd it go?"

"Scary. She thinks I should kill Edward, or incite the other vampires of Seattle to do it."

"Umm ... you're not really thinking about it, are you?"

"No. But it did give me an idea. Alice mentioned that vampires have a pack mentality and they will attack their leader if they sense that he's sick or weak. That's what Alice wants so she can step into the breach once Edward is down."

"Oh, man ... I thought she was my friend! That scheming—"

I interrupted. "Don't get too hot under the collar. A coup is fine for Alice, but for you to get anything out of this, Edward has to stay in charge. We can't trust Alice to do anything for you, but Edward has more to lose. So I'm going to stir up trouble, but not enough that it can't be allayed by the right sort of gesture—like showing that he's capable of being a nice guy by taking you back. Of course, anything else I can dig up which will help push him that direction, I'll take, but I'm not going to be handing it over to Alice."

"Did you stir up any trouble yet?"

"Not trouble, but something. After I talked to you, I met with Carlos. Alice sent me to him, but frankly, he frightens me a lot more than she does."

"Oh, yeah. Even some of the vampires are afraid of him."

"From the story he told me, they ought to be. And Edward, too. Carlos is willing to risk helping us because he hates Edward that much."

"He does?"

"Yes, and Alice hates Edward, too—though it's more an expression of ambition with her. Hate seems to be the point on which everything turns, so that's what I'll push on. But we have to be careful. I cannot risk losing control of the situation to Alice or Carlos, which means you have to disappear for a while."

"I'm not going to get in your way or do something stupid," Cameron objected.

"That's not the problem, Cam. I don't want you to get hurt if anything goes wrong, and I don't want you used against me. Once the mud starts to swirl around, Edward is bound to start looking for a person holding a stick. We don't want him to think that's you."

"But what about you? Won't he hurt you, too?"

"It's possible, but that's what you're paying me for."

"Man," he said, shaking his head, "maybe I shouldn't have asked you to do this. Maybe I should drop it."

"We can, if that's what you want ... but one of the things Carlos told me makes me think you have no real choice."

Cameron looked at me askance. "What did he tell you?"

"There's a lot more to this vampire thing than just sucking blood. I don't understand it all, but the impression I got was that without the right training and without the right ... diet, you'll just sort of waste away and die." I paused a moment, wondering if this was why Cameron didn't glow like the others.

I shook myself back to conversation. "Dropping your efforts to reconcile with Edward, or moving to another city and hoping for a fresh start, would be postponing the inevitable. And if you stay here, Edward will eventually have to deal with you as a threat to the community."

"I'm not a threat! I'm not doing anything to anybody."

"Your existence outside of the control of the community is, inherently, a threat. Think about it. And think about where to hide until it's safe to come out."

"I didn't realize this vampire gig was going to require a security expert." He stood up. "I can find a place. Don't worry about me. What are you going to do?"

"I'm going to stir mud."

Once Cameron was gone, I swallowed my trepidation and started down into the Square to seek vampires.

The night was thick with spirits trailing Grey wakes or striating the darkness with columns of cloud-light. Friday night was party night whether you were dead or alive. The historic district, with its many one-cover-price clubs and easygoing bars, was a prime location for night creatures on the prowl. I had three names on the list in this area, but in spite of my best charms, only one would talk to me. The first just squirmed around and refused to say anything before telling me to go jump in the Sound. The next one had a tale of pettiness and manipulation that wasn't much, for all his anger. The third threatened to kill me.

I gave up and was heading for my truck when I spotted a flash of red and turned my head.

Alice lounged under a streetlight and gave me her siren's smile before sliding back into the dark. As she moved, I recognized her shape in the shadow. Just like the night after I'd met Quinton—the same shape and shadow, sliding into the fog-filled alley that had led me into the Grey. She'd been teasing me, the previous night. She'd said she knew who I was. Why had she been watching me for so long?

I worried it in my brain, but was too exhausted from pushing back against the Grey all night to get an answer. I shook it off for now and headed home. I felt better as the distance increased between me and Pioneer Square.

It was almost one in the morning when I parked in a space under my building. I was tired, distracted by thoughts of Alice, and not paying attention. If I had been, I might have spotted the son of a bitch when he first stepped out of the shadows by the laundry room door.

TWENTY-TWO

Clouds and mist played around the edges of vision and I was too tired to push it back. A solid shape reached for me under the silver mist-world and I coiled back, skipping behind the nearest car.

"What in hell's little half acre do you want?" I demanded, trying to shake off the obscuring haze of Grey.

He was clean-cut, bulked buff, and dressed neatly—hardly the usual mugger. "Just you. You won't stay dead long enough."

He sprang forward, snake-quick for a guy with such bulky muscles. I turned to the side and backed up, giving him a kick in the seat as he brushed past. My high heels wobbled.

He turned, whipping out an arm to grab me. I hopped backward and slid onto the truck hood, putting distance between us.

He looked annoyed. Reached into his jacket pocket. "I'm not going to hurt you. A lot." He drew out a knife.

Bigger, faster, and stronger than me. And holding a knife like he knew it well. I didn't like those odds. I dropped onto the other side of the Rover. He started around the rear. He passed into the blind spot and I dug under the back of my jacket.

He cleared the end of the truck. I pointed the business end of the gun at his face. "Back off." I squeezed. The HK's cocking lever made a click that cracked the cold air like a hammer on thin ice.

He gaffed a chuckle that went right through me. "You're not going to shoot me." He lunged, tucking down.

I lowered aim, squeezed the trigger, twisted away.

The bullet gouged a chunk out of his shoulder. I stepped down hard and felt my heel break off as my ears shut down from the roar of the gun.

He staggered, but kept his feet and came after me, grimacing evil glee as he swung the blade.

I lurched sideways, stumbled, fell flat on my back. My skirt ripped, fouling the blade in a cloud of fabric. I tilted the pistol. Squeezed. Felt it buck, heard the underwater roar of the shot in my already ringing ears.

He swayed back, but didn't fall. Black blood dripped down the front of his jacket. He glared at me and bared a mouthful of shark's teeth.

I swallowed hard. "Oh ..."

"Hey! What's going on down there? Was that a gunshot?" The voice sounded distant and tinny to me.

The uncanny man stared up toward Rick and his dog, emerging on the upper landing. He shot a look back at me and the gun, then whirled and bolted into the darkness outside.

I slumped against the Rover, letting out a gust of breath. I was thoroughly shaken, and too watery to stand up.

"Yes, Rick!" I yelled back, feeling woozy.

"Harper?" A moment later, they popped out of the foyer door, the dog in the lead and Rick dragged behind. "Harper, are you OK?"

"I'm fine, Rick," I said, shoving the dog back. My head was throbbing and sounds were muffled by a high-pitched whine in my ears.

"What happened?"

"Huh? Just a mugger. And I want to get upstairs and go to bed."

"We should call the cops."

"What? Why? He's gone." I doubted they had a mug book of the undead, and though I didn't know what he was, normal he was not.

"You don't want me to call the cops? You're sure?"

"Yeah," I said, nodding. "I'll deal with it." I hoped.

Rick preceded me upstairs. The dog wagged like a puppy all the way, grinning a pit-bull grin of satisfaction with the commotion. He, at least, was having a great time.

I woke up in the morning sore and tired. My pumps and skirt were trashed and I had a long, deep scratch on my thigh, but my ears had stopped ringing.

While I waited for the coffee to dribble through the filter in the coffeemaker, I paged Quinton and left my office number. Then I poured the coffee into a travel mug, packed up and headed out.

I walked into my office to the sound of the ringing phone. It was Quinton.

"Hi," I said. "Something was wrong with the office alarm yesterday. Can you come by and take a look?"

"What kind of problem did you have?" he asked.

I described the alarm's nonfunction during Sergeyev's visit. I had to eliminate the plausible first, before I could go leaping to the impossible.

"That's strange. I'll be up in about half an hour. OK?"

"Great," I said and hung up.

I checked my messages and discovered one from Mara Danziger.

"Hmm, Harper, the problem with magic is getting worse. I'd be grateful for your help. Give me a ring."

Curious, I called her back.

"Hello."

"Hi, Mara, it's Harper."

"Harper, I'm worried. The blockage is worsening. To be shocking honest, Ben's no help with this, nor Albert. I simply must be finding the source. And all divinations keep coming back to you."

"Still?"

"Yes. Have you any idea why this is happening? Could it be Cameron?"

"I don't think so. But I've been mixing with vampires and there've been a few weird things hanging around."

"I told you they would—"

A knock on the door came a moment ahead of Quinton's face peeking around the doorframe. I waved him in and leaned back in my chair. "Mara, I have to deal with something here, but I have to go out to the Madison Forrest House later and look at a piece of furniture. There's something a little strange about the situation surrounding this thing." I paused, thinking, then sat forward. "Would you be willing to come with me to Madison Forrest? We could discuss this other situation then, too."

"Well ... I suppose so. I'll have Ben look after the baby for a bit. Then, what say I pick you up?"

"That'll be fine, Mara. Come by in about an hour. OK?"

"All right. Be seeing you, then."

Quinton had already begun poking around with his Multimeter. As soon as I was off the phone, he asked me to move and ran a check of the computer program. He looked at the video capture that should have shown Sergeyev, but didn't.

"I'm not sure why this guy didn't show up, but there's nothing wrong with this system and the diagnostic says there never was," he said, frowning at the computer screen. "You sure he was here?"

"Oh, yeah."

"It's a head scratcher, but the system's working fine now."

"OK."

"Keep an eye on it, and let me know if it does this again. You might try it on that client of yours, because I'm not really sure what effect some people have on electronics."

I wondered how he knew about Sergeyev. Had I mentioned him? "I'm not following you. Which client?"

"The one with the Camaro. The vampire."

"Excuse me?" I choked.

"Don't expect me to believe that you didn't know," Quinton said.

"Took me a while to be sure, but you've been in much closer contact with the guy."

"Why would you think Cameron was a vampire?"

"Lots of little signs. The weird eyes, the dirt in the trunk, the weird habits. The fangs. I've seen plenty of them around here. I steer clear of those guys. Even if they like you, you can't really trust them. 'Course, you can't trust most people. But drinking blood and turning on your fellow man is a bit worse than the usual sort of trust-breaker."

I blinked at him. He finished speaking and looked at me in silence a moment. Then he asked, "You do a lot of work for vampires?"

I shook my head. "This is my first."

"Thought so. Be careful. They're a tricky bunch. Magic kind of gives me the willies. It's cool to watch, but it's … disorienting to think about. I prefer electronics, physics, stuff I can grab on to and get a good look at myself." He played with the probes of the meter and gave me a nervous glance. "Watch your step around this stuff, all right? I can fix a lot of things, but curses and that stuff I'm not so good with."

I smiled a little. "I'll be careful."

"Good. And if you need anything, call me. I'll be around."

"Thanks, Quinton. I'll do that. I have to get going, though. I have an appointment."

"That's OK. But hey, don't get killed. You still owe me for the car," he added with a forced grin. He packed up his things and took off.

I locked up and walked down to meet Mara.

We drove east toward Lake Washington and found the Madison Forrest House Museum. We pulled into a graveled lot nearby. Mara sat for a moment behind the wheel and looked at the house with a puzzled expression.

We got out of the car in silence and walked. I had no idea who Madison Forrest had been or why his house had become a historic building and museum, but it was an impressive pile. The foundation and ground floor were built of fitted stone. The second floor and the high, pointing gables were all native cedar. Lots of glass windows shone under the wooden overhangs and must have cost a fortune when the house was built. Four gas lamps, now converted to electricity, bracketed the path from the open iron gate to the front doors. Like the Danzigers' house, it glowed, but the glow wasn't so friendly.

Mara stopped and looked at the ground. "I didn't realize there was a nexus of this size on this side of the lake. It's just a bit off the property, about … here, in the street." She stepped out a few feet from the curb. "And I can't even draw on it standing right on top of it. I'm not at all sure there isn't something rather unpleasant going on here. Maybe even the power blockage. Take a look at it sideways, like I taught you. Tell me what you see."

I peered at it from the corner of my eye. The off-color glow of the house seemed to start under her feet, like a fog that wafted toward the house. "It looks … sick to me."

"Funny way to describe it."

I shrugged and tried not to look anymore.

We walked up the path to the massive, carved cedar doors. Mara and I paid the entrance fee and began to wander around. After a while, we found the upstairs parlor and the organ. It was hideous: six feet of tortured wood flecked with ivory, bone, and gilt and upholstered with garish red fabric panels, all of it wrapped in a sucking web of black and red energy I couldn't avoid seeing. I stayed well back from the instrument, feeling ill and threatened.

"Is this it?" Mara asked, staring at it with horrified fascination.

"I think so." I got the description sheet out of my bag and compared it as best I could from my distance. It seemed an exact match.

"Oh, my," she breathed. "It's dreadful, isn't it?"

"It's pretty terrible," I agreed, feeling pain and nausea growing in my belly as a familiar anxiety began to rattle on my vertebrae. I closed my eyes, but the sense of the coiling horror in front of me didn't go away.

"No, I mean it's full of dread, though it's terrible, too. It's horrific, really. It gives me the wailing creepies just looking at it."

"What do you think of it?" I asked.

"Interesting." She made a glittering gesture and threw it at the organ. It dissolved as it hit the writhing mass of Grey. "Swallowed it … Very interesting, indeed. I think I've seen enough, what about you?"

I circled a little closer to the thing, like a wary cat, getting a better look at its shape, both physical and paranormal, while trying to keep my distance. It was impossible for me to ignore the warped, twined normal and Grey that had tangled around it, though I couldn't imagine what had caused their knotting up. Sympathetic knots tied up my nerves and muscles with pain, disgust, and despair.

"I've had enough," I gasped, backing off. "Let's get out of here."

Mara looked at me and saw my distress. She put an arm around me, which seemed to help. We hurried back to her car and sat in the front seats, staring back at the Madison Forrest House with combined horror.

Mara shook her head. "There's an incredible amount of energy flowing round that thing, but none of it seems to be going anywhere. That must be the source of the blockage. And it's so … dark. I've never seen an artifact that was dark like that one before. Of course, I've rarely dealt with them, so I'm no expert."

"Artifact? I don't understand."

She turned to me. "It's a dark artifact. That's an object that's acquired an energy aura. They store some of the energy, and if you know what you're at, you can use it—directly or indirectly, depending on your skill and the object. You can tell a great deal about the object and what's happened to it by looking at the color, size, and activity of the energy corona around it. 'Dark' is usually a misnomer. But that one is dark in fact. Means there's been something rather nasty associated with it for a long time. Bleak things, grim doings. Dreadful, as I said."

I sighed. "And my client wants it. He claims it's a family heirloom, but having seen it—and him—I'm starting to wonder."

"He must be a rather unusual person."

"I don't know if he's a human being. He's ... Grey, but I don't know what. Not a vampire, though."

"That would explain why signs point to you. I don't like the idea of a thing like that on the loose with someone Grey. Why does he want it? I mean really?"

"It's certainly no sentimental heirloom. I have a bad feeling there's a purpose for that thing."

Mara thought a moment. "We'll have to do something about it, if for no other reason than that it's blocking magic that could be useful other places." She wrinkled her brow and toyed with the steering wheel. "If we could discover why it's a dark artifact, we might be able to figure out what to do about it. I don't usually care for them, but a necromancer would be useful here."

"What? Why?"

"A necromancer manipulates magic through the auspices of death."

"Hang on. They kill things?"

"Not necessarily, though a large number of their rituals can only be effective in the presence of death, and the easiest way to get that is to kill some sacrificial animal. When I say death, I mean not just dead bodies or something of that ilk, but the change in the power state that happens when someone or something dies. Y'see, the force, or energy, of a living thing becomes free at the moment of death—it's one of the things which causes ghosts, too. The right kind of magical attractor in the immediate area can capture the energy, and a great deal of energy and information are available for a little while to anyone who can manipulate that attractor. It's terribly dangerous stuff, though, to those who can touch it at all. Many of us feel it, but necromancers are among the few who can use it. The necromancer exchanges some of his own life-force energy for control of the new energy source, so long as it lasts—giving up life for the knowledge and power of death, for a time."

"Ugh," I said with a shudder. "What good would that do us?"

"A necromancer can create dark artifacts or examine their history. Necromantic artifacts are always grim and lowering like that organ because of the thread of death tied up in their creation."

"Are they worse than any other kind?"

"Can be. The power of most dark artifacts comes from a sort of accreting process, where layers of use, power, and purpose adhere to the object and become bound up in it. Many necromantic dark artifacts are relatively harmless. Since they are created for specific purposes and only used once or twice, they don't build up that sort of power. But that one ..." She shuddered.

"All right," I said. "So why would we want a necromancer here?"

"A necromancer can look back to a dark artifact's moment of creation and see what caused it. Don't know how they do it—it's bloody spooky. If we knew what the artifact's purpose and process of creation was, we would know how to neutralize or destroy it. This is not going to be easy. If we go about it wrong, we run the risk of increasing its power by having our own sucked into the artifact."

"I'd rather not see that thing get any stronger," I said. "You don't know any necromancers then?"

"No. I find their practices a bit disgusting, and they're a dying breed. Necromancers aren't just created out of practice and determination. They're born with the potential talent and develop it as they age. It's not a very politically correct profession, you can imagine. Boys and girls who kill their pets so they can 'touch the power' usually end up in mental institutions. The right type of conditioning and therapy breaks the potential and steers them into more normal courses."

"So psychos who torture animals are potential necromancers?"

"Oh, no. One in a million children is a potential necromancer, and he—or very rarely, she—may never tap the power, never even know that there is any power to tap. They never harm anyone or anything. But some slip through and survive long enough to learn. That's the one who becomes a necromancer. They're very secretive and paranoid. Well, wouldn't you be?"

A connection closed in my mind. "Mara, what happens to necromancers when they die?"

"I suppose that would depend on how they died. I suspect that many of them don't truly die, but linger in some fashion or become something new. If they survive bodily death and still have their minds intact, they could still wield their powers, but I think it would be very dangerous for them. Casting would suck away a lot of whatever life energies they still had, and the recuperation afterward would be extraordinary. But their relationship to the power would be different, and they could probably conserve a great deal of their own energies—even feed them—by killing as part of the ritual. If they're corporeal enough to use the knife or what have you." Then she stared sharply at me. "That's a rather strange question to ask. Why did you?"

"Because I think I've met a necromancer."

"My God, Harper. Where?"

"I can't say."

She glowered at me. "You must be very careful. Use what I've taught you to protect yourself, or these powers may harm you. I know you don't quite believe it all—"

"I'm beginning to."

TWENTY-THREE

Mara dropped me near my office. Before I took another step for Sergeyev, I wanted to know more about that organ in the normal world, and though it made me uncomfortable, I knew where to start. I didn't even bother going up to the office, I just went straight to the Rover.

The street outside the Ingstrom house was full of cars. The auction of the personal property was under way and the house was packed with bidders. I wished I felt something more useful—like anger—but all I felt as I stepped up onto the screened porch was an uncomfortable confusion.

Michael was at his table inside. His eyes got wider when he saw me.

"Hi, Michael," I said.

"H-hi, Ms. Blaine."

"Is Will on the podium?"

He replied slowly. "Yeah."

"Is Brandon around?"

"Brandon's not here."

"Why not?"

Michael shrank. "I don't know. He was supposed to be here but he didn't show up. Did you want to talk to him?"

"No. I wanted to avoid him."

He nodded. "Yeah, he's not too cool lately."

I heard Will's gavel drop, and then a murmur of sound rose to a growl and people began to boil toward the outer doors. I stepped back and hid in the crowd-shadow of the table.

Michael shot me a quick look of nervous apology. "Lunch," he explained. "Without Brandon, we're running kinda late."

"That's OK."

He smiled and turned to face the first of the exiting bidders. I was pushed farther into the corner by the eddying humanity and trapped there when Will came out.

He patted his brother on the shoulder and glanced at the screen of the laptop computer. "Everything OK out here, Mikey?"

"Yeah." Michael shot a quick glance in my direction and went back to his computer and the couple in front of him.

Will raised his head and turned. He stiffened when he saw me and froze in place behind Michael's chair, until his brother elbowed him in the side.

"Hey, I'm trying to work here," Michael growled.

Jarred, Will walked toward me but kept the table between us. He stopped and clasped his hands in front of his belt buckle. His long fingers squeezed white. "What … what can I do for you?" His voice was cool, but I could almost see it, like a staff of music quivering on the air, thin as smoke.

I looked up at him, and all I could think was, "My God, he's tall!" I felt stupid, and something hurt inside which had nothing to do with recent physical bruises. "I wanted … to talk to you on a professional matter."

Will looked blank. "Professional. That's all?"

"Yeah."

He glanced at the tide of people, then back to me. "Let's take this someplace a little quieter."

"All right," I agreed, perversely reluctant to be alone with him.

"Mrs. Ingstrom left some lunch for us in the kitchen and I'm starving. You don't mind, do you?"

"No, I don't mind if you don't." I followed him toward the door.

"Hey," Michael called over his shoulder. "Bring me some when you're done. I could use a bite, too, you know. Us boy wonders have to keep up our strength!"

"Right, Mikey. I won't let you starve," Will called back.

"It's Michael!"

We walked back through the house to the kitchen. Will offered me sandwiches and coffee, too. I took a cup of coffee and watched him sit at the kitchen table to eat. I stood against a counter and sipped for a few minutes in silence as he got through half a sandwich.

"All right," he started, sitting back and leaving the rest of his lunch sprawling on the plate, "now that I'm no longer faint with hunger, what did you want to discuss?"

"First, I wanted to say I'm sorry, Will. I—"

He cut me off. "Don't start that. I don't need the extra stress."

"Yeah. Michael told me Brandon didn't show up. What's up with that?"

Will threw his hands into the air. "I have no idea! He's completely unpredictable and irresponsible. He didn't show up today, doesn't answer his phone. No one's seen him. He's even bailed on the Ingstroms without notice, and he knew Chet Ingstrom for years. No idea what he'll do next. You saw that tantrum he pitched at the warehouse. That's not the first time that he's flown off the handle recently over something minor. And we're not the only people looking for him, either. When I get my hands on the slick bastard, I'm going to shake him until he tells me what's going on."

"Who else wants him?" I asked.

"I don't know, but he must be in deep trouble. The guys who've been coming around looking for him are the sort who break legs. I don't want it to get around, though. It could really kill us."

I looked at him over the rim of my coffee cup and speculated. "Is it Brandon you're trying to protect? Or yourself?"

"Myself! Brandon's a jackass. We had an agreement, but now it looks like I've been left with the baby, again. I put equity into the business and if it goes under, or gets confiscated, then what? How could I take care of Michael if I'm flat broke and out of a job?"

"Will," I started, frowning into his eyes, "what did you invest in?"

"The auction house." He narrowed his eyes, eyebrows quirking into Ws on his forehead. He pushed his spectacles up and stared at me. "What are you talking about?"

I touched my cheek, remembering the first blow that had started me into the Grey. "I've seen this sort of thing before, and I'd say it's even money something criminal is going on."

"Like what?"

I gave a helpless shrug. "Drugs? Fraud? Tax evasion? Money laundering?"

He was appalled. "Why? How?"

"It's an easy business to hide things in—the value of an item is what you say it is, after all. Or what someone pays for it. And one of you does a lot of traveling, don't you?"

"I do, or I did until recently. Then Brandon took it over. I thought he was giving me a break to spend more time with Mike."

"That could be a cover for a lot of other activities. Has the business pattern changed suddenly? More profits? Less? Different type of goods or clients?"

Will looked askance at me. "Business has been improving..."

"And I'll bet Brandon's standard of living has suddenly gone up, yet he can't justify making you a partner, in spite of the money you've invested. Yeah, I'll bet it's doing just great for someone. And other people have noticed."

"You think the guys looking for Brandon are cops?"

"Could be cops, feds, unhappy partners at the other end, loan sharks..."

Will thought about it and shook his head, aghast. "Do you really believe that, Harper? That I could be a ... a fraud or a drug dealer—or a fall guy?"

I didn't meet his glance. Instead I put my coffee cup down and started to leave. "I shouldn't have said anything. I came to ask you a favor, but it wouldn't be right now."

"No. No, no … I'm not letting you walk out on me again." I started to flinch, but he only caught my hand and turned me back. "It took way too long for you to come back. Don't just walk out. Please."

I kept my eyes away from him.

"You wouldn't have said all this if you thought I was a villain. So maybe that's not what you think. Tell me what you think."

I hesitated, then said, "I think I don't know enough. And I think you need to be very careful, Will."

We were silent a moment. He put his hands on my shoulders; then I felt his breath move my hair as he spoke. "Thank you, Harper. And I'm sorry. I was a real jerk last week. Could we try again?"

My answer was cut off by Michael yelling from the screened porch. "Will! Hey, Novak, get your buns out here!"

Will twitched and snapped a look at his wristwatch. "Damn it." He turned his eyes back to me. "I am serious. I want to see you again and I am sorry about the way I acted. I know you didn't have to come here and you didn't have to say anything, so I'm hoping that means you'll call me and give me another chance. I'll do anything you ask to show you I mean it."

Michael shouted from the hall. "Will!"

I thought about it and knew what I wanted. I groped for something to say and picked up the plate of sandwiches. "Here. You'd better take these to the boy wonder before he starves to death. And … umm … if you're free late tonight, maybe we could … discuss some things."

"No 'maybe.' Definitely." He grinned and took the plate away with him. I stood in Ann Ingstrom's kitchen a moment longer, sipping cold coffee and writing a note on a pad by the phone. I considered just leaving it and slipping out the back, but I couldn't chicken out now. I headed for the front door. Passing the living room doorway, I looked in. Will was back up on the small raised platform, looking like a beat poet standing on a soapbox. He glanced up and smiled as I passed.

"Thanks, Michael," I said, dropping the note on the table as I started past him.

He swallowed a mouthful of sandwich and called after me. "Hey, Ms. Blaine! Harper?"

I turned around. Clutching my note, Michael got up and closed the door between the house and the porch.

"What is it, Michael?" I asked.

"Well, I just … well, I'm trying to say, like, you're not going to dump him again, are you? My brother, I mean. I mean, I know he's kinda geeky and all, but he's a good guy."

"He's a very good guy," I agreed. "And actually," I confessed, "I think he's kind of sexy."

Michael snorted a laugh. "Will?"

"Well … yeah."

Michael stared at me. "Will can't be sexy. He's my brother. You're sexy."

The blush swept over me like prairie fire. "Oh, boy. I've got to go." I could hear him sniggering as I retreated.

I sat in the front seat of the truck and stared back at the Ingstrom house for a few moments. The long-haired white cat ambled around the corner and sat on the front walk. It looked at me and yawned, showing its fangs, then raised a forepaw and began to wash as if dismissing me.

TWENTY-FOUR

It was hard to settle down, but I had a lot to do before I met Will again. Places to go, vampires to see.

Once it got dark, I drove to the university district. Since classes were still in session, there were plenty of residents out on the streets. I had to park in a pay lot and walk a ways to my destination.

The U-district has five movie theaters, several all-night restaurants, and a lot of bars. It's not the easiest neighborhood to find somebody in, since most residents are college students who come and go with the term schedule. I started at the first place on the list: the Wizards of the Coast Game Center.

The street level, filled with a noisy video arcade, owed its theme to science fiction movies, but below lay fantasyland. I walked down the stairs to the lower level, beneath the guardian glower of a giant, ax-wielding minotaur.

Here the walls were painted to resemble ancient stone and the support pillars had been elaborately draped in wine velvet swags. The baronial castle theme was carried out with fake torches and Gothic decorations. Fantastic paintings of mythic heroes and creatures hung on the walls. The lighting was dramatic, but not very practical.

About thirty young men and teenage boys had been paired facing each other at long tables, where they spread cards between them in some kind of duel to the numeric death. There was only one woman playing. Beyond the card players, a sword-and-sorcery film was playing on a gigantic screen in one gauze-draped corner, while a small group of people huddled around a coffee table in another. That was where I headed.

As I approached the role-players, one of them was saying something about casting a spell and several others offered vociferous disagreement.

"No, no, you can't cast that on a green wyvern."

"Yes, he can, but it's not going to work with the zombies there. They'll just keep coming."

They were a motley lot. Seven altogether, three women and four men—all in their thirties or so. One of the women was dressed in flowing robes of dark green velvet that didn't hide the fact that she overflowed her chair a bit as well. Her auburn hair was longer than mine had been before the elevator incident. One of the other women also wore a gown of some sort and a twisted ring of yellow and black fabric around her brow. The third woman and two of the men wore dark jeans and shirts. The other two men wore tunics and narrow trousers under lightweight cloaks. One of the tunic men stood next to the large woman, so that his cape was free to swirl around him when he moved. He was very aware of the effect.

I stopped beside them. "Excuse me. I'm looking for a girl named Gwen."

They appraised me, then looked around at one another.

The woman in jeans piped up. "You mean skinny Gwen?"

"I don't know what she looks like. A mutual friend said I might find her down here playing Dungeons and Dragons."

The standing man rolled his eyes. "You're a complete noob, aren't you? Don't even have a character yet, I'll bet."

"I didn't come to play. I'm just trying to find Gwen."

"If you mean skinny Gwen," started the jeans woman again, "she isn't coming tonight. She said she was going to see a movie at the Grand Illusion. She asked me to play her character for her."

"OK, I'll try there. How will I know her when I see her?" I inquired.

"She's really skinny, like count-my-ribs-through-my-clothes skinny."

One of the jeans-wearing men objected. "She's not that thin."

The green-robed woman weighed in. "Yes, she is. She looks like the ghost of a supermodel who died of malnutrition."

A titter ran through the group.

"All right," I said. "I'll look for the shade of Kate Moss. Thanks."

They were arguing again before I'd gone ten steps. "I still say it's pointless to cast daze on a green wyvern…"

I wondered what Mara's opinion would have been.

I climbed back up the stairs and escaped to the street, still looking for Gwen.

Part art house and part coffeehouse, the Grand Illusion is the northern anchor of the Ave. The southern anchor of this stretch of University Way NE is the University of Washington's administration building. You can walk the gamut from administration to auteurism by way of trendy trash-chic in less than ten blocks, if you don't get run down by an aggressive skateboarder on the way.

When I got to the theater, the film was already rolling. Two student-age couples sipping coffee and chatting in the café were the only people in sight. I stared at the ticket counter, trying to decide on my next move.

A young woman in a long batik-dyed skirt and a dark blue sweater set padded up behind me. "Hi," she greeted in a low voice. "Did you want to purchase a ticket? The film started about eight o'clock, so the first feature's almost over."

"I'm looking for someone who said she was coming tonight. Her name is Gwen and she's very … slender."

She gave a rueful smile. "You must mean Lady Gwendolyn of Anorexia. She went in about half an hour ago. If you want, you can wait for her in the coffeehouse."

I bought yet another cup of java and sat down to wait at a table that commanded a view of the theater door. Twenty-seven minutes later, the film ended and the audience trickled into the coffeehouse. Gwen was easy to spot.

She was a dead ringer for Waterhouse's *Lady of Shalott.* She was even wearing a long white dress with trailing sleeves. A cataract of strawberry blond hair fell in ripples to her hips, and it appeared that the Lily Maid hadn't dined on anything more substantial than a lettuce leaf and a drop of dew in years. But despite being no bigger around than a pencil, she didn't look skeletal, only whittled away.

As she entered the room I stepped forward to introduce myself. "Excuse me. Are you Gwen?"

The Grey scurried behind her. My skin prickled with cold, unaffected by her watery smile as the dark fog folded around us both. "My name is Gwen." Her voice was as thin as she. "Why were you looking for me?"

"A young man named Cameron Shadley gave me your name. Do you know who I mean?" I asked.

"I know of Cameron Shadley."

"Then you've never met him?"

"Oh, in passing, when he was still in the daylight. We never became friends. He's not with us anymore."

"That would depend on who you mean by 'us,'" I said. "He's my client. I'm a private investigator."

"Oh. I didn't know there were any of your profession for our kind. You're not one of us."

"No. I'm the daylight kind."

She giggled a little. "Let me get some tea," she murmured and drifted away to the coffee counter.

In a few minutes, she returned. She toyed with a china pot and a cup, but didn't drink. "I don't know how much help anything you hear from Lady Gwendolyn of Anorexia is going to be. I'm not much use to anyone, you know."

Her use of the nickname in the third person gave me pause. "Maybe you could be more help than you think," I suggested. "Cameron has a little problem with Edward and he asked me to intervene. But I want to know more about Edward first. What do you know about him?"

"Ned? Ned's irresponsible, but he hides it well. I suppose it's easy when you have dozens of underlings to manage the details for you."

"How long have you known him?"

"All my unlife. He made me." Her voice held no rancor, almost no emotion at all, in fact. She spoke in her thin, measured tone, as if she were talking about some other person. "In 1969, I was a carefree little chippy—make love, not war, you know. And Ned was, well, Ned. I didn't know it at the time, but he had just gained control of Seattle, so he got away with a lot. I was a mistake." She paused and sipped her tea, inhaling more of the scent than she swallowed of the brew.

"How is that? Isn't it a deliberate act? I mean, it doesn't happen by accident, does it?"

Her voice floated like petals. "No, it doesn't. What I meant is his choice of me was a mistake and his timing was poor. Long-range planning isn't his best skill. He's an opportunist and very good at it."

"What about you?"

"What about me? I'm nobody. In a community so small that every member counts, I'm only barely a member. I go to movies, because I can like those celluloid people and care about them and they never grow old and die, or stay young and become monsters. They're so nice. Even the bad guys. I like celluloid people."

"What about your role-playing friends?"

"They're not my friends—they're warms." She blinked in slow motion. "Oh. That was rude of me."

"I'm not ashamed to be warm. But if you don't like them, why do you spend time with them?"

"I like them well enough. It's the game that's interesting. I've been with the same game for three years now, but the people change. It's wonderful to feel like life and death and adventure and honor are important. It's better than just drifting along in limbo and feeling like nothing matters. Sometimes it's better than movies. It's almost like being alive. And I matter so much more than I ever did."

"What else can you tell me about Edward?"

"Not much."

"What about TPM?"

"TPM? One of his little projects. I don't know what ever became of that. He liked to play with things, buildings and businesses and things like that. It's a game. To Ned, most of the world is just a big game. He likes to win—he'll even cheat to win, but not if it breaks his own rules. He has rules, you know, they're just not the ones everyone else knows. That's all."

"Tell me about you and Edward, then."

"Me and Edward. I wish there had been a me and Edward. There was just Edward. And then, there was just me. I wasn't a very amusing plaything, I guess. He dumped me. But I get along all right, I suppose."

"You said his timing was poor."

"He was so busy that being a responsible mentor just wasn't a priority," Gwen murmured. "He let me drift a lot. Finally, I just drifted away. He takes care of me when he thinks of it, but mostly he doesn't. But poor Cameron ... Ned doesn't like him anymore. He makes things hard for him. Cameron should learn to drift, like I do. It's safer. Do you mind if I go now? The second feature is going to start. It's Jean Renoir. I love Renoir. So lovely and strange." She rose and glided away, disappearing into the dimness of the theater.

I sat and finished my coffee. This case owed more to John Carpenter by way of Fellini than Renoir, as far as I could see.

I walked back along the Ave through the still-thick throngs of college students, panhandlers, and drug dealers hanging out on the street. In some places, their conversational knots blocked the sidewalk and forced me into the street to pass. Despite the cry of the fashionable that grunge was dead, it was difficult to tell the middle-class students from the destitute street people. Scraggly beards, dirt-colored clothes, and lank hair abounded. The Goths and preppies stood out like buzzards and peacocks in a flock of sparrows. And the noise level rivaled that of any migratory-avian watering hole in spring. My ears were ringing by the time I turned off University Way and walked several long blocks to a twenty-four-hour Italian restaurant.

It was nearly ten thirty and my stomach was putting up quite a fuss over missed meals. I ordered food and drank more coffee. I thought about Gwen. Her Grey presence was almost nil; she left barely a ripple and affected me not at all. Was that what Carlos had meant? Would Cameron fade down to the same sad shadow, a memory that remained only because it hadn't yet forgotten itself?

I sighed. She hadn't been as useless as she thought, at least. Gwen was an instance of bad mentorship, too—foolish risks to the community. And she had confirmed Edward's connection to TPM back when the company was young. How deep was he into TPM's structure and how much of TPM's wealth and influence were wielded at Edward's discretion? I feared that answer as much as I needed it.

After dinner, I wasted some of my time with an undead gentleman in Fremont. I left him angry at Edward, but gained nothing directly. As I was leaving, a different and familiar sense of disquiet brushed my back. Hot and cold. I let my senses sink toward it, watching the world become hazy with the shadows of the Grey. I turned, searching.

Alice was standing in the doorway I'd just exited.

"Hard at work?"

"Hard enough," I answered, holding down a quiver of revulsion as the fever-flash heat and chill of her overt sensuality crawled over me.

She glowered. "Not quite." I felt her pressure on me increase and her voice seemed to ring deeper. "You need to move more directly against him. You should be attacking, not nibbling around the edges like a mouse."

I pushed back against Alice's demands and felt them crumble away into the cloud-swirl between us. I smothered my relief and felt sweat on my skin, panting as if I'd just done a sprint from standing.

"No. A direct attack is not what I agreed to and I'm not going to march up to Edward and make myself a target just to make you happy."

The red corona around her flared into a spire of rage. Her hands crooked into claws. "You think you can defy me? I can remove you with a flick of my hand."

I locked down a shudder. "What good does that do you, Alice? You just mop up Edward's problem without him raising a finger. He's not going to thank you for it. As long as I'm out here, Edward's got trouble, but if you really want him to hurt, you'll have to get a little dirty. Fan flames, spread rumors. That's your part of the job. Remember? If things aren't going to plan, it's not because of me."

She settled a little. "Don't overstep yourself. Lack of forgiveness is a trait Edward and I share."

"I'm not so forgiving myself. And I don't appreciate being attacked by undead thugs or having my place tossed."

She narrowed her eyes and my breath went cold. "What? You think I had anything to do with that?" She laughed flaming shards of ice through my skin. "You're not worth the expense."

"Then maybe it's Edward. If he's onto me, he'll be onto you next. You need to start covering both our backs, as you promised, or you won't have much chance to put your plans into action."

Alice glared in silence, thinking.

I took my time, breathing with care to avoid the lump of ice in my throat. "Alice, you know that if Edward thinks I'm the only source of his troubles, he'll swat me and then you'll have no opportunity to move. So let's just get on with it. You'll get your chance."

"I had best to." Alice faded back into the doorway, vanishing into the dark.

It would have been more dramatic if I couldn't see her slipping through the Grey. And that confused me. Because, if Alice didn't know what I could do or see, why had she been tailing me so long?

I shook my head, turned my back, and started walking again, looking at the list. There was only one name left, added in Alice's unpleasant purple ink.

TWENTY FIVE

Part of the corrupt charm of big cities is their acceptance of the wacky, weird, and outrageous within business as usual. But I doubt there were many other venues that hosted something as unpredictable as Radio Freeform. Format varied wildly from minute to minute; you could be scratching along with an old Bill Broonzy blues tune and smash into a cut from Lunchbox next. Your brain and ears might feel assaulted, but it would hold together. Wygan, the overnight man, had a deft touch with the mix. It was his name Alice had inked at the bottom of the list.

Late-night DJ was a pretty good gig for a vampire, I thought, and a well-known local voice wasn't likely to attack me. I drove to the row of red and white broadcasting towers on top of Queen Anne Hill and parked in the small, deserted lot outside the tiny building. I was glad that this phase of the project was nearly over. I was tired, felt low-level ill and ready to call it quits, no matter how much Alice threatened. I was a little jittery from her threats and too much caffeine, but I figured this one would be easy. Nothing could be as bad as Carlos.

Beside the steel security door was an intercom with a switch. I pushed it. A cautious voice answered.

"'Ello?"

I leaned toward the box and spoke. "Hi. My name is Harper Blaine. I'm a private investigator. Alice Liddell told me to contact Wygan. Can I talk to him?"

I heard a guffaw. "Alice sent you to me?" I recognized the soft slurring of Wygan's working-class English accent. "Sure. Why not? Hang on. I'll buzz you through. Just us chickens here tonight." The low electronic burring of the latch cut off any reply.

The corridor beyond the door was painted industrial green. The lighting was poor enough to make the dirt on the linoleum look like a pattern instead of bad housekeeping. I closed the door behind me and walked. The booth was a beacon of red light pouring through Lexan. I wondered why it was red.

I hadn't reached the booth's door before I began feeling queasy. It might have been the way the light strobed and switched to amber, but I was afraid I'd underestimated my mental and physical exhaustion. The Grey was flickering in the corners of my eyes. When I reached it, the door was open a crack and the moans of unhappy electronic instruments leaked out. I peered through the window beside the door.

A lanky, pale man waved at me. "Come on in. Mic's not live."

I stepped in. "You're Wygan?"

Leaning back in his fully gimbaled leather chair, the bony young man shot his arms straight into the air above his blond electroshock hair. "I am the eggman, I am the walrus! Goo goo g'joob!" he caroled. "Alice sent you?"

"Yeah, but I'm really here on behalf of Cameron Shadley." I looked around, trying to hold on to normal. I grasped at the first thing. "What's with the lights?"

"Keeps a certain creature away from me. He doesn't like the changing colors." He peered at me, snickering, as if he was just waiting for the punch line.

I couldn't imagine what would want to come in here. The booth was small and lined floor to ceiling with automated CD racks behind smoked-glass doors. A homemade stand in one corner had three lightbulbs arranged across the top of it: red, blue, and amber. They alternated at a slow pace. A narrow strip of white light ran over the top of the horseshoe-shaped control console, which was heavy with switches, sliders, dials, and keyboards as well as several video monitors. One of the monitors was showing old, mute episodes of *Lost in Space.* Various meters and LED displays flashed or flickered silent information. Every shadow writhed.

"Close the door, would you, love?" he asked, flipping switches. "What good's a soundproof booth with the door standing open, hmm?"

I closed the door and remained standing. I tried to hold it back, but the steamed-mirror world battered against me as I got closer to him.

"You should sit down." He grinned at me, teeth snaggled, yellow, canines pronounced and elongated. His smile was a poleax, and my knees buckled. I thumped down into an empty chair, aware of shadows pooling thicker, like oozing tar, in the corners of the room, exuding a low reek of antiquity and decay. It was an ancient and foul corner of the cold blackness I'd fallen into when I touched Cameron. My stomach flipped and tried to stretch itself around my spine. A thin halo of blue and red wavered around Wygan's head.

He cocked his head back and forth, looking like a hungry velociraptor. "Alice sent you to me about Cameron?" He gave an incredulous snort. "Pull the other one."

I shook my head. "You're not what I was expecting," I confessed, swallowing discomfort. His proximity sent ripples through every sense I had, normal or not. Carlos was a teddy bear by comparison.

"Must be my charming and sophisticated on-air personality," he quipped and brayed hundreds of hot slivers through me. "Hang on a tick—track's almost over."

He held one finger up in the air to me, then spun himself 450 degrees to face his console. His hands darted over the controls like albino spiders as a row of red numerals counted down. Then he flipped a switch and eased a slider down, leaning into the microphone. "Now here's a prezzie from me to you—a whole album side of classic Floyd from *Dark Side of the Moon.*" He flipped off the microphone and leaned back into his seat. The room seemed to roll and shift with his every movement.

He swung the seat back and forth a few times, then spun it to face me. "So Alice sent you to me. About Cameron." An eddy of darkness followed his movements. He pursed his lips and raised his eyebrows in amusement, shrugged. "What of him?"

I found it hard to speak. "He hired me and I'm trying to stir up a little dirt on a vampire named Edward."

His face twisted. "Edward Kammerling," he breathed. "Yes..." The Grey surged around him, lighting his aurora with white lightning strikes and shivering the world between us.

Sudden cold trembled my bones. "You don't like him."

He turned an ophidian gaze on me. "I'll see him to hell ... in my own time. If I'm in a very charitable mood, I might not make him eat the parts I dismember him of." He studied me with a baleful stare. I felt like a bird about to be swallowed. "They are as insignificant as fleabites, the lot of them, beside you."

I stammered, "What?" forcing words out as my stomach twisted and my lungs fought air that hung in clouds before me.

He laughed flaying knives and ice. "To think such flyspecks brought you here! I've waited so long for you." He made a motion, as if opening a door. "Why don't you come all the way in and see?" Ambient sound shushed away and a shock wave rolled out from the bright door now standing between us—the door to the Grey. The silence howled over me and shoved me deeper into the chair.

I fought my way up and started for the real door, stumbling on numb legs. This time the dragon-smoke door wouldn't lead to the white place I'd chased Alice into. It reeked of something much worse. "I don't think so," I stated.

"I think otherwise," he barked and launched through the doorway, ripping open the fine seam between normal and Grey, pushing the glowing boundary wide.

Reality split open with a roar as the Grey rushed over us, slamming the breath from my lungs. I thrust back against it and felt my protection shatter and whirl away into the flood. I gasped for air and fought the icy battering of a storm of shadows and boiling silver mist. The world shuddered and the urge to retch wrenched my innards.

White claws dug into my upper arms and held me upright. I sucked in the thick cold, eyes clenched shut, struggling, and began screaming.

Wygan shook me. "Scream! Scream, my delight, my own. There's no one to hear but me. No one, no one," he crooned, his voice moving slow and cold as a half-frozen river, deep under ice, under my skin. "Open your eyes. Open the eyes within and see your pretty new world. See what I am giving you. A gift. A gift so needful."

I fought to get out of his grip, which seemed to pierce all the way through me in javelins of ice. I felt tears streaking my face, warm tracks in a frozen world. My eyelids ground open against my will.

Wygan held me to the padded wall. His eyes glowed, and red fire and white sparks danced jagged lightning strikes around us in a world of roiling, tormented shadow and coiling mist. His eyes were snakelike. His skin gleamed pearlescent and finely marked with tiny, overlapping fringes. His ice white hair was a sculpted ridge that camouflaged the true shape of a saurian skull. The Grey surged around us like water from a broken dam, and I was drowning.

I stared back at him in strangled silence, my lungs frozen in my chest. I wanted to bolt, to claw, swim, dig my way out of there, but in the prison of his gaze, I could do no more than shake. Half a smile tore his face.

"Fear," he murmured. His breath smelled of tombs. "I could feed upon you for days. Look at my world. My prison of hunger, cold, unbridgeable distance, without touch, without warmth, but what I can steal. This is my torment, my gift. Look at it!"

He whipped me in front of him, thrusting me into a maelstrom of writhing, tortured shapes and animate cold. Twisting, arctic forms pressed against me, gaping, changing ever and ever into unending nightmares intangible and horrible, stabbing cold fingers of avarice and hunger through me. They devoured me, tore me, inhabited me in mouthless screams. I gasped and sobbed and tried to pull away from them, felt them sucking my thoughts and my life away in unraveling skeins, emptying all thought, even emotion, fear, self-preservation, draining me to bleak despair.

I sagged, and he let me fall to my knees.

"You don't see it," Wygan whispered behind me. "You haven't ascended to your proper place. Worthless fools and incompetents. They discovered you, but could not mold you as I told them to."

My mind flashed hot images: the apparently crazy man in the alley; the unkillable assailant in my garage; the break-ins … I couldn't get words to form properly, only choking out, "You … you?"

As if he could see my thoughts—or had sent them—he laughed, the sound slashing me. "You reentered this world, incomplete, half made. You needed honing to your true shape. But they failed. Cowards. Imbeciles. Faulty tools like Alice, clinging to their own paltry half-lives, petty schemes." His voice spiked upward into my skull. "Ages waited! And at last!"

He stepped to my side and crouched, a slender reptilian creature cloaked in a clot of gruesome shadow and dancing fury-light. "But you aren't here as you should be. You haven't grown to it. Imprisoned, blind, weak! You are no good to me. How can you walk where you can't see? And I must have you or cannot cross. You must see what I can see but cannot touch. Touch what I can take but cannot feel. I will make you what you ought to be."

He reached into the mist and hooked a thread of glimmering blue on one white claw. "Your power is too small. You must embrace it, must grow for me. Take this."

I cringed back with a whimper. "No. No, I don't want it," I protested, my voice a weak trickle of steam in the cold.

"Did I offer you a choice?" He pushed his tangled claw into my chest, ripping me open, unbleeding. I tried to yell, but nothing came out.

The blue thread went taut and vibrated, then shimmered and crawled over me, spreading over my limbs and up to my head. The thread passed over my eyes and blinded me a moment, then faded. The shape of it vanished, seeming to sink into me, knitting me closed again around its adamantine knot within my ribs.

The mist-world blazed and faded like fog under sun. The shape and color of the Grey changed, roaring with a tangle of light, fountains and smudges of illumination, glowing forms of vibrant color and force, lines as straight and hot as highways in the desert, as twisted as tornadoes, wild as wind.

The studio, formed of soft mist, was limned in gleaming threads around us, and the top of Queen Anne Hill spread away beyond it, through inconsequential walls, glimmering with phantom fires and falling into an ink-dark stain of cold nothingness—the Sound. In the distance, the black beast howled in rage and I felt it gather itself and rush toward us, all teeth and claws and unquenchable hatred.

The Grey was alive inside me and I felt it vibrating, coiling, binding into me like a malevolent vine growing from the living seed Wygan had planted. I could feel the pulse of it. I shrieked despair.

Wygan laughed. "Yes! You will grow to the part I need you to play. But we'd best go now, before the hungry one ruins the party."

He let go, his touch withdrawing with the same sensation as cactus spines drawn from my skin. The Grey lapped over me like a wet sheet and slid away, leaving a single, indissoluble thread that vanished between my breasts.

I was on my knees by the studio door. My clothing and face dripped. I fought nausea, gagged and swallowed bile, gasped to catch my breath again. I staggered to my feet.

"You doin' all right?" Wygan asked. He was still in his chair.

I gulped. "Alive."

He giggled, and the sound rubbed against my nerves like ground glass. "More or less. But you should be able to keep yourself that way now, until I need you. Now you see it as it really is, and you can use that. You'll need to learn the part, though, or something may hurt you."

I turned and stared at him, shivering in shock. He looked back and smiled a little, sending a breaker of cold over me. The light in the booth turned blue, though the bulb on the stand was amber.

"I … know all I can stand to."

"For now. You can let yourself out, I think."

He turned his back to me, tugging on his headphones and crouching over the console. Will Robinson pursued Dr. Smith through bars of Led Zeppelin, casting a blue shadow from the video monitor in the shape of a giant reptile, which grinned at me.

I bolted out the door and stumbled, tripping, desperate for distance, toward the door.

"Don't forget me," he called out, a shadow voice gliding on a nonexistent breeze. I heard him laughing behind me all the way.

I staggered out to the Rover and leaned against it, bowing my neck to press my face against the cold solidity of the old truck's side. I shivered and gulped mouthfuls of ordinary Seattle air to stop myself howling out loud. There was an ache in my chest where Wygan had touched me, black pain equaled by the tearing horror rampaging through my mind. I hated myself for this trembling weakness, and more so for what had happened. I crawled into the backseat and curled into a sickened ball as my thoughts screamed and raged:

What are you? Raped, ripped, re-formed. What are you, now? Ignorant fool. These are vampires; a monstrous redesign of humans, psychotic by our standard, alien, divorced from humanity. What drives them is not what drives you. It never will be. Never again. They are not human. They are not humans! And neither are you. Not anymore. Insect. Half monster. What are you, now?

I lost track of time, hysterical, quivering in a crumpled wad of misery, despair, and self-disgust. After a while, I noticed I was stiff, cold, and stinking—right after I unclenched long enough to throw up. Hanging upside down, shivering and crying, some kind of common sense reasserted itself. The nearest vampire was just inside the building, laughing still, and I was sitting like a tethered goat.

I had to drive with care, in spite of an urge to speed. I couldn't see well through my swollen eyes and the streets flickered Grey, overlaid in mist and silver, outlined in streaks of neon-bright light. I pulled over a couple of times and tried to breathe slowly and attentively until it stopped. It would not recede. The trip home was very long.

TWENTY SIX

I jerked awake at a sound and cowered under the covers. The beeping continued and the bed shuddered as Will fumbled for his pager on the nightstand.

I hid my face in my pillow and moaned, "Make it go away."

He flopped backward with the pager on his chest. "It's just Mikey, letting me know he's at work."

"He works on Sunday?"

"Usually it's me. Mike volunteered to do the paperwork so I could sleep in." He rolled over and grinned at me. "Wanna go back to sleep?"

I peeled the pillow aside. "No."

His smile got wider as he felt my toes sliding up his leg. "Feeling better?"

"Much," I replied. If I focused my attention on Will, I didn't have to think about what had happened in the night, didn't have to look at it, shimmering in the verges.

I had forgotten the note I'd left with Michael. The sight of the scarecrow figure in the darkened hall outside my home had made me recoil in fear. When Will stepped into the light, my relief flooded out as a puddle of idiotic tears and shaking. He was very sweet, even when he told me I stank and put me in the shower. I kept sliding down into the bottom of the tub and crying until Will gave up being a gentleman and got in with me. I clung to him and things improved from there, even though I refused to tell him what had happened.

Now I was disgusted with myself for having blubbered and oozed like a jellyfish.

He caught me frowning as he snatched away my pillow. "Hey. Want to take another shower?" he asked, laying on a wicked grin.

I was slow on the uptake. "Do I need one?"

"From a hygiene point of view, no. But interesting things seem to happen in your shower, so I thought it was a good place to start."

I made a rude noise, grabbed back the pillow, and swatted him with it. He dove under the covers and tickled me.

Will let the horrors of Saturday night lie and kept me too distracted to think about them most of Sunday. After an afternoon of goofing off, he even agreed to come and look at the parlor organ with me on Monday and never speculated about whatever it was we were doing together.

After Will had gone, the misery and uncertainty began to close in again. Typing up my notes sent me into fits of shivering and crying. I thought of quitting. I could not face any more nights like Saturday, but I wasn't sure I'd done enough to destabilize Edward. And if I could not move him in the direction I wanted, neither Cameron nor I stood a chance of seeing another spring. What did I have to offer Edward that was more attractive than the pleasure of taking my head off? I couldn't trust vampires. I wasn't even sure that I could look at Cameron without either screaming or putting a bullet in him—not that it would do any good.

I closed my eyes, trying to think, but only slipping around the edges. The Grey washed against me, chill and nauseating. I felt that I was standing on a dock—a world—afloat on the surface of another world, pitching with the motion of unknown tides. The disconcerting feel of electricity zipped along my nerves, but I kept my eyes closed against those twisting threads of fire. I didn't want them, or anything to do with Wygan's realm or vampires or ghosts or any of the rest of it. I felt the insubstantial ground shivering and thought of stepping off the dock...

The sound of little claws on woodwork pulled me back from the bloody edge. I picked up the ferret and snuggled her to my face, smelling the warm, corn-chip odor of her fur. For once, she didn't wriggle.

Close to that soft warmth, I relaxed, taking deep, easy breaths. Everything Grey seemed to flow like silk thread, shimmering with strands of energy, and I could feel every movement I made through it. I pushed on it and it bent, stiffening into a reflective curve around me. Even the chill was less now. I tried to push it away completely, but it would not recede below a constant bright softness lying over everything. Grids of energy gleamed on the threshold of light. Peeking sideways brought it all up to a bright blaze. I did not wish to step inside and see how the normal world looked from there.

But the constant presence was like acid on my nerves. I didn't want to be near it or anything associated with it. I didn't even want to talk to the Danzigers. Then I would have to think about it.

I shoved it back to the limits. I shivered and found myself crying into Chaos's pelt. Shuddering, I carried her off, crawled back under the covers, and hid from the ugly world.

Monday morning Will met me at a café near the Madison Forrest House for breakfast. He greeted me with a more-than-friendly kiss and we sat at a table outside. I told myself the thin golden line around him was a trick of the cool spring sunshine.

I smiled at the delicious quivers he sent over me. "When do you have to go to work?" I asked.

"Closed on Mondays," he replied, draping an arm over my shoulders, "and probably forever afterward, too, thanks to Brandon—who's not returning phone calls and seems to be dodging some guys in dark suits, sunglasses, and grim looks."

I raised my brows. "Who do you suppose they are?"

"I don't know. Mikey spotted them hanging around. They didn't bother to introduce themselves, and their cars had rental plates."

"He noticed that? Sounds like Michael could be a detective, too."

"I hope not. I'd rather admire your technique than watch Mike do it." He wiggled his eyebrows at me. "Want to show me your technique?"

I giggled. "Right here? Heck, no. What about Mike?"

"Let him get a girl his own age. I'm not sharing."

"You know what I mean."

"He's fine. Thinks it's funny. He's in school today."

"Does that mean you have nothing to do?"

He ran a finger along the curve of my ear and down my neck. "Mmm. I wouldn't say nothing."

I shivered. "Unfortunately, I have things to do that preclude dancing the horizontal tango with you all day—much as I might like to. Or had you forgotten this is supposed to be a professional meeting?"

"Spoilsport."

I poked him with a finger and made a face. "The curator will meet us in a little over an hour, so take a look at this and give me your professional opinion."

He glanced at the description sheet I offered him. "Without even looking at it, I expect that my professional opinion will be that it's a piece of grot."

"It does make me rather suspicious of the client's motives." I was suspicious of Sergeyev in general, but I wasn't going to discuss that with Will. "I need to know as much about it as possible."

"You think your client is up to something?"

"Something doesn't smell right, if you know what I mean. He said there was no rush, but he's thrown an awful lot of money at the project and he's shown up once, although he said he was in Europe the first time we talked. His check was drawn on a Swiss bank, but the rest of the packet came from London."

"I'm surprised it wasn't an Irish bank," Will commented. "The Swiss aren't as reticent about giving out information as they used to be, and the Irish make them look like pikers."

"Irish offshore banks? I've never heard of such a thing."

"It was on the horizon the last time I was in England," he explained.

"They've tried a lot of things to bring international business to Ireland. Most didn't pan out, but you don't need any special resources to be a banking power, especially if you're willing to buck the bully tactics of the US and the EU and maintain absolute discretion about your customers."

"Really? You're a guy of unknown depths, Mr. Novak."

"Yep. A diamond of the first water. Better grab me while you can."

I laughed. "I'll consider doing that."

We ate and joked around some more, then headed for the museum.

I parked the Rover in the gravel lot across the street. Will pulled his truck in beside mine. The house was forbidding, all its windows frowning and clouded through a thick bank of Grey. Even the glow of the nexus seemed to have died out. We crossed the street, but this time the gate was locked. I rang the bell on the intercom.

A woman's voice spoke from the box. "We're closed on Mondays."

"Harper Blaine. I have an appointment with the curator."

"Oh. I'll be right up."

A few minutes later, a middle-aged woman in a suit, heels, and corporate hairstyle appeared from behind the house. She took one look at Will and knew a kindred spirit. They chattered antiques the whole way up the drive.

"Nobody cares about the national heritage here," she declared as we reached the kitchen door. "You have to drag every penny of funding out of these bureaucrats' hands as if it were their own money. They'd rather spend it on a new baseball stadium. Watch your feet. There's a towel to wipe your shoes on."

We did as she suggested, leaving the mud on the towel instead of the parquet floor. She led us into the main hall and waved her hands around. "Gorgeous, isn't it? It's a damn sight better than it was when I came here. They had the interior all done in high Victoriana. Crammed with horrible gewgaws and junk, bad wallpaper, ugly, ugly colors. Totally out of period for this building."

"Then why did the museum acquire a parlor organ?" Will asked.

"Oh, yes. That's what you came for, isn't it? There was an organ on the original inventory, but it was broken and the first curator threw it out. Come on. It's upstairs. You can imagine what it was like getting it in here!" she added, leading us up the front staircase. Upstairs, she opened the door in front of us. "There you go. Awful, isn't it?"

A small sofa, chairs, and a needlework stand clustered around the hearth, as before, exuding their reassuring odor of age, must, and wood oil. Against the back wall stood the organ, outlined in gleaming red threads and writhing with vile, silent Grey snakes. Will pulled out the description sheet I'd given him and started studying it.

I felt woozy and my heart sped up. I clamped down on the feeling, but the sense of seasickness remained, tickling away, and the room had become hazy and soft like the stink of rot no matter how I tried to resist it.

Will read the sheet as we walked across the polished wood floor. Two feet inside the door, I felt sick. At four feet, my head was pounding with an instant headache of migraine proportions. I put my hand on Will's arm.

"What's wrong?" he asked.

I lied. "I don't know. I just don't feel well." I turned my attention back to the parlor organ.

It was still the ugliest thing I'd ever seen and would have been even if it wasn't cloaked in swirling energy matrices and sucking darkness like a drain. It had grown worse in just a few days. Clear vision in the Grey seemed to have come with Wygan's "gift." Storm-mist pulsed around the organ and phantom faces leered and screamed in transient gusts of paranormal wind. Creeping horror played up and down my spine. I dragged myself a step closer to it, hating the proximity. A glowing tentacle struck out and slammed into my chest where Wygan's thread was tied. I gagged and stumbled.

I tried to bend the Grey and push it away. The tentacle rippled and sucked away the strength of my push. My knees folded and I felt the floor rush up as vision went black.

Will grabbed me under the arms. "Harper!"

The tentacle pulled on me, wrapping around my insides like a steel fist. I choked, "Get me out of here."

Will picked me up and ran out. He didn't stop until we were outside, where he put me on my feet with the care of a collector placing a prized piece.

"Are you all right now? Are you sick? Do you need a glass of water, a doctor ... ?"

I slumped down on the carriage steps like a dropped sandbag. "No, no. I'm OK now. I just ... I just need some air. Go back inside. I'll be fine." I could not face that thing again. It had drained my resources too easily.

"Are you sure? We can go if you want."

"No, it's important that I know about that organ."

Will sighed. "All right. But you'll be OK till I get back, right?"

"Yeah."

He gave me several glances over his shoulder before he was swallowed again by the doorway. I sat a while, panting, and thought I heard something shrieking in the Grey. I felt better as soon as it stopped. I stood on loose legs and walked around to the front of the house.

To my eyes, the windows of the organ's den were dark. They neither shed nor reflected any light. The house that had seemed so pretty on Saturday now looked like something from a horror film, the stonework overgrown with veins of fire and writhing Grey vines. I felt a scratching along the surfaces of my bones. I slammed a mental door against the persistence of vision and scurried back to my seat on the steps.

I felt stronger by the time Will returned, smiling and chatting to the curator as they parted company at the door. She stayed on the porch.

I looked up at Will. "Well?"

He dropped onto the steps beside me, folded like a paper crane, and made a face. "Well ... it matches the description technically, but..." He shook his head. "It's not worth whatever your client's put into finding it. A lot of the decoration is bone and ivory that's ... nonstandard. Modifications and repairs aren't unusual for an item like this, but..." He chewed his lower lip and looked at the ground. "My gut says there's something wrong. It doesn't even play, really. The whole thing's kind of unsettling. But it doesn't matter, because the current museum board won't sell."

"Why not?" I asked. I looked back at the woman on the porch.

She shook her head and called out, "It's the only Tracher parlor organ they could find, and current policy won't allow us to sell anything that matches original inventory. They're freaking out over the idea of permanent reductions. Though after what Will said, I think we'd be better off without it."

I hung my head, worn out, and sighed. "I know it's an imposition, but can I bring one more expert to look at it?"

"Sure, if you think it'll help. Especially if it covers the board's butt."

"It'll have to be after hours. This guy's not available during the day."

"Oh. Well, get in touch with me and we'll work it out. I'd like to hear we didn't buy a screaming fake."

We both thanked her for her time and we left the museum. Crossing the street, I turned for one more look at the organ's resting place. The ground seemed to roll beneath my feet as I looked a little sideways of normal. The Grey snapped open, showing me an angry tangle of burning lines and shapes, boiling in a restless, sobbing mist. I jerked myself away from it, feeling a biting pain in my chest, and stumbled against Will. He held tight to my arm as we let ourselves out the driveway gate.

We stopped beside the Rover. "Are you sure you feel OK?" Will asked.

"I'm fine. Probably just something I ate."

"Bull. We ate the same thing and I feel fine." He noticed the hard set of my mouth. "You don't want to talk about it."

"No, I don't."

He sighed. "All right. We'll keep this professional. I'll see if I can dig up anything about this organ. I got numbers off the action and case, and Tracher may still have some records I can start with. I'll let you know what I find."

"Thanks, Will."

He looked me over again, shook his head. "You know Mikey's going to grill me about you this evening, don't you?"

I gave a weak laugh. "Poor Will. Terrorized by a sixteen-year-old."

"Hey, there's a sixty-year-old Jewish mother in that sixteen-year-old body. Mike's not sure you're good for me."

"Oh, I'm sure I'm very bad for you. Very bad indeed."

"Mmm ... very bad," he agreed. He leaned forward and kissed me, nibbling my lower lip. He murmured against my mouth, "I won't ask if you're OK, 'cause you're just going to stonewall me some more if I do."

I nodded. "Yep."

He sighed and backed off. "All right. But I will worry and you can't stop me. Be careful, Harper."

"I will."

"No—" he started.

"Yes, I know—you Will, me Harper."

He laughed. "You caught me!" He kissed my cheek this time and opened the Rover's door for me.

I got in and buckled up. He closed the door and watched me for a moment; then he backed away and waited for me to pull out of the lot before he started back to his own truck.

I didn't even get all the way through my office door before the client was in the office and normalcy was out.

I was startled. "Sergeyev. You're back."

"You have made progress to locating my furniture."

I sat down at my desk, buying time. "Yes, I have." I put my mouth on autopilot as my mind leapt around like a terrified monkey. "I've seen the organ at the museum and it seems to match your description—"

"Which museum? Tell the name. They must let me have it."

Some warning instinct in the monkey brain made me stall. "That may not be possible."

Sergeyev loomed over me, exuding a Grey reek and a flutter of colorless energy which didn't surprise me. "You shall make them give it," he demanded. "It is mine."

"No," I answered, my voice going hard as my stomach flipped over. The Grey pressed like a weight on my chest. I strained against it and wouldn't allow it to break through any further. "You may believe you have a moral claim, but the owners can't be forced to sell."

"It is mine!"

My words popped in the thick air like water on hot oil. "Not legally. I cannot work miracles. Can't simply make it yours. I have to work within the law."

He ground his teeth, or I told myself that was the sound. "Laws of men! Who has more right to it than I? It is in every bone, every sinew. It is mine. You must loose it to me."

I glared at him, seeing his shape slip and firm again, silver and Grey. Fury burned over me. "Don't. Push me."

He jerked his head back and glowered. "I expected better. You who can see the world should sympathize. I felt you and came for your help. But you are a silly, ignorant girl."

Now he'd pissed me off. "I am getting damned tired of being insulted by things like you. And nobody calls me 'girl' in my own office."

"You do not know with what you toy … girl."

My heart slammed around my chest like a basketball in a box and I kept smelling something like a whiff of harsh tobacco smoke. I was too mad to feel ill or to think clearly about what I was about to do. I held off my fear and revulsion in a cold, dark place and braced myself.

"Really? Why don't you show me?"

He stepped back and raised one hand, as if catching hold of the air itself. The worlds began to vibrate and hum. I threw myself across the immaterial mist of the Grey, feeling the same cold scream rip through me as brilliance burned me away. I lunged up to my feet, my office swamped and throbbing with the mirror-mist and aglow with lines of light and force. The ache in my chest grew hot.

Grey things trailing fire darted in and swarmed me, trying to cocoon me in their glowing threads. I struck at them, bending the edge of the Grey around me, and flung them back into Sergeyev's face.

"Get out!" I shouted, lashing my fists against the swarming Grey between us. A swollen blue arc spanned across my thrumming chest and arms, bowing outward as I raised my arms again and brought them down against the cloud of fiery creatures.

I felt as if I'd smashed my arms against a cement wall which reverberated, then dissolved to gritty, unstable brick. Two masses of force collided between us, shook and toppled with a crack of thunder and a stink of burned sewage. Then it crumbled away, the flames dying in an instant. Sergeyev's eyes glared at me though the haze and vanished. The world crashed back into its normal shape, thinly blurred at the edges.

I collapsed forward, landing half in my chair and half across the desk. My forehead smacked against the blotter. My arms and chest ached and burned and I swallowed again and again, tamping down the urge to be sick. Broken glass tinkled in the hall and outside. I forced myself to breathe in and out with care, settling myself around the dissipating ache centered in the knot of Grey between my breasts. Cool air coursed over my back from the broken window behind me. In a moment—or maybe it was ten minutes—I looked up and saw a face peeping around the edge of my shattered door glass. The receptionist from Flasch and Ikenabi. I waved a flopping hand to her.

She squeaked, "Are you OK? Sounded like an explosion out here."

"Uh … one of my clients … slammed the door pretty hard on his way out."

"Oh. OK. You sure you're all right?" She probably thought I was crazy, or that my clients were. I expected I'd see their offices up for lease inside six months.

"I'm fine. Honest. I just—I need to get the glass fixed," I finished.

She perked up at the thought of familiar action. "Oh! I know a board-up service. Should I … should I call them for you?"

I raised my eyebrows. "You would do that?"

"Well, yeah. If you want." A phone burred. She looked around. "Oh, no! Ohmigod, that's my phone!" she exclaimed, dashing away.

Alone, I slumped onto the desktop and tried to reorganize my brain. I was shaking. I felt torn apart and put back together with cheap glue and a lack of attention to detail. Everything seemed to ache or itch. My job was going straight to hell. But I didn't know what else to do, so I shut off the gibbering part of my brain and did what I'd been trained to do: I made phone calls.

I called the Danzigers and arranged to see them later—I had a lot of questions. Then I called Sarah, who said she'd talk to her brother as soon as she saw him and have him call me.

Twenty minutes later, men with plywood arrived to fix my door and window until I could get the glass replaced. The office felt close and dark without the windows.

In the new gloom, I picked up the Edward file and stared at it, resisting the work, aching all over. Unthinking, I reached up to rub the spot on my shoulder where Wygan's claws had dug into my flesh. The skin felt raw and hot as a sunburn. I winced as my stomach curdled around my lunch.

I'd been dancing in a minefield and was lucky to still have all my limbs. Alice scared me, but I understood what she wanted and how she wanted to use me to get it. As dreadful as Carlos was, I understood him a little, too. But Wygan I could no more understand than I could understand whales singing, and that frightened me most. I did not know what he wanted of me, but I suspected he was finished for a while.

He didn't think much of Alice, but I feared her ambition. I wasn't sure I could hold up against her a second time. I had to admit that challenging Sergeyev had been a mistake, and combined with the strange attack by the organ, whatever strength I had was near exhausted. I didn't know if it would return or if I wanted it to.

I knew my time was running out with Edward. Alice wouldn't hold off much longer. I had to use her agitation to my advantage and not be caught in the blast. But my ideas all assumed Edward's motivations were, essentially, human, and I knew that wasn't true. Ambition, power, and hate were the tools the vampires had lent me—all I had of my own was hope and a detective's steady plod. I didn't like my chances.

I buried myself in paper, trying to shut off my bodily aches and scratch the mental itch of almost-knowing. Much of the TPM file made no sense to me. I started looking for patterns, familiar words, oddities, pretty much anything that hooked to other information. TPM had fingers in lots of pies. It owned businesses and real estate all over Seattle and the near communities on the western side of Lake Washington, though TPM had nothing on the Eastside.

I started reading the list of businesses and something finally jumped out at me: TPM owned Dominic's nightclub.

Steve had said he was helping out the owner the day he spotted Cameron—except TPM wouldn't have asked him to come move furniture. Steve had given me the information just when I was also snooping around TPM's business. And Cameron had claimed Steve lied about knowing Edward, who had to work for TPM. So why had Steve called? Was he assuaging a prickly conscience, or had someone told him to give me Cameron? It had certainly pulled my attention off of TPM, and if Cameron hadn't had the insane idea to hire me, I'd never have looked further.

The tickling, nascent knowledge erupted into full form. In a short burn of energy, I scrambled for the fax of the corporate structure. Wygan had said it. The real estate lawyer had gone stone silent the moment I asked for it. But it was there on the fax: Edward Kammerling was TPM's founder and chairman of the board.

I lay back in my chair, burned out, eyes closed, and put it together. Only Gwen had said anything about TPM—she'd said it was his toy. The vampires found Edward's business activities uninteresting, or boring, but they were the key to his power base. A very sweet deal Edward couldn't afford to lose: only he had power in both the daytime and nighttime worlds, and that kept the other vampires in check. And that was why Alice wanted me—a daylighter with a foot in the dark—to take him out.

In the daylight world, he was at his weakest: just a businessman who had to hide from the light. But he might as well be in a fortress for all that the vampires could do to him there. Though I had a foot in each world, I had nothing to lose in the nightside, where his strengths were greatest. I had disturbed his foothold in the dark, and now I could threaten his foothold in the light as well. His ambition had bought him enemies, and it would allow me to move Edward any direction I pleased. So long as he didn't kill me first.

And supposing that Sergeyev didn't beat him to it.

I rolled my head, glanced at my watch and knew I was running late for my date at the Danzigers'. By the time I got to the Rover, I was dragging. My whole body ached as if I had the flu, a drawing fatigue radiating from my chest and through my limbs. Driving was not fun.

Mara answered my ring of the doorbell. "Harper!" She stopped and goggled at me. "You look flailed out. What's happened?"

"I—" was all I could get out. Then I stood there with words stoppered in my throat and couldn't think of what to say.

Mara blinked at me, then dragged me through the doorway. "Oh, my. Come into the kitchen, then. And don't be telling me this is tea-sized trouble. You look like you need a drink."

I stumbled after her into the kitchen. The house was quiet, warm, and welcoming. Only when the sensations were gone did I notice that I'd been cold, my ears numbed with a distant susurration, since Saturday.

Mara scrambled through a cupboard. "Just let me find the whiskey..."

I flopped into a chair at the kitchen table while Mara uncovered a bottle of Powers and poured us each a glass. She didn't offer water.

We both sat there and sipped our whiskey in silence a while as the kitchen beamed warm energy on us. The sick knot in my chest eased a little. Mara put her drink down and looked at me.

"All right. Tell me what it is."

I looked at my drink. "I think I need about three more of these first."

"Ah, no. Drunken revelations just leave you feeling worse during the hangover. Is this about ghosts?"

I hesitated, helplessness surging under my skin. I nodded and tried to wash the feeling down with the last of the whiskey. "Ghosts, vampires ... all that Grey crap."

Mara sat still, giving me an encouraging face.

"Why are they coming to me? These monsters, these ... whatever they are. My client—remember the guy with the organ?"

"Yes. You said he was Grey."

I nodded. "Some kind of ghost, I think. We had an argument in the Grey. He said he knew I could 'see the world.' He was furious at me for not doing what he wanted. Why do they think I can do something for them? How did I end up with every ghostly freak in Seattle?"

"Because you're a Greywalker. I warned you they would come. They hope that you can help them because you can see them and speak to them when others can't. As you can with Albert. Your arrival in the Grey must have woken a lot of creatures."

"Woken? Some of them have been lying in wait! As if I was late to an appointment." I found myself shivering.

Mara bit her lip. "Something worse than your ghost?"

I nodded, swallowing hard. "Saturday . . . ," I started. "Saturday night I interviewed vampires."

"For Cameron."

"Yes. And one of them—one of them dragged me into the Grey. He was—something worse." I couldn't get any more words out as I drowned in memory.

I sat at the kitchen table, pushing back an upwelling wail, gulping down air to force back the hard lump in my throat. It wrenched down into my chest and dissolved at a slow trickle when I caught my breath at last. My left hand hurt. I looked down and found Mara clutching it, staring at me and whispering curling blue charms under her breath. I tried to pull my hand away, but she wouldn't let go.

"What are you doing?" I demanded.

"Just holding on. Helping you hold on. You're doing much better now, aren't you? You look better."

I shuddered. "I'm all right."

"No, you're not. But you don't have to live through it again right now. Once was quite enough."

"Yes, but you don't know—"

"I don't need to," Mara stated. "Let's go find Ben. You'll not want to tell this story twice, and he needs to know."

She started to pull me up with her, but I winced in pain.

"You're hurt?"

"My skin feels roasted and I think I'm . . . broken somewhere."

"How did that happen?"

"I'm not sure. But I guess I need to talk to Ben about that, too."

I got to my feet, stiff as an arthritic spider, and crept after Mara. We went upstairs to beard the scholar in his den. Ben bustled about moving papers and books and getting us settled on the sofa, which sent up a puff of dusty book-scent as we sat down. Then he retired behind his desk and looked at us like an owl.

"Harper, you don't look so good," he said.

I nodded in slow motion. "I know."

If I'd felt better, I'd have laughed at the concerned look he gave me. "What's happened?"

I couldn't get an answer together at first. Ben looked at his wife with alarm. She shook her head.

"Is this a ghost thing?" he asked. "This problem? There is a problem, isn't there?"

"Yes," I said. "Yes. Something's wrong. The Grey isn't quite what we thought. And—and now there is a piece of it inside me."

They both jerked forward. Ben's desk restrained him, but Mara grabbed my hand again and drove an intense stare into me. I felt the track of her eyes.

"There is something there," she murmured. "But it shouldn't be. It shouldn't be like that."

Ben rose from his seat. "What is it?"

"It's sort of a knot," she answered, hesitating, then shaking her head in frustration. "I can't tell more. It isn't easy to look at. And I'm not really good at this sort of scrying." She leaned back and frowned into my face, still holding my hand. "Harper, how did this happen? What is this?"

I bit my lip. Ben teetered on the edge of moving forward, waiting. Mara squeezed my hand a little. She was doing it again and I wished it irritated me, but I was grateful.

I began again, feeling a bit anesthetized. "Saturday. I was working Cameron's case. Talking to vampires. One of them was—something I can't describe. Something beyond vampires and ghosts. Something worse. He shoved me into the Grey. He wants something from me and he called this a present. He tore me open and he put this thing inside me." I covered the ache with my free hand. "All tied up and tangled all over me. And the Grey things crawled all through me, ate me, t-touched—" I covered my face, shuddering at the remembered feel of the cold, hungry things sucking away everything. "They ripped me up, but I'm still here, and now I can't turn it off!"

Ben fell back into his seat and hung his head. "Harper. I—oh, God, is this my fault?"

Mara gave him a sharp look. "Oh, do shut up, Ben. Of course it's not your fault." She turned her eyes back to me. "And the other client, too. I told Ben about the dark artifact."

I nodded. I no longer felt like howling in pain and grief. "I went to look at it again today. It's gotten worse. It extruded some kind of tentacle toward me and I felt so sick I couldn't stand it. There's a set of red lines all around it now. It hurts to be in the same room with it. My client wants it. He threatened me if I couldn't get it for him, and he backed it up by trying to throw something at me in the Grey. And I—this thing inside me—batted it back and I screamed at him. There was sort of an explosion and then he was gone. Just gone. But not forever. He'll come back."

Mara raised her hand and started to bring it toward my chest. I shied from her, curling my shoulders forward.

"I shan't hurt you."

Wary, I let her touch me. I gasped when her fingertips pressed against me, pushing prongs of dense stillness into the center of the hard Grey knot. She looked at me a while, blank and thoughtful. When she sat back, pulling both her hands into her lap, her withdrawal left a void in the ache.

"It feels ... heavy, but elastic and smooth, like some kind of muscle—a diaphragm, perhaps. It bends if I push gently, but it won't yield to me, and the harder I push, the more it resists. It seems benign, if a little weak at the moment, but who knows what it does? It doesn't like to be probed."

Ben gave us both an incredulous look. " 'Doesn't like'? How can you say what it likes?"

"I don't know," Mara replied.

But I did. "It's alive in some way. I can feel it full of the things that live in the Grey."

Ben shuddered.

I shook my head. "I can't do this. I can't live with this. This is a nightmare. Cameron's case ... it's only going to get worse and I am not sure I can stand it. I believed he was a good guy, in spite of this. But he's a monster. They are all monsters. Inhuman, vile ..."

Ben spoke up. "Not vile. But the rest goes without saying, doesn't it? They're ghosts. They're vampires. But they look like us, so we think they are like us. And then they do something horrible, because they aren't like us. Ghosts are much closer to us, because they remember what it was like. Memory is all they are, really. And memory can hurt."

"But a vampire, I imagine, must learn to forget," Mara added. "Or surely they'll go mad. How could they live with themselves if they didn't change?"

"And Cameron is one," I said.

"Yes, but he's at the beginning," Mara reminded me. "He's still a nice boy who has a problem. You were right about that. He'll change, but you will probably never have to see it. Someday, when he's as old and twisted up with his new culture as those others, then he will be a monster. But do you want to make the decision to let him die now, confused and miserable? That's your choice."

"That's not fair," I said.

"No, it's not. You'll have to work that one out for yourself, I'm afraid. Can't put the apple back on the tree. So, what are we going to do now? That's the question."

"It's my problem," I said. "Not yours. I'm drowning. I've felt like something's sucking me dry ever since my client—ex-client, ghost, whatever—came to the office."

Ben perked up with a scholar's zeal for a puzzle. "Really? Before or after your argument?"

"After."

"Let me think, let me think..." He began shuffling through his papers and riffling books. "His attraction to the organ … physical manifestations and volition … action … Hmm." He glanced up at me from the pages of a thick tome and cringed a bit. "I'd say this guy's some kind of high-level willful spirit—that's a ghost who has volition and exercise of will—so he must be a revenant."

I shrugged, tired and wishing I had another glass of whiskey. "You'll have to explain that."

"Well, for instance, Albert's a sort of garden-variety willful spirit—some volition, but very limited will and action. But a revenant is literally that which survives. Most ghosts are kind of like etheric recordings. They don't have any will or personality—they just keep going through the motions of their lives or their message until they are released, or run down like clockwork. They're just shadows and echoes. A lot of them are just retrocognates."

I peered at him and interrupted. "Retro whats?"

"It means to know or be aware of something from the past. A medium can also retrocognate, under the right conditions. Some of them actually retrocognate when attempting psychometry."

"Ben," Mara broke in, "I'm sure Harper'd appreciate the layman's version, if you don't mind."

He looked sheepish. "Oh. Umm … Psychometry—well, I guess I'll get to that another time. But retrocognition … if you see a ghost walking through a place that no longer exists in this time and space, you're probably retrocognating, seeing stuff from the past. Do you ever experience that?" His eyes glittered.

"Sometimes," I responded, feeling more drained every second.

He nodded, then shook himself and continued. "All right, so the right medium could study the object and attempt retrocognition to tell you exactly what the connection is between your client and the parlor organ, but it would be very dangerous if it is as powerful a dark artifact as you two think."

"It's tangled up in the Grey and it seems to be drawing energy from the nexus nearby, like a battery charging up or something."

"Yes, Mara told me about it." He stopped to look at his wife, who smiled a tight smile and nodded for him to go on. "I wonder what the thing's purpose was."

"Not nice," I said. "It's black and red and very unfriendly. I think it sucks the energy out of everything that comes near it."

"Couldn't have been doing that for very long. Someone would have noticed."

"I noticed it," Mara muttered.

"You didn't say anything."

She shrugged and looked unhappy.

Ben made a rueful face. "I should call some of my contacts and see if they've noticed anything else."

I shook my head. "There's no time, Ben. I'm not doing very well, my ex-client is dangerous, and Cameron's problem may not be solvable. By me. The organ is getting worse. It's been drawing on the energy below the museum for ten months. And I don't know, but things seem to be accelerating."

"Good God! If it really is a battery, it's loaded. Anyone with control of it could wreak all sorts of havoc through the Grey."

"You're scaring me, Ben. I don't need to be any more scared than I am."

"I'm scaring *me*!" His eyes had grown wide. "Do you know anything about this ghost? Any guesses?"

"I don't know much. The last three owners of the organ, at least, are dead—all suddenly—and I suspect more. I have someone looking into its history, but . . ." I tossed up my hands feebly. "I don't know."

"A murderous ghost? That would require some big expenditures of energy and will."

"But with the organ acting as a collection and storage device, he'd have it, wouldn't he?" I asked. "And it seems to be getting worse since he arrived in my office. Just like I seem to be getting worse."

Mara looked between Ben and me and kept quiet, though her face was white and her eyes had turned dark.

"Presupposing he could access that power," Ben stipulated.

My brain engaged in the puzzle again, though I felt shredded. "If he could tap the power, why would he need me? Wouldn't he know where it was already?"

Ben waved his hands through the air. "Not necessarily. There are lots of cases where seeking ghosts can't locate even the most intimate items on their own. If he didn't know, was blocked from knowing, or had to establish some kind of path to the object before he could get to it, he could still benefit from its intimate connection to him, without being able to find it or go near it. But he wants it… Tell me everything you know or guess about him."

"I think he's European, judging from his speech. Russian or Slavic, if his name is any indication."

"He told you his name?"

"Yes, it's—"

"No! Wait! Write it down." Ben scrabbled around the cluttered surface of his desk for paper and pencil, then pushed them across to me, sending several cataracts of books and papers tumbling to the floor. "We'll just play it safe on this one, shall we?"

I shrugged and wrote the name down. "What do you mean, 'play it safe'?"

"I'm probably being paranoid, but some ghosts are attracted to their names. I don't think we want this guy looking over our shoulders, do we?"

TWENTY SEVEN

I would have laughed at our nervous glances, if I wasn't so damned scared myself. Albert haunted the doorway, as clear and solid to my Grey-sensitive sight as Sergeyev had been. Mara looked at him and made a sparkling, circling motion with one finger. Albert vanished.

"Albert will keep an eye out for us, I'm sure."

Ben coughed a tight laugh behind his books. "I hope so, but I'm afraid I'm not as convinced of our ghostly boarder's valor as you are, Mara."

"Now, be nice, Ben. You remember what happened the last time he got upset."

I looked at both of them.

"Turned Ben's desk upside down," Mara confided. "Terrible mess."

We both snorted relieved giggles.

Ben glanced at the paper I'd given him and started to chuckle.

"What's funny?" I asked.

"This guy's a sly little revenant. Generic Russian name. Basically the equivalent of Greg Stevenson. Not quite Ivan Ivanovitch, but close."

My brain was running in all directions. "It's got a Swiss bank account attached. Maybe he … stole it, somehow."

Ben whistled. "Clever. Damn, I wish I knew what he had up his sleeve."

"Yeah, but we don't have time, if you're right about that thing."

"You're right. You're right. I don't have any suggestions, though. Now we're starting to tread into the realm of magic, and that's Mara's sphere."

We all got quiet for a while.

"Look," Ben started again. "We know he wants to gain control of the organ and that can't be good. He's a revenant, and although he's got access to a big store of power, he can't just go flinging it around. Every time he does anything, he draws power. If he has plans for the dark artifact, he'll want it fully charged, so he's not going to do something until he's ready to play his cards. He already blew some at your office, so I'd guess you have forty-eight to seventy-two hours before he's going to do anything more.

"In the meantime, be extremely careful, Harper. If you wear yourself down too far, you won't have reserves to oppose him with, and we don't know what the purpose of that ... thing in your chest is. I'm afraid our help has been inadequate."

I put up one heavy hand. "Ben, stop. Without you and Mara, I think something would have eaten me by now. You haven't always been right, but that doesn't mean you're always wrong. But I've got a question. If the organ is drawing power from the nexus and everything else nearby, why isn't it draining this house, too? The house is as bright as ever."

"I don't know."

Mara smiled at me. "It's got its own nexus, remember? It's off the grid, so to speak. Can't get to us from there."

"The grid," I whispered. "The energy structures Wygan showed me—that I can still see—they're the power grid of the Grey. I think he ... wired me into the Grey."

Mara blanched. "If you're attached to the grid which is feeding the organ, then it's feeding on you, too."

I screwed my eyes shut and felt the world pitch. I remembered the draining touch of the tentacle.

Mara continued. "And whatever happens to that nexus will also happen to you and everything else on that quadrant. It must be drawing you down all the time. That thing has to be gotten rid of before it kills you."

"What about you?"

"I have this house, and I shall be very careful about touching magic outside of it. Shan't be pleasant, but I'll survive."

Eyes closed, still shutting out the overlapping worlds, I asked, "What about the dark beast?"

Ben checked. "The guardian? What of it?"

"You said it would attack a threat. Why isn't it attacking me or Ser—him? Or the organ?"

Ben's voice was gruff and ragged. "The artifact is just a storage device. The guardian won't notice that. Remember the hierarchies of threat. The threat may need to be more immediate, more active. Maybe you or he need to be doing something to draw the beast to you, like a spider down a twanging web."

I nodded, opening my eyes. "I'll try not to be a fly. That … beast is more than I can handle right now."

Ben gnawed his beard, and the glare he turned at no one in particular was ashen black. "Be careful," he repeated. "Theory says most Grey things shouldn't be able to harm you physically, but—they have. I'm afraid I'm letting you down because we've left theory behind, and theory is all I know."

I glared back at him. "Don't. Leave blame for later. Let's just get through this."

Ben looked away, chewing his lip.

I got to my feet, feeling ninety years old. "I need a nap or something, if I don't unravel first. I've still got a lot to do."

Mara went down the stairs with me, glowering the whole way.

She stopped me in the hallway. "You're not ready for this sort of thing. I could just strangle whoever did this to you."

"I don't think you'd have much luck. I don't know what to do about this," I added, tapping my chest, "but I have other things to do first and I'll do them, so long as I can."

"You must be careful, Harper. You're a stubborn, hardheaded, scientific practicalist, and all of this seems like a nightmare to you that you hope will simply evaporate when you wake up. But you don't wake up from this."

I snorted. "I've learned that already. I just have to figure out how to get through without getting killed."

"What about Cameron? Are you going to quit his case?"

I sighed. "It could be moot. And please don't try to persuade me."

"I shan't. But there is something you should know. Because a vampire can lay a geas, he can also be put under one. You can bind them to a promise in the Grey. Do you understand?"

"I'm not sure."

She sighed. "Think on it. If you must deal with them, you may need to try. Do take care, though."

"I will."

I drove home and went to bed. My sleep was tossed by fragmented dreams and nonspecific discomforts. I woke as the sun was going down. Just like a vampire.

I sat on the living room floor and contemplated the unlit TV. Its blind, dark eye stared back. Chaos jumped into my lap and nosed her way under my sweater as I sat and thought.

I had no choice, since I wasn't smart enough or coward enough to give up. Rest and the quiet of the Danzigers' house had helped ease my exhaustion, but I still felt achy and itchy and ill, and I wondered if that was doom. I played with the ferret in a desultory and desperate way until she insisted on napping. I put her to bed, then put on comfortable clothes and went out.

The first place I went was Adult Fantasies.

Carlos was downstairs, glowering at the unfortunate Jason while a firestorm of black fury whirled around them. Jason cowered, drawing in on himself.

"I'm sorry, I'm sorry, I'm sorry . . . ," the boy whined. I cringed.

Carlos's reply dripped scorn. "Yes. You are. Just clean it up and keep your wretched hands to yourself or I'll tear them off at the wrist."

Jason looked near to gagging on fear. He stumbled backward and bolted for the stairs as Carlos released him from his glare. Then the vampire turned it on me. It struck like a stone, ringing through my ribs, and I started to fold my shoulders inward. He raised his line of sight to my face and cut the intensity, cocked his head and flicked an eyebrow.

"Blaine."

I forced myself forward. Revulsion and the residual pain in my chest urged me to draw away.

"I'd like to speak with you."

He nodded and waved me toward the office. Passing him sent cold shudders through me.

The pierced Goth girl was rummaging about in some boxes. She looked up as we entered.

"Leave that," Carlos ordered.

She shrugged. "OK." I envied her lack of sensitivity. We watched her geishalike shuffle as she left, apparently impervious to the effects of Carlos's presence.

"Sit down."

I sank into a chair. Carlos settled himself behind the desk, then raised his eyes to mine. They had no light in them, and I shivered as he waited for me to speak.

"I need to meet with Edward. Can you help me do that?"

Carlos sat back, his face blank, just glowering for a while. At last he said, "Yes."

"When and where?"

"On Wednesdays, he holds court at the After Dark."

"That's in Pioneer Square, isn't it? I've never been there."

A cruel humor flickered in the blackness of his eyes. "Not many daylighters have. He'll see you. I'll take care of it."

"What time?"

"Never before ten."

"I need as many of Edward's enemies, malcontents, or neutrals there as possible. Can you accomplish that?"

"My pleasure."

"Thank you. I have an unrelated, professional favor to ask you also."

Again the silent gaze pierced me. I sympathized with Jason.

"There is an object I'd like you to look at, as a specialist."

He raised an eyebrow. "A specialist in what, do you believe?"

"Necromancy."

His brows drew down and the force of his personality bore on me like a toppled column. He growled deep in his throat and my body began to quake, the vibration of his fury beating against me. I swallowed hard and began to talk fast through my constricted throat.

"I need the services of a necromancer and you're the only one I know of. No one told your secrets. I guessed from what you told me before. I swear it."

He drew back a little. "And you need one for what?"

"I need to know the history and source of a dark artifact—necromantic, probably. Interested?"

He sat back and withdrew his fury, though a press of darkness remained. "You're a fool."

"I have no choice," I confessed, and hoped I had not made a bad guess about the Byzantine workings of his mind.

"Are you desperate enough to submit to me? I might demand a price you would prefer not to pay."

I was shivering. "You might. Do you intend to?"

He fell silent and stared into me. Streamers of light and darkness wove between us and brushed over me and I let them, though my insides clutched in fear. They slid over the knot with a chill pang of curiosity and withdrew.

He narrowed his eyes with the specter of a curious smile. "Not this time. When and where?"

"Tomorrow, at the Madison Forrest Historical House. We'll need to discuss your information with a friend, too. A witch."

He raised an eyebrow. "A true witch? Not one of those soft, powerless, New Age idiots?"

"A real witch."

"It's been a long time."

I said nothing.

He lowered his head in a half nod. "After sunset, tomorrow."

I stood up and so did he. I didn't offer my hand. "Thank you."

He stepped closer. I wanted to recoil, but didn't dare. He leaned over me. "Something of power is turning in you. Yet you seem ill." He reached out and swept something from my hair and shoulder, drew his hand down the line of my sternum without touching me. He brought a writhing piece of darkness to his face and breathed in the scent of it. "You reek of dark powers mixed with light. Have you touched the artifact?"

"No, but you could say it touched me."

He rubbed the slip of shadow between his fingers. "Disturbing. This can't be as it is." Then he wadded the shadow up and tucked it into his pocket, as before.

"I'm not pleased with it myself," I answered.

"Be wary, Blaine."

I lifted a cynical eyebrow. "And trust you at the same time?" I turned the topic. "How will we find you tomorrow?"

"I'll find you." His eyes glittered. He grinned at me and I felt as if those savage white teeth tore into my flesh. "I'll always know the smell of you now." I shuddered.

I was glad to leave his presence. I walked through the night, straight toward Alice.

She narrowed her eyes as I approached across the bar and smiled furious hunger. Sparks of violent yellow and red danced around her. "You have played far too close. I've had to expose myself in covering you. I had better not come to regret it."

"I'm too tired to fence with you. If you want to exploit the opportunity, be in the After Dark Wednesday night about nine thirty."

"Who told you about After Dark?"

I smiled with all the cold in my heart and didn't answer. Her icy acid hate slashed a storm against me, ringing off the beating Grey thing within. My knees trembled, but I stood it, somehow.

"When I'm done," I said at last, "you'll have your chance. If you move too early, you'll tip your hand, so be patient."

"Patient? I have been nothing but. And if you are double-crossing me—"

"What good would that do? I won't have a single friend in the room. In fact, you'll be the only one there who doesn't already have reason to take my head off."

I paused and turned a bit away. "Maybe I shouldn't bother. I can probably stay far enough away from you to live to a reasonable age. And I can't trust you, anyhow. You'll probably be first in line to exercise all those threats you've made."

I started to walk. Alice snagged my arm, sending heat and black ice through me. "Are you backing out now?"

I wrenched my arm from her grip, surprising us both. "Why not? What's to stop you?"

"I've said I wouldn't harm you if you did as I instructed."

"And I have, but all you've done is complain about how I haven't. So I'm screwed, aren't I? Forget it."

Alice growled.

I turned back to her and stared her in the eye, pushing against the Grey as hard as I could, hoping I had it right. "All right. Then promise that you won't harm me if I help you get to Edward. So long as I stay out of your way, you leave me alone. Promise me that."

Infinite cold bore through me as she stared. When she spoke, her voice had dropped low and resonant. "I promise I won't harm you so long as you help me get to Edward, and stand aside."

I smiled at her and turned away again before she could reconsider.

She stared at me as I left, and I felt it all the way down my spine.

TWENTY EIGHT

Tuesday started out raining. Even though I felt weak and calcified, I ran until my chest hurt from something purely physical for the first time in days. My body was fine but I was falling apart in all other ways. I ran on, amazed that I could, considering how often I had thought of simply stopping over the past few days. And I got furious with myself for my self-pity and self-doubt. I was still afraid, still weak and unsure and in the midst of the unknown, but if I stood still, there was only one possible end. At least, going forward, I stood a chance, however small.

I ran. Sweat and rain washed away my stupidity and despair. I wanted to stay in the clean downpour until everything washed away, but I had made a choice and I would stick to it.

From the office, I called the curator of the Madison Forrest House and persuaded her I needed to see the organ that night. She agreed to let us in at nine, though she was not pleased. With another phone call, Mara agreed to come, too.

I chased down some more prosaic business, keeping my mind busy, and was interrupted by a call from Will.

He sounded tired. "Hey, Harper. I checked up on that Tracher organ some more."

"That was quick."

"A lot of the records have been computerized over the last few years and I know the right people to call in Europe. Anyhow, I don't know what your client wants it for, but that organ is a fake-up."

"Totally fake? It looked old."

"Parts of it are too old, actually. The frame and action numbers didn't match. There's some additional paneling behind the mirror and over the pipes which is older than the case and shouldn't be there at all. According to Tracher, the frame came from an instrument that was damaged in a fire in Amsterdam in 1923. The case was written off by the insurance company and sold to a furniture jobber. He probably installed the action, which came from another organ built in 1902. But there's no way to tell."

"Which part is the 'action'?"

"In this case, just the keyboard—the rest wouldn't have fit. Whatever your client told you about the instrument, it's probably not true. The organ disappeared for a while and finally turned up again in a Swiss estate auction in 1957, where it was bought by the last owner of record, a G. Sergeyev of Bern. I tried to track him down, but the best I could do was a news article about his death in 1960. He doesn't seem to have had any relatives to inherit the organ, so I don't know what happened to it between 1960 and when it was shipped out of Oslo."

My ghostly client's clothing and speech predated the 1950s, so he certainly wasn't the man from Bern.

"Did the obit say what the last owner died of?"

"It was a news item, not an obituary. He was crushed by a trolley. There's not a lot else, except a partial provenance on the organ from the estate auction, but it's completely bogus. It claims the family—Mandon was their name—was the original owner, but they only had it thirty-three years, at the most, and that hardly makes it an heirloom. And there's one creepy thing: the Mandons died of asphyxia from a gas leak in the house. That's, what, five owners who all died in accidents."

I wondered how many more of its owners had met unexpected deaths. And what had happened to the organ during its lost years?

Will broke my silence. "Harper? Are you there?"

"Yes. My mind was wandering. Thanks, Will, that's helpful."

Will sounded grim. "Good, because I wanted to ask you a favor now."

I had trepidations. "Sure. What do you need?"

"This fake provenance got me to thinking about some things at work, so I looked into them. And I need to talk to the police."

"What sort of things?"

"I don't want to go into it yet. I had the impression you would know who to talk to, though. Do you?"

I didn't have to think about that. I gave him the number of a detective I knew at SPD—the most honest cop I had ever met.

"Thank you."

"Hey. Call me later?"

"Sure." He hung up, sounding distracted.

I wondered what Will had found to upset him, but had no time to explore the question. I gathered my stuff and headed to the Danzigers'; I wanted to talk to Mara before we met Carlos.

Mara and I were sitting in the living room about an hour later. Adjusting to the change in the Grey was not easy, and I had just made a hash of the same simple exercise of moving in and out at will.

Dizzy and frustrated, I pounded on the arm of the sofa. "Damn it! Why can't I do it when I want to? I can fall in and out when I'm not thinking of it, but I can't do it when I'm trying."

"You're still fighting."

"It just looks so different. It feels different."

"But it hasn't really changed. It's you that's changed. When you don't think of it, you've no difficulty. It's when your mind is in between you and the Grey that you have troubles."

"I can't not think."

Mara leaned forward and caught my eye. "You can stop fighting it. You must. We've been wrong about so much, but of this I am certain. You must accept what it is and that it's part of you. When you're fighting it, it's like a snarled rope that tightens and knots up with every tug. Relax and the rope relaxes, too. I can see it happening."

I frowned at her.

"I can see that knot in your chest if I try. It ties you to the Grey, and the harder you fight, the more taut it goes. When you simply let it be, it spreads out and you become more Grey."

"I don't want to be more Grey!"

She sighed. Shivering spears of honey gold light combed through her hair and lit the wall behind. "I am sorry, Harper. You haven't that choice anymore. Accept what is and the rest will follow. Then this will all be easy—or at least easier. Coming and going, pushing and peeking—things we've not thought of, even—will be as automatic as walking or swimming." She looked up at the beginning of sunset through the rain outside. "You are meant to be part of that world and you can only exercise the powers you have when you accept that."

I turned away to look at the soggy sunset, rubbing my hands over my face and wiping off the heavy frown that had settled there. Tension and exhaustion bore on my shoulders. I leaned my cheek on the sofa back, watching the shafts of sunlight that broke through the clouds turn pink, while the vibrant yellows and whites of the house nexus glimmered like a fairy fence between. The low, bleak cloud cover looked like the storm-mist of the Grey.

I heard Mara get up and walk out of the room. I was too tired to follow her. The floorboards sang as she returned and stopped near me.

"It's almost time to go. I made you something for tonight. I hope it will help."

I looked up at her.

Mara held out a small leather bag on a long thong. It reminded me a bit of the thing I'd seen peeking over Dr. Skelleher's collar.

"What is it?"

"It's a charm against dark things. It should help push back the organ's monstrousness a bit. Just a little thing, but can't hurt. Put it round your neck."

I shrugged and took it from her, dropping it over my head. The little bag plopped onto my sweater, right over the ache in my chest.

I gasped, feeling as if I'd suddenly breathed in clean air after a night in a smoke-filled bar.

Mara grinned. "Any use?"

"Yes."

"Brilliant. Tuck it away, though. I suspect your necromancer shan't like the sight of it."

"Why not?"

"Bit of a monster, himself, isn't he?"

"Maybe I should just wear it all the time."

Mara showed me a mock frown. "Not too sociable of you—wearing charms against your helper. Besides, it won't hold long if the artifact is drawing power. It's just a trinket."

She looked at the descending sun. "You'd best get going. Wouldn't be wise to let him get there first. I'll be along after I check on Brian and hand him off to Ben."

I braced myself and headed out.

The cloud cover contributed to an early darkness and the sky was lumpy black when I pulled into the wet gravel lot across from the Madison Forrest House. The scent of more impending rain thickened the air. I sat in the Rover, waiting and watching the front door.

An orange and green taxi pulled up in front of the museum. Carlos rose out of the backseat and stood looking at the building a moment while the taxi drove off. From this distance, his presence didn't affect me. He turned his head left and right, then was still. He whirled and walked straight toward me. It startled me and I jerked in my seat.

He strode to my side of the truck and looked in. He beckoned.

Coming to his sign seemed like I was ceding control to him and I'd done quite enough of that lately. I didn't think it would be a good idea, either. On the other hand, if he wanted to harm me, he'd had plenty of chances before this.

I rolled down the window. "You made it," I said.

"Yes. Where's your witch?"

Mara pulled in just as I started to answer. He turned to look and I got out of the truck while his back was turned.

Mara seemed to tumble out of her car. Her hair was a bit wild and her eyes were sparkling. Holding on to her purse, she rushed to the side of my truck.

"Sorry I'm late. Someone didn't want to go to sleep." She looked Carlos straight in the eye with no sign of discomfort. "Hello. Ready to go?"

He nodded. Then he looked at me. "No introduction?"

"Carlos," I started, glancing toward Mara, "this is ..." She gave a sharp shake of her head behind Carlos's shoulder. "... our witch."

He frowned, making my innards churn. He glanced back at Mara and nodded at her.

She smiled and spoke in a pleasant tone. "Tricky bastard, aren't you?"

He went still. Then one side of his mouth turned upward. "I am."

"Shall we go?" Mara suggested. "You can almost see the bloody thing glowing from here."

We all turned and stared toward the house. The upstairs parlor windows seemed to have become red glass. Shadow-light limned the trees in the yard a gory crimson to my Grey-adapted sight. I did not want to enter that building. I shot a look at Mara, who made a face and took my arm in a warm grip. With a steady stride, she walked with me to the gate. Carlos followed behind.

I rang the intercom and, after a delay, the curator let us in. "You mind if I don't come up?" she asked. "As long as I'm stuck here, I've got some paperwork to get through. Just buzz the intercom when you leave and I'll lock up. OK?"

Her relaxed attitude surprised me, until I noticed both Carlos and Mara looking very hard at her. More than one tricky bastard in this lot.

Once she was gone, we started up the stairs. At the top, I stopped and swayed, momentarily nauseated. Mara supported my elbow. Carlos brushed past both of us and opened the parlor door.

A rush of horrors poured out of the room. I jerked away before I realized I had seen more than felt them. My heart raced and I felt ice on my spine, but I could stand it.

Mara nodded at me and led the way into the parlor. Carlos was a few feet in front of the organ, staring at it. He turned his head to glance at us. An ugly smile oozed across his face.

"Amazing."

"Disgusting is more like," Mara replied. She pushed me into a chair as far from the organ as possible. "Let's get on with it."

Carlos shrugged his eyebrows and turned back to face the organ. Mara stepped back a pace and made a few sparkling signs in the air behind him. They rained a curtain of mist and white pickets. I could hear Carlos muttering, and a thin, sour odor threaded through the room. Mara walked in an arc behind him, creating a shimmering semicircle stretching from wall to wall and cutting off the pulsing miasma of the organ's aurora of light, shadow, reek, and noise.

Nightmare faces and boiling Grey began to heave into a panorama around the instrument. I saw Sergeyev's face appear for a moment. His mouth opened in a silent scream and then was sucked backward into the organ. A kaleidoscope of other faces followed, shattered fragments of terror. I didn't recognize any of them. A weird, muted chorus of grim cries and muttering rang around Carlos. His shoulders heaved once in a while and I saw his hands flicker before him. Otherwise, he was still.

A gust of black and red light burst from the organ above the keyboard. Carlos ducked, and it shattered on the circle of Mara's magic. Her shimmering sigils faded and the room was filled with a sudden howling and chittering. Carlos stepped forward and laid both his hands on the keyboard.

The organ shrieked in agony. Then came a roar, growing around the organ, pushing against Carlos like a bodiless wind. A fetid stink rose with the sound. I started up again, ready to bolt, the pulse of the Grey in my chest fluttering with my racketing heartbeat and twisting like a knife. Mara backpedaled and grabbed me by the shoulder. Her eyes were wide, and I thought she was on the verge of breaking and running herself. Her breath was loud.

Carlos raised his hands and slashed out to both sides. Silence. The Grey aura around the instrument faded, collapsing to its writhing red and black gorgon's corona again. He eased back until he had crossed the line Mara had made; then he turned and walked to us. His eyes were ablaze with a frightening excitement.

"Up," he ordered.

I got up, and he herded us to the door and stood on the threshold. "Now go," he said.

I started to turn, feeling exhausted and ill and wanting to leave.

Mara held on and remained facing him, a rock against his wave of influence. "No."

He raised an eyebrow, and the force of his demand hovered like a black swarm.

Mara glared at Carlos. "You can't push me as easily as that, Carlos. I'll not let you have it."

"You can't stop me."

"Common sense will stop you. It is necromantic, isn't it?"

His bladed half grin came back. "Why else would I want it?"

TWENTY NINE

Standing in the hall, Mara glimmered as she opposed Carlos. "If you try to take it, you'll uncork the bottle and let the genie out. Even you couldn't put the cork back in fast enough. You saw the size of the power nexus it's feeding on. It's stuffed full of energies just wild to escape. You can't use it here, so you'd have to move it. But you can't move it without unleashing the energy stored in it. It's too ripe."

He glowered and gleamed black. Something shimmered between them. I was too drained to try to see it or understand.

Mara continued. "I imagine there's only one person who can control the energy cascade that will start the moment it's disturbed. Am I right?"

Carlos stilled.

Her voice glistened and resonated, throbbing through my bones. "Answer me!"

He bared his teeth and snarled at her. His immaterial black cloak billowed ire. "Don't try to command me, witch."

"Don't be stupid!" she snapped back. "Do you want to destroy the whole fabric of energy here? That would be worse for creatures like you than for me, and I don't care to contemplate how bad I'd have it."

Carlos snarled one last time and took a step back from her, his blackness subsiding. He cast a glance over his shoulder toward the organ.

He growled. "You're right. It's too dangerous. But we can't let it remain for someone else. We'll have to get rid of it."

Mara objected. "We don't have enough reserves to contain and control it right now."

"Of course not." Carlos reached back and closed the parlor door, then brushed past both of us and headed down the stairs. I rocked back from the force around him.

Mara led me away. I felt muzzy-headed, dazed, sore, and sick. The cold ache in my chest had returned.

As we reached the foyer I asked, "Are we leaving?"

"Yes."

I gave a wobbling nod, so tired I wanted to lie down and whimper.

Out the side door, we walked back to the parking lot. Mara pushed me down into the Rover's passenger seat while she ran back to ring the curator to close up. A cool drizzle cleared away some of my nausea with the last whiff of the organ's stink as the night breeze blew gusts of soft rain into my face.

Mara returned, looking concerned. "Are you going to be all right, Harper?"

I nodded, taking slow breaths to hold down my dinner.

She looked at her watch. "We'll have to make this quick. I have a class in the morning. So," she added, turning to Carlos, "tell us about it."

Carlos folded his hands and began to speak in a low voice. The rain brushed around him.

"It is necromantic. A much older artifact has been incorporated into the structure, behind the mirrored panel."

"The old wood," I mumbled.

Carlos made a small motion of his head. "That is a box. The bones and teeth have been built into the decoration, making the substance of the deceased part of the instrument."

"What?" I asked, appalled.

His mouth quirked. "A necromantic artifact incorporates the substance of the dead, both body and spirit. The revenant is commanded by whoever controls the artifact built with its mortal remains. A door in the structure allows the spirit to enter and leave at its master's bidding."

"Could the mirror be the door?" I asked.

"Yes. It's closed now, but it was open and the spirit escaped while his last master was unaware or helpless. While the spirit was at large, the artifact was moved. The spirit killed his master and stole his name, but then he became lost. Now he wanders, still bound to the artifact, unable to be free, but also unable to return unless he's summoned or comes face-to-face with his body's prison. There's no one to summon the spirit, so he tries to find the artifact and become his own master."

"But the museum owns the organ—"

"Ownership is nothing." Carlos frowned, composing his thoughts. "The box is the original vessel, transferred from object to object, wrapped in layers of spells and wood, to hide the spirit from himself and others. He's strong and autonomous—he was a man of power while he lived and his masters rightly feared his spirit. When the instrument came to the museum, he gained the power it absorbed from the nexus. He couldn't find it directly, but he had the energy to manipulate the world again. He began to hunt the owners down and kill them."

My stomach heaved. "All of the owners?"

Carlos nodded. "Every one but this one. He killed most of his masters, as well. Each time he thought he might be free at last, and each time he was wrong. His bitterness runs deep. His future plans are dark with more deaths."

Mara put a steadying hand on my shoulder. "Who was this spirit when he lived?"

Carlos gave her a narrow look. "A mage. It would be foolish of me to say his name here. Even his adopted name is strong enough to summon him while we're this close to his artifact."

"Then how old is the artifact?"

"The box is about seven hundred years old. The rest doesn't matter. The spells and rituals worked into the artifact protect the remains from degradation until they're removed from the structure," Carlos explained. "Then they decay at once. If all the remains were removed, the spirit would be to free to leave this world. But even then, so long as a single angle of the structure remains intact, the artifact retains its stored energy, which is considerable now.

"Undirected, the energy will burst outward, like water from a dam, and destroy anything that resists it. It will blast anything that draws upon or constrains these energies. For you, witch, it would mean pain, loss of powers for a time—maybe forever."

Carlos looked at me. "For you ..." He reached toward me and I leaned away. His hand came close; then he jerked back as if burned and pulled away with a glare at Mara.

"You dared?"

"Yes, I did," she shot back. "And you know it's not against you, but that thing up there."

Carlos nodded a sort of bow to her.

Mara nodded back. "And what about Harper?"

"I don't know." He looked at me again. "It might kill you. It might just wash through you, or it might burn you to a husk. It will be interesting to find out, if I survive."

I shivered and balled a fist over my sternum. "How funny that this thing I don't even want—that one of you stuck in me—is going to kill me. But what if your theoretical dam doesn't break?"

The darkness in Carlos's eyes raked me as he shook his head. "It can't be stopped without dismantling the artifact."

"What happens if the ghost gets to the organ first?"

"Then he'll execute his plan."

I dragged my feet up onto the seat in front of me and huddled like a struck child.

"We'll have to destroy it," Mara said.

Carlos chuckled, the sound of bones rattling. "As if it were that simple. It must be done with great control. You and I together, witch, would not be sufficient."

"How many more would you need?" she asked.

Carlos thought aloud. "We require mages adept at unweaving the strands of death. Of necromancers, we'd need only one more—but there are no more nearby. Witches' strength runs in the wrong direction. One could hold it, but we'd need a dozen to break it."

My brain wasn't entirely frozen, however cold I felt. "How many vampires would it take?"

Carlos and Mara both stared at me.

"What?" Mara asked.

"How many vampires?" I repeated, my mind filled with a shape of information but not the information, itself. "They must have some powers over death, since they're the undead," I reasoned.

Carlos frowned. "I wouldn't have thought ..."

"Why not?" Mara responded. She turned and stared at Carlos. "Would it work?"

"After the spirit is released ... it might."

I laid my head on my knees, drained and battered by ideas conversely helpful and unwelcome. Wygan's voice echoed through my mind, saying that his "gift" would keep me alive, and I gave a bitter laugh.

We parted ways to plan and prepare. I chose to drink and sleep and make my preparations in the morning.

By Wednesday evening, my choices had dwindled down to what to wear for my meeting with Edward. I ended up in a slinky dress and heels and felt I was a bit overdressed for my own funeral. I'd discovered that my evening jacket wouldn't cover the holster, but the pistol would do me no good against vampires. I missed it, though. I felt less my own master than Sergeyev—whatever his real name—must have felt.

Cameron was waiting outside my office building. His eyes widened and he gave me an appreciative smile. "You look terrific."

My voice came out cold. "This is not a date, Cameron. I feel like a tethered goat."

He followed me up the stairs. "Are you nervous?"

"Why?"

"You just seem upset or something. You look funny, too."

"You just said I looked nice."

"I mean, you look … hard. Armored, maybe."

I threw myself into my desk chair. "Lovely." I felt anything but. "OK, here's the deal. I said there was something new we had to discuss."

"Yeah. What's up?"

"Things have changed."

"You're dumping my case, aren't you?"

"Would I be dressed like this if I was? No. I admit I wanted to, but it's no longer an option. And it's ethically repugnant."

He started to get up from the client chair. "But you don't want to work for me anymore. I understand."

I snapped, "No, you don't. We have something in common. We both had no idea what vampires were really like when we made our contracts. I've had some of that reality thrust upon me in unpleasant ways. But I am not becoming like you. I still have to live in a human world, by human rules. What you are and what you must do to survive are things I cannot stretch my mind over without going crazy."

He whispered, "That's what I felt," and sat down again.

"I know. That's why I'm not quitting. Besides having a contract, I'm as screwed as you are, and I need your help as much as you need mine."

I told him about Wygan and the Grey thread. He stared at me in shock.

"It's all my fault."

I rolled my eyes. "Everyone wants to take credit. It's my own fault. It can't be undone—or I don't think it can—but that doesn't mean it can't be dealt with. But that's for later. For now, we fix your problem and maybe some of mine, but it's dangerous."

The plan was simple enough, but I half expected Cameron's head to bulge under the speed and density of the information I poured into him. He goggled at me at first, frowning, asking questions. At the end, he just shook his head and looked dazed.

"That's ... seriously wack."

"Best I can come up with. If I've accounted for all the factors, if I can persuade him it's to his advantage, we may all survive."

"What if he won't help? What if he doesn't see it as you do?"

"Then we run and hope we beat the blast. Which is why you will not be in that room tonight. Find a place to lurk where you can watch the front door."

"What am I supposed to be watching for?"

"Me. Once Edward comes in, I expect to be finished with him one way or another in less than an hour. If I don't come out the front door within two, I want you to come looking for me. Do you understand?"

"Yeah. I get to be the Seventh Cavalry."

"That's the plan."

"Well, I'm not thrilled with it..."

"Nor am I, but face-to-face is the only way."

"What if he just—you know?"

"Punches my card? He could, but it's a fair bet he'll hear me out. That room will be full of his enemies, watching and waiting for a chance to take him out. Edward is not stupid. I'll be there under protection, a defenseless daylighter begging a favor. Killing me in front of that audience would be like firing on Fort Sumter. You, on the other hand, he might be able to get away with, if he's still pissed enough to try it."

Cameron didn't look happy, but he agreed to it. We left my office and strolled down the streets until we were half a block from the After Dark. The only sign was a small brass plaque next to iron gates and an iron-railed circular staircase leading down. Cameron squeezed my shoulder for encouragement, not thinking. My knees buckled as the black corners of the Grey folded over me in acid-trip lights.

He jerked his hand away, contrite and apologizing. I caught my breath and told him to get going. I walked down the stairs alone.

My heels rang a hollow clacking on the white marble stairs. The soles of my shoes slid on the cool stone. The foot of the stairs opened into a small marble foyer. It was like a very expensive crypt. A glossy pair of black-enameled doors faced me. I tapped on one of them.

The door swung back, silent as a 1910 movie. A dark man in an equally dark suit looked me over and beckoned me in. As the door closed behind me, he glanced at a list.

I was quivering as the surface of reality rolled beneath my feet. I kept my voice low. "Harper Blaine."

He nodded and held out a hand to take my jacket. He raised an eyebrow when I refused.

"I don't want to catch cold."

One corner of his mouth turned up, but you couldn't call it a smile. He led me through another set of doors, into the club proper, and pointed to a table.

"Your patron awaits." His voice was crushed glass. His mouth made another jump; then he turned and left me standing on a curve of red carpet. Glances tore me. Quick movement pulled my attention around to Alice, sidling to intercept me. I stepped into the room before she got close. Her glower cut a swath of cold down my back.

I presented an outward cool as I crossed the room, but a sick sense of impending doom writhed in the pit of my stomach. Every figure wore an outline of glowing threads, and shadows crept or stretched everywhere. Pushing back against the tidal swell of Grey was hard. I picked out faces I recognized in the crowd, illuminated by their strange lights. I didn't spot Wygan among them, but I almost stopped and stared when I saw Gwen cringing against a small table in a wash of faded green. She looked more miserable than I felt. I shook myself and completed the long walk to Carlos.

I slid into the seat that faced the door and breathed a moment's relief. Carlos and I sat almost side by side, and I could feel the weight of his darkness press over me.

"Is he here yet?" I asked.

"Not yet."

"Point him out to me when he makes his grand entrance."

"You'll know."

I tried to compose my thoughts, but they were fluttering moths in the lamplight. "What do you think of our chances?" I asked.

"Edward's no fool when it comes to his demesne."

I started to speak again and Carlos flicked his fingers in a warning signal that stroked a cold fire across my cheek.

"Himself," he muttered.

I looked from the corner of my eye toward the door.

He wasn't big like Carlos; he was slight, but his slenderness lent an illusion of height, and the fiery threads around him leapt upward, flaming in every color, tangling like sensual snakes in every other thread they touched. Sarah's James Bond description was apt: thick, dark hair over pale skin and sharp eyes, and a visible cruel streak wide as a door. Most every head in the room turned his way, even if only for a moment, acknowledging the presence of the lord of the city. I didn't allow my own head to turn, nor did Carlos.

Edward moved out of the doorway, breaking the tableau. He circled the room at a stroll, clockwise. Carlos gave a low, cynical chuckle as he watched.

"Doesn't much like this situation, does he?" I observed.

"You never know what Edward thinks until the knife is in," he warned, rising to his feet.

Edward made his way to us at last, pausing within a spreading pool of cold. Carlos glowered at him. Edward flicked a glance over the bigger vampire as if brushing away a fly.

Carlos stepped aside. "Edward."

The other grudged a tiny nod. "Carlos. Still with us."

"Eternally."

Edward gave a small sound of amused disgust. "Always angry. Such a waste, always living in the past."

"The past and the future are all now, to me."

"As ever."

Carlos spread ripples of fury. His lip curled, showing a glittering, sharp fang.

Edward locked his gaze with Carlos's. A withering, icy electricity raised the hair on my arms. "There will be another time."

Carlos stepped back, then turned on his heel and walked away without looking back. I hoped he would stay close.

Edward slipped into the vacated chair. He looked me over with a glance much warmer than the one he had turned on Carlos. It was as if he had thrown a switch. The combination of eroticism and revulsion I felt was unsettling.

"Ah, the detective. A friend of my unfortunate mistake."

"An employee of Cameron's," I corrected him. "I came to see if I can help you with a problem and repair Cameron's situation at the same time."

An anonymous server presented us with drinks. I had no idea what the little glasses held which gleamed like oil in my sight, and I had no intention of finding out. I let mine sit on the table while Edward picked his up and sipped.

"Help me? I should have wiped the little insect off the face of the earth."

"You missed your chance to kill Cameron and face no consequences quite a while ago. There are more immediate problems now, but I know how you can solve them and the issue of Cameron all at once."

One of his eyebrows rose, and he glanced at me over the rim of the glass. I smiled away the sudden thrill of sick sweat and went on.

"Quite a few of your people seem to have axes to grind with you. One tried to persuade me to take you out, but I'm not suicidal or stupid. Your community wouldn't benefit and neither would my client. There is an outside threat to all of you, not just you, me, or Cameron. If you dispose of the threat, you save the community, resolidify your leadership position, and undermine your detractors. You also have the opportunity to force your enemies either to support you or so openly defy you that you can dispose of them without fear of reprisal."

He sat back, giving me a piercing look. "You hint at something, but you say nothing. You want me to be majestic, and yet it is you who've stirred up the muck for flinging. I gave you Cameron, but you continued to sniff and dig into my affairs. You expect me to be grateful? I could rip you open and have done with it all, right now."

Ice gripped my insides, but I pushed it back. "You could. But would it be wise in front of this audience, just to quell your own discomfort? Would it be wise to kill a creature as weak as me, who comes to you under the protection of someone they all respect and fear even more than you?" I flicked a finger at the roomful of vampires. "How could they trust you then? I've been told you're no fool, but it would be foolish to kill me under those circumstances. And when I have the solutions to your problems, as well."

"You speak of a crisis upon me, but I see none beyond your annoying pricking."

"Carlos is the only one of your people who could recognize the problem, and I imagine he stopped looking out for your interests after Seville."

He raised a cool eyebrow, though I saw the momentary flicker of his corona.

I smiled a little.

He laid the weight of his gaze on mine and tried to push me. The ache in my chest distracted me enough to wrench my line of sight aside just as he spoke. "Tell me what you know and how you came to know it."

I slipped into a shooter's concentration no wider than a bullet hole at twenty yards. I could not afford to miss this mark, nor slide under his control. "I'll tell you and give you the solution, but only for a price."

Edward ground his teeth. "You defy me? You bargain with me?" Surprise and outrage broke his pressure against me.

I centered my stare back on his and kept my voice low. "I came to help you, so you would help me. This room is filled with your enemies. If you harm me—a defenseless daylighter under Carlos's protection—they will have a cause against you to rally around, a match to the powder of their hatred and fear. They will attack you on every side. If you survive, your cat's-paws and your assistants and supporters at TPM will vanish. You'll lose your ability to control your empire in the daylight world and in the nightside as well. That's the real key to your power. That's why they came here tonight. That's why they helped me and then kept the mud stirred up. They want your head. I can't stop Alice and her cronies, but if you listen to my proposition and let me leave alive and unharmed, anyone who hasn't already made up their mind will have no reason to join her against you, and the rest will back you for their own good. Carlos cannot fight you, but he won't help Alice if you give him no cause. So, are you angry enough to cut your own throat while you cut mine, or do you want to listen a moment longer?"

Edward put his drink down and propped his elbows on the table. He rested his chin on his upraised hands and stared at me. The smolder level went up and so did the albedo of the Grey, thickening to snow-light cut with brilliant neon. Silence hung.

"For a woman, you have the most amazing pair of balls." He stretched one hand toward me and glided the back of his fingers down my arm.

A jolt of something that was not pure revulsion shot through my belly. It fought with the urge to gag, but my disgust was still stronger than his casual manipulations. I twitched my arm away from him and leaned back into my chair. "I'm not on the menu, Edward."

He withdrew his hand and re-propped his chin. "I'm intrigued. So speak your piece. I promise you no harm. Tonight, at least."

I nodded and began. "There is a sort of necromantic battery sitting on top of a nexus of the magic power grid—whatever you choose to call it—in this city, diverting and storing energy. It's become overloaded and unstable as nitroglycerin. Its previous masters are all dead, and it's come back into the possession of its ghost. He's a powerful and vengeful spirit and I know he can't be trusted. He won't be kind in his use of this power, or careful."

"Carlos told you of this?" The temperature around us dropped and the air thickened.

I barked a derisive laugh, though doing so hurt. "I found it myself. I only asked him to identify it. He wants nothing to do with it," I fudged. "But it has to be dismantled—and soon—by others with power, or it will collapse. The sudden release of this power on the creatures of the nightside would be like dumping an unrestrained overload of the Hanford reactor into Seattle's power grid in one blast."

Edward's face was stone. "And we would all burn like Hiroshima." He sat back. "I see. My world has shaken. I sit in the heart of my own domain, yet surrounded by enemies, threatened from within and without and nowhere to run. And I must help you and Carlos or I shall be lord of a blasted domain—if I survive at all."

"That's how I see it. You'll have to quell this bunch tonight with minimum damage. But I don't think you'll find that difficult if you get the right people on your side early. Once you neutralize the threat of the artifact, you're a hero. After that, the few enemies who remain will be anxious to either kiss the ring or fade into the woodwork. Then you mop up as you see fit."

Edward looked down, as if the plan lay on the table, then raised his eyes again. "I mend part of the rift between myself and Carlos and, of course, I solidify my position as a wise and just ruler by returning my protégé to the fold—which also repays my debt to you, I suppose."

"It is the sort of gesture that would make you damn near unassailable."

He sighed and sat back in his seat, stretching his legs out. He folded his hands in his lap. Then he chuckled. "I don't know how much of this circumstance you brought to bear and how much you merely took advantage of, but I bow to you. You're a better tutor than Machiavelli."

I sat silent.

"Very well." He shot a glance to the side and I turned my head to see Alice, blazing fury and glaring ice at me. "If I retain my head next week, I will assign Cameron a mentor until he is capable of looking after himself to that mentor's satisfaction. Now, tell me what you require to lay this ghost and his infernal device."

I felt Alice's frozen heat edging closer as Edward listened to what I knew of the organ. Then he turned and speared her with a look.

"Alice, fetch Carlos here."

Boiling cold fury, she stalked off and returned with the necromancer. Edward brushed her aside and turned his attention on Carlos. "Tell me of this artifact."

Carlos remained standing, unresponsive. A cold wall shimmered between them.

Edward glared back a moment. Then he shrugged and sighed, the wall shattering. "Carlos, I have agreed to do this thing, and I humbly request your help. Please. Tell me what you know."

Carlos let loose his unpleasant, feral grin and told him, with a gleam in his eye. I sat back and waited as they worked out their uneasy alliance and laid plans. At last I stood up, noticing that Alice had drawn back a few steps, but not far.

Edward rose to his feet. "I am in your debt for timely warnings. And for delivering my enemies into my hands. I shall do as I've promised, but you should leave now."

I was tired and sore from the twisting and battering of being in their presence. I started to turn away, but he reached out again and caught my wrist. I spun back around, racked by the touch of waking nightmare.

"You could be an asset to me, you know." His thumb stroked over the soft spot on the underside of my wrist. I wanted to pull away, but I didn't dare.

I clamped down on my jellied nerves and managed to keep my feet. "Thank you," I whispered, "but I'm no good without my independence." I eased my hand from his and made my way to the door. Stares, speculation, fury, and curiosity ripped into my flesh as I went. I heard Edward say "Alice ... " in a gleaming, razor voice, and I bolted the last few steps to put the door between myself and the swelling pressure of imminent violence.

Outside, a shadow clutched me and dragged me into its darkness. My knees gave. A clawed hand over my mouth stopped me screaming and I gagged as the bleak, ancient depths of the Grey closed in. He spun me into the dark, but the fire-outlined snake shape and bulking horror riding it were plain.

He let me go and loomed. "Lovely performance, Greywalker. You're advancing nicely."

"What do you want, Wygan?" I demanded, keeping myself upright only by clutching the stair rail at my back.

"Just came for the show, for the feast of their rage. Your little curtain-raiser was well done. My gift is serving very well. I'm pleased."

I croaked, "Pleased? I didn't do it for you."

He laughed obsidian shards. "Nonetheless."

A fury of sound shook the doors behind us, the Grey roiling and pitching in full storm. He laughed louder, washing himself in the roar and swell of chaos, fear, and anger flooding out of the merely material doors.

"Yes, you do well," he shouted over the tumult. "I'll look forward to our next meeting. You'll be everything I could have hoped!"

His laughter battered at me, taking on a drunken giddiness which rose to a shriek of delight. He stared at the doors, reaching out to them and drinking in the pandemonium that poured out on the flood tide of furious, twisting energy. I swung around the newel-post, shoving my way up from the Grey depths, and bolted, scrambling and stumbling, ripping my stockings, my knees, and my arms on the marble stairs.

I lunged upward, gasping, to escape whatever dreadful thing had come to life below. Arms snagged under my own and slammed me back into the other world's serrated blackness whipped by stabbing light and lacerating screams.

Cameron dropped me back to my feet across the street, huge maelstrom eyes staring into mine.

"Run!"

THIRTY

We ran like two deer flushed from cover. I'd lost my shoes somewhere and my legs and arms were scraped and bleeding, but we never stopped nor turned back to investigate the storm behind us.

In the office, I collapsed into my chair, shaking and gulping air. I felt sore, sick, wretched, and tired to death. Cameron sat still and kept quiet while I pulled myself back together.

Still shaking, but able to breathe, I looked at my bruised, bloodied limbs. "I'm kind of a mess." The world seemed unstable and prone to shimmer, lighting up with strange colors. I kept talking, just for the sound of a voice. "But I think we're all right."

"What do you suppose happened back there?" Cameron asked. "I had a weird feeling just before the screaming started."

"I think it was the opening salvo of the war. When I left, Edward was about to have a chat with Alice."

"Oh. You don't think she could take him out, do you? Then we'd be humped."

I shrugged, feeling pulped. "I doubt it. If Carlos chose to defend Edward, I'd expect it to get pretty nasty. That chaos might have been something Wygan did, too. He seemed to be expecting it, he was almost—" I broke off, gulping against bile.

"You OK, Harper?"

I jerked aside and heaved my dinner into the trash can. This night was killing me. I hung there with my head down for a minute, waiting for the giddiness to pass.

Something crashed out in the hall and Cameron reentered the office carrying a paper cup full of water. I pulled myself up. He put the water on the desk and I took it with a questioning look.

He shifted from foot to foot. "Bathroom door was locked."

"Landlord'll have to fix it," I croaked. I really didn't give a damn. I rinsed my mouth and spat into the trash. "Thanks. And thanks for getting me out of there."

"I was afraid to touch you, because you always act like it hurts, but I figured whatever was back there was worse."

"You figured right. You'll make a pretty intimidating vampire someday." I coughed.

"I think I'd rather go the smooth and seductive route, thanks."

I eyed him, his blond hair a tangle, mustache ratty. He grinned. We both broke up in desperate laughter.

I gasped, clutching my very sore belly, and lay back into the chair.

"Maybe we should rethink our schedule, Harper."

"Huh?" I mumbled. I didn't think I could move. The chair was drawing me into its old, worn shape, muffling me with the comforting smell of warm leather and old files. My eyelids were as sore as the rest, so I closed them.

"You seem pretty wrecked. Maybe you should rest a couple of days before we go after that organ."

"Can't. Carlos and Edward laid plans. 'Sides, longer we wait, better chance the ghost will find it, or something like tonight happens again. Can't take much more of this. Have to cut it off, now..."

Cameron sighed a long, sad stream of blue fog. "I guess." I heard him say as the soft mist folded over me and I faded down to unconsciousness.

The buzzing of my pager woke me. My office was chill and empty but for me and a sound in the hall. My chest ached more than the rest of me.

Clank and scratch, something pushed on my office door. I started to raise my head. A flicker passed the edge of my vision. I peered sideways and the Grey blazed in sunrise colors around the door, centered on a furious, red shape. I whipped my head to look, letting the Grey well up all around, flushing the room with rippling strands and a thin, cold mist.

Alice flew through the door at me. By reflex, I flung up my hands, shoving back against the grim crimson of her fury. She stopped inches from me, teeth bared and hands like reaping hooks.

She was a horror. A long slash had rent away part of her cheek, deforming her mouth and leaving a band of muscle exposed. Her clothing was tattered and her limbs were misshapen, showing broken bones and gouges that oozed black. Fury, pain, and violence whirled around her, reeking of blood and eviscerated bodies.

Looming over me, she hissed through her broken mouth, "Trickster witch. I would shred you, but your blood will feed me better."

My heart racketed and choked me. I barely dredged up the words, "No harm, Alice. You promised."

"Lied to me. Betrayed me. You die for it."

I rolled out of the chair and leaned on my desk, weak-legged. "I agreed to make a path to Edward and stand aside. Only that. I did that. I didn't stand in your way. I told you to be patient. You misplayed your moment." Barely keeping my brain functioning, I was dizzy with fatigue, and the Grey twisted through me, wringing out my strength.

She howled rage, frozen by her promise. My geas had worked.

She leveled burning eyes at me, catching me, pressing her command against me. "I will find a way and you will stand aside. You will neither help nor hinder. You will do nothing and you will go unharmed. Break this promise, and I will kill you for days, dine upon you slowly, drinking your screams like wine."

I couldn't pull away from her. I was too exhausted to push or dodge. It wouldn't matter, though, once the organ was gone. I found myself nodding, panting, "All right. I'll stand aside."

She spun away, the door crashing behind her as I fell to the floor.

I woke at five o'clock, stiff, cold, and miserable, huddled on the floor. I dragged myself home.

A phone call awakened me again at ten. Nightmares of the night before left me incoherent when I answered, but the voice on the other end chirped, "Good morning. May I speak to Harper Blaine, please?"

I grunted and prepared to dump her into telephonic oblivion. The last thing I could deal with was a telemarketer.

"Ms. Blaine? Edward Kammerling requested that we call you and confirm your appointment and ask if everything was still on schedule."

"Uh … yeah. Edward's OK?"

"Oh, yes. He wanted you to know that everything is on track for tonight's party, but that you will have to make your own transportation arrangements. He has his own way in, of course. Will that be a problem?"

"No."

"That's what we hoped to hear. Everything else will be taken care of. Thank you and have a nice day!"

My stomach gurgled and I pitched the phone back into its cradle, burying my head under the pillow and wishing damnation on all TPM employees, living or undead.

Getting out of bed was difficult. My limbs were stiff with scabs and bruises, I felt like I had the flu, and too many sleepless nights weighed me down. The previous night was muddy in my mind, nightmare differentiated poorly from reality. The night ahead didn't promise to be any better.

I called Will, hoping to touch normalcy. Michael answered.

"Where's Will?"

"He's out at the police station."

"Is he OK?"

I could hear him shrug, unhappily. "I guess… I gotta go to class. I'll tell him you called, though."

That would have to do. I wandered around the condo, listless, aching. I kept picking up the ferret and cuddling her, hoping that things weren't as awful as they seemed and that hiding my face in her warm, fragrant fur would somehow make them better. Chaos didn't appreciate the attention and jumped out of my stifling arms, skipping off to throw books down from shelves. I hoped I'd see her again and I left a note for my neighbor, just in case I didn't.

I called Mara and told her about my meeting with Edward and what I needed from her now. She said she'd have to discuss it with Ben. Dragging my feet, I gathered up my stuff and hauled myself to the office.

I paged Quinton between bouts of uninteresting paperwork and frustrating phone calls. He strolled in a little after noon and glanced at the boarded-over windows. "What happened? Somebody try to break in again?"

"Rough client."

"Not your guy with the Camaro."

"No, the one who doesn't show up on video."

He growled, looking me over. "He roughed you up?"

"I fell on some stairs."

He shot a queer glance at me.

"It's the truth. Look, Quinton, I have a problem a lot worse than a tumble on the steps."

"What do you need?"

"I need to get past a security system so I can break something."

He blinked a few times. "Umm … that's often illegal."

"Yeah. But I can't come up with another option. If it doesn't get done—I just have to."

He frowned at the desperation in my voice. "Must be something pretty bad. Why do you need to do this?"

I shook my head at myself. "It's nuts."

"What can be weirder than putting an alarm in a car trunk for a vampire?"

"How 'bout exorcising a ghost and defusing a paranormal time bomb?"

He rocked on his heels and nodded. "OK. That's weirder. How did you get mixed up in that? Your client?"

"The guy who broke my windows. He's a ghost. I didn't know it when I took the job."

Quinton sat down and waited for the rest.

I sighed. "He hired me to find a piece of furniture. I found it, but couldn't get it for him. He got rough and I figured out what he was. I didn't want to keep working for him. He made it clear he would do whatever it took to get what he wanted and if I stood in his way, he'd go through me. I can't run from him—he's a ghost—and I can't imagine what he's capable of. I figured the only way to get rid of him was to find out why he really wanted the thing. Now I know. And it's terrible. There is no option but to stop him."

I closed my eyes a moment, tired, but relieved to have gotten it all out. I wondered if Quinton thought I was crazy yet.

He mulled it for a moment. "Why does this job fall on you? Why do you have to stop it?"

I played with a pencil and didn't look at him. "I'm afraid that this thing will hurt me, too. I'm a little bit ghost or monster myself, connected to all of this stuff. Horrible things have happened, and I'm just too much a coward to let this happen, too. This is the only thing I can think of to stop it."

Quinton was quiet. I continued playing with the pencil and breathing around the stone in my chest.

Finally he asked, "So what building are we breaking into? Give me all the information you've got and I'll hunt down the rest. By the way, when are we doing this?"

I glanced up. "Tonight."

"Tonight? Oh, boy … Miracles 'R' Us. I assume that we're not going to go and ask permission for this."

"I already offered to buy the thing—the museum won't sell.

That's what made my client so angry. If I could think of another way, I'd do it."

"All right," he sighed. "Let's get to it."

I sketched out the plan and gave him everything I knew about Madison Forrest House security. Quinton soaked it up without taking notes.

"OK. I'm going to the library. I'll call you when I've got it figured out."

I thanked him, but he was already heading out the door.

Mara called later in the afternoon. With an edge in her voice she told me she would do it, but needed a lift to the museum. She didn't give me time to ask any questions.

At six, Quinton called.

"I got it. I can do it. I'll see you there a little after sunset, OK?"

"OK," I agreed.

I drove up to Queen Anne to get Mara. The house did not look quite as inviting as normal, the color of the light in the windows an unpleasant green. Albert met me on the walk again. I limped to the door, alarm racing my heart.

Mara answered my knock. Her face was pinched.

"Come in," she clipped out. "Ben's upset."

"Oh?"

"He doesn't want me to go. Now that he knows the threat is real, he thinks I can't help and will be in harm's way needlessly. Imagine!"

Ben stepped into the arch from the dining room. "I'm worried about you. What's wrong with that? You're my wife, our son's mother. I don't want anything to happen to you. I think that's reasonable."

She turned to glare at him. "Now that it's down to theory versus practice, you don't really believe in magic at all. You think it's just feel-good hocus-pocus and dancin' naked under the moon with a bunch of March-hare feminists."

"That's not true!"

"'Course it's not, but it's what you think—" Somewhere in the house a tiny sound started up.

I waded in. "Stop this. I need Mara. I know she can do it, because I've seen her do it. It has to be this way."

"I could come along."

"No." The sound grew into a distant, hiccuping cry.

Ben and Mara both looked toward the stairs.

Mara looked panicked. "Someone needs to stay with Brian. Besides, if something does go wrong—"

"Then you admit that something could go wrong, that you may not be competent to—"

Mara's panic turned to ire. "I certainly do not admit I'm not competent! I only meant that no plan is completely foolproof. Don't assume you know better than I what I—"

Ben cut her off. "It's too dangerous! It's irresponsible and unsafe and—well, it's destruction of private property! It's just not right! Harper," he added, turning to me, "you know this isn't right."

I cocked my head at him and leaned against the doorframe. "What is right? Letting the ghost do whatever he wants with it? Allowing everyone who treads in the Grey to be fried like an egg when it blows up? If you have a better plan, I'd be glad to hear it, because frankly this one stinks, but it's all I've got."

Brian was at full wail now. Ben stared at me. Mara gaped at me, her mouth forming a little O.

Ben blinked. His face crumpled and he turned toward the stairs. "Brian needs me. And Harper needs you, Mara. She's right. She's right. You'd better go." He stopped on the first landing and glared back at us. "But you had better come back. Brian and I need you, too."

Mara began crying, flew up the steps, and threw herself into her husband's arms. "I love you. I will be very, very careful, I promise. Thank you, love."

Ben looked on the verge of tears himself, his head hanging over her shoulder a moment before he turned to give his wife a kiss.

"I know you'll be careful, sweetheart. I know it. You'll be fine," he added, letting her go. "You two had better get going. It's going to be dark soon." He turned and marched up the stairs.

Mara plodded to me, reaching for her purse by the door as we went out and swiping at her eyes. Albert blinked owl-like at us from the porch, but made no move to come along.

Dejected, Mara sat in the front seat. "I wish I could have Ben with me … though you look like you'll need more help than I. You look one step from dead."

"I think I felt better when I was."

I drove out to the museum and told her the plan. Mara nodded. I felt miserable. Nothing within or without didn't ache with bruises or a wearying, bone-deep illness, and everything I saw was aglimmer with streaks of color and coils of Grey.

I did not park in the same lot as on the previous visits, but several blocks away and around a couple of corners. We got out and walked to the museum.

Clouds obscured the moon, but that wasn't the only source of darkness. The Grey around the building had thickened into an artificial midnight, a twist of realities from which light seemed to flee. Quinton had been leaning against a tree by the fence line and now ambled toward us, emerging from the coil of darkness like a ship from fog. I did not introduce my companions to each other. They didn't mind.

"Hi," Quinton greeted us. "I've already got stuff in place and I can control what the cameras see, so the security guys shouldn't be alerted. The perimeter alarm is off at the side door. It's not locked. Don't touch any exterior doors or windows and don't make too much noise." He began to lead us up the darkened edge of the drive, in cover of shadowing trees and shrubs.

I murmured to him, "How'd you manage all of that?"

"I don't want you to know."

"Thanks. Will you come inside?"

"Only as far as the kitchen, where the electrical box is. I want to stay near the switches, in case anyone starts prowling around."

"OK. Have you seen anyone else yet?"

"Vampires and ghosts? Not yet, but I might not see them at all. They're sneaky bastards. Besides, it's barely dark yet."

"'Sneaky.' Charming description." We all turned and faced Edward.

He stood in the shadows under the covered driveway. "I hope I didn't miss much. Eavesdropping is one of my best techniques."

None of us blushed.

"Who else are we to expect?" I asked.

"Only Carlos and Cameron. With your friend here, it should prove sufficient."

"No one rallied to the flag?"

"There were volunteers, but I didn't get to be the lead dog without having some teeth. Occasionally, it's necessary to prove I still have them. It wouldn't behoove me to ask my people to do what I wouldn't. Besides which, they will be busy creating the illusion that all of us were busy elsewhere tonight."

Quinton muttered under his breath, "Teeth and balls. Nice combo—for a pit bull."

Edward turned his gaze on Quinton and skewered him with it. Quinton squirmed a bit, but didn't look down.

"And for lone wolves," Edward added. "Just be careful whose pack you run across this time."

I looked at them both. "You guys know each other?"

Edward gazed at Quinton. "By reputation."

Quinton gave a slight nod and we all chose to look toward the side door.

Edward pointed to it. "Shall we go?"

We went as stealthily as wet gravel would allow—a train of phantom follow-the-leader—and let ourselves in. Quinton stood aside and waited for us to pass.

"I'll stay here until I see another vampire," he whispered.

"And Cameron."

"OK. Stay quiet, all right? Neighbors like to walk their dogs around here, even in the rain."

Carlos and Cameron joined us as we started up the stairs. We all hesitated at the top, glancing about. I don't know what made the vampires scope the area like that, but in my case, it was fear. Mara looked nervous and overwound. She cast a look at me and sketched a sign in the air between us. It sparked a moment and shed warmth on me, then faded.

We went to the parlor. The door was sheathed in a blanket of ugliness that oozed and seeped around the edges, flowing onto the floor, creeping like a spreading puddle of blood. Carlos brushed past the rest of us and touched the door, whispering. The darkness squirmed aside. We followed him in. He closed the door behind us.

The room was swathed in the rolling, icy blackness that had retreated from the door. Carlos pushed it back with his hands, clearing space. We moved furniture to his direction, shuffling in aching silence. Mara and I were sweating before we were done, and I moved at an old woman's pace. I had to give the organ a wide berth. Every time I came near, it sent a tentacle of darkness toward me. Carlos pinched them off with a smell of burnt flesh.

With all the furniture pushed up to the farthest walls, we rolled up the rug. We stood back as Carlos began to chalk symbols on the floor. Mara held one of my hands and chanted something that kept the Grey back from us. The Grey web inside me buzzed with exhausting activity, crackling and arcing over my nerves and joints as the energy from the nexus hummed through me. I watched the darkness lap at the arc of chalked sigils. After a while, Carlos motioned to Edward and they began to push and pull on the organ. Judging from their grunts and stifled noises, it was terrible work.

Cameron started forward to help. Carlos waved him off.

"Better for us to do it." He gave a rictus grin. "We are old in our own evil."

Once the organ was a few feet from the wall, Edward fell back, looking as ill as I felt. His face and neck bore thin, white weals that had not been there the night before. Carlos crept around the floor, singing in a low voice, drawing a careful circle of runes and symbols that writhed and connected into an endless, glowing gyre enclosing himself and the organ.

Then Mara began a larger circle of her own, outside and around his, that encompassed most of the rest of the room. She muttered as she walked, making a trail of dim sparks along with her chalk line that pushed the darkness into a heavy, gathering storm around the organ. She left a small opening opposite the door. I went to stand by it with her, facing the door. I could feel the organ's power surging.

"The scent of blood to draw him," Carlos said and looked toward me and Mara.

She glared at him.

Carlos watched me and started to reach for my hand.

"No," Mara snapped, her words coming out of her mouth sharp gold and scintillating. "And not mine, either. You know that."

Edward raised a languid hand. "Don't be cruel, Carlos. It's poor form to repay our friends in that coin. I'd give mine, if I had any."

"Maybe your friend downstairs," Carlos suggested. "I could call him here."

I tried to glare at him. "That's not fair."

Carlos growled, "Fair ..." Cameron started to say something, but Carlos shut him up with a look. "Very well, then. Cameron, open the door for our guest."

Cameron edged around the circle as Carlos, mumbling something that sounded more like curses than spells, drew a small knife from his clothing. He slashed it across his right wrist.

Nothing happened. Then Carlos closed his eyes. His lips moved but no sound came out. His chest heaved as though from heavy exertion and dark, slow drops of blood welled along the wound, then dripped to the seething floor. They splashed loud as cymbals. Carlos flung his hand in an arc, dark droplets splattering over the organ's mirror and stops with the sound of shattering crystal.

Stillness and the sickening stink of corrupted blood held us. I was panting as I called out, "Sergeyev. Grigori Sergeyev. I have your vessel. Come and get it."

A wind burst up from the floor with a roar and a shape rushed through the door. It crossed the edge of the first circle, racing toward me. Mara dropped to her knees and closed her circle with a word. A wall of white light leapt upward. The Grey shape smashed against the barrier and recoiled with a howl of frustration, collapsing into the form of my spectral client, trapped between the two charmed circles.

He cursed us all in vociferous Russian. Cameron stood spellbound by the door and I cowered behind Mara, oppressed by the ghost's withering hatred and battered by my own fear, pain, and exhaustion.

"There's nothing he can do to you, so long as the circles remain intact," Mara whispered, as I held her shoulders. "The only one at risk is Carlos, and no ghost wants a taste of a necromancer's fury if he can avoid it." She looked uncertain and pale with fatigue, hands wound into her circle's spell, keeping the ghost confined between it and Carlos's circle of necromancy. Her own power strained to maintain the circle's integrity as Sergeyev stormed against it. I hoped whatever flowed, pulsing, through me was helping her, but I didn't know.

Carlos reached out and yanked one of the stops out of the organ. Sergeyev turned with a jerk and threw himself against the inner circle with a shriek. The ivory decoration on the knob crumbled to dust and sifted to the floor, frosting the blood with a thin coat of white. Carlos dropped the knob and reached for another.

"Nyet!" Sergeyev screamed, followed by a babble of Russian sounding imploring and threatening by turns.

Carlos answered him. "We come to release you, you ungrateful wretch. Seven hundred years of torment and all you can think of is revenge. Against whom?"

Sergeyev spat out a name, stalking in frustration around the perimeter of Carlos's circle. His appearance wavered and flickered through a vertigo-inducing montage of every person he'd ever worn, stolen, or devoured. I leaned one shoulder against the wall, which flickered with strange lights.

"Dead," Carlos snapped back. "A long time dead. I knew of him." He yanked out another stop. "From his torments, I release thee. From this prison, I release thee..."

The revenant shrieked and howled, clawing at the air between them and cursing in gouts of fiery storm until my knees shook and I thought my ears would bleed. Carlos screamed back at the ghost, long, entwining words that wove around the spirit, loosening and thinning him as the vampire dashed more and more of the organ to the ground. Music rails and preset knobs rattled to the floor and sloughed into dust. Keys groaned as they were wrenched from the boards and fell away in slivers of memory.

The hallway boomed. I was slow to turn my head, but heard Cameron scream and fall.

"What a lovely party," Alice hissed from the doorway. "And I wasn't invited." The flesh on her face still showed deep gashes, but her hair, face, and dress were covered in fresh blood.

The sight staggered me, and I leaned one hand hard onto Mara. Quinton ... ?

"Bitch," Edward spat, whirling toward Alice.

She laughed and darted forward, tearing a hole in the circles on the floor. She snatched the mirror from the organ. "Mine!" she shouted. Colors and streamers of power roared around her, twining over and through her. "I am your mistress now. Attack the ones who would harm you!"

Sergeyev howled unholy glee and rushed into the inner circle, pouncing on Carlos and the organ.

Mara sobbed and rocked backward. We lurched back against the flickering wall, cringing.

Edward flew toward Alice, who danced sideways from the circle, clutching her prize to her chest. She howled mad laughter and shouted, "Edward! It's only you I want! Run away, mice! Run and hide, or I'll eat you, too!" She fired a cold glare of triumph at me and laughed harder.

Cameron lurched to his feet near the door, his neck and head looking lopsided and loose. He snatched at her, missed, and swung his arms again.

Carlos had fallen back against the organ, his arms up, warding against Sergeyev's slashing energies. Shrieking faces and savage blades of light lashed from the instrument. Single-minded, the necromancer swiped at the music rail, dislodging the last of the spindles, which dissolved and powdered on the floor as they came away from the instrument. The ghost yowled and wavered a moment, then attacked with savagery.

Mara struggled up out of my arms and flung a ball of blue light at the ghost's back. It splattered across him and he howled as Carlos howled, too.

She winced. "They're too close together. We'll have to reclose the circle. Come and help me."

I tried to move and felt ice tighten on my limbs and a sharp shortening of my breath. Sickness and revulsion held me back with a muttering in my brain: "Neither help nor hinder ..."

Mara threw herself onto the floor and began to crawl, drawing new symbols and chanting in gasps. She looked up at me, desperation in her eyes. "Come on!"

I stumbled a step back. If I moved forward I felt the weight of Alice's geas against me. But I could go and nothing would happen to me—she had promised me that, screamed the chittering voice in my head...

Mara tore her gaze from me with a frightened face and kept crawling, painfully, across the floor.

I backed toward the door, curling against the shuddering, battering of the Grey in violent discord, while the double-pronged battle raged around me, cutting me with stray blades of energy that played tearing chords on my chest.

Sergeyev smashed at Carlos, oblivious to every counter his opponent made. Even as his substance faded, his strength, drawn from the artifact, seemed to grow, and his wrath burned a reeking red and black pall around them.

Edward and Cameron flung themselves on Alice from opposite sides and grabbed her. She fought and screamed, slashing and biting, tearing flesh wherever she touched them, a whirlwind of fury. Cameron caught her flailing arm and yanked it backward. A sickening pop and a rending sound—Alice shrieked and wrenched toward him, jaws gaping. Edward snatched at her head, tangled his hands in her flying red hair and yanked, twisted, jerked…

Her neck snapped with a crunch and she flopped onto the floor, thrashing like a gaffed fish and gnashing her teeth. The mirror dropped and smashed. Cameron grabbed the nearest thing: a needlework stand. He knocked the embroidery hoop off and plunged the long spindle of wood down, into Alice's chest.

Her scream shook the house. I sprawled to the floor as Mara crawled the last few feet to close the circle. The rush of magic as the circle closed rattled my teeth, and the temperature plummeted ten degrees.

"Mirror!" Carlos yelled. I could see his groping hand for a moment under the barrage of Sergeyev's assault.

Edward grabbed a ragged piece of the broken mirror and threw it. Carlos's hand reached for it, dark, dead blood flying wide. The ghost flung himself against the sparkling shard of mirror. It cut into his form, slicing the hot threads of power that cloaked them, melting and flowing into him.

Alice's heels beat the floor into buckling ripples and her teeth snapped as she pawed at the rod through her chest. Beside her, Sergeyev shimmered silver and red, inching toward solidity as his appearance slid and wavered over his uncanny surface.

The room heaved and shuddered. Sergeyev screamed and dove at Carlos, slashing him with razor hands. Cameron and I both lurched forward. I pulled up short, held back by a stab across my chest.

Mara snatched him back. "Don't break it or we're done for," she cried.

"Fire!" Carlos shouted, one hand groping as he tried to roll away from the glittering monstrosity that tore at him. "Please!"

Mara caught her breath and Edward froze. He gave a jerking nod and Mara scrabbled in her pockets, yanking out a wooden kitchen match. She struck it and tossed it over the chalked circle.

The lines and charms blazed upward in flame, then bit into the dry wood of the floor. Beyond them, Carlos muttered, gasping and waning. Edward backed from the fire, stumbling, blind, over Alice, while Cameron pounded the floor with his fists, howling, "No, no, no!"

I looked toward the door and saw more flames. The fire was spreading on the lines of force. Alice dragged herself from the floor, lurching for Edward through the growing inferno. I couldn't move to stop her and live, and I couldn't help Carlos. Only stopping Sergeyev would save anyone, but I'd made the wrong choice—under the weight of Alice's geas and my own fear, my own weakness—and my friends would die for it.

Dead if you do and damned if you don't. I wouldn't survive if Sergeyev won, whether Alice took me out later or not. But if she needed to threaten me, then I must have a choice. And she'd have to find me—or my body—first. I started crawling forward, pushing against the pain in my chest. The house shook, bucking and roaring with a sound like a freight train bearing down.

A gut-tearing chill ripped into me and I rolled onto my back. The huge shape of the black guardian beast burst from the flame, vaulting upward, through the ceiling, trailing fire and smoke, then rushing back toward us, frenzied, roaring. Its maw gaped an infinite, lightless pit above me as I lay cold in motionless terror.

I pushed my hands uselessly against the pressure rushing before the monster and felt fire sear along my arms. "No, no, not me," I gasped, "not now." The knot in my chest burned and twisted like a blade as the jaws closed over me. I was too slow, too late, and I couldn't help anyone now. I sobbed and let go, not caring what the monster did to me. Who cared if the Grey swallowed me whole?

I gave up struggling. I let it have me.

I felt the knot in my chest loosen, blooming open, pouring the writhing, living Grey through me, knitting it into my body and mind. I let it wash across me and I felt bright as the soft snow-mist that enclosed me.

Then the floor slapped my back and I looked up into a blaze of light, streaming and boiling around a black void. The guardian breathed out an odor of tombs and poised above me, confused. I pointed at Sergeyev.

The beast reared back, spinning and shrieking, and its tail of pure pain lashed across me. I gasped and sank toward the dark as screams erupted nearby.

The creature plunged toward Carlos and Sergeyev, forms of fire and shadow, engaged to death. It whipped a circle around the two figures. For an instant, the awesome horror reflected in Sergeyev's shifting mirror, spinning, its terrible jaws agape. Then the beast reared and the ghost shrieked as the black creature swallowed him and dove down, through the buckling floor, vanishing under a boil of black smoke and the reek of inferno. The scream swelled and roared, consuming, powered upward and outward by the flick of the flaming tail.

Crackling and groaning pierced the vacuum of sound left by the monster's rushing exit. I rolled to my knees and looked around. Alice lay still nearby, skewered to the floor between Edward and Cameron. The house was still shuddering, the flames of the circle now gobbling at the floor and walls, gouting noxious smoke. Behind the ring of fire, Carlos struggled, making weak, broken movements, pulling himself up against the organ, which shivered and collapsed against itself, sending him to the burning boards.

Cameron leapt up, but Edward grabbed him before he could cross the fiery line. I curled into an anguished crouch.

Edward touched my shoulder and I shuddered. "Out," he ordered. "Before the house collapses."

Mara dragged me to my feet and toward the door. The house seemed ramshackle and doomed, staggering beneath us as we stumbled and crawled for the stairs. I glanced back, blinded by smoke, tears, and pain, ears ringing, seeing the parlor in flames, three dark shapes moving within it, tearing the organ to pieces.

Halfway down the tilting staircase, Mara and I met Quinton coming up. He grabbed me by the shoulders and I winced, yelping, the pain so sharp I gagged on it. Ignoring that, he hustled both of us out through the kitchen at a furious pace, yanking something out of the electrical panel with gloved hands as we passed.

I gasped. "Cameron, Carlos—"

Quinton snapped at me, "They can take care of themselves. They're vampires. We're not!"

I whimpered and folded myself around the memory of pain at my core. Quinton and Mara dragged me down the rain-washed driveway and out the gate. I was all heels and slippery ankles. Between the two of them, they shoved me into the backseat of the Rover. Mara climbed in beside me, shaking. Quinton pickpocketed my keys and drove through the grim, ash-darkened rain. Finally, he parked on a side street and turned to look back at me.

"I think this is a safer place, but you can see it from here."

My head clearing in fresher air, I raised my head. "See what?"

"The museum. It's burning."

THIRTY ONE

Car alarms shouted in the distance as frightened people tottered into the street and toward the hellish glow. No one seemed to find it strange that we were sitting in our vehicle, looking dazed and injured. They were all as confused and frightened as we were.

As we three battered humans sat in the Rover, we could see the Madison Forrest Historical House Museum consumed in a conflagration even the rain couldn't slow. A column of fire crowned the night-darkened hillside, the shape of the house becoming obscure in the black smoke, white steam, and flickering yellow light. For a while, only the sounds of the car alarms made any impact on the night. In a few minutes, fire crews arrived in their hopeless cacophony, attacked the fire, but fell back, bewildered by its fury. They turned their hoses on the grounds to keep the fire from spreading and then gave up and watched the mansion burn. We stared at it and at each other and felt as helpless as the firemen and the wandering neighbors.

The shape of the building remained bright as noon to me even as the walls began to crumble, Grey memory holding the energy in place as the grid reabsorbed and distributed the overflow in its own time. How long would the ghost of the house linger? I wondered.

Someone tapped on Mara's window. We all looked and saw a white face streaked with black under a tangle of gold and black straw. Mara opened her door.

"Cameron! You're all right!"

He pulled a face. "I'm kind of crispy around the edges." His long hair was gone below the shoulders, singed off by the heat of the fire. The rest was ragged, smoke-shot and heat-fried, his mustache just blackened stubble. "Carlos isn't doing so great, though."

"Where is he?" Mara demanded, stepping out of the truck into the running gutter.

"Over there," Cameron said, pointing into a darkness of bushes.

She looked into the truck at Quinton. "Come on," she ordered.

He looked at me. "You OK?"

I suppressed a cough and answered, "Yeah."

He nodded, then got out of the truck and followed Cameron and Mara into the dark. In a minute or two they returned, supporting a blackened, shambling figure between them. His head hung and he seemed much smaller, as if the fire had consumed part of him. His three guides helped Carlos into the rear compartment. He collapsed on his back and lay still in a settling funk of wet ash. I peered at him over the seat back, my guts twisting. The others scrambled in.

Mara frowned. "He doesn't look good."

"He got pretty burned up," Cameron explained. "I don't think he can see, either. I—I hope he'll be all right. Edward said he would..."

A thin whisper floated up. "Eventually." Carlos sighed and lapsed back into stillness.

I shivered. "Can we get out of here?" I begged.

Quinton started the Rover and crept through the throngs of stopped cars and wandering humans.

"What about Edward?" Mara asked.

Cam fumbled with his seat belt in blackened fingers. "He got Carlos and me out to you guys, then he left."

"Ungrateful bastard," Quinton muttered.

"No," said Cameron. "He had a lot of other stuff to take care of, what with Alice and everything else. He didn't have a choice."

"Alice was that harpy who attacked us? Is she dead, then?" asked Mara. She shot me an odd look.

Cameron gave a hollow laugh. "Well, yeah, but I don't know what happened to her. She was still pinned to the floor and we had to finish breaking up the organ, so we left her there. The circle kept most of the fire back for a little while, but by the time we were done, the whole room was blazing like hell. We had to bail out a window and I couldn't spot her. I guess she burned up with the house, but Edward wasn't sure. He thought she'd crawled away somehow. I didn't think anything scared vampires, until tonight. That fire ... like some nightmare that's going to come for you and eat your heart." He shivered. "It would have eaten us if it could have."

Mara faked a reassuring smile. "You finished your job, in spite of it. That's courage."

"Or stupidity," Cameron added.

"Hey, where are we going?" Quinton interrupted.

"My house. Ben will be having kittens by now."

Quinton remembered the way and pointed the Rover toward Queen Anne Hill. The rest of the trip was silent except for the grumbling of the engine and the hiss of the wet road beneath the tires.

Albert glowered as Mara and Cameron helped Carlos down to the basement. He glared at me and made a face I interpreted as frustration before vanishing after them.

I huddled on the porch step. Quinton handed me my truck keys. I took them in shaking hands. "Are you all right?" I asked. "I was worried—"

He shrugged. "I'm fine. But I've got to go. I've got a few things to take care of myself. I didn't expect something like this to happen, so I need to take care of that little oversight. Don't worry. It'll be all right. I'll be in touch."

He backed away a few steps, then waved and turned, disappearing down the stairs. I got up and stumbled into the house.

Ben Danziger stood in the entry looking dumbfounded. He

jammed his fists through his hair, making it wilder than I'd ever seen it.

"Oh, you're all right!" he cried, grabbing my shoulders.

I moaned and everything got black around the edges. He carried me to a couch and sat me on it. "Wait here! I'll get you some water. Don't move, no, lie down. Yes, lie down..."

I slithered down the upholstery and closed my eyes. Ben woke me to give me water a few minutes later.

"You look terrible," he said, holding the glass for me.

"Thanks," I croaked. "I look better than the other guy."

"Oh, God, yes! What happened?"

"It burned. The museum burned down after the guardian came and ate Sergeyev. And I almost got them all killed because of Alice..."

It was hard to explain what had happened, especially since there were details I couldn't tell Ben. I was saved, after a while, by the arrival of Cameron, Mara, and Albert from the basement.

Between them, Mara and Cam thought that Carlos would recover, though it was going to be slow. Being dead to begin with had its advantages, but he was still in very bad shape. He'd spent a lot of himself, first for the spell, then fighting Sergeyev and the organ, and the fire had almost finished off what was left. Cameron declared that he would tend him.

Mara sent Cameron back downstairs and Ben upstairs to look after Brian, then sat on the sofa next to me. Albert hovered behind us. Mara picked up my hand and stared at it. "Why did you hesitate? Why did you pull away?"

I couldn't look at her, giving tiny shakes of my head. "I couldn't ... couldn't do it." Geas. I swallowed the word like bitter medicine.

"But you gave yourself up to the Grey. That saved us. I saw that."

I felt a smile jerk and die before it reached my mouth. "Lucky timing."

She scowled. "But why did you—"

"I can't say. I don't know." I pushed myself up, swaying with weakness and fatigue. "I'm going home."

She stood up, too, and tried to catch me. "Not like that."

I twitched away. "It's not a request. And I won't stay here." I glared at Albert. He slipped farther from me.

"You won't make it."

"Then send someone with me. Send Ben. I won't stay."

Ben drove me home.

I turned off the phones and locked the doors behind me. I spent several days curled up with Chaos in my lap, surrounded by the muttering hum of the Grey.

The first morning, an impressive white card arrived in the mail, thanking me for attending a fund-raiser at TPM the night of the fire. I showed it to the investigators who showed up a couple of days later. I told them I had a bad case of the flu, which they didn't question, since I looked like something scraped off a locker-room floor. They went away.

A few days later, the newspaper reported that the fire was due to a ruptured gas tank in the basement and a smoldering cigarette dropped by a workman. The arson investigators didn't like it, but there was no accelerant and no sign of tampering with the tank. I doubt they ever really closed the books on it, but they let it lie.

They wouldn't have believed that the fire was started by a desperate necromancer and a witch, or spread by a furious beast that devoured ghosts and prowled the edges of the world between worlds. They wouldn't have believed that the fire had fed on magic as much as on dry wood, varnish, paint, and cloth. They wouldn't have believed any of it. What kind of crazy person could? I wished I didn't. But I felt it every day, the untied knot of Grey knitting deeper into me as the flow of power corrected itself and sang across my bones, illuminating the world in threads of fire that gleamed through an ever-present silver mist.

Eventually I returned to work. Cameron turned up at my truck the same night.

He'd had to clip his hair much shorter than mine, and his face had changed under the mop of angelic curls that resulted.

I kept the Rover between us and touched my own upper lip. "Hey, no mustache," I commented.

"Nah. I figured I should change my look for a while." He glanced down and sucked in his lower lip. "Harper … I owe you a lot more than money. Carlos is getting better and I'm doing all right. I moved him out to Bellevue with me. Got tired of squatting in the Danzigers' basement. Besides which, Albert drove Carlos crazy."

"He's like that. How's your sister handling the invasion of the vampires?"

"She moved back in with Mom. After they stopped acting like total wenches, they actually get along OK. Especially since they can both complain about me now. Sarah's pretty good for Mom. She freaks out less whenever I come around. We're getting things worked out. I'm not going to go back to school for a while, though—Carlos needs me too much and I figure I'll get a pretty good education just talking to him about stuff. He's got a lot in his head after knocking around so long."

"I imagine so."

"Anyhow, I just wanted to let you know things were working out."

I smiled at him and we talked about money a bit, but I was glad to see him go. His presence in the Grey was already changing.

Three days after the museum burned, Brandon McCain fired Will, disappeared with the company funds, and was arrested in Los Angeles for fraud two weeks later. Will called me a week afterward, and we had the first of a lot of dinners. I loved sitting in the mundane world with him.

Over dessert on our one-month anniversary, he said, "I'm not going to have to testify against Brandon."

"So you did find something, that day."

"And a lot of days afterward. When you got me looking into that organ's provenance, I started thinking about the paperwork on some of our stock, and I looked into that, too. I found all sorts of stuff in the paperwork, once I figured out where to look. Brandon foisted a lot of fakes off on people, and he used my reputation to do it. I warned him … but he fired me." He looked sick over it. "Anyhow, that's over. He, uh … what's the phrase? Took a plea?"

"Copped a plea. He made a bargain with the DA so he wouldn't have to go to jail."

"Yeah … and he's supposed to make restitution, but there's nothing left to make restitution with. He grabbed it all and hid it somewhere. Everything else is going to be sold off to pay people back, so … I've got nothing."

"What are you going to do?"

"Well … savings are running low and I need to look after Michael. But I got a call…"

"Oh?"

"Yeah. To go back to Europe. To England, actually. Investigating provenances. It's what I really like doing—what I should have been doing all along—and it'll get my career back on track. It's a good job."

My heart fell and I bit my lip. "Oh. Yeah, that's a great job. How did you hear about it?"

"The curator from the Madison Forrest House called me about it. She's going over to do related work and told me about the opening. Do you remember her?"

"How could I forget? The place burned down right after we went there."

"Yeah. Well, that's another thing."

"What thing?"

"You. You have secrets. Weird things seem to happen around you."

"That's the way my job is, Will."

Distress boiled off him in sickly green waves. He took my hand and held it too tightly. "It's not just the job, Harper. It's something about you. It's like there's an invisible wall between you and the world, and only part of you is walking around out here with me. I am … I'm crazy about you, but after Brandon, I can't live with secrets like that. Not right now. I need a simple life for a while."

"You're dumping me."

"No! I will stay in touch. I do want to—I don't know, stay with you? But I can't."

I eased my hand back from him. "I understand, Will. It's a great opportunity and you need a break. It's all right."

"Harper …"

I kissed him on the cheek, though it seemed an icicle stabbed through my heart. "It'll be all right. Someday the wall will come down. But not yet." He looked fit to cry when I stood up. I didn't shake his hand. "Stay in touch."

He rose from his seat and stared at me. "I will."

I faked a smile. "Yep. You, Will. Me, Harper."

I walked away.

I walked a long time and ended up at my office and sat in the dark for a while. I just sat in the reupholstered client chair and stared at my desk from the wrong side and remembered the stink of uncanny fire.

That night at the Madison Forrest House had burned down my resistance to the Grey. It burned away much of what I had believed, but it had not taken my friends before, not quite. Not even sweet, lunatic Quinton, who still turned up to take me for beer and rounds of disastrous pool. Not even the Danzigers, though Mara often gave me speculative looks from the corners of her eyes.

I couldn't look at any of them without seeing the reminder of their stark faces that night and the threads of living color that tangled around them, diving in and out of the orderly grid that hummed in low registers below the normal world. It didn't make me sick to my stomach anymore—only sick to my heart.

Close as they were, none of them were like me—whatever I was. With Will who hadn't been there, I had, I thought, passed for human. I guess I didn't pass well enough.

Someone knocked on my door, the new glass rattling a little in the frame. When I didn't answer, I heard the swish of an envelope through the mail slot and the thin thump as it hit the floor. I left it a while, until I was sure the messenger was gone.

I turned on the desk lamp and cut the envelope open. There was a private check with a lot of zeros in the amount line, signed by Edward Kammerling. The note on the check read, "services to the community." I put it in my desk drawer, knowing I would never cash it. I wasn't like him, either, and I wouldn't be bought.

I left my office in the dark and went home, brushing past the shapes of things we do not see, into shadows of uncertain futures and pasts that don't lie down.

Don't miss the next book in Kat Richardson's Greywalker series, published by Piatkus Books:

Poltergeist

Meet Harper Blaine. She doesn't just see dead people…

Harper Blaine was just an average small-time private investigator until she died – for two minutes. Now she's a Greywalker – walking the thin line between the living world and the paranormal realm. And she's discovering that her new abilities are landing her all sorts of strange cases.

In the days leading up to Halloween, Harper's been hired by a university research group that is attempting to create an artificial poltergeist. The head researcher suspects someone is deliberately faking the phenomena, but Harper's investigation reveals something else entirely – they've succeeded.

And when one of the group's members is killed in a brutal and inexplicable fashion, Harper must determine whether the killer is the ghost itself, or someone all too human.